THE MEGAFIRE SERIES:

PROJECT R.E.D.D.

Fyra B Ginn

This is a work of fiction. Any resemblance to events (past or present), characters (living or dead), names, or other elements is purely coincidental.

This work was created by the author without the use of AI technology. The author did use automated grammar and spelling checks. No portion of this work is permitted for use in the training of artificial intelligence technology.

ISBN: 979-8-9883135-6-4
Published By: Phoenyx Honor Publishing

www.fyrabginn.com

To Ang,

For always having my back.

Chapter 1

As if in water, she floated weightlessly through space. Darkness touched her skin but there was a certain freedom among the stars. One particularly bright supernova pulsed, beckoned a touch. She reached outward, and in spite of knowing the vast distance separating them, she felt its heat burning her palm, her fingers, traveling upward and into her chest. The pain that followed pulled her, reminded her that something wasn't right here.

Earth's gravity pulled her back, suddenly, and in one second she fell from space landing in soft, wet grass. She lifted a hand, tried to support her weight, but her body felt heavy, vast contrast after her space flight. It took concentrated effort and will to affect the earth, to place another muddy hand just above her shoulders and push upward. After ages of effort, she rocked back on her heels and knelt, covered in mud. Her lungs heaved with effort, and she slowly lifted her gaze from the earth.

She met dark, dead eyes stuck inside a stringy body, absent of muscle. Grey skin on top of bones and tendon, the thing hissed, inches from her face, before lunging forward…

Arda woke up panting, sitting up in her soft bed. After a moment of confusion, her racing heart began to slow. She heard the familiar beeping of her alarm, and felt her tense muscles begin to relax as her breathing slowed. She unclenched her hands from the sheets of her bed and looked around at the room that had always been hers.

She was safe.

She was home.

It was only a nightmare.

Her Virtual Assistant, Joy, greeted her in a cheery voice that sounded strange juxtaposed against the remnants of her terror.

"Good morning, Ardora." Chirped a digital amalgamation of a human voice.

"Good morning, Joy." She stretched, trying to relieve the tension in her shoulders. Familiar surroundings greeted her. The small, but well-furnished bedroom housed her bunk bed, a desk underneath, several holographs of famous scientists, and her cello with a single chair. "What is the time?"

"The time is six hundred and fifteen hours. Your quiescence report shows a lower level of deep sleep than normal. REM sleep was turbulent, and your pulse rate was faster than average during dream cycles. Do you wish to report the nightmare?"

"No, Joy. My doctor doesn't need to be made aware of every bad dream I have." She sighed loudly at her VA, who was a great help most of the time, but its repetitive nature irritated her sometimes. They were "helpful" even when unnecessary.

"If the nightmares continue, Ardora, you could fall under the counseling threshold. Are you sure you don't wish to report the data to make it convenient if you see a therapist?" They were also very efficient.

"I can report it myself if I so chose." Her words were clipped, her jaw clenched. "What's for breakfast?"

"Your mother is making eggs. I've added additional vitamin D to your supplement for the day, as the weather is overcast. This will help you be productive."

"Thank you, Joy. You may go." The beep told Arda the VA was on standby. She wondered if her mother would let her get away with programming another off command, perhaps, "go away, robot." She chuckled at the thought but knew it wouldn't happen. Her mother didn't have her sense of humor.

Arda stretched again and touched the quilt which always covered her sheets while she slept, handmade, rare in this city. Her grandmother, Hope, had fashioned it from cloth and used it to wrap her mother in as a baby. When Arda was born, she was wrapped in it as well. Purple and blue squares reminded her of her dream, floating in space, before the Beta attacked.

Arda had always been a dreamer, a mark against her in a society who owed its existence to science. While most children stopped dreaming around the age of twelve, somehow, Arda continued having vivid and beautiful sleep journeys, some that were also terrifying. She granted herself a few precious seconds to remember how it felt to float through space in the dream, before she shoved the thought aside and rose for the day, becoming sensible and efficient.

She removed the quilt and climbed down from her bed, walking out of her room and into the small bathroom afforded her family. After eliminating, she placed her hands into a small receptacle that sanitized them with UV light. To the left was a circular chamber. She removed her clothes and stepped inside, the door sliding shut silently behind her. She placed her feet as indicated and placed her face forward, pushing a button as she did so.

The chamber opened on top as her face was sealed. She felt the rush of air as her body was sanitized head to toe. Her eyes were covered for protection as her face was cleansed as well, then the seal was removed. She stepped out of the air chamber completely clean and germ free. In school, they'd been taught about the world before the Omega Fire Disaster, how there had once been oceans full of water, the resource so abundant people would bathe in large pools of it with abandon. *Shamefully wasteful.*

Now, water was a valuable resource used for drinking and practical applications only. Everyone drank six glasses a day, and the penalties for not doing so ranged from a scolding by your parents to medical intervention. The health of citizens was of utmost importance. Poor health led to poor work performance, and a direct negative impact on the city. Here, every person mattered.

"Joy, can you analyze the shower sample for me?"

"Normal on all parameters including dirt and bacteria, however, the levels of sweat produced are directly related to the increased pulse rate you experienced during REM sleep. Are you certain you do not wish to report this to Medical?"

She rolled her eyes. "No report, Joy. You may go."

She took the sonic cleaner from the wall and placed the crescent-shaped end in her mouth, surrounding her teeth. She bit down and pushed a button, feeling her head vibrate as her teeth were cleaned thoroughly. When the vibration stopped, she removed it and placed it back in the wall, hitting the sanitizing button. She was finished, cleaned, and ready to dress. She hit another button and the entire wall rotated, revealing a smart panel that also functioned as a mirror. She could see her body in it, not too tall or short, not too wide or skinny. By many accounts, she seemed average. Her face held soft features, and her eyes were deep rather than vibrant. Her brown hair echoed the standard, but her skin was a little too light compared to most others.

She touched the side of the panel and a menu opened. She navigated to clothing and previewed the various outfit patterns her mother had purchased. Finding what she wanted, an ensemble in the same purple and blue as her grandmother's quilt, she hit a button, and the panel scanned her body. She waited for several seconds while the clothes were printed, putting them on her form as they came out, first undergarments, shirt, then pants, followed by footwear.

When she was clothed, she walked down the white steps. They were lucky to find a two-bedroom, two story home in the Alpha district. Being the most populated city of the five remaining, real estate was scarce. Their kitchen had a FoodGen, but her mother stubbornly refused to use it, preferring the tiny fridge and archaic stove to cook her meals. Arda knew her parents were old fashioned, but why they felt the need to be wasteful was beyond her. Still, eggs were eggs.

"Joy tells me you didn't sleep well last night," her mother said, focusing on the eggs she expertly folded.

"I'm fine. I just had a bad dream." Arda could feel the pressure building behind her eyes. Sometimes it was hard not to get angry. Why did Joy insist on telling her parents? She was supposed to be loyal to Arda.

"Don't be mad at Joy. I hear it in your voice. You know that even though she's yours, until you're out of academy this year I have override privileges on your VA. Do you want to talk about your dream?" Her mother set her eggs down in front of her and smiled gently. "Sometimes it helps."

"It was the Betas. One attacked me."

"I see. Why do you think you had that dream?"

"We started the Genetics unit in our history class this week. We were discussing the structure of society. We talked about Betas yesterday."

"So, you think it was a dream based on a subconscious fear? Do you fear Betas, Ardora?" Her mother's face went from gentle to amused. "You know that no Betas exist in the districts. Planning on leaving the Alpha district any time soon?"

No one respectable leaves the districts. "No, Mother."

Laughter erupted from her mother's mouth. "Then you have nothing to fear. Steadfast, come in here and cheer up your daughter." She heard movement in the office.

"Stepdaughter," Arda whispered. It wasn't that she didn't love Steadfast. He raised her. She just wished she knew more about her real father. Her mother never discussed him.

Her mother chided her with one look, and Arda focused on her eggs.

A tall, skinny man entered the room. He rubbed his glasses in his hands and smiled at both women. Her mother reached over to kiss him on one cheek. They were a picture: her mother's red hair catching the sunlight and her stepfather's short golden curls. It made Arda want to gag.

"Should I eat this in my room?" She asked. The adults laughed. Arda didn't know why. Nothing was funny. Her lips pursed as she stared them down.

"Faith, dear," her dad said, "will you please give me a protein shake? I have to leave early. Springtime brings troubled youth."

"I just cooked eggs! I actually cooked for you, and you want a protein shake?" Her mother, though the words were harsh, kept the polite expression on her face. "Are we disputing the value of real versus synthetic food again?"

"I know better than to argue with you, Love. I'm just late. I have to leave in five minutes."

"Fine. Here's a protein shake." Which meant that Arda got two servings of eggs. Without asking, her mother plopped them onto her plate.

“I don’t need this much protein…”

“Hush. Eat what’s given to you.” Her mother began loading the dishes into the DishGen. She wouldn’t use synthetic food, but it was hard to argue with the convenience of having instantly clean dishes.

“Can you drop me at Academy, Stead?” Arda managed as she shoveled eggs into her mouth.

“Can you be ready in three minutes?”

“Bag is packed. I’m ready now.” She quickly downed her vitamin supplement, grabbed her bag containing her learning tablet and her lunch, and followed Stead out the door, before her mother could scold her for leaving food on her plate.

“So, your mother tells me you had a bad dream…”

Arda rolled her eyes. *Here we go again.*

Public transportation was available to everyone, but Steadfast had to travel around the district for his security position, so he was one of the few people to have a small flyable car. It only sat two people. Arda enjoyed the quiet peace of the small vehicle over the bustle of public transport. Large groups of people always made her nervous.

She took out her tablet and logged on to her account, checking to make sure she completed all of her coursework for the previous day. She glanced over to see her stepdad looking at camera footage from the night while he slept. Humans couldn’t be trusted to drive themselves, so you merely entered a destination, and the car would take you there. All stops were handled by operators and programs, in order of urgency.

It must have been an important day for her stepdad because they didn’t have to stop at all to get to her school. She

wondered vaguely what could be going on. In a walled off city, not much changed overnight.

They pulled up to the Academy of Highest Learning and Arda gave him a quick shoulder hug. "Thanks," she said sweetly before stepping out into her section of the world.

She heard a familiar, deeper voice shout from across the campus, "Arda!" She turned just in time to be wrapped up in a bear hug by her tall and handsome classmate.

"Hey, Chaste. Put me down! *Chaste*!" Though touching was prohibited, they'd been friends since Early Learning. No one would report him, but they were still becoming adults soon. Kid stuff like hugs had to be over. "I'll report you!"

Chaste laughed. "No, you won't," he dared her, but he dropped her gently to the ground anyway. She looked up smiling into his dark features, brown eyes catching the sun. Little pools of gold shown in his irises. While she was an average height, Chaste towered over her. He was popular and loveable. Everyone thought so. "Ready for Genetics?" he asked.

Arda groaned, her eyes rolling and her shoulders tight. "What are we going to learn this year that we haven't learned in Early, Intermediate, and Advanced learning?"

"Never know, they might throw something new at us." They began walking into the school. "Maybe actually tell us something about how the Betas came to be."

He looked over at Arda, who gave him a skeptical look. "Right, and then they'll tell us how to unlock the genetic potential of pigs to induce flight."

He shrugged. "It's possible."

She glared, exasperated, but he began to walk off.

Chaste walked inside the large white building, nodding his head to his classmates. They moved out of the way in deference to him. Not only popular, he was also an athlete, whose father had sat as District Chief for several years, and she was the quiet daughter of a security guard and a financial district worker. He was someone important, and she was his friend.

They entered the classroom and Arda walked to her usual seat near the back wall. Chaste sat directly beside her. Others fell in, the chatter slowly dying down as the clock neared seven and thirty hours.

Precisely timed to the second, the lights in the room dimmed and the holographic teaching VA was projected at the front of the room. Human tutors often taught the small amount of very wealthy children who could learn from home. Most city academies used virtual renderings of famous individuals lectured on their areas of expertise. For the History of Genetics unit in Advanced learning, Dr. Gregory Jackson graced the room, the father of modern Genetic Modification Technology and founder of the North American Genetics Institute.

"Welcome to the History of Genetics. I am your instructor for the last six weeks of your history education at the Highest Learning Academy institute number 13. I will be instructing you on the origin, experimentation and implementation of genetics for your level. Failure will not be tolerated. Please press the green button on your tablet to show compliance."

After everyone had pressed the green button, a picture of the real Dr. Jackson displayed on screen. "This is the father of genetics research. His lab was based out of North America in the late half of the 21st century, before Omega Fire occurred…"

I was right. Same boring lesson. By this point the students knew the answers by heart. She went through the motions of learning, but in her head, she was reliving her dream. She could write about "Genetics" in her sleep.

"Prime, Arda?" the VA chirped.

Arda looked up to find the whole class looking at her. "I'm sorry, VA. What was the question?"

"Please note that failure to learn this subject matter will result in the dismissal from the academy. I will repeat the question once. What was the Great Mistake?"

Arda, without lifting her head, stated, "The Great Mistake was a series of events that lead to OmegaFire."

"Elaborate."

"A synthetic genetic event among early subjects called the Mythics caused a catastrophic world event called OmegaFire. No knows what started it, but it devastated every habitat on earth except the immediate areas around the five districts. After the Great Mistake, genetics research was banned except by three companies."

"And can you tell us, Jackson, Chaste, the names of those three companies?" the VA continued. As it was a computer program, it had no idea it was talking to the great nephew of his originator.

Chaste cleared his throat before he answered, "the European Institute at Gamma district, the Asian institute at Delta District, and the North American Institute at Alpha district."

The VA went on to talk about the importance of primary missions. Europe's mission was to extend the human lifespan, Asia's primary mission was responsible for improving our physique to survive in the new climate created by OmegaFire, and the North American institute was kept around mostly because Dr. Jackson wanted a second chance to start over. Though he never touched a research experiment personally again. This institute's primary mission was to keep Omega Fire from recurring.

Arda left school that day learning absolutely nothing new. Bored, and slightly stressed out, she decided to walk home. A headache throbbed at her temples. Chaste offered her a ride, but she felt sluggish from her dream, and she wanted exercise and fresh air.

Her home was several blocks from the school, but the walk would take about a half hour. With no VA to tell her not to, she decided to take a short cut through the park. Wildlife and plants were essential to the district, so the park was a central area where one could go to see various contained habitats preserved after Omega Fire. They were all sealed in hard, shatter proof glass and climate controlled. How her mother managed to get so much fresh food out of so little was beyond her. Most people chose to use the synthetic FoodGen machine instead. Instant meals, no waiting. Arda loved the animals though.

Alpha station was lucky enough, being the Capital district, to have the largest selection of animals, and five distinct habitats, Arctic, Desert, Temperate, Tropical and Oceanic, her favorite. She loved watching the colorful fish swim around. Sometimes a dolphin would look at her sideways. She was so grateful to the districts for saving as much as they could. She wondered what water felt like when it was all around you, submerging you. She knew she couldn't breathe through it, and for a moment, her dream came back to her, her pulse racing and her breathing fast. Her hands became fists as she stared, comparing the ocean to the vast blackness of that abyss.

Lost in thought, she didn't feel the hand sneak into her bag. She only felt the weight on her shoulder being lightened. She turned and saw a dark-haired man running away with her tablet.

"Hey!" She shouted at him before running full sprint to catch up.

He rounded a corner and went down an alleyway. She did the same. He threw a garbage can down in her way. She ran around it. He turned, going left and Arda kept pace with him. She was no athlete, but the penalty for losing your tablet could be up to an extra month of instruction time to graduate. She was not going to let that thief keep her bored in school.

Down the road they traveled until the tall figure took another left. She was gaining on him and was sure she would catch him around the turn. However, as she flew around the corner, she stopped, confused, because a large brick wall stared back at her. There were no holes in the brick, no way of jumping it. The only other exit was a sewer drain, and no one in their right mind traversed those ancient tunnels anymore.

She had no choice but to report it and go home. Her parents would not be happy and...she was right. Her parents were furious, questioning why she had to walk through the habitat alone. Arda was chided and put to bed, after eating a healthy piece of chicken for dinner.

She shut her door and removed her clothing from the day. "Joy, analyze the clothing sample," she said through gritted teeth. Her movements were quick and swift as anger at her helplessness overcame her.

Joy took a few seconds longer than normal to respond. "I detect normal levels of bacteria, however, there are some unusual fragments found only in the sewer."

The sewer? Had he really... "Joy do not send data. Destroy the sample." She did not need anyone thinking she had gone into a restricted zone.

"Are you sure you wish me to destroy the sample? If a bacterium from the sewer were to invade the populace it could be catastrophic."

"I didn't go into the sewer today, Joy. Destroy the

sample." Her voice commanded it. With the only evidence gone, no one could report her.

"As you wish."

"You may go."

Arda placed the robe over her shoulders, ready to go to bed.

"I'm so glad to hear you say that." A baritone voice, unfamiliar, with a strange accent, seemed to whisper behind her. She turned, questioning if she was dreaming. Bright blue eyes glowed back at her. Glowed! She didn't know eyes could do that, be so vibrant a blue as to mesmerize her. For a moment there was silence, but before she could summon the courage to scream, a feeling of safety washed over her. This man was no threat.

"I'm so sorry that I had to borrow your tablet. I'm returning it to you unharmed. My apologies for your parent's anger. I could hear it from my spot on the roof. They weren't lying when they said you should no longer walk home alone. Thieves are everywhere." And with a wink, he was gone.

The safe feeling left her immediately, replaced by panic. Her breathing and heartrate sped up so much that Joy came on.

"Warning. You are exhibiting signs of distress. Is something wrong?"

"No Joy, I'm okay. Analyze the room please? Has anyone entered or exited but me?"

"One heartbeat has been present in your room for the past ten minutes. You are alone."

Who, or what, is he then?

In the morning, with her pad safely back in her hands, Arda convinced herself that she had just misplaced her tablet.

Surely the unlikely set of circumstances the night prior was a dream. No human had glowing eyes. No one was robbed in the park. She almost believed it until she saw the look on her parents' faces at breakfast. Today it was more eggs.

Her mother said nothing as she dumped eggs onto Arda's plate. Her stepdad cleared his throat, thought about speaking, but decided against it. It was up to Arda to start the conversation. She took a deep breath, the tightness between her shoulder blades straightening her back, and began.

"I found my tablet." Relief. There, it was out. Her mother turned away from the stove and gave her a quizzical look. Sharing a glance with her husband, the two then looked decidedly away from Arda. "What? I found it. It's a good thing." She took it out and placed it on the table, eyeing them both, adjusting the strap of her bag uncomfortably.

Steadfast looked in her direction. "Unfortunately, Arda, I'll have to take your tablet to examine it. You can use one of mine today."

"Why?" Arda couldn't keep the irritation out of her voice, felt her temple begin to throb with a stressful headache.

From the other room, he answered. "Because, Arda, we don't know who took your tablet or why they decided so benevolently to return it to you. It's worth much more if it's sold. I'll need to investigate this. It's my job."

Arda sighed. So much for *normal*. "Fine. Do you have a tablet I can use?" She tried to keep the nervousness out of her voice.

Her mother removed her plate and handed her a vitamin supplement. She took it and swallowed. *Still not talking to me, I see.* Arda didn't bother to curb in the loud sigh that echoed between them.

Steadfast came back a few moments later to give her an

old, worn looking tablet. Compared to what the other kids had at academy, she might as well take a computer. It was decades behind the times.

"This is what I get?" she asked in disbelief. The tablet was thicker than actual paper.

"Be lucky you have one at all," her mother chimed in. "Some students in your situation would just be kicked from academy because their parents have no extra tablets."

Steadfast made a couple quick swipes with his finger over the ancient screen. He actually had to touch the screen to make it work. *Gross.* She would be a laughingstock.

"All downloaded. Though it doesn't have holographic, you should still be able to perform the necessary functions with it."

"Thanks," she mumbled. Her mother sent her a look of exasperation, signaling that Arda couldn't quite keep all the sarcasm out of her voice. "I mean, thanks, Dad."

Steadfast stood up. "I'll drive you. Let's go."

Chaste was the first at Academy to notice. He gave her a look, and she glared right back, daring him to say anything. Instead, he leaned in and whispered, "what happened?"

"My tablet was stolen. This is Stead's."

"Classic."

"Yeah, whatever. You want to trade?" She shoved his shoulder gently. However, while she was doing so, another student noticed. Standing rather quickly, the rascal grabbed it from her desk.

"Oh, what's this?" Everyone looked at him. They all knew who he was, and they were all surprised he was still here. She expected him to be kicked out ages ago.

The boy took the tablet and started to touch the screen. He wasn't as tall as Chaste, who began to stand, but he was fast.

And thin. His blonde hair was way too long for a respectable boy at academy. He wore homemade clothes with worn shoes that needed recycling badly. While most students in the Academy of Highest Learning came from middle or upper class backgrounds, he was raised outside the walls in the poor district.

Still, he had enough friends in the room to block Chaste from getting the tablet back. While Arda and Chaste tried to move around his friends, he continued to swipe away.

"I really don't want your germs all over my tablet. Give it back!" She clenched her fists as he simply ignored her, jumping over and around desks as he continued to pry into equipment that was not his own.

A warning beep signaled the start of the lesson. They had fifteen seconds to be seated. Arda was getting worried.

"Willful, give it back!" Arda shouted at the boy. With a smile at his name, the boy, sitting in front of her, unceremoniously handed the tablet back to her. "Here you go. Only old surveillance videos anyway. Nothing worth hacking."

She breathed a sigh of relief as the lights dimmed, and the lesson started, but Arda was curious as to what he found. She'd check on that later.

"Good morning, I am Dr. Jackson, and this is day 2 of your genetics unit. Today, we will be discussing a very uncomfortable subject, that being the failure of the big three and the resulting consequences."

A map popped up in the center of the room. It showed the earth, all seven continents as if seen from space. "This, is our home. Though a small colony of scientists has landed on Mars, this is our home, and we, Alphas, are its keepers."

The map zoomed in. "This is our continent. North America. We are here..." it zoomed in again, "in the Alpha district. We already know the faults of our forefathers here. We were responsible for OmegaFire. We can't take it back or wish it wasn't so. It is our burden. But each facility and district shoulders one of these burdens. With heavy hearts, we will discuss those today."

"Rogue, Willful. To what am I referencing?"

With a sigh, the vagabond answered. "You're referencing vampires and werewolves, Sir."

The class erupted in laughter, Arda included.

The VA waited for the laughter to stop, then turned back to Willful. "While you are technically on the right track, vampires and werewolves do not exist. Can someone be more specific?"

Several hands reached for the red button to indicate they were prepared to answer. Arda did not. Thea, short for Theasaura, was chosen to answer and stood, perfectly reciting a textbook. Her back was straight and proud, her black hair falling free like silk. Arda knew she had striking blue eyes, but not eyes that glowed…

"Early study of genetic modification focused on prolonging life had severe consequences. Test subjects suffered from vitamin deficiencies, and a rare blood disorder that requires frequent blood transfusions, however, they aren't vampires." She shot a disdainful look at Willful, who only smiled widely in return. "In addition, during the first phase of Asia's enhancement project, while looking for ways for Alphas to survive using less resources, a group of test subjects also experienced adverse side effects. These included unsightly hair growth, emotional instability and physical strength deemed too dangerous to possess, however, they are not werewolves."

"Exactly." The VA was silent for a moment before continuing. "What happened to all test subjects in both projects?"

Willful turned toward Arda and motioned across his

neck with his finger. The gesture was obvious and unimpressive. Why was he distracting her so much today? She glared back, a finger to her lips.

"Prime, Arda? Care to answer?"

Arda stood, and somberly, respectfully, stated, "all test subjects were… disposed of."

"Yes. And why was this significant?"

Chaste answered without raising a hand. A bit of anger could be heard in his voice. "Because it depleted the remaining population of each lab's district by half, severely limiting the district's ability to function and sustain humanity. If not for Alpha district's intercession by sending residents to booster their population, those labs and their districts would be a total loss."

"And this is bad because?" The VA asked the entire class this question, but there was no emotion in his voice.

"Because then the human race could all die out." Willful couldn't hide the anger in his voice either. "And because a lot of people *died*."

Everyone was silent for a moment, while the VA stated, "please refrain from emotional responses to adult situations. While the developments there were tragic, we still gleaned a considerable amount of data from those failures that will ensure that they do not occur again."

Another pause occurred. "Let's delve deeper into the data we were able to gather from these experiments."

Arda leaned back in her seat. This would be a long, hard lesson.

Arda waited until lunch break to attempt to look at the surveillance footage on Stead's tablet. Chaste sat down next to her, a massive amount of food in his lunch box. Loaded with protein, he was allotted more because of his athletic ability. Arda had a piece of chicken and standard veggies and fruit.

"What are you doing with that ancient thing?" he asked. As others walked by, they gave their salutations or tapped his shoulder. Being generous, he acknowledged everyone, but listened intently to Arda.

"Willful apparently hacked Stead's tablet…"

"Right, because he's so *bad*…"

Arda laughed. "Well, he thinks he is."

"Indeed."

She thumbed through the files, mostly standard surveillance of public areas. "I'm just checking to see what he found. I don't know how to hack, so."

"Honestly, Arda, I don't think he does either." They laughed again.

Surprisingly, Willful took a seat across from Arda. "Anything good?""

"What do you want?" Chaste demanded.

"Calm down, just seeing the result of my many skills. Arda? Any top-secret files?"

Arda just glanced in his direction briefly. "You know, if I told Stead about this, you could be kicked out…"

Willful laughed. "Right. Six weeks away, not enough educated populace, smaller than normal class sizes and expanding job markets. They aren't kicking anyone out anytime soon."

Arda continued combing through the files. One did catch her eye. "They have surveillance in the sewers? Why?"

"Sewer slimes." Willful stated, as if they would come attack them at any moment. "Did your dad get some good videos of some slime?" He leaned over and stole the tablet from her.

"Give it back, Will." Arda was annoyed. She only ate half her lunch, and their time was growing short.

"Just a minute…" Will tapped the tablet in several patterns before returning it to her. "Here, let's watch the whole video after school, okay? It's kind of long."

With a wide and unconcerned smile, he handed it back, walking away swiftly to his small group of friends.

"Talk about slime." Chaste looked at her, hoping to make her laugh. She chuckled but was starting to get worried. What was Stead doing monitoring sewers? Her mind drifted back to glowing eyes for a moment, then the vastness of the oceanic habitat. She shook her head to clear her thoughts, eating her protein quickly as others began to move back inside.

Getting through Physics at the end of the day was tedious for Arda. Though she understood the concepts, she was only half listening as she reflected on the incident the previous day. Things were starting to add up in her head, and she didn't like where her thoughts were leading her. Sewer on her clothing, sewer video, a boy disappearing near a sewer… The official line was that no one lived in the restricted area, but if no one was there, why all the cameras and expense of installing and maintaining them? Something didn't add up, and her curiosity was often her biggest hurdle.

Arda looked over at Chaste. He was her best friend, but he was also the son of the former District Chief, as well as the great nephew of a man that shaped their world. She highly doubted that he would be up for helping her, even if she begged him to. She sighed, realizing that he wouldn't be an ally in this.

Willful, on the other hand, was the first of his family to possibly graduate from the Academy of Highest Learning and seemed to have the necessary skills to help her figure out what was going on. Arda tried to reason her way out of this adventure, telling herself all about the dangers and punishments that could befall them both. She struggled with her nature until the end of the day.

Walking out of the building, it wasn't until an impulsive last second that she started toward Will, who was waiting toward the side of the building for her.

Chaste grabbed her arm, firm yet gentle. "Arda…" he whispered. "What are you doing?"

Her heart pounded a bit too fast, her stomach tied in knots, but this seemed important. "I just want to watch the video. Maybe see some sewer slime. That's all."

"You remember what happens to hackers, right?" An image of a famous one being hauled away by Stead several years ago came to her mind. He had disappeared without a trace. She'd asked Stead about his trial, and the response had been, "it's…been dealt with and we are safe."

"He'll cover his tracks. Erase the tracking data. I bet Stead didn't even want it on his tablet in the first place. No one will know. Want to see slime or not?" She added a wink and a smile, but half of her agreed with Chaste. *What if we're caught?*

Chaste was thoughtful for a moment, before he released her arm and took the lead, walking toward Will. Surrounded by a group of his peers, Will didn't acknowledge them until they were close by.

"Well, well. Two of the top ten coming to my little circle. Decided to watch it, then?" His smugness did nothing for his appeal, but two girls giggled as he winked at them. Nothing seemed to faze him.

"Yes, Will, let's get on with it." Chaste stood behind Arda, seeming to guard her from the other students.

Will looked around him, at her. She tried to stand as stone, but something in his eyes seemed to peer inward in a way she didn't understand and was not comfortable with.

A smile spread suddenly on his face, and with another wink, he said, "not here. Let's take a walk."

After an inordinate number of secret handshakes and goodbyes, Will started walking away. Arda and Chaste followed. They walked in silence past several blocks before Will turned toward the park. "Let's try here. No internet around the animals. Lots of corners to hide in."

"Lots of thieves to steal your stuff…" Arda mumbled. Chaste gave her a look but kept silent.

Will managed to find a small indent in the oceanic habitat where a worker could release feed into the large basin. There was a small glass bench that shimmered with the glow from the water. Will sat, Arda sat and Chaste looked around uneasily.

"Relax, it's fine. No one comes back here unless they're feeding animals, and that only happens at 700 and 1700 hours. We're good."

Chaste made a noise of exasperation and continued to look around. Arda opened her backpack and removed the old tablet. She handed it unceremoniously to Will, who once again used his fingers to touch the screen. She thought about sanitizing it later, even though his fingernails were as clean as hers. She didn't know why that surprised her. He was poor, not unhygienic.

"Here we go. Ready to see some sewer slime?" Placing the tablet in between them and enlarging the image, Arda and Will began to watch.

The picture was old, and the images were not clear, plus some of the data must have been corrupted, because for several seconds the screen would go dark. The scene displayed showed old, stone sewer with a river of cringe next to it. There was a ladder leading upward on the left, rusty and unused, and a small path next to the grossness crossing horizontally on the screen. A single light was visible, shooting straight out from the camera.

"It doesn't look like much is down there." Arda was slightly disappointed to have her mystery turn mundane.

"Then why is it so long, huh? Someone bothered to comb through this and save it. Must be a reason." Will's eyes never left the tablet. "Just wait for it."

After several minutes of waiting for it, Arda convinced herself that nothing was there. She was about to tell Will to stop this nonsense when a dark image appeared on the screen. Entranced, she watched the figure climb down the rusty ladder as if they weighed nothing. Two more joined the leader. They conversed with each other in shadow for a moment before the leader turned toward the camera. Familiar, glowing blue eyes seemed to lock onto Arda's through the screen. A second later, the data ended.

While Will jubilantly displayed his pride by replaying the data for Chaste, who was surprised and amused, Arda instead felt a growing sense of dread. Who or what is living in the sewer, and why had they targeted her? Should she tell her friends, or keep quiet? She couldn't decide which path would lead to the best outcome, and the more she debated with herself, the more the unease in her stomach grew.

Chaste, having watched the video, did not respond as joyously as Will. He stood, calm and collected, and turned to the other boy, stating only, "erase it now."

Will, a perplexed look on his face, thought a moment before his hands nimbly touched the tablet again. "Yeah, yeah, no problem. That was always the plan, right? I mean, getting rid of evidence of *live* vamps firsthand is no biggie."

Chaste chuckled. "That was a trick of the camera. Vampires don't exist," With that, he turned and started to walk away. "Coming, Arda?"

Except Arda was having a difficult time moving. Will handed her back the tablet, and she stood on shaky feet. "You look like you've seen a Beta." Will remarked, his voice no longer carefree, but concerned. He reached out to grip her hand, a show of support, but she recoiled from it.

"I'm fine." Arda shook off the terrible feeling she had. "Chaste!" She ran to catch up to her friend. "Will you walk me home?"

Chaste, putting an arm around her shoulder, a bit possessively, answered. "No problem."

The two friends left the park and turned toward home, Zone 3. They didn't see Willful take out his own tablet and replay the scene once more on it. "Erase it. Right, slime." Will replayed the video several times before packing his tablet away and standing to go home. He left just in time to see a park employee place feed in the habitat. He stopped around the front of the exhibit to see several larger fish attack the food. *Poor little guys, stuck in there instead of the real ocean.* He watched the colorful fish swim in schools, unaware that a camera was watching him.

"Chaste," Arda asked as they turned onto her street. "Can you keep a secret?"

He turned and looked at her quizzically. Their society advised against that practice, with a long list of valid reasons. "What?"

"You have to promise not to say anything."

He laughed. "We've been best friends since Early. I've got so much dirt on you already. A secret won't destroy you."

Somehow, that didn't have the calming effect she was hoping for. But she felt she had to tell someone, and if that was her parents, she could be dismissed from academy. She purposely forced her hands to relax, for her shoulders to relax just a bit. She forced her breathing to be even and her voice to come out smooth and unperturbed.

"Yesterday, my tablet got stolen."

"Well, I assumed that when you brought Stead's tombstone tab with you."

"No, but…" Arda paused. "When it was stolen, I chased them and- "

"Oh, no! You mean you ran in public? For shame!" He laughed then, loud and boisterous. "What will you do with your wicked self?"

Arda sighed and tried again, feeling that he wasn't really listening to her in the way she needed. She placed a hand on his arm, sincere. "I lost him near a sewer drain. When I got back to my room Joy told me that I had sewer residue on me. Then today, that video…" Why had she left out the glowing-eyed man?

Chaste was silent for a moment, then placed both hands on her arms, just above the elbow. He stood near her, but not so near that she could feel the warmth of him.

"We only have six weeks of Academy left." He gently moved both of his hands to her shoulders, rubbing at the spot that was always stiff from stress. "I'll walk you home every day to help you feel safe if you want. Or we can take the bus. Whatever you want. Getting something stolen is no joke. I want you to feel safe."

Arda felt her shoulders slump forward a bit, as she realized she was getting nowhere. She suddenly lost her nerve. Something was keeping her from telling him the whole truth. Maybe she needed to reflect on it a bit more.

"Thanks, Chaste." They crossed the street, steps from

her building and walked inside.

Chapter 2

She walked through the door first, her mother and Steadfast standing in the tiny kitchen. Arms crossed, face red, Faith stood tapping a foot on the floor. Steadfast smiled politely and began to speak.

"Arda," he began, "how was school?"

"Great. Tablet worked fine." Setting her bag down, she didn't quite understand the tone of the room. She should be careful. "No one complained. Thank you for letting me borrow it."

He smiled. "I'm glad it worked. Just because the tech is old doesn't mean it isn't useful. Can you have a seat a moment?"

Arda pressed her lips together and sat. "Sure. What's up?"

Faith began. "Arda, we need to talk to you about your future." She paused and sat next to her daughter. "You have five weeks of classes left. I realize you've always been an avid dreamer, but you need to take some time combing through possible professions you may wish to choose."

"You're worried I won't be able to get a job?" That never happened in the Capital.

Steadfast laughed. "No, no. We are worried you may not get the right job. It matters. We've lived in Zone 3 our whole lives. We don't want to see you move to Zone 5."

That's where Willful lives. He seems fine. "What's wrong with Zone five?"

Faith gave an exasperated sigh. "No one chooses to live outside the walls with the merchants, Arda. You have to take your CAT seriously if you want a good job. With your scores, you might even be able to do better than here."

Only one residential area was better than 3. Zone 4, where the politicians generally lived. Chaste's father chose to remain in Zone 3, despite being eligible for Z4. "Why does my career aptitude test matter so much? I thought it was just to help us figure out where we would fit best."

Faith sighed again. "That's what they tell you so that you don't feel any pressure. This is the single, most important part of your education that will set up the success or failure of your family for the next generation."

"Thought we weren't supposed to feel pressured, Mother."

Steadfast laughed. "We don't want to pressure you; we want to prepare you. Now, I know you're seventh in the top ten of your class. By itself, this gives you extra points, however it's not enough to secure a good score. The point we're hoping to make is that you need more than the education you get at Academy. I know it, your mother knows it. We want that for you because we love you, so you're going to be studying with me at my office after school, every day. Faith will pick you up and drop you off."

"More studying? Why?" Arda felt defeated. Her hopes of more time to dream vanished. She'd considered playing the cello more, as well.

"It's what's best." Faith stood and began to make dinner. Chicken and vegetables. Again. "Your first lesson starts now. Go with Stead."

He stood, moving toward his office. Arda followed reluctantly. She wondered what more she could possibly learn that she hadn't in physics, biology, chemistry, history, integrated studies, applied studies, calculus and genetics.

Steadfast sat down in his office chair, urging Arda to take a seat to his left in the small room. She complied.

"First, I'm going to ask a series of test questions ranging from easy to extremely difficult to see where you are failing. Think of this as a practice test."

Arda sighed. "Fine." The throbbing headache at her temple returned.

Stead turned to her, his glasses making his eyes appear bigger than they were. "This is all about you sweetheart. You'll do fine. It won't take that long. You'll see." He handed her a tablet with a timed quiz on it. "Try to complete it as fast as you can."

Arda swiped her finger over the start button and began.

Falling into bed that night, she sighed heavily, covering her face with her arm. If the test had shown her anything, it was how much she still had to learn. Tossing and turning, she fought to go to sleep. Thoughts of oceans and Betas tugged at her, the cello tugged at her. She always felt more centered after practice, and it had been so long…

Waking suddenly, she asked, "Joy, what is the time?"

"The time is 315 hours."

Looking around to see what had startled her, she stated, "lights, please."

The room lit up. Her window was open. Had she left her window open? Standing, she walked slowly to it, as if it might attack her. "Joy, did I leave the window open?"

"No. The window was opened ten

minutes ago by an unknown force."

She froze, halfway there, her heart in her throat. A breeze flowed into her room, framing her face and fluttering her hair gently. Slowly, she walked to the open window and looked down. No one. Sighing, relieved, she reached up to grab the window and forced it back down.

Before she could, a strange creature, too skinny to be a healthy human, jumped into her room, landing on top of her. Arda screamed, and clawed at the creature, trying to get it off of her. It grabbed her arms, holding them above her head. Looking her in the eye, it hissed and bit her neck.

Arda woke to a dark room, dripping in sweat. Breathing heavy, she looked at the window. It was shut. *Just a dream.* She heard her mother's voice in the hallway. The lights to her room came on, and her mother stepped inside. Steadfast was behind her.

"Arda, are you okay? Joy, is Arda okay?"

"I'm fine- "

"Arda experienced a nightmare. This is the second in a week's time. Should I report this?"

"No, I'm okay."

Faith sat by her daughter. "Believe it or not, I once had dreams too. Report it, Joy."

"*Mother...*" She wasn't a child that needed coddling, and the irritation showed in her voice.

"I'm not putting you in counseling, but when you scream in your sleep loud enough to wake the neighborhood, honey, I can't *not* report it." Her mother's eyes were a bit too wide, and Arda realized how much fear she was trying to hold back, for her sake. She relented, merely settling back into bed.

"Report received. May I be of further assistance?"

"Dream serum. Small."

"I'm not a *kid* anymore." She hated how whiney her voice sounded, instead of being assertive, like Chaste was capable of.

"You're someone having nightmares. Probably because of the pressure we put on you about this test. Let me help you." Her mother lovingly pushed a tendril of her hair away from her face. Arda was always jealous of their curls, the both of them. Her hair was straight and plain.

Arda sighed. "Fine. Just not grape, please."

"Strawberry dream serum complete."

A small hole in the wall opened. Her mother looked over the small glass filled with a pink liquid. "Drink up."

Arda swallowed the sweet, medicinal drink. Seconds later, her head hit the pillow and she was out. Her mother turned off the lights and shut the door. Turning to Stead, she said, "Just a nightmare. Nothing to worry about."

"Are you sure? Remember what happened with you?"

"My daughter will not have the problems I was born with. She'll be fine. You'll see."

"For her sake, and for ours, I hope so."

Faith kissed her husband on the forehead and said, "let's go to sleep my love."

Smiling, they turned and walked away.

Arda had to admit when she woke the next morning that she felt refreshed. Mostly, now, she woke up feeling tired. Maybe the serum wasn't so bad. Today was her one day off from school. She wished she could say that she was spending it with her friends, reveling in their childhood freedom for one of the last times in her life, but no, she already knew what her day would bring.

Trudging down to breakfast, her mother handed her a protein shake. "No eggs?" she asked.

Faith said, "After last night, you need the extra vitamins. Eggs tomorrow. I added cognitive boosters for you so you can optimize your study session. Don't worry…" she said as she heard Arda sigh, "It's just a morning session. This afternoon, we're going to tour Zone 5."

"Why?"

"Because it's important to know where you can go, and where you want to go in this world. You're a dreamer. You romanticize life. It's a wonderful trait, until it destroys your future. You need to see how people live there."

"So, this is encouragement?" She eyed her mother blankly.

"This is education. It's just not the kind you get at Academy."

Her mother walked into the living room, while Arda walked slowly up the stairs to the office. Steadfast was already hard at work.

"You're here. Good." He turned to her, handing her a tablet. "This is the entrance exam for my job. It combines tech knowledge with mathematics, science and has quite a bit of technical reading. It's forty questions long. I'd like you to be able to sample some tests for different careers to see where your natural aptitude lies. This is the first. I have seven more. Let's have a great morning, shall we?"

Handing her the first test, Arda fought off another sigh and quietly began. She just wanted to get this over with.

Seven hours later, she emerged from the office, a headache throbbing between her tired eyes. Her mother was ready with what she assumed was a pain serum. Gulping it down, bitter and metallic, she was correct. However, the headache faded almost instantly.

"I know it's a lot, but he'll use the data to help you shine. I promise. Let's go." Taking the keys to Steadfast's car, they left the house.

"So, what will we be doing in Z5?"

"Observing. I got a special pass for the day that allows us to trade with the merchants. It's old fashioned, but the people selling there are trying to feed families like the rest of us. Knowing this, the government allows us to go once a month. You will find something you like, and you'll barter to pay for it."

"What's bartering?"

"It's the art of negotiating price."

Arda looked at her mother, who was placing directions into the car's automatic system. "Huh?"

Faith looked at her daughter. "This is exactly why you need more knowledge than what Academy gives you. They're so worried about creating the next line of genetic engineers that they don't give any thought to practical skills."

The car began to move. "I still don't understand."

"Say I want to sell you this car. I want twenty thousand credit for it."

"Okay. It's a good car. Probably worth twice that."

Faith sighed. "No, no. You don't say that. You think it. What you say is that you smell smoke. Has it been in an accident?"

"Why? It hasn't been in an accident, has it?" Her throat

tightened, her heart beginning to race. That barely ever happened anymore.

"No, dear. You say that to get the price dropped."

"I want to drop the price."

"Yes."

"Why?"

"Because then you pay less."

"But I thought we were supposed to be helping them. How is paying less for something going to help them?" She crossed her ankles, confused, not entirely confident that her mother understood modern life.

Faith sighed. "Let me start over." Arda sighed as well. Looking out the window, she watched as they passed the park, wishing she could watch the fish.

One free day a week. You could go to the park, you could take a walk in the gardens, tour the shops of Zone 2, or go to the merchant's quarter in Zone 5, where a bazaar of homemade goods and foods were on sale. The only zone located outside the walls of District Alpha, they handled all shipments coming from other districts and handled all factory work.

As Arda stepped out of the car, remembering what her mother had said, she coughed at the quality of the air in the district. Her mother gave her a look. Arda couldn't help it. Something smelled rotten. She felt her cheeks redden as several people around them sent a glare her way. They couldn't control the air quality, and she had no right to judge them.

"It's from the factory smoke." Grabbing her arm gently, Faith led Arda into the middle of the bazaar. "Don't go far from me. We're safe as long as we're careful."

Walking up to a random stall, her mother started to talk

to the vendor who was selling homemade quilts, much like the one her grandmother made for her. "Oh, that's cool." Arda spoke softly, half listening to her mother.

"How's the weather been?" Her mother's back was very straight and proud, all of a sudden.

"Pretty fair down here. And you?"

"Oh, couple of rainy days. Nothing to complain about."

Arda gave her mother a quizzical expression but said nothing. It hadn't rained in three weeks. Her mother squeezed her arm, compelling her to remain silent. She wondered if this was a sign of declining memory adults sometimes struggled with. She'd ask her mother later if it was time for a memory supplement.

"How much for one of your fine quilts?" The smile was warm and genuine.

"Fifty credits. Takes me a week to make just one. I take my time. Look at this one." Snatching a gold and orange fabric from the pile, the merchant said, "goes so nice with your features. Brings out the blush in your cheeks."

Her mother laughed but eyed the fabric. The shopkeeper was right. Her mother did look beautiful against the contrasting colors. "I was actually interested in your preferred stocks."

The vendor grew serious, looking her mother up and down. Then, she did the same with Arda. Inclining her head, she said, "preferred stocks are for adults only."

"Right. Arda, dear, go grab yourself a sandwich from next door and wait there for me."

Handing Arda a small bag full of real credits, a mix of gold and platinum, Faith followed the woman into a small shop behind the stall. Arda was a bit perturbed. She liked the look of some of the quilts and would have been interested in a purchase. She eyed the credits in her hand, and walked away slowly, wondering what her mother expected her to learn if she just left her alone.

Walking to the vendor next door, she looked over their menu. The older man running the grill smiled wide at seeing her, and it seemed somehow familiar. "Ah, young Miss. What can I do for you today?"

Arda half smiled back, a little nervous, having barely glanced at the menu. "I'd like a sandwich." She handed him the credits her mother had given her.

"Of course, you do. Of course. What will it be? Chicken, turkey, beef, pork, we have them all. REAL meats, too, no synth stuff. My family contracts with a local farm. Want to try a sample for free?"

If she took a sample, she had to buy something from the stall. That's what her mother explained to her. Nothing here was really ever free. "Sure. Do you have the turkey?"

The man moved away and kicked the foot of a boy sleeping in the corner. "Wake up lazy head, we have a customer."

Arda watched as the boy stretched. He was tall, but not as tall as Chaste. Blonde hair, too long… Standing, the blanket was removed, and she stood facing Willful, her heart pounding a bit fast in surprise, her eyes a little too wide. "Hey."

Will turned to her and smiled, knowing she was out of her element, and a bit happy about that. "Top ten. What brings you to the market?"

"My mother is here. Is this your family's stall?"

"Yeah, every sale helps." He stood, dusting off the dirt from sleeping on the floor. "Dad, this is Arda, she's in my class."

"Oh, a friend of my eldest son? You won't pay today." He walked around the counter and gave her back her credits, patting her hand softly.

This was the part where she was supposed to protest. "I

really don't mind paying-"

"Put it *away*, child. Here you go. Something tells me you need a lot of veggies today."

Handing her a plate full of sandwich, she smiled and thanked Will's dad. Will showed her into their small home and sat her at a tiny table built for two. "This is all you've got?" Her table was easily four times as big.

Will turned around, looking to see if anyone had heard her. "Listen, let's just not mention the décor. I don't want my mom feeling judged. We do the best we can here in Z5. Just eat your sandwich."

Arda did so. She was amazed at the taste of the first bite. "This is so good!"

Will laughed. "Yeah, cause it's real. Real turkey, real oil. Real rosemary that my mother tends."

"My mom feeds me real eggs and chicken sometimes. I've had natural food before."

He seemed impressed. "You're lucky then. Not many people know what good food is."

Arda munched away as two small children ran through the house from the front to the back, where a small park sat, shared between all the houses. Instead of a swing set and a slide, like at Arda's family park, there was a large garden in the center. "Why don't they have any toys to use?"

Will looked at her curiously. "The vegetables and herbs are more important than a slide. We play in…other ways."

"Oh, I see." She felt very out of her element. As she was finishing her sandwich, her mother walked in, laughing with Will's father. "Arda! I had no idea you were in the same class as Will. We've met so many of your other friends. Will, I'm Faith. I went to school with your father, Frank."

"That you did Faith, and you haven't aged a day. No idea

this was *your* daughter."

"It's good to see you. Arda, would you mind if I sat and talked with an old friend for a bit? Oh, I'd love to meet your wife."

Willful stood, motioning for Arda to follow. "We'll leave the adults alone, right? I can keep an eye out for her."

Faith smiled. "Thank you Will. Have my daughter back here in two hours please. Enjoy the bazaar, sweetheart." Patting her head, Faith sat in one of the small chairs in the room, completely unperturbed by the small, compact house. In fact, she seemed to suddenly fit in, as much as Arda stood out. Will was leaving, so she scampered after him.

"So, Top Ten, what do you want to see today?" Will placed his hands in his pockets, turning toward her. His hair, normally tied back in a ponytail for school, was loose and free, the wind picking up tendrils of it. She watched it reflect in the daylight, and thought that he would be handsome once he filled out. His hazel eyes held a wicked smile, as if he were up for any manner of shenanigans, if she was so inclined.

She stopped staring and cleared her throat. "I'm supposed to buy something. My mom wants me to learn to barter."

Will smirked, a lopsided smile sassy on his face, his eyes narrowing. "You don't know how to barter. That's…" He chuckled, until she glared at him, daring him to say something condescending. "You just let me know when you see something you really like, and I'll handle it if you want. You can tell your mom you did it yourself."

Arda sighed. "I could do it if I wanted to. I'm just," looking around, she stared at all the people, "I'm not used to all the commotion I guess." The noise, the bustle was a lot for here. She felt overwhelmed, an outsider in a throng of people.

He saw her discomfort and walked close, saying, softly, "lead on Top Ten. I got you."

Walking through the crowds, it wasn't long before she found something appealing. However, Will vetoed all her choices, referencing the vendor's character. Finally, they approached a small scarf vendor, selling beautiful hand-crafted silk scarves.

Will didn't say anything bad, so Arda approached a bit closer. Will placed a hand around her shoulder, a gesture she wasn't completely comfortable with. Chaste had a pass with casual touching, but Will didn't know her. He winked and whispered, "play along."

An old woman approached them from a rocking chair near the door. "Ah, young Willful, I see. How are you, you dashing rogue?"

Will laughed. "About to be the first person to graduate from the Academy of Highest Learning, Mama Bear."

"Yes, well, you are smart enough, huh? Always getting into tech, taking perfectly good things apart. I work with your Ma in the plant. She talks about you. And what do we have here?"

The woman held out her hands to Arda, who had no choice to but let he take hers, rubbing her calloused thumbs over her palms. "Soft hands. This one does not work in the plant with me. What is your name, dear?"

"Her name is Melody. Melody Stock." He urged her to keep quiet. "She lives in the fringe."

The woman looked her up and down. "Boy, are you playing a trick on old Mama Bear? This girl's clothes are too good for the fringe, her hands not worn from the work. Fringe, you say. Ha!"

Releasing her hands, she turned, "and she is no Melody."

Picking up a beautiful scarf, light blue and purple, she turned and held it up to Arda's face. "There we go. Beautiful, makes your silver-grey eyes shimmer. This is no scarf for a fringe girl, though."

Will laughed. "Oh, Mama Bear, you know me too well. She lives inside the walls."

"Ah, honest, my boy." She pinched his cheek. "You can't get past Mama Bear."

Hanging his head in false shame, he said, "May we buy a scarf anyway?"

Smiling, she said, "Well, as long as I won, you just owe me a few gold. Have it as a treat. This girl, has an air about her."

Handing her the scarf, she held out a hand. Before Arda could reach for her purse, Will was handing her two solid gold from his own pocket. *Gold coins*, not credit. Turning quickly, they walked away. "There is more to a barter than price, Top Ten. Sometimes, the best thing you can do is give them a good story, a good piece of gossip. They live on so little."

"Why did you pay for it?" She eyed him accusingly. She wasn't one to rely on the charity of others. Her brows furrowed in confusion, her stance wide, her shoulder straight.

"That purse you're carrying is a dead giveaway that you are not from here. It tells them how wealthy you are and puts you at a disadvantage. You've got a lot to learn in two hours."

"Where did the gold come from?"

He smiled, and said, "everyone needs their secrets. Consider that one of mine. Hand me some credit."

She did so without showing off her purse. "Good. There you go. Let's go buy some gloves to match that scarf."

"Is this really what you want to do with your day?"

"Getting to show up a Top Ten?" His crooked smile flashed again. "Best day of my life. Let's go."

Arda followed him to another vendor, ignoring his teasing. He was right. She did have a lot to learn.

Two hours later, bags in both arms, Will decided they should head back. "Your mother will be impressed with your skills." He nudged her arm. "You got a whole outfit with that gold, and you still have some to spare." He slung one bag of hers over his shoulder, perfectly comfortable to help her with her new clothes. Permanent clothes. Ones that wouldn't taste the shredder at the end of the day. Like her grandmother's quilt. There was a comfort in that, that softened the set of her shoulders. It had been a good trip.

"Thanks for the help. I still have to pay you for the scarf." Turning, she began to take the credit out.

"No, Top Ten. It's fine. We won't starve."

"But-"

"NO." He said it so firmly she felt the commanding force of it. Her eyes widened and her smile faltered, worried she'd insulted him, somehow. He sped up and turned the corner, Arda following quickly. As she went to do so, however, someone bumped into her, forcing her to the ground. The man said "*sorry*" and ran away. Will looked back, glanced at Arda, and shouted, "stop him!"

Running faster than she thought possible, he gave chase. Arda slowly stood, her pocket light all of a sudden. Reaching for the small purse, she couldn't find it. So, the man had stolen from her. Walking quickly in their direction, she held on to her bags tightly. She had no clue where Will had gone.

Glancing right, she thought she saw him at the end of the next street, but there were too many people for her to be sure. What did she do now?

"I finally have you to myself," a voice behind her almost whispered. Her eyes flew upward and she gasped. She couldn't be sure, but this looked like the person who had stolen her tablet. "You!" She got ready to scream, but before she could, his eyes lit up bright blue.

"What do you want?" she asked, softly, dazed. *What's happening?*

"Only to introduce myself. I'm not here to hurt you." The glow from his eyes faded, but Arda still felt calm.

"Who are you?" She couldn't move her arms, which lay relaxed at her sides. Her hair flowed in front of her face, courtesy of the strong wind.

He smiled, then, gently moving her hair out of her eyes. "My name is Mayne. You… *remember* me." He sounded surprised.

"You stole my tablet. My mother was mad." Her body swayed with the next gust of the wind. He reached out two arms to balance her, knowing she couldn't do so herself.

He chuckled. "I apologize for that. Listen, I know who you are. Your name is Ardora Prime. You were born on the summer solstice almost eighteen years ago. I've been observing you for some time."

"You don't go to Academy." The calm was starting to fade. Her fingertips twitched as she regained control, slowly.

"No, I don't. We don't have much time. You'll remember meeting me, but when you try to tell someone else, you won't be able to. This is necessary. I'm about to prick your finger. It won't hurt, I promise."

Standing there, she asked, "Why?" She watched as he held up a mobile testing machine to her finger. In spite of wanting to curl it back, all she could manage was another quick twitch. She watched her finger as the metal pricked it, then the small laser as it seared the wound back together. The scar would fade in a day.

"To see if I'm right. To see if you are who I think you are." He put the device back into his pocket, as her hand began to clench. "You might turn out to be very special, Ardora. Goodbye." With a soft smile he walked away.

As he moved on, Ardora was back to her old self. *What the hell was that?* Looking down the street, she saw Will jogging back to her and sighed with relief. "Will." Her voice betrayed her emotions more than she wished.

She placed a hand on his shoulder, trying to tell him what had happened, but she couldn't. the words wouldn't come to her.

"It's okay, Top Ten. I got your purse back." Placing an arm around her shoulder, he continued. "Little punk didn't know what hit him. Left him on the ground, grabbed the purse and walked back. You're shaking." He rubbed his arms up and down hers. "Are you okay?"

"Yeah, I'm fine." She wasn't really, but she couldn't tell him that.

"It happens, you know. Some people are just not well off like my family. They're just trying to make sure their dependents have food."

I nodded, but the words I wanted to say didn't come to the surface, so I gave up. "To think that people still experience food insecurity…"

He nodded. "There is a lot to the world outside of those alabaster walls." She wanted to ask more, but those words were stuck inside of her, as well.

They arrived back on the familiar street where her mother awaited them. Faith turned away from Frank and who Arda assumed was Will's mother, and hugged her daughter. "Did you have fun? What did you get?"

"Will helped. I got a whole outfit."

Placing a hand on his shoulder, Faith said, "good. Good. Are you ready to go home?"

"Yes." That, she didn't have to lie about.

"Will, you have to stop by sometime after school. Steadfast would love to meet someone so gifted with tech."

"Thank you." The surprise and pleasure in his voice were genuine. "I'll take you up on that."

"Goodbye Frank, Constance." With that, her mother turned and walked away, taking Arda with her. "I had no clue you had such a diverse group of friends, dear."

"Will is really smart, but I wouldn't exactly have called him a friend before today."

"He is a great person to know. If he graduates, if he passes, Steadfast can get him a job in security. It would help his family. I can't believe that's Frank's boy. I feel so old sometimes."

"You're not old mother."

Looking at her daughter, she said, "you did a good job today. Let's go home and you can see what I bought for dinner. It's a rare delicacy. It's called pasta."

Getting into the car, Faith entered the coordinates to their home. Looking out of the side mirror, Arda drew in a quick breath Mayne stood there, waving goodbye to her, as if he hadn't just violated her and possibly run illegal medical testing on her. Looking away, she locked the door.

"Is everything alright?" The car began to move out of the space. She risked a glance back, and saw no one, then calmed.

"Just a shadow I guess…"

They sat in silence for some time before her mother spoke again. "Arda, I am so glad that you know so many people, we really are doing a better job of helping students achieve upward mobility. And I know his father and his mother. They are great people, wholesome, so I'm sure Will is also…"

Arda waited for her mom to continue, but she didn't. "He's okay. Why?"

"Well, after you get assigned a job, you know what happens next." Her mother sounded…embarrassed, and Arda was wondering why.

"Two years of working, then I'm placed. Are you worried about that?" She rolled her eyes.

"Well, I don't want to sound mean or rude, but I'd always assumed it would be Chaste that you were placed with."

This was getting uncomfortable. "Mother…" It was a warning.

"Oh, I know, it's not any of my business. Listen, my concern is that, with all the politics going on, Will might not get a chance at upward mobility. He might not get out. If he doesn't, you shouldn't be close to him anymore. Still friends, but distant friends. It's a hard truth, but you will not be placed with someone who isn't qualified to live in the same Zone as you."

Arda sighed. "That's so far away though. Besides, it's not really up to me, is it? The computer generates matches and we pick from a list of three. Right? That's what the chemistry chip is all for?"

Faith hesitated before she answered. "Your job, like your placement, is your choice alone. The government will try to tell you who to love and what job to do, but it's your life. You have to live it."

"If it's my choice, then why do they bother with all the testing?"

Faith took another pause before saying, "they mean well, but they can't know what's in a person's heart. You're the only one that knows what's best for you."

"So, all the times you told me that you knew what was best for me, were you lying?"

Faith laughed. "No, but you're almost an adult, and I'm just realizing that I need to prepare you better for the new world you're about to face. That's all."

Arda nodded. "I learned a lot today. It was a good day."

"I'm glad." Arda looked at her mother, and wondered why she looked so concerned if she was so happy for her daughter. "Is something wrong?"

Faith looked her directly in the eye. "No, dear. I'm fine."

Arda let it go, but she'd been raised by this woman. She knew when her mother was lying.

Chapter 3

Steadfast sat down to dinner, holding a tablet in his hands. Faith handed her a plate of something she'd never tried before. It looked squishy. She didn't like it. "What's the sauce made of?"

"Tomatoes, garlic, basil. Standard pasta sauce. Try it. It's great."

Taking a bite, she chewed slowly, wondering if she would like this dish. She did. Her taste buds did, anyway. "It's good."

"I'm glad you like it. Your grandmother used to make it all the time before the wheat shortage." Putting a bowl in front of Stead, she turned away.

"I've compiled a profile for you to look at that shows how likely you are to qualify for the various upper-level jobs. What I'd like to do is go over the results after dinner and figure out one or two areas that you'd like to concentrate on. We'll focus on reviewing the skills for the job you want."

Arda, with a mouthful of pasta, said, "okay. Can I have more?"

Faith looked at the pan. "Uhm, sure. There's about enough left for another serving."

"That's a lot of carbs for her, Hun." Arda eyed the man that would stand in the way of the tasty sauce.

"She's young. It's okay. How many more nights like this are we going to have, right?" Dumping the rest of the pasta onto her plate, she sat down and ate a smaller portion with a sensible salad. "How did she do?"

"Great. They did a good job giving you all the basics.

You passed almost every test. Usually someone will only pass one or two of they're lucky. With scores like these, I'm wondering why they placed you at seventh."

Arda shrugged her shoulders. "I'm in a class of overachievers."

Stead laughed. "Right. Well, then, that just means tougher competition. There are, what, thirty of you in your class?"

"Yes."

"That's so small," Faith said.

"Remember dear, small is good." He touched her hand, a look passing between them she didn't understand. "So three or four of you, assuming you all pass, will be accepted to each of the various industries. Some industries may be full so they may not even be accepting new employees. Your choices, in my opinion, based on your scores, should focus on any of the three following areas: Genetics, Medical or Counseling. All respectable fields."

Her mother beamed. "That many choices. Well done, sweetie."

Arda turned and said, "What if I don't want to work in any of those?"

Stead seemed taken aback. "Well, the next areas were arts and agriculture…"

Faith interjected. "We understand that you're nervous, but believe me, knowing beforehand what you're good at and what you're interested in will help you when the time comes. Now I think we should start with his top three, since we know you're likely to succeed in them, just for now. He did do a lot of work to get those results for you."

It wasn't that Arda didn't like those choices, but they seemed dull. She was no doctor. Nor was she going to sit and listen to people's problems all day. "I suppose... genetics?"

Steadfast beamed. "The hardest one. Good for you. Challenges are the spice of life."

Faith clapped her hands together. "My girl is going to be a geneticist. Oh, how exciting." Grabbing their plates she began to load them into the DishGen. "Steadfast, will you have the material by tomorrow?"

"Yes, dear."

"Good. Arda, you can have the rest of the evening to finish any work for Academy tomorrow." Kissing her forehead, Faith motioned for Arda to be dismissed. Walking complacently to her room to begin her work, Arda wondered why she didn't test well for arts. With her ability to dream, she'd be a great writer. Maybe it was time to stop being a child and find a way to be excited about what she tested well for. Still, she didn't fail at art. Steadfast said it was number four.

Taking out her tablet, given back to her after a thorough inspection, she opened it to see a message from Will. *Great.*

Opening it, she saw a picture of the turkey sandwich she ate that day for lunch. Underneath, he had typed, "want me to bring one for you for lunch tomorrow?"

Arda thought about what her mother had said, but that sandwich was delicious. She found herself smiling, so she hit reply and typed, "sure." Sending it, she opened her lesson to review for the morning, tired but determined.

Chaste was waiting for her outside school the next morning when Stead dropped her off. It was awkward thinking about what her mother had said. She wasn't even thinking about that in her life. Her smile must not have been convincing, because he tilted his head at her.

"What's wrong?" He placed an arm around her shoulders. "Didn't enjoy your day off?"

"Oh, it was educational. We went to Zone 5 to shop."

His arm tightened slightly. "Everything go well?"

"Yeah. It was fine. How was your day off?"

"Not as exciting as yours. My dad wants me to understand council procedures should I decide to go into PUTT."

PUTT stood for Politics, Utilities, and Teacher Training. It was the program that trained officials of the state. "He wants you to be district chief, huh?"

"Yeah, but I don't know. It's a big decision. I guess it's in my blood but…" He looked off in the distance, quietly. "What do you think I should do?"

Her mother's voice echoed in her head. "It's your life, your choice."

He chuckled. "Right, but do you think I'd be good at it?"

"Doesn't matter what I think." He stopped, suddenly. He was so still that she wondered if she'd said the wrong thing. Shouldn't it be his choice?

"It does to me…"

Will bounced up before he could elaborate and handed Arda a storage unit used for food. "Here's your sandwich."

Arda smiled and said, "thanks."

"Hey, Will." Chaste didn't exactly sound welcoming. His arm tightened around her a little more.

Sensing the tension, Arda followed up. "Will lives in Z5. My mom knows his dad from school. Stead is going to help him get a job in security."

"Oh, cool man." Chaste moved away from Will, taking Arda with him before she could talk. She wondered if this had to do with her mother's conversation with her. "What are you doing?"

Chaste didn't respond. "Hey, Will."

Will turned, looking at Chaste. "Good luck, man!"

And the conversation was over, for now. They walked inside, Chaste high fiving people all the way to first period. Arda sat down in her usual spot, Chaste beside her. Will sat in front of her. She smiled and got out her tablet to start the day.

The VI came online. "This is Dr. Jackson and this is week 2 of the history of genetic modification. Today we will be looking at the evolution of this industry as it pertains to life in the five districts…"

Arda saw Will turn, stretching. A note, written on paper, very old-fashioned, appeared. Taking it, she quickly unfolded it in her lap. It said, "I'm coming over tonight to see your dad. I hope that's okay with you, Top Ten. See you then."

She couldn't respond anyway because unlike some people she had no access to archaic writing supplies. Could she even form the letters correctly anymore? They hadn't practiced that since Early. Will apparently had skills she was unaware of.

Folding the note and placing it in her pocket, she focused her attention back on her VI. If this was going to be her career, the grade in this class could make or break her. She had to do well.

Sitting down for lunch, which they were eating outside today, Arda took out the turkey sandwich Will had given her. Chaste saw it and inquired, "is that from Will? You two become friends yesterday?"

Ignoring the ring of jealousy in his voice, she breathed deeply, smelling the fresh herbs in the sandwich. Her mouth watering, she replied, "sort of," and took her first bite. This sandwich tasted even better. "His dad makes great sandwiches."

"I see. I thought we didn't like him, though." His eye brows drew together, his nostrils flaring.

Arda tilted her head. "Turns out he's not a bad guy."

At that moment, Will chose to sit down next to Arda. "How do you like the sandwich?"

She had a mouthful of delicious turkey, so she gave him a thumbs up. Will turned to Chaste. "How's it going, man?"

Chaste smiled, but it didn't quite reach his eyes, which had turned cold. "Great. Arda and I were having lunch. You're free to join us."

Arda didn't get that, because he was clearly already joining them. Unconcerned, she chomped and chewed the delicious food. A friend that could cook this well would benefit anyone.

"Listen, Arda," Will said, "I've been thinking about that vid we found. You think I could show you something after school? When I come over?"

"He's going to your house?"

Arda put her sandwich down. "What's the big deal? My dad wants to help him out. Come too if you want." Was she going to get to eat this delicious sandwich or not? Rolling her eyes, she tried to ignore the both of them.

Chaste looked at her for a long second before he said, "sure. I'd love to. I can keep you company while you work for her dad."

Will laughed. "Hey, man, it's not a big deal."

The tone changed. "Whatever." Chaste stood and walked away. Arda looked at Will. "What just happened?"

Will looked at her. "You really don't know?"

She shook her head and picked her sandwich back up. She could talk and try to figure out male behavior, or she could eat. "No." She took another bite.

Will pressed his lips together and thought for a second. "He's jealous."

Arda thought about that for a moment, her suspicions confirmed. "I'm not placed with him or anything. What does he have to be jealous about?"

Will laughed, his hazel eyes dancing. "Have you looked at yourself lately?"

Arda didn't know how to take that so she frowned. "Every morning, in the mirror."

He nodded, his lips together, as if he wanted to say more. "Well, he looks at you the same way I do. I don't want to create any problems. If it's not okay for me to come over that's fine. I appreciate your dad's offer to help me, but I can do it on my own, too."

"Over Chaste? No. We're friends. He'll be fine. I think." Looking at Chaste, playing basketball, seeing how the other girls were watching him too, she guessed she understood. Now was not the time for this to happen, though. They had enough to worry about.

"I'm just focusing on my career right now. That's what he should be doing, too. What we all should be doing."

Will smiled in a strange, warm way just then. "Very true," he said, before standing and joining his friends. Arda sat eating the tasty sandwich by herself, thinking on the strange behavior of boys.

When school had ended, Will and Chaste escorted her home. It was awkward, silent, and tense. On arriving, seeing that Faith nor Steadfast were home, they sat in the small living area and turned on their tablets.

"So, Will, what job are you hoping for?" Chaste asked this without looking up from his tablet. Arda, however, glanced at him, wondering how long he intended to keep up that cold tone of his. She wasn't fond of it.

"Ideally, I'd like anything other than factory work. My family's been stuck in Zone 5 for generations. I'd like my kids to grow up in Z3."

"What's wrong with Z5?" Arda inquired.

"Nothing, if you like low air quality, tons of people in small spaces, and no access to sustainable tech."

Arda thought about her mother's appreciation for the market and said, "I'm sure there's good things about living outside the walls, aren't there?"

Will looked at her then, eyes squinted just a bit, as if he was wondering what she was thinking. "If you mean constant Beta attacks and lacking resources, sure. Seriously, you don't want to be there unless you have to be."

Chaste snorted. "She just hasn't been outside the walls much."

Arda turned to him, glaring angrily. "So?"

Chaste looked up then, and measured his words before continuing. "So you don't understand what it's like. That's what Will's trying to tell you. You've always been raised in Z3."

"But you understand it?" Arda was puzzled, and a bit upset.

"My dad was Chief, remember? Yes, I understand."

Will chimed in then. "As much as you can without actually living there, yes."

Arda didn't agree with either of them. To her, since her recent journey there, Z5 seemed like a culturally vibrant and open place with good-hearted people who shared what little they had.

Turning her attention back to her tablet, she changed the subject. "Any jobs you're hoping for over others?"

Will thought a moment, then said, "medical, probably. I'd like to help people stay well."

Arda smiled at him, then, the anger gone. "That's a great profession. Steadfast suggested that for me as well."

Chaste snorted again. Arda turned to him, trying not to show her exasperation. "What?"

Chaste looked at her as if she didn't understand something she should. "You'll be a geneticist."

Though Arda had been leaning that way, she didn't like the fact that the choice seemed to belong to everyone but her. "I'll be what I think is best for me."

Chaste looked back at his tablet. "You'll be a geneticist."

Will chuckled, but with a look from Arda, focused on his own work. She was angry, again, and she couldn't quite place her finger on why. She didn't like Chaste's tone. It was as if he were trying to speak for her, as if he knew her future when she hadn't decided it for herself yet.

Sighing, she stood and went to the eating area to get a glass of water. Her mother's words echoed in her ear. *Your job, like your placement, is your choice alone. The government will try to tell you who to love and what job to do, but it's your life. You have to live it.*

When her parents arrived at the house, she was handed another tablet. This one was state of the art, with holographic display and VR capabilities. "What's this for?"

"I have a friend that works in the education center. He was kind enough to allow me to access some sample tests for you to try out. They won't be exactly like your exam, but they'll help you understand what will be expected of you. I geared each of them toward your intended path, Will gets Medical, Chaste will get PUTT and Arda, I found the most rigorous tests for genetics I could find for you. I'd like you to take them now."

Turning, he walked away. Chaste whispered in her ear,

"see? Told you it was genetics."

Smug. He was being smug, and a bit condescending, and it was grating on her nerves. As if he were trying to prove he knew her better than Will. Taking a slow, controlled breath, she focused on her test, but a fire was growing inside her. One she knew would eventually need to burn.

She woke from a nightmare that evening, sweat dripping from her forehead. Breathing heavily, she rubbed her eyes. Slowly, looking around her room, she calmed down. *Another bad dream.* Why were they suddenly so real and vibrant?

"Ardora, your vitals indicate you experienced a nightmare. Shall I report it?" Joy's voice was pleasant, but it still startled her.

"No, Joy. I'm fine."

"As you wish."

"Sleep serum, Strawberry Dream."

A moment later, a vial appeared in the small alcove to her left. She downed it and passed out.

Immerging from the shadows, his eyes glowing, he looked down at the girl before him. She smelled… different than most. She didn't know what she was. He did. Touching her face, gently, he smiled slightly, and raised her left sleeve. Producing a vial and syringe, he placed them together and injected the thick liquid into her arm. There was no way he would let them destroy her uniqueness. She would not be forced like he was, not in any way.

Taking the vial with him, he gracefully and silently jumped out the window, landing on the ground. He walked away and faded back into the shadow.

Chapter 4

Arda stood looking at the museum in Z1, her head tilted in curiosity. It was less an official building and more of an old, ruined estate. This used to be the home of Dr. Gregory Jackson, Chaste's ancestor and the founder of the society they now lived in.

Arda felt a strange sadness as she looked at the columns, foundation, and decaying building. This place had potential once, and now it was like an old memory, faded and dying. This was ground zero, where the accident had occurred, where Omega Flame had changed the face of the planet forever. She imagined the cries and screams of those outside the protective border, what they must have felt, and her eyes began to burn from it, but she held back tears.

They'd been here before, but as seniors, they would be granted access to sensitive areas of the house. Arda turned to Chaste, who stood at her right. He gave her a half smile. She wondered what he was feeling, as this must be daunting for him. He kept his face and emotions cloaked, though.

"Are you feeling well?"

He placed an arm around her shoulders. "Yeah, it's fine. I just can't imagine living in a house this big, you know? So wasteful."

At the front of their small class of thirty, an actual person came out of the building to greet them. This was strange as normally tour guides were also virtual. Several of the other students whispered the sentiment among themselves until she signaled that she was ready to speak.

"Welcome to the Museum. I am the Keeper. My name is Wisdom." Her face didn't held the smile of welcome most officials used, but remained hard, unreadable. Arda began to feel uneasy about what they would learn today. "You are the senior class from the Academy of Highest Learning, here today to observe sensitive areas of interest that remain confidential. As such, you have access to me during the tour. I will answer any questions I can, but first, you must open your tablets and agree to the confidentiality clause. This is standard procedure for this tour. You are not to mention what you see here to anyone. If you feel uncomfortable signing this document, you will be unable to continue."

She hit a few spots on the screen of her tablet and Arda's made a beeping sound, letting her know the document was sent. Opening it, clicking "I agree," Arda didn't even bother to read what was in front of her. The government had kept them alive thus far, so she trusted them.

After a few moments, Keeper Wisdom looked up from her tablet. "100% completion. Thank you for the quick response. Please be aware that any attempts to record with any devices will be thwarted beyond this point and security will be notified." Though the electronic wall was not visible, a blue light was used to show where the video recording was not allowed. "Let us go inside and begin."

She continued talking on the way into the building, but Arda already knew the basics. She tuned out the tour guide as someone whispered in her ear. "*Some contract, huh?*"

She tensed, the soft breath tickling, sending goosebumps up and down her spine. She turned toward the source and saw Will. "Did you actually read it?" Her eye brows raised. It was a long contract, and she was impressed that anyone could read it that fast.

Will nodded. "Some of it. Heavy stuff. They're serious about all this. I wonder what's so important that we have to sign a contract like that to even be let in on it." He was smirking, curiosity clearly increasing his adrenaline.

Arda nodded. "I guess we'll find out." The group paused at the bottom of a great staircase that had been restored completely. Arda looked up. The upper level was new to her, and another blue electronic barrier stood at the top of the staircase. They weren't lax in security.

Keeper Wisdom stopped at the foot of the stairs, where several motion sensing lasers were actively moving. She hit a few buttons on her tablet, and the lasers were removed. "This is the beginning of the real tour. Everything encountered upstairs is confidential. Let's begin."

They walked up the staircase and turned to the right, walking down a hallway and into the farthest room on the left. "This was Dr. Gregory Jackson's private quarters." She opened a pair of double doors and Arda gasped, eyes wide. She'd never seen such opulence.

Real wood everywhere, on the bedframe, the walls, the windows. The bed looked large enough to fit a family of four. Dressers and furniture, completely restored, were strategically placed around the room. Real cloth curtains hung over the windows. *This was the room for just one man?*

"Now, let me assure you we didn't waste too many resources compiling the furniture in this room. Most of it came as donations from Z4. You know the original structure was in ruins following Omega Fire, so we had to approximate what this room looked like. This is a fairly accurate recreation. This is where our founder slept at night."

The students were released to look around. Will opened a door leading to what Arda assumed was a bathroom, full of strange water wasting devices. Opening her tablet, she brought up the online descriptions. This was something called a bathtub, in which someone would immerse themselves in water. This was an old-fashioned toilet, and a large sink. Chaste moved on quickly, but Will stared at the large marble tub.

"What is it?" Arda asked.

His cheeks turned red, and he shook his head.

"I didn't mean to embarrass you." Concern filled her features.

"No, you…didn't." He looked to see if anyone else was around. "We still have some tubs like this in Z5 for emergencies. This one looks like it could hold more than one person. I was just…contemplating why that might be."

"Let's move on," the Keeper said, before Arda could think on that. They walked out of the bedroom and turned toward the center near the staircase. She opened another set of double doors. "This was his office, and a very special place, as this is where the Omega Fire incident originated."

Stepping into the room, the students started to frantically whisper amongst themselves. At the back of the group, Arda couldn't see what it was until they began to file in. She caught her breath and fear gripped her throat as she understood the whispers. In the middle of the room was a glass structure, rising all the way to the ceiling and beyond. Inside the glass structure, was a single, black flame. Arda felt fear rising within her. Was that what she thought it was? *Surely, they wouldn't keep something so dangerous here.*

She glanced at Chaste, who appeared unperturbed, then at Will, who was struggling like she was. Did Chaste already know about this because he was the son of a former District Chief, or was he just that good at hiding what he was feeling?

"Silence, please," the Keeper stated. She waited a

moment, then began. "You see before you the very spot that the Omega Flame began. You are in the presence of the most destructive force ever created. For some reason, this flame could not be extinguished, no matter what methods we used. It has been protected since the beginning of this colony and has provided us with a great deal of information. Obviously, now you understand the importance of the contract you signed. If people were to know that this was still here, it might cause a panic. The information gained from this single flame has been essential to the survival of our colony. We are protected in a large part because this flame has never died. Any questions?"

Arda was still in shock from what she'd learned, but several hands raised in the crowd. One was Thea. "What kinds of information has this flame given us?"

The keeper smiled. "Everything from preventative clothing resistant to its effects to housing materials needed to keep homes from burning. This tragedy cannot be repeated."

Will raised his hand. Arda looked at him and saw a strange angry expression on his face. Luckily, the Keeper couldn't see him at the back of the room. After a few minutes, he put his hand down and gave up. Arda turned to him with a questioning look on his face, but he shook his head.

"Now wasn't really the time or place to ask anyway," He rotated, walking toward the flame. The keeper was leading the class away, to another part of the museum, but Arda didn't want to leave without Will. She placed a hand on his shoulder as he touched the glass. He seemed startled, but said, "touch it. It's cold!"

She placed her hand next to his, gasping as she did so. No heat was coming from the flame. As they watched, the flame that had been burning brightly flickered slightly toward her hand, as if it was reaching to her, as if it wanted to get to her. As if it needed her. Smoke rose from it, and something tugged at her mind, seeming to whisper to her. She couldn't make out the word, but part of her wanted to break the glass, and set the flame free.

The thought scared her so much that she quicky removed her hand and her breath quickened in her chest. The flame went back to its normal teardrop shape.

"What was that?" Will asked. Arda shrugged her shoulders and turned away, struggling to control her breathing. That flame made her feel uneasy.

She found herself thinking about it for the rest of the tour. As they exited the building, Will caught up to her.

"That was strange, right?"

Arda looked at him blankly. "What was?"

"Oh, come on. You know what I mean. You made the flame move. Somehow."

Arda felt fear race down her spine, and she glanced to see if anyone was close. They were alone, Chaste wandering a few feet away. "We aren't supposed to talk about this, Will."

Sighing, he relented, "fine, but that was weird, and you know it."

Walking away, he joined another group of students as they walked back to the school. Arda couldn't shake the way she felt, and worse, she couldn't talk to anyone about it. She didn't feel it was right to keep that flame alive. She didn't quite believe the Keeper when they said nothing could extinguish it. Frustrated and afraid, she followed her class back to their building.

"You're very quiet tonight," her mother told her over dinner. "The museum trip during senior year was hard to get through for me as well."

Arda turned her eyes from her food to her mother, her brows furrowed in confusion. "We aren't supposed to discuss it."

Faith and Steadfast laughed. "Oh, honey, yes, but no one is going to report you if you talk about it with *us*. We're your parents." Faith reached over and squeezed her hand, showing support and affection.

Arda took a breath and gathered her thoughts before she spoke, trying not to think about whispering smoke. "I can't believe we've kept something so dangerous within reach for hundreds of years. If I had my way, it would be gone."

Faith looked at Steadfast, who answered her, "many young people feel that way after learning it's there. However, you have to look at all the good that's been gained from studying it."

"And that good could be gone in an instant if it was somehow released."

Steadfast laughed. "Arda, it's secure. It hasn't moved, has been there for generations. It's not going to rise up against us. It's how people used the flame that was dangerous, not the flame itself."

Arda thought on that for a moment before saying, "from what I've learned, the flame itself can still do a lot of damage."

Faith spoke up. "Yes, but all attempts to destroy it have failed. We live with it, protect it, secure it so that no one will have to be subjected to its destruction again. It's part of the hard life of being an adult in this world. A world you will join in a matter of weeks. It's our duty to safeguard and protect ourselves and the flame."

Arda looked back down at her food. "I wish I could study it myself. There must be some way to destroy it we haven't thought of."

When she looked back up from her food, her parents were staring at her as if she'd said something horrible.

"What?" Arda was confused. "Wouldn't that be the best route? To have a way to intercept it's destruction, neutralize it, so no one was hurt?"

"It's just not something that is safe to say. Everyone that has studied the flame up close has died a violent death. We don't want that for you." Faith grabbed her daughter's hand. Steadfast grabbed the other. Arda smiled reassuringly, but in her mind, a fire was blazing. Today had changed her, and she wasn't going to let this go.

"May I be excused?" she asked. They nodded, and she walked up to get ready for bed. In a few weeks, she'd be living in her own apartment, working instead of studying. She'd be alone with her thoughts, no parents to calm her. While it was a scary thought, living alone, she was also excited to do so. Excited for the next stage of her life. Today she had grown up, just a little bit more.

She walked into her room and shut the door behind her, sitting in the chair by the window. She placed the cello and began to play some scales. Music was a dying art. The only reason she had a cello was because her grandmother had been a prominent artist. Now it was all visual effects and synthesized noises, much different from the organic, natural sound of string on wood.

She was so immersed in her practice that she didn't see him enter until his eyes locked on hers. His glowing eyes instantly calmed her. Her hands slipped from the instrument, and he set it aside before crouching before her.

"We need to talk, you and I."

Arda couldn't quite think. It was as if a fog had settled over her brain. "About what?"

"Oh, I imagine you would have a lot of questions for me

if your brain was working. I could tell you who you really are, or how your government is lying to you, but I mainly wish to talk to you about your future tonight."

"My future?" Arda was confused.

"In a few weeks, you'll graduate, and a world of opportunities will be opened for you. You can ask for any job you want and it will be given to you. You have power that you don't know you have. You saw a piece of it, today, with the flame. It's important for everyone that you choose the right career. When they ask you for a decision, I want you to consider being brave, and saying two words. 'Project R.E.D.D.'"

"What's Project R.E.D.D.?"

"You'll find out if you're brave enough to say them, at the right time." He stood and began to move toward the window.

"What makes me so special?" The fog was slowly lifting from her brain.

He turned back and said, "you'll also understand that, if you work on Project R.E.D.D."

When the fog cleared completely, she turned, but he was gone. She remembered everything as a dream. She was almost wondering if she'd merely fallen asleep while practicing, but no, the cello and bow had been placed carefully to the side.

Questions filled her mind. Who was he? Why was he so interested in her? Why were his eyes glowing? What is Project R.E.D.D.? How did he know about the flame today?

Rubbing her eyes, she said, "Joy, scan the room. Is there anything unusual?"

"Scanning," Joy responded. A few seconds later, she said, "Other than a raised heartbeat, you and the surrounding environment is normal."

"Sleep serum, strawberry dream."

It appeared before her. She knew she would be up all night with these questions unless she forced herself to go to sleep. Drinking the liquid, she shut the window and locked it, then climbed into bed and was out a few minutes later.

When Arda awoke the following morning, she vaguely remembered dreaming of glowing eyes. As she went about her daily routine, she couldn't shake what he'd said the night before. Walking down to breakfast, she sat to eat, and devised a plan, with a small lie, to see if she could get more information.

"Mother," she began, carefully, "I had a dream last night about someone with glowing eyes."

Her mother stopped cooking and turned to her. "What?"

Arda felt her heart beat speed up, and wondered if she'd be revealed. She struggled to keep her breathing even, but her hands were balled into fists below the table. "I had a dream about someone with glowing eyes last night."

Faith took a deep breath in and shouted, "Stead!" Then she sat down and waited for him to enter, pointing at the empty seat.

"Repeat what you said to me, honey." She took her daughter's hand and a big, warm smile lit up her face, but there was worry in her eyes.

Arda repeated herself. Steadfast took a deep breath and said, "You're sure it was just a dream?"

She nodded, lying. "I mean, people with glowing eyes can't be real, right?" She looked back and forth between them, hoping for any nonverbal signal that may give her a clue.

For a long moment, no one answered her. Faith looked at her husband, who eventually spoke. "Arda, I know you've been under a lot of stress," he began as he took off his glasses to rub his eyes. "Maybe it's time to see a counselor."

Her hopes for an information session plummeted. "What?"

Faith rubbed her hands together nervously, but her shoulders weren't tight. Her body language confused Arda. "These dreams have been going on for weeks now. I agree with Stead. I'll arrange everything. Just one session, to make sure you're in the best health. What do you think?"

Thought she felt uncomfortable, she said, "whatever you think is best." She wasn't particularly upset about counseling: she was upset that she hadn't been successful in getting any information out of her parents. Whatever they knew, they didn't believe they needed to share.

"I'm ready for school." Arda knew better than to push too much at once. There were other ways to get information.

When she arrived at school, she sought out Will. He knew far more than he should and was the perfect partner to help her get some answers. She looked for him in the morning, but Chaste didn't make it possible for her to talk to him alone. Frustrated, she tried to broach the subject several times during the day unsuccessfully. She half listened through their lesson on Betas and consequences of inhumane research, wondering the entire day which words were right to say, and what she should avoid.

Luckily, she had her chance as school ended. She slipped past Chaste and ran out the door before he could stop her. Turning, she found Will outside the school, already on his way to her house to study with Stead. Catching up to him, she turned and began.

"I need your help."

He turned to her and smiled. "With what, Top Ten?"

She took a deep breath and rushed the words out before

she could think. "I've seen the glowing eyed guy, from the video."

"What video?" he asked, looking genuinely confused.

"The surveillance video we watched earlier."

He looked at her with a blank expression on his face. "Huh?"

It was then that Arda realized he had no clue what she was talking about. "You don't remember?"

"Guess not." He placed a hand around her shoulders and said, "so, end of the year dance is coming up." He leaned close to her and whispered, "*too many ears. Later.*"

"It is." He released her shoulder and walked beside her a respectful distance away.

"We'll get our Chemistry Chip."

"Yeah." She had thought about that, as well.

"Are you nervous at all about them constantly monitoring our vitals?"

She shrugged. "For me, it's not any different than my VA, Joy doing it."

He nodded. "I don't have one. It feels…invasive, to me."

She forgot that he lived a different life in Z5, and wouldn't have access to that type of tech.

"Your data is kept in a secure file. They can't just access it. All of our data will be secure. It's just to see who our best match is."

"I get the science. Your body responds to the people you're interested in, and the chip compiles the data into your most compatible option. I'm just struggling with letting a computer know how I feel about…" He stopped himself before he finished his sentence. "About…everything, all the time."

"Stead works in security. I'm sure if you have any questions or concerns, he'd be happy to clarify the risks with you.

You can refuse the chip, you know."

He sighed. "That...takes me out of the gene pool. I want kids."

A sudden image of him snatching up a small child and dangling them in the air, as Stead had done with her, popped into her head. She smiled, feeling as if he'd be a fun father.

He looked at her, seeing it, and her face became a mask. She looked down and her brows came close together, worried he would tease her for it, but he didn't.

"I'll ask Stead about it, then. I want to be matched with..." another pause. "The best option, when that time comes."

They walked home talking of boring things, but it was hard for Arda to ignore what he said. Why was he worried about ears? Did he mean microphones? Spying on citizens was illegal, wasn't it?

Walking into their home, Steadfast sat down and helped the two study. Hours went by before they had a chance to speak alone. She pulled Will into her bedroom and shut the door.

"Hey, at least buy me dinner first," he joked. She narrowed her eyes at him. "Just kidding. May I sit?"

She sat on her bed, he sat on the chair by her desk. He looked at her for a few moments before saying, "what do you want to know?"

"I want to know everything you know about glowing eyes."

He rubbed his hands together. "I don't know much."

Arda smiled then. "Maybe not, but you're smart. You can hack. You can figure it out."

"I think you're overestimating my skills a bit. Why is this so important to you?"

She sighed. "Because a stranger with glowing eyes keeps

telling me odd things. Isn't that enough of a reason?"

He looked at her face, scanning for emotions. "You really did meet one, didn't you?"

"Yes, that's what I said. One what? What is he?"

He pressed his lips together and paused a moment. "When I was five, I was curious about the stories, you know, vampires, werewolves, kid stuff. I read in one of the books that to this day, vampires live in the sewers. Being a kid, unsupervised in Z5 where there aren't many security cameras, I went down into a manhole late at night with a buddy of mine. We saw this creature with glowing eyes. It scared the crap out of us. We couldn't get out of there quick enough.

"When I got home and told my parents, they put me to sleep. The next day, instead of going to school, I went to my first counseling session. They did everything they could to convince me that what I had experienced was only a dream. What I didn't tell them was that I stubbed my toe on the way out of the sewer. It still hurt. I knew it was real, but my friend, when I saw him again, he sounded strange. Like if we talked about it, we'd be in trouble, so I learned to say what they wanted and haven't talked about it since."

"So you saw one, too?'

"Yeah. I didn't say anything when we took the video because you never know who's watching. I didn't trust you yet. Maybe I should have."

"They're real?" She swallowed hard as her stomach churned.

He nodded. "No one will believe us if we say that, though."

"We have to keep this to ourselves."

"Yes. I will look into it when I can, but for now, I think it's best if we don't screw up our careers poking around."

She nodded, agreeing. "So we wait, until after we know where we'll be, then we investigate this."

"Sounds like a plan. Anything else?"

She paused, unsure, but finally blurted it out. "Do you know anything about a Project R.E.D.D.?"

He shook his head. "No. What is it?"

"Just…something else I want to investigate." Arda wasn't ready to reveal everything. She would have to think on this for a long while before deciding exactly how much to trust him. One thing was certain.

"I'm glad I'm not the only one."

He smiled. "The man…with the glowing eyes. He didn't…hurt you, did he?" Concern filled his features.

Why she felt warmth inside her from his question was beyond her, but it caused a smile to form on her face. "No, just… spoke in riddles and was gone."

He nodded. "Arda…" he shook his head, as if the words weren't good enough. Then he locked eyes with her, his arms folded in front of him. "If this man comes to see you again… let me know. If I can help, if I can…" He stopped again. "I want to help keep you safe. Please let me know if you ever need that…from me."

He walked past her and out of her bedroom abruptly. She felt a blush creep up her cheeks, remembering her mother's words on boys and dating. That time was fast approaching, and she had no clue where her preferences would lie. But then again, that's what the Chip was for.

Chapter 5

Arda turned and looked at her mother, who stood with a strange expression on her face, as if she may shed a tear or two. There were two weeks left until graduation. Tonight was their Year End Dance Social. Arda chose a pastel purple gown that shimmered in the right light. Her hair was tied back and curled. Her mother had even allowed her to dip into her make-up tray, an ancient, archaic tradition that was frowned upon during the workweek and allowed only for special occasions.

Glancing at herself in the mirror, though, she gasped. She looked like a painting.

"You're beautiful."

Arda turned, "Beauty isn't important."

Catching a strand of hair that had fallen out of place, her mother fixed it to her head. "Yes, in the realm of life, not much. I bet your two friends will appreciate it though."

"Mother…" There was a warning in her voice, and she felt her cheeks begin to heat. She didn't want to be teased. Not now.

"Oh, I know." Stepping back, her mother turned and opened her bedroom door. "Five minutes." Alone now, Arda glanced again in the mirror. Her friends would be surprised. Even though she knew beauty didn't serve a survival purpose in her world, she was quite pleased with her appearance.

Taking the shawl her mother handed her, she walked out of her room. She was ready to go. Walking down the stairs, Steadfast handed her two sets of a small flower arrangement. One was white, one a dark purple so intense it was almost black. "What are these?"

"It's called a corsage. You received two. Generally, you get one for each boy who is interested in dancing with you. The dark one is from Will. The white from Chaste. You wear them on your wrists."

She stood while he placed the flowers around her wrist. The center flower was each a single rose. She sniffed and sighed a little. The flowers were real, non-synthesized plants. The smell was much more fragrant and richer than what came out of the PlantGen.

"Time to go." Stead opened the door to drive her to the dance. In her head, she went over the etiquette expected of her. This was not just a dance. They would gather compatibility information from the VI's that chaperoned the event. It was her choice who she talked to, who she danced with, but those choices would affect who she was eventually placed with. It culminated at the end with implantation of the Chemistry Chip.

She took a deep breath and slowly let it out. Steadfast must have sensed her apprehension, because he said, "don't worry. It seems like a big deal, but it's not. It's more important to have fun and use this chance to get to know people. Talk to whoever you want., and if you get nervous, try the punch." He squeezed her hand and pulled up to the school entrance. "Remember, Arda, like your career, these choices are yours."

Stepping carefully out of the car, she walked into the school whose entrance had been set up with glowing lights, wasteful, but it did give the school a special ambiance. Opening the double doors, she turned to the large common room that would hold the dance. The entrance was glowing with artificial lights and decorated with paper flowers. As she entered the room, a mechanical voice said, "Arda Prime recording." Her heart leapt in her chest. *Great.*

Thea walked over to her. Though they weren't close, they

did occasionally exchange pleasantries. She also wore two corsages. "Hello, Ardora. Lovely evening, isn't it? Mind if we chat for a few?" She glanced around. "This is slightly awkward for me."

"Me too. What would you like to discuss?" The two moved over to a small table where they sat and debated some ethically relevant topics of the day. Thea began listing the career paths she was considering, which seemed to be every career path. Arda smiled and was polite, but her stomach would not allow her to forget where she was.

They had some of the most esteemed chaperones tonight. Dr. Gregory Jackson stood to the side with a recreation of Leonardo da Vinci and Madam Curie. As she glanced around, she saw other prominent pioneers they'd studied.

"It's weird." Thea was speaking. "It's weird that our vitals are being analyzed, but you know, when we get our careers, they'll be doing this every day, so we should try to adjust to it now, I suppose."

"I know, I just can't convince my stomach." Placing a hand over the middle of her abdomen, she gave Thea a helpless look.

"I know. It's dreadful in there. One moment."

Her friend stood and walked to a table set with food and punch. Filling two glasses, she returned to Arda and handed her one. "This should help. I must admit my stomach isn't cooperating either." She took a sip.

Arda looked at the red liquid in the cup. "What do you suppose they put in this?"

"Mood enhancers, anti-stress meds. Try it. My father said it would help, that it wouldn't hurt us. Since he's the head of Medical I trust him."

She hesitated putting the liquid to her lips, but after a

moment, complied. The liquid made her feel instantly better. "Do you want some more, Thea?"

"Sure."

As she stood to get more of the punch the mechanical voice announced Will's entrance. She was tempted to turn and look, but the punch suddenly seemed very important. Her pace quickened, even in the heels. Reaching the punch, she picked up the ladle and began to fill Thea's glass.

A hand at the small of her back startled her. "You look beautiful." Turning, she stared at Will, while Thea stared at them both. "You aren't supposed to talk to me until I talk to you."

He shrugged but looked her up and down in a way that made her want to blush. With a smirk he added, "fine, I'll be over by the back entrance when you choose to talk to me." He winked and left.

Returning to Thea, she downed the second glass, feeling much better.

Thea smiled at her and said, "let's go talk to some people." Grabbing her hand, the dark-haired girl walked her to a group of guys, saying, "I intend to talk to everyone, so they match me with the right person. Let's start with these guys."

Except while Thea was all about the data, Stead's words were her guide. She didn't feel the need to talk to everyone. Most of the teen men they chatted with did nothing to her vitals. She was even slightly bored as they talked about their careers and goals.

Moving on, they spotted a large group of girls surrounding Chaste. Thea approached him, dragging Arda with her. Practically shoving her into him, she said, "you're turn to talk to him." Some of the other girls even moaned out loud. She looked at her friend and smiled. "Hey, Chaste. I like the flower you gave me."

He smiled, big and wide. "I'm glad. Been waiting for you to get here." The other girls were dispersing. Thea grabbed his arm, hanging on. "Hi, Chaste." Arda watched her beam at him. She was clearly more interested in him than anyone else they'd talked to.

"Hi, Thea. Good to see you." Arda looked down and saw the white rose corsage on her wrist as well. It was normal to send them to your most interested. Chaste apparently liked them both.

"Want to dance?" She was so different from her usual self. This Thea was not a cold and distant bookworm, but a vibrant and open woman. It was nice to see this side of her. It made her real in a way she wasn't to Arda before.

Chaste turned to Arda, giving her a strange look, before saying, "sure."

The two walked off, leaving her alone. Around her there were groups forming, talking and chatting. At the back of the room stood Will, right where he said he would be. He seemed lonely. She didn't like that, so she walked over to him. His eyes didn't leave hers, and his arms were folded over his chest.

"Hey!" She stood next to him, leaning against the wall.

He smiled. "You had the punch, didn't you?"

"Sure. Two glasses." A look of disappointment shone on his face. "What?"

"Nothing. Did you speak to a lot of people?"

"Mostly who Thea wanted to talk to. You?"

He chuckled. "Everyone knows where I stand, so no, not many girls have talked to me."

She tilted her head. "What do you mean? How many corsages did you give out?"

He sighed. "Just the one."

She wondered why. "Just the one to me? Why didn't you give out more? Chaste gave away at least two. Don't we want data?"

"I…" He sighed, struggling with what to say. "How did you like the corsage? I made it myself."

That made her smile, knowing he took the time to do those kinds of things. Then it hit her, that he was from Z5, and while Chaste could afford multiple flowers, the cost of just a single corsage might have meant that Will could only give out one.

"It smells great." She smiled wide.

Looking at her, he held out a hand. Though it was unconventional, she allowed him to take her to the dance floor. Her normal rigid exterior was vanishing, in part thanks to the punch. "Do you know how to dance?"

She shook her head. "I have no clue. Let's just copy everyone else."

A large group of people was forming in the center of the room. They joined, everyone mimicking everyone and danced to several songs. When a slower song came on, though, Chaste found them.

"Mind if I take this one, Will?" He confidently twirled her away from the other boy. She laughed, chiding her best friend. "That wasn't nice. Besides, I'm supposed to ask you."

"I'm so popular that you might not have gotten a chance. I saw how Will approached you when he came in. Knew you would be okay with a small breech in protocol."

She wrapped her arms around his neck, hugging him tightly. "Do you remember when we were young, and it was okay to give giant bear hugs?"

"I don't remember you being this strong, though." She released him. He spun her around the dance floor and as Arda watched, the floor began to clear. Chaste had the advantage of growing up as a Chief's son, so dancing was natural to him. She followed his lead as the song played, until eventually they were dancing alone. The steps were easy, right foot, left foot, right, then in reverse. Matching him step by step, they fit together, relaxed and open. She smiled up at him as he twirled her occasionally and supported her around the waist, so she didn't fall.

As the song ended, she became more aware of everyone watching them, and her worry returned. While they stood, clapping started. She looked at Chaste, who was nodding his head, thanking them for their applause. Turning her head, she saw that Will was the only one not doing so. The look on his face was carefully blank.

Three girls approached Chaste at once to ask for a dance. She walked to Will, smiling. Though he looked relaxed, she sensed some tension in him. As she got closer, his gaze grew more intense.

"If I didn't know better, I'd say your eyes were glowing at me." She was trying for a joke, but as she chuckled, he reached out, took her hand, spun her low so she had to cling to him, and his lips were suddenly on hers.

An alarm sounded, and as quickly as the kiss had begun, it ended. Everyone was looking in their direction, and two armed security guards started to approach them. His breath near her ear, he whispered, "*I didn't need the punch to know who raises my vitals.*" Before she could whisper anything back, they were being separated and he was escorted out of the dance.

Chaste came up to her. "Are you okay?"

She wondered that herself. She felt very strange. Her heart couldn't seem to slow its beat, and her body felt hot. Her breath came quickly, and she rubbed her hands together, nervously. Taking a moment, she leaned against the wall before answering, "I'm fine. Why?"

"They have these rules for a reason, Arda. The punch, the chaperones, they're so people aren't attacked, like you just were."

"Oh, Chaste, don't be so formal."

Gently taking her hand, he said, "Girls approach the guys this time. It's important for accurate data. He had no right to kiss you."

Her lips tingling, she laughed, a strange response, given her normal behavior. The punch must have been affecting her a bit too strongly. "It was less an attack and more a declaration. I didn't mind it."

His expression changed then. "You didn't mind him…" Sighing, he paused before pulling her tight against him and placing his lips on hers. Before he was escorted out, he said, "he's not the only one who cares about you."

She watched as he was taken away. Thea came up to her and locked arms. "Oh, wow. Two men disregarding protocol to kiss you. Are you okay? Do you need anything?"

She nodded, but part of her didn't feel okay. Part of her felt very confused. "I think I had too much punch."

Hours passed, the two girls socializing, dancing. Arda excused herself to the rest room and returned a few moments later. As she looked around the room, her attention was drawn to a dark figure standing in a shadowy corner. Somehow, she knew. It was him.

Walking toward him as if she was drawn to him, she couldn't tell who he was until his gaze landed on her, the same glowing eyes calming her.

"You look very lady-like tonight. How are you enjoying the dance?"

"It's wonderful." She twirled around but kept her voice low. "What are you doing here?"

He touched her elbows gently, and said, "I'm here to give you this." Their eyes closed, and an image came unbidden to her mind.

Someone was strapped down, receiving an injection, but it burned as it went in. The person screamed, their eyes lighting the room blue. When the light dimmed, the person was gone.

The alarm sounded again, responding to her vital signs. The armed security approached her, his last words for the night, "don't have any more punch." He disappeared as if sinking into the shadow.

"Sorry miss, but did something frighten you?"

Remembering that he couldn't scan, she said, "I think I saw a rodent." She placed a hand over her racing heart. The security began to search with flashlights. Finding nothing, they said, "must have been the punch."

The End of Year Dance Social was less a dance and more a collection of data needed to place the most promising young adults with an advantageous match. At the end of the dance, each person was given a small round microchip that would track their vitals daily for two years, ending in the selection of a romantic partner.

As hers was placed on the skin between her thumb and forefinger, Arda gave no second thoughts to the process. This is what people had done for generations, and it had brought her mother not one but two great loves. She trusted the process and the outcome.

As she walked out of the dance, Will and Chaste stood on the sidewalk outside the school, softly talking. Their movements indicated that the topic was far from pleasant. Arda approached them both, the punch draining from her, her brain sharp.

As she moved closer, they stopped their debate and smiled at her. She smiled back, but that was her only sign of softness. The rest of her body language was firm, her shoulders back, her face neutral.

"What was that about, gentlemen?" She was proud that her voice sounded even, despite the fact that the memory of their lips on hers kept coming back to her.

They looked at the ground, at each other, everywhere but at her. "I'd like an answer as to why you broke protocol, sacrificing your data for the night."

Will was the first to make eye contact with her. "Neither of us cares about data."

"If you don't care about your future, what is it that you care about enough to throw it away?"

Chaste met her gaze and gently touched her right hand. "You."

It was said softly, as if he were afraid she would run. Will took the other. Understanding now, Arda sighed.

"These systems are put in place to work. If either of you would like to be placed with me, you have to abide by it. By taking part in the system, you're respecting me, and my wishes. You think I want them to place me with someone who isn't the best choice? Someone inferior?"

"No." They replied together.

"Then you need to participate. Did you get your chip?" Changing the subject, she was hoping to leave this mess behind them.

They each showed her one, in the same exact place hers was located. "Good." Stead pulled his car up to the street, and she knew their time was up. "Good night to the both of you."

Releasing their hands, she walked away, stepping into the car and shutting the door.

"How was the dance?" he inquired excitedly.

She briefly relayed the events of the night to him with a frustrated voice. He listened politely until she had finished, only then starting the drive home. As the car made its way back to their house, he said, "Arda, I remember being a young man, once. Be patient with them. Hopefully, they learned their lesson, and won't repeat such behavior in the future. It is sometimes difficult to be male in our society."

"What do you mean?"

He looked at her sadly, and said, "just… cherish the moments you have with both of them while you can."

She looked out the window, hiding the foreboding feeling his words gave her. Even though she knew that life was stable here, she couldn't help but feel that change was coming. His words did not give her any hope that the future would be positive.

Today was usually her day of rest, but now that she had the chip, she was expected to accept dates during this time, within reason. While you weren't forced to spend time with anyone, it was strongly encouraged to spend time with varying potential partners so your data was comprehensive. Spending time with just one person was frowned upon.

Waking up and getting ready, she wasn't as excited as she expected. It was hard for her to think of some event two years away, when she had so many burning questions about her career path, a decision that would occur in two weeks.

Her heart was not fluttering as other girls might be. She

found herself distracted by glowing eyes and hidden secrets. She was still struggling to understand the decision to keep Omega Flame burning.

Turning, walking out of her room, she walked down the steps and prepared for breakfast. Faith and Stead, unlike other days, were nowhere near the kitchen. No food was laid out for her.

Confused, she turned to the small living room and gave them a quizzical look. Faith nudged Stead, who turned and looked at her.

"Oh, good morning. I know we normally feed you, but…" he paused, taking off his glasses to clean them. "…but you have several dates to look through today, one offering you breakfast."

Handing her his tablet, she looked over the page in front of her. While at the dance, the girls chose, the protocol for dating allowed differing initiations to create accurate data from each sex. This week was the male's choice. Before her was a schedule that left her very little time to herself. Noting that Will was the one who was offering her breakfast, she clicked to accept. She needed to talk to him anyway.

As soon as she had done so, the doorbell rang. Looking up, her parents were smiling broadly.

"He's prompt. He was probably waiting for you to accept on our doorstep. How sweet." Faith stood and went to open the door. Will stood outside, waiting. Faith hugged him and almost pushed Arda out the door. Shutting it behind her, they were suddenly alone, and she felt awkward.

"I…wanted to be your first date." He spoke carefully. "I get your attention for the next two hours. How are you?"

"I'm feeling a bit strange, honestly." The memory of the brief kiss clouded her mind, in his presence, and made it hard to focus on other topics.

"Me, too. We'll feel strange together. I know it's weird. I don't really care for the whole system." He took her arm in his and they walked over to one of the few businesses open to cater to young, dating couples.

A small café stood across the street from her house. You could sit and order from your table. It was similar to home other than you could sit outside and eat. The workers were responsible for giving the place a romantic atmosphere. Flowers hung everywhere. Several small puppies and kittens would roam between your feet to be snuggled. Everything was warm, friendly, and comforting. The chairs were covered in soft silk and velvet, and you could sink into them.

"I haven't seen much of you or Chaste since the dance." Arda didn't know what else to say.

He smiled gently. "Well, we heard what you said, and pretty much made a pact that we'd both follow the rules from now on. I wouldn't want you thinking I don't think the best of you, or that I don't take your autonomy seriously. I'm...sorry. For kissing you without your permission. It won't happen again."

She smiled, but the blush came to her cheeks. She quickly looked down at their menu. "Wow." She was taken aback by the rich food they collected in their database. There were things on the menu she'd never heard of. What was French Toast?

"I have no clue what to get. Have you ever had this stuff?"

Looking over the menu, he mumbled, "not much of it. I've had pancakes. I have no clue what crepes are. I guess we just pick something and order it. If we don't like it, I have enough credit to get you something else."

She glanced at all her options and felt overwhelmed. After several minutes of silence, she decided to try something called, "Irish eggs benedict w/ potato pancake, corned beef, poached egg and hollandaise sauce." She chose it because she had no idea what any of it was. *How do you "corn" beef?*

Placing her order, she turned her attention back to Will. "So, what do we talk about?"

"Anything you want. How's the career path going?"

She sighed. "I still haven't decided. Have you?"

"I'm thinking Medical. My mom raised me with a healthy respect for your body and natural healing. I think that will help me in that field. They desperately need good doctors in Zone 5."

"So, then you're thinking of small clinic work instead of working at the main hospital?"

He nodded. "You don't make as much credit but living in Zone 5 has really made me aware of how much need there is."

"You want to work in Z5 but live in Z3?"

He looked at her. "If I get placed with you, Arda, we'll live wherever you want."

She blushed a bit. "That's rather intimate to discuss at this point, don't you think?"

He reached out to grab her hand. "I know, it's just that I want you to be clear on where I stand, that I'd take care of you."

She glanced up and saw the earnest expression on his face. "I believe you."

They chatted until the food came, and as they ate, it became easier to relax and talk. The time ticked away, as she got to know Will's hopes and dreams, his favorites and his dislikes.

A timer sounded, signaling that they had fifteen minutes left of their time together. He stood and began to walk her home. Realizing that they hadn't discussed what she wanted to, she leaned in close and whispered to him.

"We need to figure out how we'll communicate when we start our new jobs. If we're going to investigate glowing eyed people, I mean. How are we going to do that?"

He shook his head slightly and said, "Not now, not on our first date."

Reaching her door, he asked, "may I kiss you again?"

Her eyes grew wide, her face turning red, but she was able to nod her head. Yet, he didn't lean down to kiss her lips like she'd hoped. He instead placed a careful kiss to her forehead. He leaned back and smiled, saying, "enjoy your day, Top Ten."

He opened her front door, and she walked through, then he shut it softly behind him. Her first official date was over.

Faith and Stead were in the living room, waiting impatiently. "How did your first date go?"

She smiled, feeling something heavy in her pocket. "Wonderful."

Stead handed her the tablet, and she noted she had five other dates she could attend that day, ending with dinner with Chaste. Sighing, she wondered why so many people wanted to get to know her. She'd never been as smart as Thea, or as pretty as the other girls.

She gave Faith a look, and her mother must have understood something she didn't, because she said, "Let's sit for a minute and I'll explain." Arda complied.

"Listen, dear, our family is special. Our last name is Prime. You know that, but you don't know why. I got a lot of attention when I was younger because our name means something special."

She paused, thinking. "Your great-great-grandmother was a baby at the time of Omega Fire. She was an orphan. No one knows who her parents were, but the founder, Dr. Gregory Jackson, raised her from birth. When they logged families for the district, some ten years later, she was the first family registered, and given the name Prime.

"This association, connection with the founder, has always kept us in good standing, making us somehow more viable candidates. He took an orphan into his home and raised her, protected her, and gave us our legacy."

Arda nodded. "Why didn't you tell me sooner?"

"Because we don't brag in this family."

"Brag?"

Faith laughed. "Education these days… Bragging is saying that you're more valuable or important than another, publicly."

"Oh. I understand, I think. She was disadvantaged but raised with the Founder. That could give us sentimental value over other families. And to say that in public, would make us seem…conceited."

"Sort of. Chaste is aware of the connection, too. That's why we figured you would be drawn to him, but there are a lot of options for you to consider. My first dating day, I had four dates. You've got six."

Arda smiled and looked at the next person who wanted to take her to the park to talk. She swiped to accept. She had a half hour to herself before she'd have to be ready.

Before she knew it, the day was over, and she was sitting down to eat at another outdoor venue overlooking the park with Chaste. Lights hung around, soft violin music played.

Chaste held the chair for her and she sat down. "Thank you."

He pulled the chair close to her, instead of sitting across from her. Putting an arm around her chair, he leaned close to her. "I've been waiting all day to spend this time with you."

She placed both of her hands in her lap. The normal easy

feeling between them was dissipating quickly, replaced by the same awkward feeling she had with Will. "I don't know what to say to that."

He chuckled and opened the menu. "Have you enjoyed your dates so far?"

"They were all very pleasant. I'm exhausted."

"Me too. How many dates did you have?" He reached for a glass of water, sipping on it.

"Six." He choked, coughing. After a moment, he said, "Well. That's a lot of data."

She shrugged. "Isn't that the point?"

"Six, huh?"

"Is that high? How many accepted your date?"

"Three."

"Oh." Was she more important than the founder's ancestor? "My mom told me the story of my family. How my great-great-grandmother was an orphan and was raised by Dr. Jackson."

He nodded. "I've known all my life. Do you have any questions?"

"Is that why we're friends?"

He looked surprised but he said, "no. We're friends because of what we've been through. Don't think I won't use it to my advantage though. I plan on winning you over."

She smiled and glanced at the menu. "Don't worry about that. We're best friends. I know what you'll like."

He swiped a few buttons and her order was placed. She wasn't sure if she was comfortable with that or not. He was the first person to order for her.

When the food arrived, she took a bite and sighed. He had good taste. She loved it. Looking at him, he leaned in close and said, "I told you."

The night was over far too quickly, and before she knew it, they were standing outside her door. "Well, thanks for dinner, Chaste."

He leaned his arm around her shoulders, pulling her close to him. "Any time." He placed a kiss on her cheek and left.

Arda walked into the kitchen, exhausted. Faith and Stead were still up, waiting for details. After a short conversation, she retired to her room to get ready for bed. As she sat brushing her hair, the highlights of the day flashed through her mind.

The more she thought about the day, the more she gravitated to thoughts of Will and Chaste. The other boys were sweet, but they were her friends. A pleasant warmth in her chest, she laid down to sleep.

He came out of the shadows and placed the file on her desk. It was ancient, sealed with a string. She was getting lost in the glamour of this life when she should be asking for answers. He didn't blame her. It must be amazing to be above ground. The air was lighter, the smells sweeter. He turned to leave, the offering on her desk, full of questions more than answers. She was the first person in a long time to be able to confront this horrible secret. If she didn't, no one would.

Chapter 6

The Beta stood in front of her, foaming at the mouth. She wanted to move, to run, and she couldn't. Her hands and feet were shackled to the earth. Another Beta appeared from the fog, shambling toward her. As her breathing sped up, she turned. Some dark figure was standing on the side, watching her. Looking up, making eye contact, his eyes glowed blue. As she waited, frozen, he was suddenly in front of her, protecting her.

Turning, he smiled at her. It was the same man who she'd met before. "Don't get distracted. If you do, people will die." Turning back, he walked toward the Beta and ripped off its head.

She awoke in a sweat, breathing heavily. *Not another nightmare.* Joy inquired as to her condition, but she ignored her as she saw the stack of papers on her desk. Slowly, she walked over and opened the file.

An hour later, she hid the file under her bed and got ready for school with shaking hands. Trying not to think too hard about it, she put what she had read at the back of her mind. Now was not the time. She had finals to take, interviews to conduct.

This week was the week her life would change forever. By the fifth day, she'd have a placement and a diploma. The following week, she'd move into an apartment near her new career, and get her first stipend to buy furniture and food of her own. It was scary but also exciting.

Walking down the steps, she was too nervous to enjoy her breakfast. Noticing, Faith placed a nutrition bar in her bag. "For later, if you can eat." Kissing her daughter's forehead, she said, "Good luck, sweetheart."

Stead was waiting outside in his car. The ride to Academy was short and quiet. Stepping out in front of the building, she saw her friends, as solemn as she, walking with a sense of doom to their first test.

Will smiled but didn't speak to her. Chaste placed his arm around her shoulders but was silent as well. She walked in and sat down, breathing deeply, waiting for the VA to give them the rules for their test. In the back of her mind, she felt panic rising in her. What if she failed? For a moment, she couldn't even breath, couldn't think. Her mother's words echoed in her head, one more time, giving her courage. Her life, her choices.

During the hour break between tests, they called random students to a room where they would interview with the heads of the various industries needed to run the district. The more you knew, the more you convinced them you were needed, the better your chances that they would ask for you. If they asked for you and you scored well on that test, the career would show up in your top choices. Contracts would be sent, and the final interview would typically consist of one to three offers.

She understood the process but this didn't make her less nervous. One by one they called students down. Fifteen minutes later, the student would come back, asking for someone else.

Most came back without saying much of anything. A few came back in tears. This didn't make Arda feel any better.

Wondering what she would say, how brave she should be was tough. Being an adult was not turning out to be easy.

Chaste squeezed her hand, and she released her lower lip, not realizing she'd bitten down on it in nervousness. Will walked by with his group of friends, winking at her. Some of her other dates inclined their heads in her direction, reminding her of another choice she'd have to make, eventually.

The bell rang for their next test. She walked in quickly. Ten classmates had gone through the interview process today, but neither Will, Chaste, nor herself had been through the process. If this continued, by the third day of testing everyone will have been interviewed. This didn't make her feel better.

"How do you think you did?" She stood outside the academy, talking to Chaste and Will. It was their first actual conversation of the day. The apprehension of testing dissipated as they walked away.

"Oh, the questions were rigorous, but I think I did okay." Chaste placed his arm around her and Will shuffled his feet.

"What about you, Will?" She tilted her head at him and smiled softly.

With his hands in his pockets, he said, "Well, I don't think I failed. That's something, right? You?" He smirked in her direction, and she tried to keep from blushing. Since the dance, it had been hard to keep thinking of both of them as just classmates.

"I did fine. Studying with Stead really helped me out."

"Nervous about the interview?" He locked eyes with her, his solemn.

"Yes." She released a long breath, steadying herself.

"Have you decided on a career yet?" Chaste squeezed her shoulder.

"No." That was a tough one with the new information she got this morning. Her mind drifted back for a moment, thinking of death and sacrifice. Glowing blue eyes and a folder on her desk....

"I'll decide when I decide, I guess." Her brow furrowed, and she was a bit frustrated at herself for not knowing what career she wanted. It was time to decide.

The three friends dispersed, Arda awaiting Stead's car. She couldn't wait to get back home and examine the files a little bit more.

The next day, none of the three had been interviewed, still. Anticipation was making them nervous. They decided to take a walk to the park to relax.

Arda sat staring at the desert habitat with its lizards and snakes. She couldn't imagine living in a place with so much sand. She watched as the snakes slithered on the ground, as the lizards sunbathed themselves.

Will and Chaste stood arguing about some topic she wasn't interested in. The air chilled around her as she watched the reptiles slow and eventually pause their movement. Turning, she almost gasped to see her mysterious friend, or enemy.

"Don't do that." She whispered, angrily.

"Sorry. Turn back and look at the exhibit. I don't want anyone to see me except you." His eyes were no longer glowing, but a vibrant bright blue.

She did so, but only because she needed answers.

"Why did you give me that awful file?" She met his eyes in the reflection of the glass.

"Because it happened. It's the district's dirty history that everyone ignores." He looked angry.

"But why me?"

"Someday you'll answer that question yourself. For now, let me just say that you are gifted. You have people depending on you to help them, and that file is the beginning of your journey. If they find out you have it, you could die. Be careful, be smart, be paranoid. Tell no one. I'll find you after you've started your new life. We can discuss this more then."

Then he was gone. She walked to the two boys and took both their hands. "I'd like to go home now."

"Is everything okay?" Chaste looked around while he said it.

"Yes, I just…the stress must be getting to me."

"We'll walk you."

When she got home, she walked into her bedroom and opened the file again. She would be called to interview tomorrow, and she wanted to examine what she should say and what she couldn't.

The file was a gathering of medical data based on early experiments with Omega Flame. The test subjects were, she assumed, the same subjects that had been eradicated when the experiments were determined to be unethical. However, the data obviously still existed.

The first page was a list of possible symptoms, some check marked. As she read through them, they seemed superhuman. Breakdown of red blood cells, needing transfusions. Check. Inability to absorb Vitamin D. Check. Accelerated hair and nail growth. Check. Need for long periods of rest. Check.

Turning to the next page, it was harder to continue reading. This was a series of paragraphs explaining various stimuli given to the subjects. As she read through these, tears fell from her cheeks. This didn't seem like an experiment. This seemed like torture. Who voluntarily electrocutes people? Who burns victims to test their healing time? Who places someone in isolation to determine how long it takes for them to go crazy from silence?

The third page didn't make her feel any better. They were vital readings that coincided with the previous pages paragraphs. Page four was possible ways to continue the experiment and suggestions for improvement.

Page five was a chart, filled with results for various groups of test subjects. One group was labeled Control, one Group A, Group B and so on. The last column had the percentage of fatalities vs. survivors. Most were above fifty percent.

As she combed through the remaining pages, containing everything from nutrition to sleeping patterns to activity, she felt her heart break. How could anyone at any time think this was okay? This was the great use of Omega Flame? This is what her people had to go through to get to where they were today? This was the cost of their perfect society?

The file gave her more questions than answers. Sliding the file under her bed, she tried to think of something else, anything else. Her mind drifted to Will and Chaste. She remembered their first date, how kind they'd been. The quick kiss they'd shared at the dance. Her heart eased and she felt a little better. She had a team. People on her side. They would help her get to the bottom of this.

The third day of testing started like every other. They crammed into their first classroom and prepared for their genetics test. This was important for Arda, as it would be used if she decided to pursue that career. With Steadfast's help, she plowed through the test, easily finishing first. Thea was done a few moments later.

The two girls walked out of the room, as was protocol, and straight outside without discussing the test. Once they were out though, Thea turned to her.

"Did that seem easy to you?"

"Actually, yes. Yourself?"

"I've been prepping for this all my life. It's always been my dream career. My mother works there. You're obviously interested as well, or you wouldn't have studied."

"Yes, it's one of my top choices."

"Well, may the best geneticist win."

Arda smiled, and the two girls talked of other things until every student was outside. This was it. She'd be interviewed today. It was hard to focus on her friends or the conversation, with how her stomach was tied in knots.

As they all sat, waiting, she noted fifteen minutes coming and going. Thirty minutes. She noticed that not one single student had been called to interview.

"Something's wrong." She said it softly, so softly she wasn't sure anyone would hear her, but they did.

"What do you mean?" Thea asked.

"They aren't calling anyone."

Will stood and shouted, "anyone been called yet?"

No one raised their hands. Another fifteen minutes passed before they were summoned back for their next test. This was the last official test to be given. After this, they would have a day of rest, followed by graduation and placement.

It was hard to focus on the medical exam because of the strange occurrence. Everyone was wondering the same thing.

What had happened to warrant breaking protocol? The hours passed slowly as she attempted and sometimes failed to keep her thoughts focused. She'd just received too much new information recently to be great at this.

Finally satisfied that she'd done her best, she submitted her test and walked out. She was one of the first ones finished, but she went straight home by herself. She had to ask Faith and Stead about this. She wondered if she'd done something wrong. She was worried about what this meant for her future.

However, her parents were not home yet from work. She was an hour earlier than normal. Walking up to her room, she shut her door and reviewed the file.

The front door slamming startled her, an hour passing too quickly. She placed the file under her bed quickly as she heard her name being called. Collectedly, she hurried downstairs.

What she saw didn't reassure her. Faith sat at the kitchen table with a cup of synthesized tea. Stead stood behind her, rubbing her shoulders. Both of them looked as if they'd been crying.

"What's going on?" Arda spoke softly, afraid even her words would cause more damage.

Faith looked at her. "Oh, my precious girl. Sit down. We need to talk."

"Did I do something wrong?" Her heart was instantly racing, her eyes wide. Her body felt tense, her muscles ready.

"No, no." Faith waved her hands in the air. "Nothing, you're perfect, amazing. It's just that something has happened, and we need to tell you what to expect."

"Does this have to do with why I didn't receive my interview today?"

Stead reassured her. "Yes, but it's nothing you've done. They've just suspended the education process for now.

However, with your exams finished, you can still be placed when…"

"When you get back." Her mother finished slowly, as if each word pained her to say. She could count the number of times she'd seen her mother cry on one hand, yet she was visibly shaking, and the tears flowed. Arda wanted to comfort her but wasn't sure how. Normally, her mother was that person.

"Back from where?" Arda had no clue what was happening.

Faith took a slow, deep breath, sipped her tea and began. "District four and five have declared war on District two and three."

Why would anyone do that? "Why?"

"Complicated politics, mostly." Stead didn't elaborate. "The important thing is to know what our role will be in the coming months."

"What is our role?" She felt frozen, still. A fog began to cover her brain and she realized it must be shock.

"The leaders here have chosen to remain neutral and provide a safe harbor for both sides as they fight it out. This means that a neutral territory will be set up to treat wounded and hold prisoners. Our marines will not be fighting, per say, but will be in an active war zone."

"What does that have to do with me?"

Faith looked at Stead, her breathing heavy and broken. "Ardora, your class is so small. The reason they stopped the interviews is because…"

"Because they only intend to interview the survivors. For the time being, you will all be called to serve in the marines, to help where you can as the districts resolve their differences."

Arda took a deep breath, afraid her voice would break. "Am I going to die?"

Faith stood and hugged her daughter. "No. No, I won't let that happen. You will be changed by this experience, though. And some people you know, they might not come back."

"It's important to have your feelings here, at home, where it's safe, where we love you, where we can support you. They are sending the seasoned troops to the area tomorrow. A week from now, you start basic training. We have a week to prepare you for this awful turn of events, Arda, and we will do everything we can to insure you come back to us."

She didn't doubt her parents, but she couldn't fathom what war was like or how she would be able to survive it. She'd seen marines occasionally, at festivals or events. She'd seen their scars, some without limbs, and knew physical danger is what they signed on for.

But what about the people who didn't volunteer? She knew the laws. She knew that the government reserved the right to call anyone at any time. Still, was it best to send people like her? Soft spoken, unathletic brainiacs would save the day?

A knock at the door had her turning. "Who is that?"

Faith gave a half smile. "Someone else we'll be helping. Come in."

Will walked through the door, his eyes somber, his shoulders slumped. Gone was the charming rogue, replaced with a serious adult. The change was a bit unnerving. "I heard. What do I do?"

Faith motioned to a chair and said, "You and Chaste bring her back to us. We'll help you do that."

He sat next to her, and underneath the table, he placed a hand on her knee, squeezing lightly. He didn't meet her gaze, but her parents also didn't object to the physical contact. She looked down at his hand on her knee, and slowly covered it with hers. She heard him sigh softly, and she realized it had taken a lot of courage for him to reach out. In that moment, she didn't care if the protocol for adults in her society was to get by without physical contact. She was grateful he was here, treading new and terrifying territory with her. She wasn't alone, and she could get through this.

Arda paced back and forth in her room, uncertain how she would sleep that night. How could this happen? People were going to die. Will, Chaste, Thea, herself… It wasn't right. Her body wanted to move, to expend energy. She couldn't stop breathing rapidly, and her fingers kept clenching and releasing.

Then it hit her. He knew so much already. Maybe he would have some advice or insight. How to find him, though. Glancing at her door, she decided now was the time to be brave.

Locking it, she turned and headed to her desk. Taking a magnet from one of the drawers, she slid it over the chip. After a few seconds, it fell off of her hand.

"Joy," she said. "Run a self-diagnostic, comprehensive."

"If I do so I will be unavailable to take your data tonight. Do you wish to continue?"

"Yes. Full defragment as well."

"As you wish. Powering down sensors."

And just like that, she was free. Grabbing a couple objects that could be used as weapons, she placed them in a bag and opened her window. Carefully, as she'd done as a child, she climbed down the tree and walked out of her yard.

She kept to the shadows so no one would see her. Anyone caught out after curfew lost privileges. She could be putting her career in jeopardy, but with the possibility of war and death, she didn't care.

Waiting for the patrol car to pass, she walked quickly

across the street into district 3. The park loomed before her. It was time for the world to give her some answers, instead of handing her a constant barrage of questions. Her heart pounded so loud as she ran into the park. She was surprised she didn't have an instant headache. All of her senses seemed heightened. She was aware of every little movement and sound.

Retracing her steps, she found the sewer where she had first lost him. Taking a deep breath, she opened the manhole and started to climb down. The light faded until she was surrounded by darkness. Her foot hit solid ground and she let go of the metal bars.

Fumbling in her backpack, she brought out a multitool with a flashlight and turned it on. Before her stood a large circular hallway leading in two directions. She had to decide on left or right.

For a moment she pondered, but how could she possibly determine where each was headed? Knowing that the park continued to the right, she chose that direction. She walked slowly, as if something would jump out at her any minute. Her nightmares could exist down here. She could turn the corner and run into the grey-skinned Betas, who would tear into her flesh. She debated going back, but she was already this far. She focused on her breathing, willing first her lungs, then her heart to slow. For a while, nothing happened. She eventually relaxed, her pace quickening until she was traveling at her normal gait.

Taking another right, she noted the downward slant of the sewer, leading deeper underground. She followed it until it opened into a wide cavern. She couldn't see much with her flashlight, but she saw faint, glowing candlelight scattered around.

These were buildings. Where there were buildings, there were people. Turning her flashlight off quickly, she hugged the side of the cavern, her fear overtaking her. People where here…underground.

Her breath quickening, she heard voices, movement. *This was a stupid idea.* There were thousands of lights. They had no clue who she was. How was she supposed to find one person in this sea of candlelight?

Doors opened and shut, people coming out from their homes. She began to see glowing eyes everywhere. She swallowed hard, her heart beat pumping so fast and loud she thought she might have a heart attack, right there.

"You shouldn't have come here." Arda wasn't sure if the voice was coming from her head or someone else, it was so soft. Like the wind was whispering to her. She looked behind her, greeting a familiar pair of glowing eyes.

Before she could respond he placed a hand over her mouth and backed her away from the approaching candlelight. People were searching for a disturbance. Hiding behind a wall, he shielded her from sight with his body as they passed.

Several heartbeats pumped through her chest before the light vanished. When it did, he whispered, "do not speak. They can hear your whisper. Just listen. Turn around, take two rights and get out of here."

"I need to talk to you." She said it as softly as possible, but he still covered her mouth. Looking around, he waited a few seconds before he spoke again. "I will come see you tomorrow if you leave now."

She nodded her head, a sign of compliance, and he released her. Turning to go, they were suddenly surrounded by a group of glowing eyes.

"Well, what do we have here?" The voice didn't bother to whisper.

His head down, he said, softly, "if you know what's good

for you, you'll let us leave."

"Oh, I don't think so. This is my neighborhood, and you brought a donor in without sharing. I think you owe us some donor blood."

Keeping her pinned to the wall, he slowly lifted his head, his long black hair flowing as if a wind brushed it, yet there was no wind down here. "You don't know who you're messing with, thug. But one more word, and I'll show you."

A round of laughter ensued. "Really? One of you, five of us. What are you going to do?"

One chuckle escaped his throat before he acted. She couldn't see well in the candlelight, but she knew they were fighting from the sounds. Something thudded to the ground as if thrown. A grunt as if someone was kicked in the stomach. Another loud thud. It happened so fast that she couldn't follow it with her eyes.

At the end of it, the boy was no longer shielding her, and four pairs of eyes were gone. The last was pinned against the cavern wall, the man lifting him one handed by the throat. "Please, I didn't realize, please let me go, Mayne."

"If I let you go, how do I know you won't speak on this?"

"Even if I did, I'm a nobody. No one will believe me. Please…" The brave eyes had been reduced to begging. Arda wondered what was happening briefly before the boy's hand released his prey. They all ran, faster than she could follow.

Grabbing her hand, he said, "let's move," taking her back out of the cavern. He walked so fast that she had to run to keep up with him or she risked tripping. Up and back they went, until they were standing in front of the metal bars she used to climb down.

"Go." He was firm and it took grit to stay still.

"Not until I get some answers."

He didn't appear to like that. He grabbed her and lifted her body over his shoulders, climbing the bars as he did so. Her breath caught in her throat as she locked down, afraid of being dropped. She froze herself to keep that from happening.

Reaching the top, he pulled the switch to open the manhole and tossed her above ground, shoving her legs out of the hole and shutting it firmly behind him.

She tried opening the hole again, but it was stuck. He'd somehow locked her out. Frustrated, fuming, she gave herself a minute to breathe, to calm down, before she stood and headed home on shaky legs.

Climbing up the tree to her room, she took the clothes she had worn and disposed of them into the trash. She didn't want anyone to know where she'd been. Putting on her pajamas, she walked into the bathroom and took a quick air shower, deleting the results by hand. The evidence gone, she retreated into her room and tried to sleep.

When she headed downstairs the next morning, she was greeted by Stead and two officials. One was dressed as a marine. She would get no time to process this, though.

"Good morning?" Her eyes flicked between the two men.

"Good morning, dear. Please sit down. We have something to figure out." She complied and Stead continued. "Last night, your chip went dark."

"Oh, yeah, I noticed it wasn't on this morning, but Joy did a sensor check last night so I couldn't report it. She's still down."

"Convenient." The marine looked at her with cold eyes. "You'll need a replacement." He opened a small case, taking a new chip from it. "Please hold out your right hand." She did, and he placed the chip between her thumb and forefinger. "Whatever happened to cause the chip to malfunction, please try not to repeat it."

He left the house, and they both breathed a sigh of relief. "Arda, what happened?"

"Since when do the armed forces handle faulty chips?"

"Since we are in the middle of a war, and sometimes, scared people try to abandon their duties. They look for incidents like this to keep people from defecting into the wastelands. That your chip malfunctioned the night after you were told you would be called to serve…they take that very seriously."

"Oh." She didn't offer any other information.

"I can see you're scared, but you don't have to be. I'm on your side. I'm just curious to know what happened. You're not the type of person to shirk your duties. I know that. Tell me."

It wasn't hard to let her embarrassment show. "I was playing with magnets and I guess one just got too close."

He laughed. "Is that all? Arda, stay away from magnets for now. They definitely cause the chip to malfunction."

She smiled and nodded, as Faith walked in and began to make her breakfast. Her mother's movements were brisker and more business-like, as if she were trying too hard to appear normal in an abnormal circumstance.

This was supposed to be her last free day, a day of relaxation before they were supposed to graduate. With the war beginning, she had no clue what that meant for those plans.

"Do we still have graduation tomorrow?"

"No, unfortunately that has been postponed until the end of the war, solely because no one is getting placed at a job until you return." Her mothers movements sped up even more, and Arda could tell this was weighing on her, too.

"What do I do now, then?'

"When Will arrives, I will prepare you both for war." Stead squeezed her fingers as her mother set her plate in front of her, full of various breakfast meats. She was supposedly expected to up her protein intake, significantly.

"What's with all the protein?"

"You'll need it with the training you'll go through, to build muscle tissue. We need to start that today so you're ready for basic training. Without prep it can be…brutal."

"Great." She mumbled it under her breath and ate silently.

Will knocked on the door just as she was finishing. "Come in," she shouted as she placed her plate in the DishGen. He complied and Stead came out to greet him.

"Will, good morning." Extending his hand, Will shook it. "First lesson, firm grip. When you shake someone's hand, they test your character. Try again." Holding out his hand, Will clasped it more roughly. "Yes. Perfect."

Turning, he said, "Arda, you should change into more suitable clothes. Your training starts with a run around Z3."

'The whole thing?" She was shocked. Z3 took up at least twenty blocks.

He blinked and nodded. She turned and reluctantly trudged upstairs to change. She heard him giving advice to Will in the background. Entering her room, she was surprised to find her mother standing inside, pacing.

"Mother?" She tilted her head, quizzically.

"Oh, Arda, just tidying up in here. I'll take care of your room while you're in training, don't you worry."

She felt a twinge of fear run through her at the thought of her mother finding her file. She'd have to find a new hiding spot. "It's okay, you don't have to start today."

She sighed and said, "I know, it's just… sit, dear." She sat on Arda's bed and patted the area next to her.

Arda obliged. "Hold out your arm." She complied. Her mother produced a syringe and poked her skin without another word. It pinched, more than normal shots. She hissed in a breath but didn't say anything until it was finished.

"Isn't it a strange time for me to get a vaccine?" She felt heat running up and down her arm and flexed her hand several times until it felt normal again.

Faith didn't look up. "This isn't a vaccine. Arda, this is something else. Our secret. You can't even tell Stead."

"I don't…understand."

Her mother rubbed her hands together, nervously. "It will help make sure you are safe in the future."

"Will it hurt me?"

Faith turned and hugged her daughter. "No, dear, this will, if it works, save you. Not a word to anyone."

Turning, her mother left, and Arda sat dumbfounded. What was going on? Pushing it away, she dressed in exercise wear and walked back downstairs. Smiling softly at Will, who looked unsure of himself, they walked out the door to start their run.

"I've never ran this far before." She was worried she might not make it.

"I have. I'll help you pace yourself. It's just the first day. It'll get easier. Let's start with a jog instead."

She complied, hoping she wouldn't let anyone down.

Half an hour later, Will walked back into the house, holding a passed out Arda in his arms. Stead stood from his spot at the table and said, "what happened?"

"She was fine for a while, but then she had trouble

breathing. She passed out." His eyes were wide and his breathing uneven. He brushed the hair out of her face quickly. Stead checked her pulse.

"Get her to her bed. I'll grab my first aid kit. Faith!"

Will walked her to her room and sat gently on her bed, sitting across from her by the desk, his legs shaking. Her parents weren't far behind. "Her lips are blue. Do you think it was an asthma attack? Joy, run a medical diagnostic on Ardora."

"Running…Done. Ardora is suffering from constricted airways. I recommend the following injected into her arm, quickly." A syringe appeared and Stead lovingly pricked her skin, sliding the medicine in.

She awoke to the three of them standing around her bed. "What happened?" She blinked several times, her head dizzy.

"You have asthma." Will said, softly.

"I do? I've never had a problem before…"

"Yes, this is most curious, almost as if someone dosed you." Stead didn't look toward her mother, but eyed Arda carefully. He obviously cared about her, but what he was suggesting was considered dishonorable, another method of keeping people from serving.

"What do you mean, dosed me?"

Faith spoke up. "Why would someone go through the risk of getting illegal drugs to give to our daughter?" She was wringing her hands nervously.

"Why indeed. It could just be from the strain and stress you're experiencing. We'll continue with weight training in an hour, give you a break to relax your lungs. We'll try the run again in the morning."

He left the room, followed by Will. Who looked back at her with a strange expression on his face that she couldn't place. When they had gone, her mother shut the door. "Oh, honey, I'm so, so sorry."

"Sorry for what?" Her head was still spinning and it was hard to follow.

"I only gave you a little. It wasn't supposed to block your airways like that, merely slow you down. So you wouldn't pass your entrance test, so you'd be safe."

Arda was surprised at her. "You… you did this?"

Faith had tears in her eyes. "I'm so sorry. No more. I promise." She hugged her daughter, and whispered, "please don't tell Stead."

Her mother was shaking. Arda knew how much her mother loved her. How much Stead cared for her. She tried to put herself in her mother's shoes, watching her own child go to battle, where they may be hurt or injured. Her own heart swelled, and her eyes burned. Whatever her mother had done, however dishonorable, she had done because she was worried about her daughter. Arda didn't agree with her actions, but she could understand how her mother had come to that conclusion.

"I won't, but no more. I have to be honorable, mother."

"I know." Her mother brushed her hair out of her face, as she had done when Arda was young.

"Where did you even get this?"

"That day, at the market, in Z5."

Arda desperately wanted to ask another question, but the words wouldn't leave her mouth. Maybe it was that she loved her mother and didn't want that perfect image of her ruined, or maybe it was fear that stopped her, afraid of the answer. How had she known, weeks before it was announced, that there would be a reason to douse her daughter with illegal drugs to keep her from going to war?

Arda barely made it to her bed that night. Every muscle ached. She'd had to use heating therapy in her shower to make her feel relaxed enough to move around. She'd never been so exhausted, and this was only day one. Her head hit the pillow, and she was out several seconds later.

Mayne entered her room silently, trying to rouse her unsuccessfully. Walking to her desk he saw that she'd attempted to scribble the word, "war" onto a piece of paper. He crumpled it in his hand and placed it in his pocket.

He knew what was happening around him, knew what the government intended to do. He would come back another night, but before he left, he produced a syringe and injected it into her arm. She wouldn't die in a war if he could help it.

Chapter 7

The next day was not better. Arda still couldn't run very far or fast. She was beginning to think that this was the best she could do, but the rules were clear. If you couldn't survive basic training, you didn't move on. It wasn't something she intended to let happen. Sure, war was scary, but if she didn't go, who would look after Will and Chaste?

She struggled through every day, making small, incremental progress while Will flourished. He lapped her several times on their last day of training. He'd run the whole zone three times, while she'd only gotten half done before giving up and walking. It was frustrating for her.

"I don't… remember… having this many… problems when… I was a kid." She said it slowly, as it was hard to breathe.

"Arda, it's okay. Not everyone can be a soldier." Sweat dripped off of his brow, and down the middle of his chest, outlining the muscles that were quickly growing. The tall, lanky boy was quickly being replaced by a well-muscled man.

"I have…to go. For you and…Chaste." Her eyes began to burn.

He stopped and grabbed her shoulders, turning her to face him. "That's not what I want. I want you safe. Why would I want you in an active warzone? Believe me, this is a good thing. I'm relieved that you'll be safe."

Her eyes welled with unexpected tears. "I need to be there in case. I want you to come home safe. I want to protect you as much as you want to protect me."

He hugged her then, tightly, rubbing her lower back. She didn't care if others stared at them. She wrapped her arms around his waist, leaning into him for support, as well as from exhaustion. "I'm fine, Chaste is fine. We are okay, we'll come home. Your breathing is too weak for you to stress out. Focus on controlling it."

She tried, summoning her will to force her emotions to subside but it was no use. Her breathing quickened and she started to hyperventilate. Will picked her up and began walking the distance back to her house. The worst part was that as they walked, people stared at her as if she'd just suffered a trauma. She hadn't, she was fine, but the embarrassment made everything worse. Eventually, she just hid her face to keep the thought away, to try to calm down. The harder she tried to shut down her emotions, the more her body reacted, quaking in his arms.

By the time they reached her house, her breathing was back to normal. Her shaking over and her eyes dry. Will set her gently on her front step. His arm muscles had filled out, and it wasn't at all difficult for him to do so. "Sorry." She twisted her hands in front of her.

"For what? Caring?" He laughed. "You don't have to be ashamed if you feel something for me. I'm flattered." He leaned in close and placed his forehead to hers. "I'm grateful that we've become close."

The door opened, Steadfast standing inside. "It happened again?"

"Yes, sir." Will helped Arda move forward.

"This is unfortunate but it can't be helped. Tomorrow you both leave for your initial testing. Arda, if you don't pass, realize that it's still okay. Not everyone is meant to be a soldier."

She rolled her eyes a little, used to hearing that by now. It didn't seem right. If she had suffered from asthma as a youth, she would have gone through gene therapy to fix it. She would be able to make sure her friends came home. As it stood, she was out of time, and unprepared. She pushed the what ifs to the back of her mind, hiding from her worst thoughts from the fact that she was for the first time in her life, a failure at something she deeply wanted to succeed.

"I have someone I need to introduce you to Will. He's waiting in the next room." The two of them left Arda alone in the kitchen. Faith was at work, so she was on her own with food. Opting for a protein bar, she walked up to her room, faintly hearing their conversation.

"Will, let me introduce a dear friend of the family, Sergeant Tyrus Keating."

"It's wonderful to meet you, young man. Stead tells me…"

And then it was gone. Her stepfather really had a wealth of friends. This made her feel better. If they had someone with authority looking out for them, it increased their chances of survival.

Walking into her room, she shut the door and got out the file. Each night, she fell asleep exhausted. She hadn't talked to Mayne, save the vanishing note, hadn't received any of the answers she needed. Tonight, though, she'd try to stay awake, and hopefully, he would come.

Combing through the files, she tried to find any new connection, anything to justify why this was allowed to happen to people. For an hour she remained alone, in her room, searching for answers she couldn't find.

When her door burst open, she jumped, shutting the file and turning toward the door. Will shut it behind him and came to her.

"What are you reading?"

"Uh... nothing." She stood with the file and tried to walk to her bed, but Will managed to take it from her. "Will, really, it's nothing. Give it back."

"Too interested, Top Ten. Share." He opened the file without permission and his eyebrows narrowed.

"I can't. Please?" She began grasping for it, but he turned away from her. His solid body was too sturdy for her to reach around him.

He sat at the desk and began to read the file. She sighed in frustration and sat on her bed. For a few moments, he read silently, then he closed the file and set it on her desk. He rubbed his face with his hand and looked at her. "Is this Project R.E.D.D? The one you mentioned before?"

"I think so." It was barely a whisper.

"Where did you get the file?" His voice was harsh, commanding.

"A friend." Her voice cracked as she said it. She swallowed hard.

"What's their name?" The firm tone implied anger.

She thought for a moment before saying, "No one."

"No one gave you the file? Funny." He stood, and knelt in front of her, his hands on either side of her knees. "Seriously, though. Who gave it to you?"

She looked down at him, studying his face. It was contorted with anger and fear.

"I can't tell you." That was true. Every time she tried to talk about Mayne, nothing came out. She was grateful for that, right now.

She watched his jaw clench, his hands ball into fists. He swallowed hard, and said, "Arda, having that file is dangerous."

The concern in his voice touched her heart, warmed it. She leaned forward and took his face in her hands, saying, "I'll be ok. No one knows I have it but you."

He looked down at her lips, then up at her eyes. "Arda…

please tell me how you got it."

She didn't answer. Standing, she took the file and shoved it under her bed. When she stood and turned around, he was in front of her. "Burn it, get rid of it. Whoever gave you this put you in great danger."

She tilted her head, feigning confusion, though she had read the file more completely and knew exactly what he was talking about. "What do you mean? Do you know something?"

"I did some digging after you asked me the first time, yes, but what I found was so disturbing that…I had to stop."

"What did you find?" Now she was curious.

"Nothing you need to know about. Arda, this stuff is…unimaginable. It's degrading to our history. We can't let anyone find out we know about this. Please, if you care about me, let this go, and get rid of the file."

She looked at him then, the worry clear on his face. She took his hand in hers and kissed his cheek. "I can't." Though it was just a whisper, the words felt heavy.

The sigh of defeat came from him softly. He took her face in his hands and smiled, then. "When I get back, you'd better be alive. You stay safe, you stay smart. I'm not letting a war come between us." Then he lowered his head, touching his lips to hers gently. Her first real kiss. Not brief, not firm like the dance, but soft, careful.

She leaned into his chest, letting his arms wrap around her. Her breasts pressed against his rib cage. She felt his abdominal muscles clench, his arms tighten, yet his lips remained soft against hers. Light butterfly touches that caressed first her top, then bottom lip, that sent her heart racing in a different way, filled her head with fog and her body with heat. Goosebumps ran up and down her arm, and she shivered lightly. His hands moved along her spine as he felt it, tried to comfort her. His courtesy made her want more, and without thinking, she flicked her tongue across his bottom lip.

He stilled, his entire body frozen for a moment. She mirrored him in response, wondering if she'd gone too far. His muscles, still tense, reached for her arms, drawing her away from him. She whimpered at that. She wanted more of him, not less.

He waited until she was steady, then their eyes met. His mirrored her desire. He scanned her face, her lips, her body, then a wall came up between them. She saw it, how his demeanor changed.

He shook his head, and then he was gone, out the door and out of her life, for now.

Tears welled up in her eyes again, so she smothered her face in a pillow, and began to cry, the mix of emotions overwhelming her. She drifted off to sleep after several moments, awaking to the darkness, unsure of what had disturbed her.

Stretching, opening her eyes, she gasped as Mayne stood near her. "Finally, I get to talk to you." She sat up, intent on getting answers, but the moment she looked into his eyes, the calm overcame her.

"Stop this. We need to talk." Her voice was even and calm.

"You will not go to war. You are too weak. You will stay here. You will join Project R.E.D.D. That is your destiny. Say it."

As if in a trance, she repeated his words. He grabbed the file from under her bed and turned to leave. Through the fog in her brain, she said, "It was you…that drugged me."

He turned back. "You have no clue the thank you I'm owed for that. We won't speak again for a while. When we do, you'll be a different person. Good luck, Ardora."

Arda walked away from the testing ground feeling like a complete failure. She'd done her best, kept up in sit-ups, push-ups, until the running test. Though she had continued to improve, it wasn't good enough. She hadn't passed out, but she had failed. They took one look at her time and said, "go home. We don't need you."

Looking one last time at her classmates, all of them passing, she saw the wall come up. Her on one side, Chaste, Will, Thea, everyone, on the other. She'd never felt so alone in her entire life, so rejected and miserable. They stood on the other side of the arena, wiping their faces with towels, their eyes on her, sympathetic, kind. She locked eyes with Will, who gave her a half smile. He mouthed the words, "*go home, Top Ten.*" She turned and walked away, her chest tight, knowing she wouldn't be joining them, that the issue was settled.

She didn't want to go home, not yet. Her emotions were huge. She wanted to wait until she was stable. Walking to the park, she spent an hour near the oceanic habitat. Watching the flow of the water and the fish calmed her troubled mind, allowed her emotions to dim just enough.

Faith and Stead gave her a warm, empathetic look as she entered, hours later. She couldn't speak, so she shook her head instead. Faith hugged her silently and Stead breathed a sigh of relief. "Oh, good. You don't have to go."

The frustration and turmoil came through as she choked out the words. "I was willing to. I wanted to."

"I know, but war is…war. I'm glad my daughter isn't going."

"Me too." Faith brushed her hair out of her face.

"Everyone but me passed. I *failed.*" Her eyes burned as

she forced out the words.

"But from this failure you are left with a great opportunity. Sit down." He waited a moment, she sat, holding back tears, and he began. "You're the only person who will graduate this year. Your failure with the armed services gifts you with any career you want. You can bargain for a better apartment, or better working conditions. Arda, you're the only candidate they have. They'll fight to get you."

"Really?" Somehow, that helped. She wiped the tears away and felt the weight in her chest lift.

"Yes."

"Wow." She took a moment and thought about that. What did she want to do? What should she do? "I guess then I have some decisions to make about my destiny."

"Well, make them quickly, because tomorrow you interview."

"That soon?"

"Yes. They're already a week behind. They'll have to try to catch you up."

"Understood. Dad, who was the man you introduced to Will?"

He paused for a moment, looking at Faith. "An old, dear friend."

She nodded, satisfied for now. Turning, she walked up to her room to think.

Arda sat down in the large interview room, a dark room with cameras and screens. She waited for the equipment to work, for the screens to light up. She had no clue what she would say, no answers coming to her. Her head ached from all of the emotions she'd experienced within such a short time. It was hard to focus, to keep Will and that kiss out of her thoughts.

The screens lit up all at once. Seven people in business suits sat at desks, adjusting ties or shirts. One was drinking a glass of water. The largest man, in the middle, spoke first.

"Ardora Prime."

"Yes." It came out smooth and even. She was proud of that.

"You are here to be evaluated for career placement. I will introduce the board. I am Dr. Wickenstone, head of genetics. To your left are the heads of Medical, PUTT, and Agriculture. To your right are the heads of Arts and Pop Culture, Counseling, and Security. As you failed your test, we have decided not to include the General of the Armed forces."

She nodded, willing her cheeks not to redden. "It's a pleasure to meet all of you."

A small woman with olive skin answered her. "Believe me, speaking as the head of Medical, it's a pleasure to meet you. It's hard to fail at something. The difference between the seven of us and the rest of the District is we didn't let that affect us. How do you feel about your recent failure?"

She thought a moment before she responded. "I will never forget it."

The head of PUTT spoke up. "That is a wise attitude. I like that you took the time to think about your answer before you gave it. Looking at your test scores, I see you've done your family name proud. How do you feel about being the first family?"

"The first family?" She let confusion fill her features.

"Oh, don't be modest. We know you're a Prime, your ancestor was raised by Dr. Jackson himself. How do you feel about your legacy?"

Again. This was not the line of questioning she'd

prepared for. "I think that it's my duty to continue to be honorable and steadfast under that name."

Now the head of Counseling…" Ardora, what do you feel is the most important part of life in the district? What keeps us together? Keeps us thriving?"

"I think that we thrive together. Or fail together. Our biggest resource is our people."

They jotted down some notes on paper then. "And what do you think is the biggest threat to the continued security of our existence?"

The moment of silence dragged out so long that one of the advisors said, "Speak up, girl. We know you have a brain. Use it. Don't be afraid."

She swallowed hard and began. "I disagree with the continued existence of Omega Flame. In my opinion, it remains the biggest threat to our society."

"Spoken like a Security Officer." The head of that department sounded impressed.

"On that line of questioning, then," the head of Genetics asked, "how do you feel about the study of genetics? It comes from the flame, and with your outstanding scores, it looks like you're considering that as a career..."

"I believe that at the beginning, using the flame might have been a necessary evil that we had to tolerate, however, with what we know now, it's outlived its usefulness. Genetics itself is necessary and vital to our survival."

"So how do you feel about genetically engineered food? Do you have a FoodGen in the home?" This from the head of agriculture.

"Yes, we do, but my mother also provides real produce when she can."

"You'd say they're both necessary?"

"They were for me, and I feel as if I've benefited from both."

"Fair enough."

"Ardora," a lyrical voice began, "what inspires you to greatness?" This was from Arts and Culture.

"What do you mean?"

"Would you call yourself a creative person?"

"I play the cello, I can't draw. My mother believes I'm a dreamer..."

"Ah, the organic sound of the Cello. Do you like it? Or do you prefer synthetic sounds?"

"The cello sounds more…authentic and beautiful to me."

"And if you could play that for a living, would you want to do so?"

She hadn't given herself the opportunity to think of that. Her grandmother had chosen that path. "I would be honored to follow in the footsteps of my grandmother, Hope. It is a tough decision."

She sat back. "Give us one moment, Ms. Prime."

The screens went dark. She sat in the silence for several moments. This interview was nothing like she'd imagined it to be. No quizzing, but only questions about how she felt. How did that help anything? After a few more minutes of silence, all seven screens lit back up.

"Ardora, normally this would be the time to debate between your top three choices, however, under these unusual circumstances, it has become necessary for all of us to be included in the negotiation process. Now, that being said, you did wonderfully in your interview. As we don't want to appear unseemly, we will retire this interview and instead send you digital copies of our offers. You will have a week to review them, maybe with your parents, and then we will speak again, and you will give us your decision."

United, they ended with, "thank you for your time."

The screens went dark, and it was over.

Arda walked into her home and saw her parents busily looking over the contracts which had already been sent.

"Arda, sit down sweetheart. We have a lot to discuss with you." Faith handed her a glass of water, which she downed before sitting. "That was not what I expected."

"It never is. All those questions about, who are you? What motivates you? It's hard to answer, but they're the best in their fields, so I trust them to run an interview."

"Now, dear, we are reviewing the contracts. I know how hard the last few days have been, so you can either sit here and do this with us or you can rest for a while. We can always give you the highlights later."

"No, it's my career, I should be included." She picked up a tablet and began to read.

> The party of the first part, hereby referred to as Politics, Utilities and Teaching Technologies, or PUTT, does agree to hire and retain the party of the second part, Ardora Prime, under the following conditions:
>
> A primary residence will be provided for the first two years of internship to the party of the second part.
>
> A salary allowance of 1000 credit will be applied monthly to an account controlled by the party of the second part.
>
> A vehicle will be assigned by lease to the party of the second part for the duration of the internship.

As Arda continued to read, she realized she might have chosen unwisely. She had to stop several times to ask her parents questions about the wording of the contract. After several hours, she had finished her first one.

She stretched, looking up from the tablet. Faith and Steadfast waited with their hands folded. "Are you ready for us to walk you through what we read?"

"Sure." She thought she got the hang of the first offer, so she was ready to hear the next.

"I have the contract from Security." Faith showed it to her. "They are offering you an apartment in Zone 3, a car for your internship, a salary of 1000 credit and a bonus of five extra vacation days in your first year after internship."

Steadfast gave her his tablet. "I have the contract from Agriculture…" She listened intently as they continued to speak, trying to take all of it in. They got through the first three contracts, but the night had snuck up on them.

"Go to bed, honey. We can do this in the morning."

Yawning, she complied, walking slowly upstairs, thinking about her offers. They'd go through the rest tomorrow and her mother would help her start the negotiation process.

Turning into her bedroom, she examined how many remnants of her childhood she would leave behind in just a few days. A snugly unicorn stuffed animal, the quilt from her grandmother, the cello, were all things that she wouldn't be able to fit in her new apartment. Interns were expected to devote themselves to learning their trade. Anything not related to your intended job was a distraction.

She thought about the long day she would have tomorrow. Her twenty-nine classmates would begin basic training. Will would have to cut his hair. She laughed at that, not sure she could picture him without his long locks. The girls would have to, as well. She tried picturing Thea with a buzz cut. She just couldn't.

She lay down to sleep, without a serum. Only children were allowed to do so without a script from a counselor. It was time for her to grow up, not to rely on childish things. The dark came quickly.

She'd slept in later than she would have liked. In a rush, she stumbled out of bed, getting ready as soon as possible.

Running downstairs, her parents were already discussing the contracts. Faith looked up and motioned to her to eat her eggs. As she sat down, she was handed a tablet.

"We didn't want to wake you. As an intern, you'll lack sleep. We combed through the offers and compiled a chart of data for you. The best offer seems to be coming from…" he glanced down, swiping through the chart, "genetics. They offered you a larger starting salary, ten vacation days after internship and work housing on the resident floor, as they noted you would be the only intern this year. That means a larger apartment with less restrictions. It's very nice of them, but before we accept that offer, let's see what we can do about these others."

They walked her through the process, teaching her to refine her bargaining skills. This was different than the market, as she wasn't trying for a comb or an outfit, but her future. All set, she sent the reply emails asking for more than she thought they would give, but not too much.

Noting the time, she said, "I have to go see my classmates off."

Faith nodded. "We're coming with you. Ready Stead?"

Leaving, they got into his car and drove to the town hall, where the induction ceremony would take place. After its conclusion, the cadets would spend weeks in basic training, isolated from everyone except their class, learning to be soldiers. Then they would leave immediately to help the doctors secure the medical tents at the war front. This would be the last time until the war concluded that she would see them.

They walked into the large hall that was usually reserved for trials or official meetings. Today, the room was packed with family members saying goodbye. She scanned the crowd for Will, Chaste or Thea. Panicking, for a moment, she couldn't find anyone. Then a hug from behind pinned her arms against her sides. When they let go, she turned to see Thea.

"Sorry if that was awkward, but…" Her gaze lowered.

"I get it, I think." Arda hugged her back. "Is your family here?"

"Yes," she turned behind her. "My father came."

"Have you seen Will or Chaste?"

"Yeah, they're around somewhere." She looked behind Arda. "There." She pointed. Arda turned and saw Chaste. He was more muscular than she remembered.

Ignoring Thea, she walked to her best friend and focused on breathing as her emotions became unstable. She paused, but when his eyes locked on hers, she continued. As she approached, he placed his hands in his pockets.

"Ardora." That sounded official, but he smiled.

"Chaste." She wrung her hands together, worried now. "How have you been?"

"Busy. You?"

"Worried."

He looked at his feet. "No need. We'll be back soon. My dad doesn't think this war will last over six months. No one has the population to keep it going for very long. Since we're neutral, we should be safe. Don't worry." He wrapped her in his arms for a quick hug, despite onlookers staring. He clearly didn't care. Then, he gave her a last brave smile and walked away, finding his seat next to his father, who, as a former Chief, was surrounded by well-wishers and politicians.

She scanned the crowd, looking for Will. Walking around, she was able to find every classmate of hers, except for him. Where was he? Had something happened?

The bell was called for everyone to take their seats for the ceremony. Feeling defeated, she found her parents and sat down. Chief Richards started his speech, and a hand rested on her shoulder gently. She glanced behind her, aware of how different he looked, his hair shortened. She smiled at him, and he smiled back. He was okay.

His speech ending, they began calling names. One by one the students walked from their seats to the front of the room, as their families cheered and clapped for them. Arda felt shame at not making the cut. They would be leaving, and she would be alone, unable to help. They called Chaste, then Thea, all the while his hand resting on her shoulder. When it was finally his turn, his hand slid down to her elbow and placed a piece of paper inside, where no one could see but her.

"I'll come back to you." It was barely a whisper, but it held weight to her. Her eyes started to swell with tears, so she pinched herself trying to stop them from flowing. This wasn't about her or her emotions. She needed to be strong for them.

She watched as they were all given the code of conduct, as they recited their pledge to serve and as they left, walking out of the room from the back. Another speech was given commending the families for raising such fine children. Arda touched the piece of paper in her pocket. Whatever it was, she couldn't look at it right now.

When the speaker was finished, they rose and began to file out row by row. Arda's parents were approached outside by several others, including Will's father. They exchanged pleasantries, but Arda felt very out of place around so many older adults. She was out of her depth, and she knew it.

"Hang on to that note," someone whispered behind her. She turned, standing face to face with a tall, red-haired man. She didn't think anyone had red hair anymore, except her mother. Most people were a shade of brown. "Excuse me?" she asked politely.

"I don't miss much. I actually showed Will how to make it." Her father turned and noticed them.

"Ah, Ardora, you've met Tyrus. Good."

He held out a hand to her and she shook it as she'd been instructed. Firmly. "It's nice to meet you."

"And you, daughter of Faith. How are things, Stead?"

"Well, and you?"

"Getting these recruits ready. And don't worry, I'll be with all of them every step of the way." He placed an arm on her shoulder, but there was a weight to it she couldn't understand. As if he was trying to send her a message, but she didn't know the language. Stead's attention was diverted, and he pulled her near him.

"I know someone drugged you. I'd like to know who." Panic filled her. Looking at him wide eyed, she was frozen. Before he could say more, Faith interrupted them.

"Oh, Tyrus, it's lovely to see you. Do you ever age?"

He laughed as he hugged Faith. "Not very much, apparently."

She lovingly tapped him on his arm as if they were old friends. "Come sweetie. We have to go."

"Yes, I'll talk to you after the war is over and your friends are safely home." Turning, he left, and Arda let out a breath she didn't realize she'd been holding. Faith gave her a look but took her hand and walked her toward their car. The day was over, her friends gone.

Arda silently shed tears in the car on the drive home. Faith and Stead were silent, aware of them, but unable to offer any comfort. She decided it was silly to cry. She wasn't going to war. She was getting careers handed to her. She didn't have anything to lose…except every one of her peers.

"Is there anything I can do from here?" She finally spoke up.

"What do you mean, honey?"

"Anything I can do for the soldiers from here?"

"I'm sure some of the women in Z5 will organize some packages to be sent with blankets, socks, treats, things like that. If you would like to add anything I can talk to some of my contacts and see what we can do."

"I'd like that. Thank you, Mother." She clenched her jaw, her eyes burning, and swallowed hard trying not to cry. It was silly.

As they walked in the house, she was greeted by the beeping of tablets, letting her know that the emails had been returned. Faith and Stead sat down to look through them, but she felt guilty. Excusing herself, she went into the living room and sat on the couch, resting her eyes.

She awoke screaming later, from a dream steeped in death. Her mother was near her, Steadfast watching from the kitchen. She rubbed her shoulders and her hair. "It's okay. You're safe."

She didn't feel safe. She couldn't remember her dream, other than many, many people dying. "I'm okay." It came out shaky, but she tried to believe it. Standing, she stretched, and said, "How did the offers go?"

"Everyone is still in, the best being from security this time. They upped their stipend significantly. Arts and Culture is willing to give you more vacation days, though."

"And genetics?"

"Holding firm on their first offer."

"I see. What do we do now?"

"We narrow down your choices to the ones you do want, to make them fight harder for you."

"Okay, so how many do I have to pick?"

"Four."

"Genetics, Medical, Arts and Culture, Security."

"Alright." Faith began to write out the next set of emails, suggesting things to her daughter. Arda just nodded, but her mind kept drifting to her classmates.

The day ended with another better offer, this time from Security. Her eyes tired, she walked up to her room and remembered the piece of paper Will had given her. Taking it from her pocket, she opened it slowly, confused as to how he'd folded it so complexly, in the shape of a crane.

Finally opening the note, she gasped at its contents. It was a picture of them both, drawn by hand, embracing each other. At the bottom was a note that read, "This is what I'm holding on to." She had no clue he could draw so well. It made her blush, but she was also proud of him. She placed it in her drawer, making certain it was folded flat. Her lips tingled as she remembered their kiss, hoping that it wasn't the only one she would ever have.

Three days later, she was back in the interview room,

staring at the four screens. On each screen was someone hopeful she would choose them, but the words couldn't quite leave her mouth.

"Ardora, have you decided?"

She knew what she wanted to say, but she felt compelled to say something else, as if the words would burst forth from her whether she wanted them to or not. She wrestled with the thought for a few moments, silently.

"I know this is a big decision. Would you like an additional day to contemplate your future?" This from Arts and Culture.

She shook her head, but still the words wouldn't leave her mouth.

"Is there anything you need to ask us before you decide?" Genetics seemed patient with her.

She looked them each in the eye, took a deep breath, and let the words leave her lips.

"Project…"

Chapter 8

The screens went dark before the second word was even uttered. Surprised, she sat in silence for a few moments before one screen lit back up, however, a new face stared back at her. He wore glasses, was dressed completely in black, and his hands were carefully folded in front of him.

"Prime, Ardora, daughter of Prime, Faith, grand-daughter of Prime, Hope, great-grand-daughter of Prime, Patience, great-great-grand-daughter of Prime, Regina. Correct?"

"Yes."

"My name is Swift. I have no last name. I am very curious as to how a Prime, such a distinguished line, has come to hear of our Project."

She thought a moment. She couldn't reveal her source. What should she say? Her face blank, several moments passed before he continued, "I see. I too have sources I wish to protect, but from someone so young… impressive."

He looked at her face for a moment, as she tried to keep a blank expression upon it. "I represent the office of Reconnaissance, Espionage, Decryption, and Defense, otherwise known as Project: R.E.D.D for short. Why do you wish to work for us?"

This was easier to answer. "You're a secret government project. Doesn't get more exclusive than that."

"I see." He glanced at several screens she couldn't see. "I have some basic questions I would like to ask you to see if you're a candidate or not. These questions pose a list of open-ended scenarios. We would like you to tell us what you would do. Are you ready?"

"Yes."

"Scenario One: You're out with your friends, at a park, and you notice a file sitting on a bench nearby. Do you look at it?"

He was playing with her. She hadn't known what a file was until Mayne had handed her one. "What's a file?"

"A stack of papers."

"Why isn't it electronic?"

He laughed. "Okay, moving on." He pressed more buttons. "Scenario 2: A small child stands in front of you in Z5, holding a red balloon. The child is accosted by a man with glowing blue eyes. What do you do?"

Again, he was testing her. "I wake up."

"Excuse me?"

"I wake up, because people with glowing eyes don't exist."

He looked at her for a moment before laughing out loud. "Oh, you have a sense of humor." He wiped a tear away from his eyes and hit more buttons.

"Scenario three: You find an old tablet on the ground. It isn't yours, but no one claims it, even when you ask. You pick it up and notice that some files are encrypted. Do you hack the data?"

"I don't understand why anyone would ever need to encrypt data, let alone hacking someone else's personal property."

He snorted at that. "Last. You're in competition with your classmates and everyone but you have passed. How do you handle that failure?"

That was…incredibly personal. She realized he was trying to elicit an emotional reaction. She looked down, then back up when she was ready to answer, locking eyes with him. "I join a secret organization in hopes I can help them in a different way."

He stared at her a long moment before placing both hands back in his lap. He sighed and began, "Loyalty is good, if it is tempered with wisdom. You lie very well. No tells. That's good. I don't care what or who brought you to us, but after checking your scores, it's clear you're a candidate. I must be very clear with you. If you choose to join our Project, it is a lifelong commitment. Don't expect special privileges like the other departments were willing to give you. If you get something, it's because you earned it. Understood?"

She nodded. "Now. You're the youngest person ever that has inquired about the project, so if approved, in spite of your age, Steadfast will hand you a written contract, sealed by us, when you get home. You will open and review it *alone.* If the terms are to your liking, you start work the following day. If not, you will come back here and be able to choose among the other disciplines. I expect a response by 900 hours tomorrow. If I don't receive it, I'll assume that you decided Project R.E.D.D. was not the best career for you."

The screen went blank before she could answer. Standing, she exited the room. Faith was waiting for her. They'd walk home together, as Stead was still working. Faith put an arm around her daughter and asked, "I'm too excited to wait for Stead! What did you choose?"

"I…" she paused, "I need another day."

"Oh." Her mother seemed disappointed. "That's okay. We'll celebrate tomorrow then."

They sat in the kitchen when Stead came home. They heard the car door slam shut, louder than normal. He opened the kitchen door, his face red. He looked angry.

Slamming the door, Faith jumped. "What is it, dear?"

He paced back and forth for a while before he began. "Arda, what did you do?"

"I don't know what- "

"Don't lie to me!" He grabbed her by both shoulders and picked her up out of the chair.

"Stead!" Faith stood, trying to grab his arms to protect her daughter. "What is the matter with you?!"

"What…did…you…do?" Arda just stared at him, a hard stare that showed she didn't appreciate what was happening.

After a moment, he let her go, and walked back outside. Faith turned to her and softly said, "are you okay?"

Arda nodded, although tears were threatening to fall. He came back moments later with a file, a single red strip of tape sealing it, without any other marking. He dropped it on the kitchen table. Faith looked at it, with its lack of a label or return address, then back at her daughter, her face blank.

"What's wrong, mother?"

Her mother, instead of answering her, walked away. Stead's face was losing its rouge, but his hands remained on his hips. "Arda, do you have any clue what you're getting into?"

Before she could answer, he walked away. Alone, now, she picked up the sealed file and walked slowly up to her room. She shut the door and opened the file, hoping her parents would forgive her.

Ten minutes later she rubbed her eyes, taking a break. She had never seen such specific jargon, such wordiness. Words she had never heard before filled the page. Rubbing her head, she had no clue what she was going to do.

A knock on the door disturbed her peace. "Come in," she spoke so softly, it was a wonder the person heard her. Her mother walked in. She tried to hide the file, but her mother motioned her to be still.

"Arda, it's okay." She looked at her daughter. "I'm the one person in your life that you can talk to about Project R.E.D.D."

"You know about it?" Her eyes grew wide.

Her mother was silent for a moment before she said, "Dear, I'm on the Board of Directors. If you join, I'll be your boss's boss."

"But the way you left the room…"

"For Stead's sake. He is aware that the Project exists, but not that I work for it. He would worry. So I used my face to conceal my involvement, a small omission. And if Swift interviewed you, then you have the capacity for it too. I'll tell you as a mother, this makes me both upset and strangely proud of you. How did you even know?"

Arda lowered her head, saying nothing. "You've always been a quiet girl, Arda. That will help you. Let people fill the silence. They'll tell you much. Can you tell me why you chose this career?"

She felt her chest fill with pressure, her eyes burning, her throat closing. "I…have to do *something*. I can't sit back while they risk their lives and not help them. If I can't be a soldier…I'll be the spy."

It was out, and she breathed a sigh of relief. Even if Mayne hadn't compelled her, she would have chosen this path.

"I can understand and respect that." Her mother's voice was soft. She knelt beside Arda and cleared her throat. "Now, on to your contract."

Her mother grabbed the file from her desk and sat down on the bed. She scanned the document for a moment, before saying, "Standard contract. Lifelong commitment, until retirement or death, quarters at the institute with off base privileges after internship…" She paused a moment, reading some more. "Stipend of…" She turned the pages, "500 dollars a month plus travel, food, business expenses paid…" Again, she turned the page. "And a bonus for completion of each contract, starting with a 20,000 credit for completing internship. Wow. I only got ten thousand."

"That's a lot of credit. Why would anyone need that much?"

She looked at her daughter and smiled. "You'll use it all at this job, believe me. Arda, are you absolutely sure you wish to pursue this?"

She thought a moment before she asked, "Do you think I can do this?"

Her mother's smile widened. "I think you'll do wonderfully."

"Then yes."

"Alright, then we need to go over the rest of the contract. You'll contact Swift tomorrow at 800 hours."

"He said by 900."

"First rule, they always mean an hour before. Being on time in this Project means being late."

She nodded, then looked at the clock. "I'm not going to get much sleep, am I?"

Her mother gave her a sympathetic look. "I'm afraid not. Now, let's go through the rest…"

Four hours later, they ended their discussion. Arda had all the rules and procedures down. She set the clock for four hours later, hoping she would be able to wake up and function.

Sleep did not come easily. She thought of Will, of Chaste, thought of what they were doing right now. She thought of Mayne, the glowing eyed man that had led her here. She thought of her future, still not sure exactly what Project R.E.D.D. was responsible for. She decided, though, if her mother was involved, it couldn't be all bad. Her mother, after all, was a good-hearted woman.

Turning, she thought of the picture in her desk drawer. She wondered how long it took him to draw it. She wondered what he thought about her, if he was thinking about her now. The guilt she felt over being the only one not to serve came and went, threatening her to tears. Lastly, she thought about the red-haired man, Tyrus, who had known that she'd been drugged. He scared her, but her family insisted that he was a friend. Confused, she finally drifted off to sleep as the sun began to rise.

The alarm woke her far too early. She sighed as she realized how little sleep she'd gotten. Crawling out of bed took every ounce of willpower she had. Walking down the stairs, her mother handed her a purple serum.

"You don't want this to become a habit, but it will help." She downed it, and the aching, tired feeling left her almost immediately, replaced by a bright-eyed woman.

"Wow. What is that?"

"Don't worry. We have an hour to draft a response. I'll help you. Eat your eggs and sit down."

She did, surprised that the serum made everything taste better. Her mother worked with her for an hour, drafting a response. As it was sent, a knock sounded on the door. Faith took her hand, and said, "no matter what happens next, I want you to be brave. I made it through this. You can, too."

Arda didn't understand, but she walked to the door anyway. Opening it, Swift stood before her, two security guards behind him. "Hello, Ardora. Faith. May I come in?"

"Of course. Welcome to our home."

"Lovely little place. I'm glad we pay you well enough to

afford a two-story apartment."

She looked at him oddly. "I could afford more, true, but I like Z3. People are more…honest."

He folded his hands behind him. "Ladies, we are in a unique situation, as interns usually do not come from the same gene pool. I'll admit I'm curious Faith as to why you would allow your daughter to continue. You know what lies beyond your front door."

He was saying more than what he was saying. Her mother understood him, but she didn't. "I'm curious, Swift, as to why someone in your position would dare question a board member."

"My apologies, Seer Prime."

"Accepted, Recruiter."

You could cut the tension with a knife. "Ardora, I have come to collect you. You will leave your home with nothing on your back except the clothes you wear now. By tradition, this next test will prove whether you truly have what it takes to be an intern with our organization. It will be tough, but you'll be better for it. Are you ready to take the next step forward in your life?"

Her mother squeezed her hand gently before letting go. Arda looked at her mother, locking eyes with her. When would she see her again? "It's okay dear. If you really need me, I'll be able to find you."

Standing, she said, "I'm ready. Let's go."

Swift gave her a half smile, bowing to her as he did so. "You're chariot awaits, then." He waited for her to exit the house, then followed. A large luxury car stood blocking the road. "In we go." He opened the door and she stepped inside.

Once the door was closed, she breathed in a strange smell, like that of the roses in her corsage. She inhaled on instinct, and then the darkness surrounded her.

Feeling a breeze on her skin, she returned from the dark, slowly. She felt cold, damp earth beneath her fingers. *That's strange. Her bed isn't dirty.* As her thoughts formed, she remembered the car. She remembered her decision. Slowly opening her eyes, she began to panic.

She was surrounded by trees on all sides of her. This was like the temperate habitat in the park, only she was inside it. Ground beneath her, the trees stretched higher in the sky than at the park. So high they blocked out the sun.

She sat up too quickly and the world spun around her. Her head ached. Touching her forehead, she tried to focus. Slowly, the effect wore off, and she tried to stand. Looking around her, panic rose as she realized that she had the clothes on her back, and no other supplies. This is what he'd meant? What had she gotten herself into?

Now is not the time. Now she needed to survive. She needed to find a way out of there. She turned, and a small scream escaped her lips. There, sitting on a log, doing something to the wood with a knife, was the red-haired man, Tyrus Keating.

-*This is what I'm holding on to* (Will Draws Arda 1)

- Retrieved from the R.E.D.D. archives, 154 o.f.

Chapter 9

One year later…

Arda sat working at her desk. She was starting the first day of her second year of internship, and she was grateful. Grateful to have made it this far, to still be alive, to be working with such amazing people. She was just, so *grateful.*

She practiced it again until she believed it. This year had been hell. She'd never been lonelier, more isolated, more broken than she was now. She couldn't let that stop her though. She had a mission, and she would succeed.

Glancing through the various news articles, she stopped when one caught her eye. She was supposed to be looking for bias, but instead, she clicked on a simple article, not more than a paragraph long.

> After a year of fighting, it is with great pride that we announce the successful conclusion of the war. All soldiers will be returning home to begin their internships shortly. The winning districts, 2 and 3, are offering significant rewards for our neutral help, to be negotiated by our Chief. Districts 4 and 5 have reunited with the cause, agreeing to a ceasefire in exchange for mercy. Let's welcome all our soldiers home!

She clicked off the article as soon as she was done, worried someone would be watching too closely. Though she was thrilled at the conclusion of the conflict, she was not willing to let anyone know it. Turning her attention back to the online articles, she continued in silence.

A voice startled her an hour later. "Jeez, Ardora, you're making us look bad. Slow down a bit." Anger welled inside her, but she turned and forced a smile. "Shadow. So good to see you this morning."

"You as well." He smiled, but his eyes remained cold. Foolish for you to let me read you so easily. "Did you hear the good news?"

Yes. "What good news?" She let her eyes close slightly.

"Your classmates are coming home. All twenty-five of them." He locked eyes with her. She almost slipped, almost gave away her thoughts, but her training stopped her. A year of hard, grueling training that taught her to conceal her emotions, and sharpened her survival skills. "That's wonderful. I should very much like to see them."

"Well, you're in the middle of your internship, so that's highly unlikely. Maybe I can talk to some higher ups, see what I can do."

She wanted to stab his pretty face. "Oh, that would be lovely. Thank you."

He held his coffee to his lips, drank slowly, his eyes never leaving hers. "Don't mind helping a colleague, especially one as talented as you."

Oh, bite me. "You're too kind."

"Anytime, Ardora." Turning, Shadow walked away. He was a year ahead of her, but his internship would not be over any time soon. To officially complete it, you had to fulfill a contract. While he talked as if he was a god, he still hadn't completed a single one.

Arda turned back to her work, foregoing the coffee that

was a luxury at this office. She didn't like how it made her feel. In this line of work, control over your emotions was everything.

A new email was placed on her virtual workspace, so she quizzically opened it. She couldn't help the smile that briefly covered her face. The sender, Fortuna, was a codename for her mother.

After a brief visual scan to verify she was herself, the words popped up. From an outsider's perspective, they made no sense. Gibberish, a combination of random words put together on a page. To her, they were a code, one only she and her mother knew. She couldn't write anything down, so she'd adjusted to decoding the language in her head.

Contract. That was the first word. She began to get excited. Park. That was the meeting place. Hot Snow.

The first two were obvious. Her mother had a contract for her. This would be her first official one. The park was their meeting spot. Hot snow, though… Hot could mean time of day. So, the hottest time of the day at the artic habitat. That made sense.

Deleting the file, she closed her computer down for her break. Standing, adjusting her dress, she began to walk toward the elevator. Though no one stared at her, she felt eyes watching her. Probably Shadow. He was always trying to sabotage her.

Closing the doors, alone in the elevator, she relaxed just a bit. She was excited. When she met her mother, when she completed this contract, she would officially be able to skip her second intern year. After being cooped up in this building for a year with only the occasional walk to the park, she would love to skip more grunt work and finally have a private place to live.

The elevator opened into a lounge, quiet and peaceful. Plants grew along the walls, potted flowers sitting on the receptionist's desk. Beyond her were two security guards, by the only entrance and exit to the building. Showing her ID, giving them her thumbprint and eye scan, they allowed her to exit, saying only, "be back in fifteen minutes."

She nodded with a smile and left. As soon as she was out of sight of the building, she quickened her pace. It would be hard to get all the information she needed before her fifteen minutes of freedom was over.

Her mother was waiting in the park, sitting on a bench overlooking a lovely group of penguins. Arda knew the routine by now. No direct contact would be initiated, as eyes were everywhere. Her mother wasn't technically allowed to help her, but she'd been an invaluable resource to her daughter anyway.

Walking in front of her mother, Arda put a hand to the glass. "Aww, you're so cute," she said, pretending to enjoy the view. She'd stood right in front of Faith, blocking her view. Her mother stood, walking to the side as if to see better. As she did so, she slipped a small, almost weightless object into Arda's pocket.

"Some people. Watch where you're going!" She turned and walked away. She used an implant to disguise her voice. She sounded nothing like the warm mother she knew. This voice was cold, calculating. She loved it.

For a few more minutes, she stood, staring at the penguins. Turning, she walked into the public restrooms. Closing a stall, she quickly took the small device out and touched her watch to it. Lights flashed, the transfer of data. She would have to pass through a metal detector to return to work. Keeping the chip was not an option.

When she finished, she flushed the chip and left the stall, sanitizing her hands. She walked out and started back to her job.

Smooth. She was quite proud of herself and her mother

for finally believing in her. On her wrist was the key to a promotion, the key to her freedom. Though her shoes ached in the heels she was wearing, she walked quickly back to the facility. She didn't want to be late.

After work was over, after she'd rejected offers of drinks or unofficial dates, after dealing with Shadow and his humungous ego, she finally stepped into her small apartment, throwing off her heels and sighing with relief.

She desperately wanted to look at the contents of the contract, but now was not the time. Walking slowly, she sat down on the small couch she'd purchased last year and turned the view to the arctic habitat. Penguins, polar bears and ice filled the screen. Rubbing her feet, she waited.

After a few minutes, her mother's face filled the screen instead. "Arda, are you busy?"

"Just rubbing my aching feet. How are you mother?"

"I was so grateful when I became an agent and could wear something other than heels. They're the worst. I don't know why they still require such an archaic and outdated set of footwear for women. Men certainly don't have to wear them."

"You and I both, mother."

Her mother continued talking, but a red light swept the room. Arda continued what she was doing, used to the procedure. When the red light was finished, she stood and began to talk freely.

"How are you, really?"

Faith laughed. "About to go home to your father. Is there anything you want me to tell him?"

"Did you hear? They're coming home."

"I did hear that. Would you like Stead to give them a

message?"

"Yes. Tell them I'm so happy they're home."

"Will do. Did you get the contract?"

"Yes. Thank you, mother."

"Don't thank me. Read it. Your room will be secure for the next two hours. It's a lot of information to digest. This is not easy, Arda. You will have to be skillful in completing this. Your time frame is two weeks. I have to go."

The screen went dark. Arda immediately ran to her tablet and connected her watch. Thanks to the program she'd built herself, the screen downloaded the data and decrypted it almost simultaneously. Looking at the first page, she began to read...

Two hours later, she deleted the information with a heavy heart. Her mother was right. This wouldn't be easy, but if she could finish it within the two weeks, she'd complete it before someone else got a chance to.

Walking to the tiny FoodGen, she ordered her dinner and ate quickly. She would have to get a good night's rest if she wanted to get this done on top of her normal duties. Finishing her meal, she undressed, ordering a sleep serum and passing out some moments later.

She stared at Tyrus, for a moment not moving. "Where am I?"

He looked up from the wood. "You're alone."

"But you're here."

"No, no I'm not. If anyone asks, you're alone right now."

"Okay."

"I'm here to make sure you don't fail. It was a courtesy I gave your mother when she joined the Project. I'm giving it to you too. I owe your family."

"How old are you?"

He laughed at that. "Older than you think. Now," he threw the knife down on the ground in front of her. "Pick up the knife."

She reached down to do so, holding it in her hands.

"Your first lesson. Always, always have a knife."

"Okay."

"You're second lesson is on its way."

"What's the second lesson."

He smiled. "Don't hesitate."

He jumped up in the tree, climbing up so quickly she wasn't sure he was human. That's when she heard the growling. She turned and looked behind her, seeing the wolf.

She gasped, sitting up in bed quickly, checking the time. Turning, she noted the wolf pelt on the wall. It was a good thing she hadn't hesitated that day. Rubbing her eyes, she stretched and got ready for her day, pushing the dream and the memory away. That same knife went into a hidden sheath she'd made herself, where no one would suspect.

The morning went according to plan, keeping herself busy, doing odd jobs that entry agents didn't want to do. Monitoring residences, updating car routes, reporting possible threats, light work. She kept glancing at the clock, waiting for her break time. After break time would come more work, but then, when she was home, the real challenge would begin.

When her break came, she gladly left, walking to the park and standing in front of the temperate habitat. Watching the wolves inside it, she began to remember. Images came to her*, the wolf jumping on top of her, fumbling for the knife, the bite of the wolf as it latched onto her arm. The feeling of stabbing it's neck, rush of blood.*

"Arda." A voice behind her crooned. Turning, she didn't recognize the man before her. He was tan from the sun, his hair short, his body stocky. His eyes looked sad, but there was something familiar about him. The memory floated to the top of her mind. The last time she'd seen those eyes had been a year ago. They'd been happy then. Her heart began to beat fervently, despite her training.

"Will." She breathed it, but he had heard. He sat next to her on the bench, his hands careful not to touch her. After a moment, he looked down at the ground and asked, "how has this year treated you?"

Thinking of the rehabilitation she'd undergone from that bite, the removal of the scar tissue, the extreme dehydration and fear she'd experienced, she merely said, "I am well. And yourself?"

He looked at her, and said, "I am well."

She knew in spite of her difficulties, the training, the sleep deprivation, that nothing in her life compared to what he must have experienced on the front. That he could react as if everything was normal said a lot about his resolve.

Her look softened then. "I'm glad you're well. When did you get back?" She fought to keep her breathing even. Her entire being wanted to wrap her arms around him and not let go.

"A few hours ago. Listen, Arda, I wanted to talk to you before anyone else did. I know we've lost a year, but no matter what you hear, I still feel the same way about you."

What a strange sentence. She felt her mask of professionality come back up. "What am I going to hear?"

"You're going to hear a lot of lies. Don't believe them." He gave her an unrest gaze, as if he would say more, then he simply turned his back to her and walked away before she could ask any more questions.

She wondered what had happened, but her time was almost up. Realizing she could be late, she stood and jogged in her heels back to work. Will would have to wait. The longing in her chest would have to wait.

Returning to her desk, she'd been working ten minutes before two security guards came to get her. Not sure where they were taking her, she nervously followed them, but her body language showed only confidence. They boarded the elevator and hit the seventh floor. Though she did nothing, she was getting worried. The seventh floor was off limits for interns, residents and anyone except the board and elite agents. What did they want with her?

The doors opened and the two security guards motioned for her to enter the hallway, but they did not follow. Once the doors shut, a small, round woman came to greet her. "Ardora Prime?" Her voice was pleasant, if high pitched.

"Yes."

"Follow me please. No questions."

She did so, as the woman lead her down a hallway of dark glass. You couldn't see anything beyond it. Turning right, they walked halfway down before she opened a door that appeared out of nowhere. "Please step inside for a conference call."

Arda complied and the door was shut behind her. She didn't know what was going on, but this was no wild wolf. She could do this. Adjusting her suit, she waited patiently.

After several seconds, in which she was certain they were observing her vitals, a screen came into view. Swift sat, facing her. "Ardora. What a pleasure to see you surviving."

"You as well, Recruiter Swift."

"I notice that you went to the park today. You saw your old friend Willful."

"I did." Her face was blank.

"I need to know what you discussed."

"You really want to know?" She smiled alluringly.

"I need to ask."

"He talked about how much he missed me, how he

wanted me in his arms. How he longed to kiss me…" she sighed convincingly.

"Really."

"Really." She even winked at him.

"Ardora, as an employee I was responsible for hiring, I feel the need to be honest with you right now."

Sure you do. "By all means."

"Willful is being investigated for claims that he deserted his unit, resulting in the death of three of your classmates. It's a serious charge. We will be handling the investigation. As an employee of Project R.E.D.D, I shouldn't have to remind you about breeching protocol."

"I'm aware of the protocol."

"Good. I'll expect you to follow it instead of succumbing to your…urges. If you're caught lying, you realize you will share his sentence."

"I do."

"Good day, Ardora."

The screen went blank, and the woman opened the door, instructing her to follow. She had no clue what was going on with Will, or what she could do to help. She had to focus on herself for the next two weeks. Once she gained her freedom, she could figure this out. Then, everything would resolve itself for the better, at least, she desperately hoped it would.

Chapter 10

Arda walked into her tiny apartment, ready to start her work. She had four, maybe five hours of time to research before she had to sleep. Going without sleep was not possible in this line of work. Sitting down, she hit a button on her watch and a virtual screen appeared. It was tough at first, swiping on air to form words, but she'd gotten the hang of it over the last year.

She closed her eyes before she began, visualizing the contract.

Directive: Discern the identity of a traitor.

Time: 2 Weeks

Credits when completed: 20,000

Handler: None

Primary Agent: Faith Prime

The primary agent was the one responsible for setting up the contract. She had no handler, which meant she was on her own. The rest of the contract had given clues and various events that would eventually help her identify the traitor. This was it. This was her first real job.

Opening her eyes, she began her search. She knew this had to do with the war, someone from D1 was giving information to both sides. As a neutral party, D1 should not have become involved. This person possibly tipped the scales to favor one side over the other. That was a violation of the District Treaty.

She didn't think about the consequences. Obviously, this person was dangerous and deserved what they got. She understood why her mother was giving this to her. She had twenty-five contacts in her classmates that she could surveil and gain intel from. Any other intern or agent would be less effective than her. Combing through their military files, she started her search.

When the five hours she had available were over, she rubbed her eyes and shut down her watch. She'd go to bed, wake up and continue tomorrow. She was slightly frustrated. One day was down. She only had thirteen more, and the information she was receiving online was useless so far. Twenty profiles down, and not one detail that narrowed her search. She could still eliminate all of them, or none of them. She would have to go about this in a different way. She'd ask her mother to allow her leave. Only a board member could override intern sequestration.

As if she were watching, the red light covered the room, securing it. Her mother came onscreen and said, "how is it going?"

"Online files are almost done. Most is useless to me right now."

"I thought so. What do you need?"

"Face to face time."

Her mother thought a moment. "I'll see what I can do. Prepare to go to work as you normally would tomorrow. Arda, this contract isn't just about you. It's very important that you be the one to complete this. I love you."

The wolf pelt hung around her neck, creating a blanket from the cold. Nights in the forest were especially trying. It'd been two days. She'd been out here for two days, and she still had no clue what was expected of her.

Thanks to Tyrus, she had a knife. She'd unsuccessfully tried to kill a fluffy bunny that morning, a squirrel later in the day. She was starving, but she had found water. She knew it wasn't sanitary, and she knew she was running a fever, but she was alive. She was still alive.

He came back to the site, checked her forehead. "You still have a fever. Eat these."

She looked at the green leaves in front of her. "What is it?"

"It'll lower your fever, so you can sleep. Remember it's shape. They'll ask you about it when you get back."

Taking the leaves, she shoved them in her mouth and swallowed. He watched as she did so, focused on her breathing.

"Why are you helping me?"

"You want me to leave?" She expected a smirk, like Will would have given, but there was only concern in his face, and a bit of sadness she couldn't place.

"No, but aren't people supposed to do this on their own?"

"A generation or two ago, people could have done this on their own. Maybe someone from Z5 would still have the knowledge. Your generation of bookworms, though, you'd never make it. They worry too much about teaching you the wrong things."

He sat down, producing a rabbit. He began to prepare it. "Light the fire."

She sighed. "I can't."

"Yes, you can. You just haven't yet. Try."

She looked at it but didn't move. He noticed. "Arda, if you want to eat, we need the fire to cook this little guy. Or you don't eat."

Feeling defeated, she grabbed a stick and twisted it like he'd shown her. Her hands were raw from trying to do this for the past two days. She ached everywhere. Her skin was blistered from the unusual strain. Thinking about Swift, who put her here, she got angry. Her mind drifted away from her task, focused on that man's stupid face. After a few minutes, smoke started to form. She didn't let up, even though she was rubbing away skin. Eventually, the fire started.

"Good! See? You did it!" Before it could go out, he picked up a dead branch and lit the leaves. The fire grew. Finally, she felt her feet warm

again.

Sometime later, fed and warm, she curled up under the pelt and tried to sleep. Tyrus watched over her, whittling a walking staff. She was out instantly.

The dark room mirrored the dark woods for a moment. The walls were trees, the bed earth. She saw it as her dreaming mind followed her body in waking. She watched as the trees slowly faded back to walls, as her breathing slowed, and knew she was no longer there, no longer in danger. No wolves would leap out at her as she slept. The sweat dripping from her brow was wiped away, her meditation techniques quickly working on her lungs and her heart.

She shook the memory off and began to wake up, though she couldn't quite control the shaking in her hands as she ordered her clothes for the day.

When she walked into work an hour later, she was composed and ready to tackle her contract.

Today was no ordinary day, however. Two security guards approached her, taking her by the arm into the elevator and hitting a top floor. . This was twice in three days. Her colleagues had stared after her. She was proud that she hadn't looked at any of them, had focused on keeping her gait even and her breathing slow, her face a mask of nothing.

Back to the dark room she went, following the same small woman from the other day. She sat, letting them check her vitals, knowing her heart rate and pulse were steady. When the screen lit up, it was not her mother who was present as she had expected. It was Swift.

"Ardora Prime. So good to see you again."

"Recruiter Swift."

"It's actually Investigator, now."

"Investigator." *An overnight promotion?*

He nodded. "I don't have a lot of time but I need your help. You are…in a unique position for a project I'm trying to resolve. Your mother contacted me this morning, demanding I keep you out of this, but unfortunately, you are the only one who can help me."

Nice work, mother… "I'm very focused, as you know, on the many duties of my internship."

He laughed. "Oh, we all know that's foolish busy work. Wouldn't you rather be doing something that actually helps your District?"

"I like my job, where I am, but I am always available to be of service for my society."

He nodded, smiling. He liked that answer. "Before I tell you your assignment, I must offer you the conditions. Upon completion of this assignment, you'll be graduated to Agent. However, you should not expect any bonus, as this is my operation."

Of course, you want to keep the money for yourself… "I understand. That's generous of you to include me at all."

"I'm aware. Now, if you are caught doing anything other than what I've instructed you to do, I will have to immediately terminate your involvement. Understood?"

"Yes." *Coward.*

He went on to explain the same assignment her mother had already given her. As a board member, she couldn't be seen giving her own daughter any help. However, if it came from someone who didn't even like her, it stood on its own merit. She'd made Swift her lackey, and he didn't even know it.

Walking out of the room, her steps felt lighter, her body energized. She had been extended temporary Agent privileges, meaning her sequestration was over. While she would maintain the same apartment, this meant she could leave the facility whenever she had official duties. She struggled not to leap or run from the happiness spreading like shockwaves through her chest. She knew her eyes would be beaming with it, so she made certain to keep her gaze down.

He just made her contract completion plausible. This would give her the access she needed. Then, she'd go around Swift, collecting the money by handing her findings to her mother. Once she was a full Agent, he couldn't touch her.

She didn't even bother to stop by her workstation. She walked out of the lobby and opened the doors to her future. It was difficult not to breathe deeply, so she did it as she walked, over a period of ten steps. Breathing in freedom, trust, and autonomy.

Her first stop was a small apartment in Z3. She looked at the one-story home in the old district. Unlike her house, in the newer honeycomb pattern, this house was a box. A small square of a home. Getting up her courage, she walked up to the front door and knocked briskly.

"Coming." A few seconds later, an older woman opened the door. Seeing her, she smiled broadly. "Oh, Ardora Prime, is that you?"

"It is, ma'am. Is Thea available?"

She gave her a sympathetic look. "Yes, dear, but…" She looked inside, silently signaling to someone. "Oh, okay. I suppose you can come in."

She walked into the charming, vibrant home full of color. The door shut and she was enveloped in a hug instantly. Thea was stronger than she remembered. Hugging her back, she looked around for possible locations for a surveillance bug. Clothing was destroyed at the end of the day. She needed a more permanent location.

Her emotions threatened to overcome her, in spite of her task. This was her childhood rival, but before the war, at the dance, and during exams, there had been a softness between them that was slowly developing into friendship. She'd missed Thea, her *friend*, more than she had allowed herself to believe. The hug lasted a long time, and she let it. When Thea released her, it took all her willpower not to give away any expression, to keep her burning eyes from releasing tears. Meditation kicked in and helped, but in her mind, she was jumping for joy that her friend was safe. Then she saw her face, and realized that maybe, she wasn't safe enough.

Where there was once long, flowing black hair, there was short stubble. Where there was once a smile, a continuous expression of fear. She had a scar starting at her left eye and moving all the way down her face and neck. On her left hand were two fingers, burned so the skin stuck them together.

"Thea." She said the word with weight.

"Oh, I know." Thea stepped back and adjusted her shirt, nervously. "I know that I've changed. Don't worry, my dad said he would get me the best plastic surgery Medical has to offer. In a couple weeks, I won't look this way anymore."

Though Thea smiled, it no longer reached her eyes. "Thea, I was wondering if you'd be willing to catch up with me for a bit. I have a few free days off work- "

"Where are you working?"

"Financial." Banking was controlled by security, which was controlled by the Project. To be hired in Financial was the back story most agents used. Easy to remember.

"Oh, good for you, Arda." She sat on the couch,

motioning to her friend to sit as well.

"I don't mean to pressure you," Arda began, sitting next to her, and placing a bug underneath her cushion, "but I wanted to let you know that while I don't understand what you went through, you're still my classmate. I…" she grabbed Thea's hand, squeezing gently. "I care about you all a great deal." This time, she let the burning. She let a few tears fall.

"I know you do." Thea tapped her hand with her own, silently supporting Arda. "I got the care packages you sent. The cookies were my favorite."

"I'm glad you liked them." She paused. "I guess I just want you to know I'm here for you. If you need anything I can give you, I hope you'll allow me to help."

"If I think of anything, I'll let you know."

"Have you seen Will or Chaste since you got back?"

Her eyes darkened. "Chaste is alive. I saved his life, as he saved mine." She stood, walking away and standing near a window, gazing out. Arda noticed she seemed to be doing a breathing exercise of her own, and wondered if they had another experience in common. Nightmares that haunted their day, though the content would be different.

Arda couldn't help that her eyes widened. "I…hadn't heard that."

Thea turned back, waving the thought away, a sign that there was more to the story. "I have no clue about Will. The last time I saw his face was in the prisons after he left our squad mates to die. Chaste and I were the only ones to make it out. Of the five casualties our District suffered, three were from our unit."

She walked across the room, pacing back and forth, her shoulders hunched forward. Even with her back to Arda, it was clear she was breathing quickly. The nightmares were overwhelming her, as they once had with Arda. She knew the look but couldn't do a thing to help. "I think you should go for now."

Arda stood, sensing her panic, holding back for her friend's sake. "As you wish. Good day, Thea."

Arda's heart broke a bit as the door shut. She heard the wails of her friends cries as she walked down the street to her next stop. One thing was for sure. Had she been anyone else in the Project, Thea would have slammed the door in her face. She really was the only one capable of helping them, of getting to the bottom of this.

Hours later, as the sun was setting, she walked back into her apartment. Her feet ached, her body ached, but today had been more successful in eliminating potential threats. Getting to her room, she kicked off her shoes. On the couch, was a set of new pumps. Right. She was an agent now. She smiled thinking about how much more comfortable the black pumps would be in the field than the heels.

Silently Thanking her mother for them, she set them near the door for her work tomorrow. Opening her watch, she started her own file, notating the results from her various visits and the elimination of several classmates. It disturbed her that she couldn't eliminate Thea yet. The girl had been through enough, but she wasn't an exception. Almost every soldier had come home disfigured. She was just grateful for Medical, who couldn't erase the memory, but could erase most of the physical damage.

She'd visited ten. Ten of her former classmates. She still hadn't seen Chaste. She was almost afraid to face him. What Thea said about Will also made her uneasy to approach him. Made her heart ache. The thought of him being a traitor… Her hand paused in the air, and she pushed the thought away, stubbornly refusing to believe it could be true.

She would need different sets of data. More than just home surveillance. She would need to interact with them when their guard was down. When they were at ease, and when they were together. They needed to trust her enough to talk about those topics in her presence.

She would finish her home visits, but then she would need to change her strategy.

She woke in the forest, the wolf pelt around her. The fire was out, tendrils of smoke snaking through the air. She stretched, her muscles aching. Her belly wasn't as hungry as before, her fever broken.

Looking around, though, Tyrus was nowhere to be found. She debated shouting his name but didn't want to attract predators. That was rule number 3. Move quickly but quietly.

She stood, searching the site for clues to his disappearance. All she saw was the walking stick he'd made and an arrow in the dirt pointing away from the sun. That was self-explanatory. She picked up the stick and began to walk, though the first steps were stiff and awkward. Her ankles were swollen, from the times she'd twisted them on uneven ground. She was not used to the winding up and down of forest paths.

The hours stretched before her, her legs pulsed in pain, her fever returning. She had been walking for so long that she couldn't feel her feet anymore. Her shoes were worn, starting to break down. The synthetic clothing wasn't made to be worn much longer than a day. She was lucky she still had clothes.

The sun shone high in the sky when she found the next arrow, a big formation of stones, guiding her through the trees. Every so often, now, she would find a marking on a tree, leading her through the brush. When did Tyrus have time to do this?

She was grateful for the walking stick. It gave her something to lean on. It was thoughtful of him to make it for her. She switched hands every so often, giving that foot a much-needed rest. The sun was had almost vanished before she heard it. The low hum of civilization, the activity of the bazaar.

She was suddenly filled with adrenaline. She ran, getting closer to home. She could see the bazaar, its lights shining bright. The faint sound of a guitar drifted to her ears, followed by laughter. She continued her run, until she was through the trees and the light shined again on her face. Kneeling, she almost cried. She'd made it. She was home.

Chapter 11

She stood at the gateway to another two-story apartment in Z3. This was her last stop. This one made her the most nervous. Knocking softly, she waited for someone to answer, wringing her hands nervously. She didn't bother to hide her feelings, and hoped she didn't need to.

Chaste's father answered the door. "Good morning, Chief Jackson."

He smiled at her, taking both her shoulders in his hands, but not quite hugging her. "Good morning Arda. I was hoping you would be by soon. Have you come to see Chaste?"

"Yes, if that's okay." She felt her training fade, just a bit, and she was returned to the schoolgirl she'd been a year ago. She even bit her lip.

"Come in. Come in, dear."

She walked into their apartment and waited for him to shut the door. She placed a bug under the kitchen table while she waited. When he faced her, he motioned her to go upstairs. "Is he in his room?"

He said nothing, only gave a half smile and a nod. She walked slowly upstairs, dreading what she would find. Was his experience painful? Would he even be conscious? How bad were his injuries, not only physical, but to his mind? In the two days she'd been seeing her classmates, no two people were alike in their scars. What had happened to *him*? To her best friend?

She knocked on the door and he said, "come in." At least he was awake. The door opened, sliding away, and she felt her eyes burning, her chest tightening, as she gazed at him for the first time in over a year.

He was fine. Like Will, he didn't seem to have any injuries. Though he'd filled out like they all had, he was whole. She sighed visibly, relief and guilt flooding her system.

He saw it and smiled. "Hello, Arda." He set a tablet down that he'd been working on and stood. "Sorry, my back is not as good as it used to be."

She went to him then, slowly, the tension between them thick. He saw the earnestness in her gaze, and stood, as she leapt into his waiting arms. She squeezed so tight, afraid to let go. Burying her face into his chest, she felt a piece of her control fade, and she wasn't concerned, as she should be. She squeezed him tightly, as a chunk of her world she thought she'd lost was suddenly returned to her.

"Come on, Arda. I can't really breathe." His hands relaxed on her shoulders.

She let go and backed away. Her hands smoothed down his arms then took his hands in hers. "Are you well?"

He gazed at her features a moment, silently debating some thought, then stepped forward, closer to her face and whispered, "I am now." He moved forward, and she released his hands so he could wrap one around her waist, the other gripping her hair gently. His body flushed with hers, he lowered his head as her heart began to pound, and firmly pressed his lips to hers.

For a long moment, she blissfully allowed it, even sunk into it. She was no longer an agent investigating his unit, but just a woman, feeling the intense heat building between herself and a man she admired and trusted. As she pressed herself against his chest, more firmly, she felt his hand in her hair tighten, felt him grip her waist possessively. His hard body leaned into hers as if…

With regret, she backed away, knowing that the tension between them couldn't find an outlet beyond their kiss. For a few moments, they adjusted, in the silence, and her training kicked back in.

With him, she felt she could be less formal. "Was it awful?"

He nodded, his face carefully neutral now. "It was. You wouldn't… couldn't understand. You weren't there."

"I know. It's just that…well, I can be here for you now. I don't know what I can do, but…I'm here." She shrugged.

"Well, thank you for that. You know," his gaze landed on her, and a smirk crossed his face, "the kiss helped."

She laughed then. "Don't think you're getting another."

He grabbed his chest. "Oh, it hurts. I may need another... to recover."

"Stop it." She playfully punched his shoulder as she had done a thousand times as a child. His hand reached out, lightning fast and grabbed her wrist. Then he froze, his face distant.

"Chaste?" It was said carefully. "Chaste, are you okay?" Her stance shifted to a defensive one. He was her best friend, but if waking nightmares plagued him too, she wasn't going to allow him to hurt her.

For a few moments he seemed to be somewhere else. Then he blinked several times and came back to her. "Sorry, Arda."

"Oh, no, I shouldn't have punched you." She silently filed away the change, for later, to add to her report. He wasn't the only classmate of hers to show that face.

"No, no. You always did that, before…"

"I know but now we're adults. Maybe it's best if we remember that, and keep a professional distance between us, while you heal?"

He cupped her face, pulling her toward him, but didn't press his lips to hers. "Arda, the last thing I want from you is distance." His thumbs traced her cheekbones, before he dropped his hands, walking away to stare out his window. He gazed out at his backyard.

She got back to her job. "So, have you seen Will lately?"

He looked at her, guilt showing in his face. Strange, Thea had anger, he had guilt. "Not since we got back."

"Thea told me he deserted you."

"Thea should keep her mouth shut." His jaw was tense.

"So, he didn't?"

He turned to face her and searched her features. She knew what he was looking for, so she plastered on a concerned and quizzical expression. He could read people too.

"No, Arda, he didn't. I can't really say more than that because I know *people* are investigating it." He stared her down then, trying to send her a message. It could have been one of two things. Either warning her away, or that he knew she was.

She let her eyes widen, in apparent surprise. "By all means, please don't put me in the middle of that." She held both of her hands out from her body, as if pushing the thought away. "It's just that he's approached me, and…"

Chaste didn't answer right away, still searching her face. "Arda, he's one of the greatest men I've ever met. He's my brother. You shouldn't avoid him. He needs you like I do." Her heart melted a little at his lack of jealousy, at the bond they'd grown over the year she'd been out of their life.

She didn't think she should push any more, but there was definitely something there. "So, what are your plans? I know they give you some time off before you'll be given your career choices. How much time do you have?"

"About ten days left." The same as her deadline, which couldn't be a coincidence. The leaders of the city wanted this dealt with before a permanent career placement made the issue harder to confront.

"Any plans?"

"Yeah, I mean, I don't know where you're working now, but- "

"Financial." She almost said that too quickly.

"Fine, but we are getting together tomorrow night actually to hang out, relax. You're welcome to come by. There'll be punch. I know how much you love your punch."

She blushed at that, unable to stop it. She still couldn't control everything. "Got you there, didn't I? You remember that kiss."

A little breathless, she said, "of course I do."

His gaze softened, the silence stretching between them for a moment. "Well, Arda, we are adults, and I have to get ready for my day, so I think I'll talk to you later if that's okay."

"Certainly." She stood, walking out. "Good day, Chaste."

"Good day, Ardora." He shut the door behind her. She walked down the stairs, said goodbye to his father and let herself out. She turned immediately back to her building and walked briskly. This changed everything and she needed time to think.

The elevator stopped on her way up. Shadow stepped in beside her. The door closed and they were alone for two floors. *Great. Just what I need right now.*

"Ardora." His tone was professional, with a touch of mockery.

"Shadow." Hers was completely neutral.

"I heard you've been temporarily promoted. Congratulations." A slight hint of jealousy.

"Thank you." She let pride out, just a tad.

"It must be hard for you, knowing you've only completed a year of internship." The goad.

"Oh, I can think of many people that have more experience than that but are less qualified." The retort.

"True, true. What do they have you working on?"

"Nothing much, I'm afraid." Nonchalant, with a hint of boredom.

"Right." It was obvious he didn't believe her. "Well, I'm available if you need help."

I need your help like I need a kick in the stomach. "Thanks for the offer. I'm fine for now."

He placed a hand on her shoulder in a seemingly apologetic and friendly manner. "Don't worry, we're all behind you." She knew what he'd just done, but she didn't give it away.

"Yes, you obviously are far behind me." The door to her floor opened, allowing a quick exit. She walked quietly to her apartment and opened the door, shrugging off her coat, and checking for the bug. When she found it, she cursed him silently.

Dropping the bug on the floor, she squished it. *Take that, idiot.* She turned away, forgetting him and focusing back on her work. She sat, activating her watch and began to connect the dots.

Will, Thea and Chaste had all been in the same unit. Included in that unit were three of the four classmates that didn't return alive. Something had happened to them that was awful, and as it resulted in death, it would be investigated. This is where they got the notion that Will was a deserter, but did that make him a traitor? Could he have ran, knowing that he was leaving Chaste and Thea to die? If he did that, though, then why did Chaste defend him so strongly? Thea hated Will, Chaste loved him.

One thing was certain. She needed to talk to Will again.

Needed to get him comfortable enough to discuss something that would be hard for him, without making him feel betrayed. She knew she was the only one who could find the truth, but was she willing to sacrifice their potential relationship to do so? She'd need to be very, very careful.

The following night, she stood, trying to choose a dress. One of her first classes had been on attire. Agents were expected to blend in, except when they shouldn't. You had to know what colors incited what response in the average person, what to avoid and what to flaunt. Red was almost always too aggressive, black too stern. You could wear neutral tones like brown or grey for certain occasions, but at social events, you had to be careful not to stand out too much from what others would be wearing.

In the end, she chose a pink dress. It was form fitting about the waist but flowed at the bottom. Causal but fun enough for a party. The soft pink would make her attractive, but the pastel color would not intimidate any of the other girls there. She would seem pretty, but not gorgeous. She decided it was perfect.

Cringing, she chose heels to match. She hated wearing them, but it was what was appropriate given the occasion. She would be meeting Chaste in an hour at his place. She needed to get going.

Taking a small purse, she walked out of her apartment. The elevator opened, Shadow inside it again. It was late for him to be going down. She wondered if he just rode the elevator in his free time, trying to intimidate his colleagues. She wouldn't put it past him.

He looked her up and down in a way she wasn't entirely comfortable with. "Arda," he began, "you clean up nicely. Must be great to have Agent privileges, even if it's just for a short time.

I don't blame you for using them. Who's the lucky guy?"

"It's just a bunch of friends getting together." She kept her stance defensive.

He laughed. "Sure it is." He relaxed purposely, letting her see it. He didn't want her to think he was trying to intimidate her.

She couldn't wait for the elevator to reach the bottom floor. "Where are you going so late? You're still an intern."

That was very direct, but she couldn't help it. He got under her skin. "Checking in with someone in the lobby."

"I see." She wouldn't give him any more than that. He didn't try to touch her, this time. She didn't need to fear he would leave a bug attached to her.

The doors opened and she stepped out. Walking straight through the lobby, she saw them through her peripheral vision. A dark figure stood, waiting for Shadow. *Must be his contact.* She showed no special attention toward him and focused again on her work. She turned toward Z3 and began the long walk.

He found her halfway to Chaste's apartment. He grabbed her arm, pulling her into a side alley. In the dark, all she could see were his glowing eyes. "Mayne, what are you *doing*?"

He stopped, releasing her. She faced him, still the same height and weight as he was a year prior. He'd kept his distance, as promised, until now, apparently. A couple walked by, glancing in their direction. Without looking toward them, he leaned one arm against the wall above her head, as if they were there to make out instead of talk business. "Arda, what are *you* doing?"

"Walking." She didn't completely trust him, after all he'd done, even if he'd been right about her career path. She wouldn't have been happy in any other job.

"No, I mean what are you doing chasing after a nothing contract when there are bigger things to worry about?"

He knew. How did he know? Her glare spoke the words

she didn't have to. "What, you think I got you this job without having any connections? Spill."

"I'm doing it to speed up my internship. This contract is simple enough. I'm trying to get my freedom back."

"I didn't help you get here to investigate quibbles. I helped you to inspire great change. Don't get so into their little squabbles that you forget that file."

"They know you gave it to me." A small risk, but she wanted to see if he knew they knew. And he did.

"So? The people that keep secrets are…good at keeping secrets."

She sighed at him then. "It would help if you gave me more information."

"Not now, while you're on this. I understand what you're doing. Finish this contract, and then we'll speak about the real injustice going on in District 1. And Arda, be careful. Your friends are more intuitive than you believe they are. Make sure they're still your *friends* before you open up to them. Just…try not to take another before we investigate what *I* need."

He turned and walked out of the alley, in the opposite direction of her destination. She composed herself a moment, then followed, turning toward Chaste's street. It was time for her first undercover assignment, and she was spying on her friends. *Not trust them? Maybe they shouldn't trust me...*

Chaste was waiting outside when she walked up. "Still don't have a car?"

"No, sorry. I don't mind walking, especially after I failed that physical."

"I get that. Here." He produced a set of keys from his pocket and pointed to his father's car. "We can take this for now." She got inside and he put in their destination. She noted it was in Z5. "Where are we going?"

He smiled, placing his arm around her like he'd always done, but his eyes seemed too cold for such a friendly act. "You'll see."

Though she smiled and adjusted her dress, Mayne's words gave her pause. Was she really seeing coldness in his gaze, or was she projecting that because he'd primed her to see him that way? She had a lot to sort through tonight. It would be interesting to see which of her friendships survived, and who the traitor ultimately would be.

"You're quiet. What are you thinking of?" He grazed his thumb across the soft skin of her shoulder. She felt goosebumps rise from the light, ticklish sensation. *That move is new.*

"Just, worried. I don't exactly fit in with all of you. You have this huge, shared experience that I just…am not a part of. Are you sure I'll be welcome?"

He half smiled at her. "Arda, you'll be fine. If anyone starts anything, Will and I have your back. Thea, too."

"I appreciate that." His hand moved from her shoulder, finding a loose curl of hair to place gently behind her ear. She looked down, suddenly aware of the small space between them in the car.

After she didn't speak for a moment, he slid his hand down her arm and entwined their fingers. "Really, Arda, it'll be okay."

She wanted to believe that, to believe him, but she couldn't shake a feeling in her gut that told her his cold eyes were a problem. A moment of panic almost showed on her face before she stopped it. They'd been gone a year. They'd been to war. They'd seen things, heard things, experienced things she couldn't imagine. She had no clue what they went through, or if they were even the same people. What was to stop all of them from ganging up on her, making her talk? What was her exit strategy?

Scared that she didn't have one, she sighed loudly. Chaste laid a kiss upon her fingers and said, "just relax and have some punch when we get there." The blush came quickly. He laughed at her. "At least I know how to break the tension with you." Giving her back her hand, he leaned away from the wheel, stretching his back. Arda smoothed her dress again, awaiting the inevitable.

They pulled up to their destination, a small vendor that served punch and good food. They walked in, seeing their classmates fill up the room. Tyrus sat talking to Will. Somehow that didn't surprise her. Everyone was dressed up and the restaurant had closed to welcome home the troops.

A small dance floor lay behind the bar. Several tables sat between the entrance and the dark wood. Arda took in everything, impressed with the decorations and the atmosphere. The lighting was soft, the décor warm and sleek.

As they entered, Thea approached wearing a stunning blue dress. It brought out the color of her eyes. Though her hair was short, she wore a scarf around her head and shoulders, making her appear very feminine. Arda was impressed with her wardrobe, strictly on a professional level.

"Arda, you came! Wonderful. I was hoping one of your two would invite you." She punched Chaste in the arm. He didn't mind her touching him. Probably trusted her, after all they'd been through.

She felt a twinge of guilt at not being there, not serving like they were forced to do. Before she could do anything else, Thea led her to the bar and ordered blue punch. A moment later they appeared. "Chug." Thea tapped her glass to Arda's and drank, downing the punch in one gulp. Arda tried to copy her, but it didn't work out well. Thea laughed and patted her back.

Arda wasn't worried about the punch. She knew she was

working. She'd taken a serum that would counter the effects of the punch. She could have up to three and not feel a thing. No way anyone would drink more than that.

"How are you, Thea?" She had to shout over the music to be heard.

"I'm doing okay. Taking it day by day, you know. Yourself?"

"Just trying to catch up for lost time with all of you."

"Where did you say you worked again? Isn't it strange for interns to have so much free time?"

"As I was the only one left, I got my pick of disciplines. I work in Financial."

"Right, Financial. So, you count credit."

"Yes. Pretty boring. When I heard you were coming back, I put in the time off. I wanted to do everything I could, since…" she drifted off, not sure how to finish her sentence.

"Hey, it's okay. No need to be sad. You got to stay here, where it's safe. Believe me, you got the better end of that deal."

"I don't mean to complain. It's just that I would have helped, would have been there if I could have been."

"We all know that. We were there at your testing. We saw the asthma attack. I just don't remember you having that issue when you were younger. Did you?"

"Not really, no. I have no clue how it got so bad, so quickly. What was it like?"

"What was what like?"

"Oh, being away from the district, tending wounded, anything. I just want to know how you are."

She ordered another punch, downing it in another swig. "I'm not quite ready to answer that. Let's go chat up some other people that have mentioned you." Smiling, she took Arda's hand.

Thea led her away to talk to some of their classmates.

She followed, mentally filing away who was grouped with who, taking everything in to help her do her job. She also made effort to remember who seemed happy to see her and who thought of her as an outsider. She made sure she spoke to everyone that she could.

An hour later, after another punch, she was satisfied that the group was starting to loosen up. She attempted to emulate their behavior, which consisted of laughing at nothing, smiling a lot and lots of dancing. And casual touching. Apparently, they were no longer actually adults.

A hand on her back had her turning to see Chaste. "Having fun?" He smiled as he said it, apparently feeling the effects of the punch.

She smiled back. "Yes. I like the red punch."

"Me too. Talked to everyone?"

She nodded. "Except you and Will. It's the least I could do, considering."

"Considering what?"

She looked at him. "Considering I couldn't go with you."

He eased her to the side of the room where a wall stood. Leaning against it, he relaxed her into him. "Arda, I didn't really want you there."

"I feel like a failure, not serving." She hated that this kept coming up, that she was having a hard time letting it go. She was supposed to be extracting information, not giving it away.

"I get that you were the only one, that you felt left out, but I have to be honest with you, war is awful. I watched four of our classmates die and I couldn't save them. The one thing that gave me some peace of mind was knowing my best friend was safe back home."

"It's kind of hard to get to know everyone again when no one seems willing to talk about what happened."

He gently combed her hair behind her ear as he'd done in the car. "Give us time. That's all we need. Patience and time."

"Anything you can tell me about it?"

He looked away before looking back. "I missed you."

She didn't want to push too hard. "I missed you too."

Thea approached them, and the three friends spent the next hour exchanging old stories, tales of their childhood, reliving some of their more devious exploits. A few times Thea would relax and talk about the war, enough so Arda got a glimpse of what it was like. She talked of the medical tents, how it wasn't always sterile, the fact that they had no restrooms, and games they would play at night to keep themselves awake on watch. Finally, someone was opening up to her, and it felt great. Placed in among the conversation were several jokes that Arda just didn't understand.

Chaste handed her another drink. She had to remember that this was the last one. She still had more information to gather. Standing, she thanked him and moved to the one person she hadn't been able to chat with. Will still sat next to Tyrus. His elbows on his knees, leaning forward, so that others couldn't interrupt. As she approached, their conversation concluded, and Will's serious expression gave way to a smile. He stood, relaxed and she saw a familiar smirk cross his face. For a moment, the carefree boy returned.

She wasn't worried about Tyrus telling Will. He'd sworn to keep her secret, and after those three days in the woods, she had learned to trust him. She smiled back at Will and stood in front of him.

"I've been looking for you." She smiled, sipping her punch slowly.

He laughed. "That's not how we drink."

She gave him a sidelong look before she tilted the cup to

her lips and swallowed it all. Setting the glass down, she turned back to him. "Happy?" Was the room always this…twirly?

"Very." He looked at her and at Tyrus.

"I'll leave you two be for now." He reached her and placed a protective hand on her shoulder, then looked at her companion. "We'll talk later, Will."

Walking away, she watched Tyrus start to converse with Chaste. She had a sneaky suspicion that something was going on. Will grabbed her hand before she could think on it too much and sat, pulling her with him until she plopped into his lap.

Laughing a bit louder than she should, she smacked his arm lightly. "What are you doing?"

"Making you more comfortable. You look stiff. Like you aren't having as much fun as everyone else. Maybe you need more punch."

"No, I've already had three."

"Your choice. How are you, Arda?" He placed a hand across her thighs, rubbing his hand along the skin at the bottom of her dress. His other was wrapped around her waist, so she leaned into his chest, relaxing.

"Worried about you." She hadn't meant to say that. How had that come out? Her head felt light, weightless like in her dream. Maybe she hadn't understood the pill she took.

He sighed, softly, and her floating head wanted to make him make more sounds like that.

"I…am aware that some organizations are looking into my behavior, but it's not something I want you to worry about."

"I have to."

"Why?"

Before she could tell herself not to, she whispered, "*It's a secret. Shh.*" She laughed again, this time snorting. Why had she almost given herself away?

"A secret huh? Is that secret that you're into me?"

"Uhhh, no. I mean," she laughed again. "I mean, that's not the secret, but I like you, Will."

"I like you too, Arda. Quite a bit. I saw you came with Chaste."

"Yeah, except his eyes are cold." Probably should have said that…

"Cold, huh?" He brushed his hand over her thigh again, and she found it difficult to concentrate.

"Yes. Hot then cold. As if he can't make up his mind about me, anymore. I'm not even sure he wants me as a potential match."

"I can guarantee you that he does. He's a good guy."

"Hey," she laughed, "that's what he said about you." She poked his chest with her finger and snorted again.

"Well, *now* you're on our level. Let's dance." He stood, leading her to the dance floor, as the song changed from fast to slow. Pulling her very close, he swayed with her, back and forth to the beat. This was different than their social. He stood much closer, and his hands massaged her back as they swayed. She wanted to pull away to talk, to get some information, but the warmth of him cajoled her into pleasant silence. She leaned her head against his chest, and thought she heard him sigh again, softly. Before she could convince herself to get to work, the room spun, and blackness clouded her vision.

When she awoke, she was in a quiet room. She was on something very soft, but firm. Lifting her head slowly, she saw a fireplace crackling loudly in front of her. Her head spun, aching. She thought back on the events of the night and realized she'd been drugged. Surrounded by people she knew, she'd been violated. Anger and fear rose within her, but as she tried to stand, the world swam in front of her again. She wouldn't be going anywhere anytime soon. She thought back on the protocol for this situation, which had been covered in simulations during her first year.

Looking around, she tried to find something she could use as a weapon. Nothing on the couch, nothing on the floor, no tools near the fireplace. She wasn't sure what she could use. Reaching to her side where she kept her knife, always, she found the sheath empty. No glass lay around the dark room. She was out of options. Reaching for her watch, she found it taken from her. Great, she couldn't even call for help.

Muffled voices came from behind a doorway to her right. She saw two shadows soon after. She tried to stay balanced but was unable to. She was unprepared for whoever was coming. Fear closed her throat, had her lungs aching, which made the room spin faster. She held her head in her hands, willing her breathing to slow, to be even, for her heart not to pound. She would need every ounce of control and willpower to neutralize a threat if it walked through that door.

Her stomach clenched as the door opened, but Tyrus and Will came through. She breathed a sigh of relief. "Good, it's you." Tyrus sat in a chair he pulled from the shadows while Will took a seat next to her on the couch. He wrapped an arm around her, pulling her into him, kissing her forehead gently. "How do you feel?"

"I was drugged." He smoothed his hand down her arm and back up again, as if trying to soothe her. She felt his body brace, tense up before he softly replied, "I know."

She thought a moment before fear rose in her. "Did you drug me?" She didn't have the strength to push away from him, to see his face, so she knew he wasn't lying.

She watched Tyrus look at him, then back at her, but the older man said nothing.

"No, I did not." He resumed rubbing his hands along her skin.

"Then who did?" Her voice was returning, becoming more alert, more commanding, and less helpless. The room spun a little less.

"I did." A voice said from behind the couch. She felt her heart drop as she recognized Chaste.

"Why would you *do* something like that?" The betrayal in her voice was thick, real, and accusing.

"Thea tried the first time. It didn't work, so I tried the second. Arda, we had to get you to a secure area we could control. That restaurant was surrounded by…" Tyrus coughed. She looked at the older man, whose turquoise eyes were filled with regret. He'd planned this, all of it, and was sorry for it.

"Drugging you allowed us to move quickly and safely away from those who were surveilling our group, on the pretense of getting you medical attention. It was an unfortunate but necessary step to get you here, where we can actually talk freely, without any…"

Tyrus looked at her then, pointedly. He wanted to convey a message to her alone, and he wanted to make sure she was listening, that she understood. "Where there are no extra eyes."

She knew of protocols where agents under assignment could have implants placed into their cerebral cortex, that allowed them to record everything without anyone knowing. They were Cloaked agents, lethal and deadly, who had gone through some horrific circumstance that allowed them to declare themselves legally dead. They worked in connection with Project R.E.D.D., but no one outside of it would be aware of their existence. She knew from the woods that Tyrus was aware of the project, but that he was aware of Cloaked agents meant he was…more connected than she previously thought.

"I don't understand what is so important that you had to go to those lengths to talk with me."

"You will. Then I hope you can find it in your heart to forgive me." His voice broke on the last word, and he walked out swiftly. Will still had one arm wrapped around her shoulders. She eased away from him, slowly. "Did you know?"

He took her hand, and she watched as he swallowed, hard, before he said, "yes." That's why he'd held her so closely. He rubbed a thumb lovingly over her knuckles, and his hazel eyes met her grey ones, with an earnestness and intensity that surprised her. He very much was asking for forgiveness, without saying the words.

Tyrus cleared his throat. "Listen, Arda, they brought you here because they know that you trust me, so I'm asking you to keep doing so for a few hours so we can sit down with you and explain everything, give you the information you need, so we all leave on the same page. Is that acceptable to you?"

"I suppose since I don't have a choice that yes, it is." She gave him a blank stare, and something drifted into Tyrus's eyes, then. Pain, regret, and something affectionate. He didn't want to be at odds with her, either.

He opened his mouth, as if he would say something, but closed it and simply stated, "would you like some water?"

"Is it drugged?" It came out flat. Will snorted beside her.

He gave her a sympathetic look. "No."

"Then sure, after you have a drink."

He chuckled, took a sip from the glass, then handed it to her. She drank the water, her throat parched.

"Now, I have to start at the beginning…" He began to tell his tale, and as he continued to speak, it was as if Arda could imagine it happening in her mind. Something about his gaze allowed it to be real to her. "It started a year ago, after your classmates completed basic training…"

Chapter 12

His eyes began to glow green, and Will squeezed her hand. That was the last thing she felt before being swept up in Tyrus's memory.

He watched the recruits file in, getting out of the transport. He'd be in charge of the medical tents. It was his job to make sure that everything ran smoothly, that the doctors were supported and the soldiers well.

He watched as the young men and women lined up before him. They'd been given additional conditioning to survive this war, mental and physical. The advances that they'd made in genetics helped the unit form faster, more cohesively.

"Recruits!" He shouted it, a big booming sound that had several of them jumping.

"Oo-rah!"

"I'm Sergeant Keating. You'll be under my supervision for the length of the conflict." He motioned behind him, and six other soldiers came out from their operations center. "These are your team leaders. They've all been under my command before. Each team guards a tent. You're responsible not only for keeping the doctors and patients safe, but you will do whatever is asked of you, immediately. One team will be with me. Willful, Chaste, Theasaura, Titan, Sharp, and Eagle. Step into command so I can brief you. The rest of you, listen to your names and follow orders."

They saluted him before he turned his back and walked with his recruits to the tent. They filled the small area they had, ready to help. He sighed, looking at the four boys and two girls before him. He'd make their very difficult jobs as easy as he could, but this was no picnic.

"We have a different mission for your team. I have orders from District 1 that require discreet, clever soldiers to handle sensitive information vital to the war effort. You will be in charge of securing the data when it

arrives, and insuring it gets to the correct authorities at the correct times. Any deviation or failure will not be tolerated. Do you understand?"

They nodded, although, as he thought about it, there was absolutely no way they could understand. He turned, looking at the table in front of him. Red pieces stood for D2 and D3. Blue stood for D4 and D5. The old soldier in him was tired of this, but he knew he had to play his part, for now.

The image changed, faded as Arda sensed time passing…

His team filed in. He looked down at the table, moving red forward, blue forward. The fighting had started in earnest. The medical tents were set up, ready to receive patients, and the soldiers were ready. It was time that his team did their part.

"You will break into two groups. Blue and Red. Will, Titan and Eagle are blue. Chaste, Thea and Sharp are red. Your job is to surveil the war zone. I'll be giving you radios so you can communicate with me. Your job is to record the events from each side of the battle. I won't lie to you, it's bloody. We need this recording to document the war. You will be out there for a long time. Rations will be sent to you.

"We are ten miles away from the combat zone. Every five miles, I want a man from your team. I've set up stations at each point with food and water. Climb the tree and you'll see it. When the recording runs low, a warning will be sent to us. You'll be responsible for relaying the new recording device to the next station. You'll change stations once a week. Understood?"

Given their instructions, they left to secure their posts. He stayed in the tent, waiting as the bombs began to drop.

Time passed again…

He rushed out of his tent, toward the critical ward. Something had gone wrong. Team Red had one man down, team Blue had two. Will stood, outside the tent, a recording in his hand.

Tyrus took it from him, saying, "where are your other two?"

Tears threatened Will's eyes but they didn't fall. "Gone."

"What happened, scout?"

"It's on the recording, sir."

"I want to hear it from you."

Will took a deep breath and said, "I cannot tell you under the circumstances."

He grabbed Will by the back of the neck, pulling him close enough to whisper. "Do you realize that refusing to answer a commanding officer is only allowed if you've done something traitorous, as a defense, so you don't incriminate yourself?"

"Yes, sir, I understand that is usually the reason. If you watch it, you'll see what I mean."

"I'll have to arrest you."

"I know." His eyes were determined and clear.

He called an escort over, and they took Will away. Entering the tent, he saw the Red team inside. Thea's face and neck were being stitched back together. In her hand was a burnt recording device, fused to her skin.

Chaste was covered in blood, but he was standing tall. Tyrus walked to him. "Report."

"Blue team didn't radio us to let us know they were falling back, that they were targeted. We tried to get away, but Sharp…" his voice broke, "I carried them both back, but…"

"You did good, Chaste. Sit down before you fall down."

He obeyed. "Why didn't Blue Team radio you?"

He shook his head. "I don't know."

"What were their colors?"

"Sir?"

"The enemy who attacked a peacekeeping force. What were their colors?"

"They didn't wear any. They were dressed in black."

His heart skipped a beat. Wondering what the hell they were doing there, he left the tent and walked to the other side of the camp. This was the camp for the captured, those that weren't injured but had lost, who would not be returning to battle. Two buildings stood, concrete slabs that contained dozens of men and women, waiting for the war to be over. When it was, these unlucky ones would not be going home. They'd be switched to the enemy district, to build new lives there. It was not an easy transition, and one he knew would result in suicide for at least a quarter of the people that survived the war. Sometimes, he hated the Districts.

He walked over to a white tent, in the middle of the compound. Inside, a tall man was wiping blood off his knuckle. In the middle of the room, tied to a chair, was Will, already beaten badly for leaving his men behind. He'd be considered a traitor unless Tyrus proved otherwise.

"You know why you're here, Will?"

"I left my team behind."

"What else?"

"I didn't radio team Red."

"What reason can you give me for not doing those two things, for ending lives today?"

"I didn't end their lives. The Dark Riders did."

Sometimes, he was surprised at how clever Will was. "How do you know about them?"

"I listened to the soldiers in Zone 5. My dad's buddy served in the last war. He told me."

"Then I won't waste the official line on you. You know they're no myth." He sat a chair down in front of the recruit and placed his elbows on his knees. "Will, you saw them, and what happened?"

"It's on the recording…"

"I want to hear it from you."

"I was recording, as you told me. The Dark Riders came out of nowhere, onto the battlefield. They started slaughtering men on both sides. It was awful. I stayed as long as I could, but I had to get this back to you, sir."

"You ran, ten miles, without stopping to check on your team."

"They were already dead."

"Why didn't you die?"

"Check my right pants pocket."

He did, noting some sort of cloth was inside. Pulling it out, he unfolded the cloth. It was a hood, thin but resilient, with no holes where the eyes and mouth should be. He wouldn't have believed it if he hadn't seen it himself. This was the hood of a Dark Rider. They were cleaning up, and his whole unit was in trouble.

"Will, where did you get this?"

Pure rage shone on his features, tensing his body. The pulse in his neck jumped, his jaw clenched. "Off the dead bastard that killed my team."

Tyrus's heart sank. The boy had no idea what he'd just done. The Dark Riders lived by a code. It was ancient and specific. Blood for blood. No rider when unavenged. They wouldn't stop until Will was dead. Still, part of him was impressed.

"Someday, I hope I get to hear that story. For now, the safest place for you to be is inside one of those concrete buildings. Don't worry, Will. I understand what you were doing. You're no traitor."

His eyes stopped glowing. She was back in the room, Will's hand still in hers. Tyrus's memory faded from her, but the emotion remained. She swallowed hard, not quite ready to speak. Millions of thoughts flooded through her mind.

Will was obviously the center of this investigation. He'd recorded something he wasn't supposed to, as was his job, and they were coming after him, through Project R.E.D.D. She had no clue who these Dark Riders were, but she had a feeling someone was involved. Was her mother involved? Did she know about all this? Should she protect Will, or turn him in?

How could she? Looking at his face, waiting patiently for her to say anything… *how can I turn someone in for doing the right thing?*

"Tyrus..." It was a whisper after a long moment of silence. "Does Will know?"

He shook his head. "No."

"Does Will know what?" He said it playfully, but she

turned to him and took both his hands in hers.

She sighed, making a decision she knew there was no going back from, but it seemed like a night of hard truths. "Do you remember the talks we had before the war?"

"Yes, I remember every moment I spent with you."

She almost blushed at that. *Not now.* "Do you remember me mentioning something called Project R.E.D.D.? Remember the file?"

"What file?" Tyrus threatened.

"In a minute." She faced Will again. "Do you remember?"

Will's face went blank as she said it. "I remember."

"Will, I work for Project R.E.D.D. now. I'm an intern, but right now, I have agent privileges because…" She took a deep breath and pushed the words out. "Because I'm investigating…you."

He pulled his hands away. "Arda…"

She stood, turning away from him. "Except now that I know all this, how can I investigate you? I mean, you did what you thought was right. You acted with nothing but integrity and these Riders just go around killing people? I mean, it's not right. Something more is going on here. Why is Project R.E.D.D. worried about you? I mean, that recording was the truth. Don't we value the truth?"

He stood as she continued to speak. "What are they hiding? What are they planning on doing to you? Why did I get this assignment?"

She paced back and forth, a horrible thought forming in her mind. She turned to Tyrus as Will walked toward her. "What if she knew?"

All of the information she'd received was too much.

Panic settled in, her heart pounding in her ears, and her breath came in uneven waves. She began to shake, all remnants of composure evaporating. Will grabbed her as her knees gave out and brought her back to the couch.

"Tyrus…" She felt her body begin to shake.

"I'm sure she didn't know."

"She *gave* me the contract."

"I'm sure it's because she believed in you. You would not only learn the truth, but you would do what was ultimately right."

"I'm sorry, but I'm stuck. If I don't turn him in, I'm the traitor. If I do, I have to live my whole life knowing I... What do we do?"

"You go back to work, make it look like your investigation is progressing. I'll investigate why Project R.E.D.D. is involved."

"How deep in are you?" She made herself look at the older man, who simply smiled and stroked her hair. "In the world of clandestine agencies, Project R.E.D.D. is a baby among giants. They're good at what they do, don't get me wrong, but if we're dealing with Dark Riders, here, this is a whole other level of subterfuge. Will, I've kept you alive this long. You'll stay here in Z4 until this whole mess is solved. And Arda, I'm not letting anyone sacrifice a young soldier to keep a dirty secret quiet. We don't have answers, yet, but we will find them."

Arda walked into her building in the middle of Z2. The cameras would not see her heart rate increase, not see fear in her eyes. She'd taken a calming serum before she left Z4. Walking up to the elevator, she pressed the button, and it opened immediately. Riding it up alone, she waited for the elevator to get to her floor.

However, the elevator refused to stop at her floor. Wondering if it was malfunctioning, she watched the floor increase, continuing to the top of the building. She steeled herself for whatever might be happening.

When the doors finally opened, she stood at floor eight. No one got to floor eight. This was the apartment for the Director of the Project. She'd never even seen his picture, let alone knew his name. Stepping out of the elevator, it closed behind her. A hallway led to two double doors some ten feet away. She walked forward, and unsure of herself, knocked quietly.

It was so long before someone answered that she'd actually thought this must be a mistake and had called the elevator to come take her to her floor. Only then did the door open, and a gruff voice said, "Come in."

Walking through the doors, bright lighting shone from chandeliers and a fireplace. Windows looked over the zone, the lights from the night sky twinkling like stars. It was quite a view.

"Ardora Prime, please take a seat."

His back was turned to her. All she could see was a dark suit, brown hair. She approached the chairs in the room and noted that her mother was sitting in the chair to her left, so she sat in the right.

"Mother."

"Ardora." She reached out a hand, and Arda took it, noting she squeezed it twice, instead of once. Be alert, her mother was secretly telling her.

"Why am I here?"

The Director swiveled, and she met his face for the first time. Very few people, other than those that knew him personally, would know his face. Sharp angles, a triangular nose and chin, but deep grey eyes met hers. "Because, Agent, there are some things that we need to discuss."

It had been such a long night for her. She was already feeling beyond tired from crying. She didn't want to sit and have this discussion, but you didn't refuse the Director. "Such as?"

"What happened tonight?"

"I was drugged, but my friends saved me, took me somewhere that I would be safe."

"That somewhere was?"

"Out of the restaurant."

He gave her a sarcastic look. "Oh, *clever*, but I need to know the exact location." She watched as his eyes softened, just enough, for her to see the strange look Tyrus had given her, mirrored in him. A mix of affection, regret, and fear. Why would either of those men look at her like that?

"When I woke up, I was in a car, and they were dropping me off at Z2." The security cameras would show that, as they'd just done so.

"There was some time lapse between you leaving the restaurant and arriving in the car. You don't know where you were for that time?"

"Isn't it on the security cameras? Or my watch?"

He sighed. "Unfortunately, no, it is not. The car evaded security. Whether or not that was purposeful is unknown, and your watch suffered a malfunction that caused it to reboot during that time. Why were you in that restaurant tonight?"

"Swift had given me a contract to fulfill. I was given temporary Agent privileges to complete it."

"Ardora, I understand that in this situation, you were the correct candidate…"

"Even though I *knew* this would happen." Her mother grabbed her hand, and tears were about to fall from her eyes. She squeezed tightly.

"Yes, Faith, you've made your objections to this very...*public.* Ardora, please continue." But a look passed between them that piqued her curiosity as well.

"I was to find out if any of the soldiers had been involved in traitorous activities."

"And what is your conclusion thus far?"

She swallowed. "I don't want to let you down, Director, but I haven't reached any conclusions yet."

He paced back and forth behind his desk, his arms clasped behind him. "Well, then, let me pose this question to you, agent. Do you think you were drugged by the traitor?" Anger, just a small sliver of it, was in his voice. That made sense, if one under his command were harmed, to be angry at that.

"It's possible."

"I see. You have no clue who drugged you?"

"None." Even toned, a bit of dismay and fear. Perfect.

He took a deep breath in and considered her carefully. "I'm going to do something unprecedented tonight. Your mother came to me as a personal favor, concerned that something had happened to you tonight. Thus far, the investigation has been conducted as a solo operation, and I understand that you want to complete it to become a full agent, that you'd be unwilling to accept help because of that." He hit a button on the desk, and said, "send him in." Her heart sank as she thought of the last person she would want to walk through that door.

"However, Ardora, we don't have so many agents that we can continue to risk your personal safety as you continue to lead this contract. So, I'm assigning you a helper, someone to watch your back, to take some of the pressure off of you."

The doors opened, and Arda turned to see who had entered. She was right to be concerned as she watched him swagger in.

"Ardora, you know Shadow. He's been working with me on some related but not directly coinciding objectives. You are now partners in this, and so you don't argue, I'm giving you both permanent agent status. You'll move apartments in the morning to the upper floors. You'll be given full access to the materials you need, just send the request directly to my office, code Fifth War. Can you do that for the Project?"

Without looking at her, Faith squeezed her hand, letting her know she should say yes. The problem was that Arda didn't want a chaperone making her life even harder, especially if that person was as inept as Shadow. Still, she had to be the one to steer this investigation away from Will.

"I agree, Director, and thank you for the consideration."

He smiled, but it was guarded. "I knew you would. The two of you will be given a small office for this op. I'll have your watches updated to give you access. Congratulations to the both of you. Tonight is the last night of your internship. I'm sorry it's so…unofficial, but desperate times call for ingenuity." He gave her a last long glance, then turned away.

That was their dismissal. Standing, she waved goodbye to her mother and exited with Shadow. He called the elevator, and they waited until they were both inside before either of them spoke.

"Should of let me in on it from the beginning." Shadow chuckled as he said it.

"Shadow, I wouldn't let you in to a boat if you were drowning." She couldn't help it. The anger over working with him for a year bubbled over and out of her voice, as it rasped with distaste and anger. She felt her teeth clench. Not only did she have to find a way out of this for Will, but also now had to protect him from Shadow.

He reached out and hit the emergency stop on the elevator.

"*What are you doing*?"

He had the audacity to hold up a finger, as his watch hummed and beeped. After a moment, he locked eyes with her, moving forward so that they were only several inches apart. Anger was evident in his brown eyes.

"Well, we *have* to work together now, so anything you want to say, anything you need to get off your chest, say it. Get it out so it doesn't affect this op. The program on my watch has given us a safe space. Get it out here, now, so we can work together."

"How dare you. You think this is about you?"

"Isn't it? Come on. I can take it." He leaned against the bar so his arms were on either side of her. He leaned in and sighed loudly.

"You suck at your job." It was out of her mouth before she could stop it. "I don't want to do this op with you because you are just…an *awful* agent. I would trust my life to the wolf I killed in the wilderness before I trusted it to you."

He sighed, the anger leaving his body language, replaced with a relaxed posture that somehow managed to irritate her more. "You know what this 'awful agent' has been able to learn from everyone dismissing him?"

She thought a moment and laughed loudly. "Are you expecting me to believe that this is all a facade? That's your argument? You don't suck at your job, you're doing it on purpose?" She tried to turn away from him, but he gripped her wrist and turned her to face him.

"The maids on our floor can be bribed with candy to plant bugs. The secretary of the building has had three miscarriages. Swift is estranged from his whole family because he spends more time at work than at home. The Director calls in your mother once a week for a private meeting. He likes his coffee black, but your mother takes hers with…"

"…two cream and two sugar." We said it together.

Oh. Maybe his strategy did work. "I see."

She didn't know what else to say. She felt her cheeks turn red as the embarrassment over judging him sunk into her. How had she let him get under her skin so much?

"I mean, I can go on, but sure, write me off. Lord knows I don't have a parent on the Board so how useful can I be." That helped the anger return, covered the guilt, helped her continue to be strong. But when she looked at him, she saw a hint of a twinkle in his eye.

"That's not fair. I didn't know my mother was in the Project when I applied."

"Wait, she didn't get you in?" Surprise, real surprise, and curiosity.

"No, I got myself in." Raised eyebrows. He was impressed by that.

He thought for a long moment. "Fine. We can work together."

"We have to." She hit the emergency button and they continued to the intern floor. Parting ways, she closed the door to her apartment and instead of going to sleep, searched it top to bottom for bugs.

In the morning, she flushed three of the four she had found. One, she put in a metal box, to block the signal. It might turn out to be useful later. She'd had a restless night, but the day had arrived, and she had to arrive with it.

Walking to the elevator, she met with Shadow. With full

Agent status, their clothing had changed, from form-fitting uniforms to professional attire. She walked in a black dress with her pumps, and he complimented her in a business suit of grey and blue. "How'd you sleep?"

"I found the bugs, you *creep*." She watched as he tried to hide a smile, and that almost caused one to form on her face in response.

He chuckled. "Not like I got anything useful. Your room is always secured for the important stuff."

"My mother doesn't slack off."

"No, she doesn't. She's quite a legend, you know. Do you know her contract completion rate?"

"I haven't had a chance to look."

"Huh? Seems like something you'd want to know."

"What is it then?"

"Ninety-nine percent. Almost a hundred. Word is that she only ever failed one contract she took in her entire career. How awesome is that?"

"I guess that's pretty great."

"Pretty great? For comparison, the Director's completion rate is eighty-two percent. The next highest operative was at seventy-four. Your mother is more than pretty great. She's a legend."

Though she knew he was probably pruning her to get information, she couldn't help but feel pride in her mother for that. "Then why isn't she the Director?"

He looked at her as if she'd grown a second head. "You really don't know?"

Arda shook her head.

He looked down at his feet. "I don't think it's my place to say."

"Oh, come on Shadow, don't start worrying about my

feelings *now*. You're the keeper of secrets. Divulge this to me, great one."

Anger appeared in his gaze, but was quickly removed, replaced with trepidation, "Arda, she was up for the position, but then she announced she was pregnant with you."

It took her a moment. "Why did that stop her from becoming the Director?"

"In order to be the Director of the Project, you must have no attachments. You aren't allowed marriage, and a family, and a life outside of the Project. Until she conceived you, it was as simple as walking away from a husband. But a child? She couldn't…wouldn't walk away from you. She stepped down from consideration, and instead, applied to be a member of the Board, so she could oversee the Director, but remain an employee of the project. For someone with access to a board member, you seem ignorant of what goes on here."

She couldn't argue with him there. "I guess so." She looked down at her feet, suddenly wondering if she'd ruined her mother's life. She felt her lip quiver and the sting of tears threatened her eyes, but they didn't fall. She'd clear that up with her mother when the time was right. Now, it had to be about work. She eyed Shadow, wondering if he was manipulating her, and at the even sway of his shoulder, concluded he likely was. She would need to be very careful around him, from now on.

Chapter 13

Their office was not that impressive. Two desks sat facing each other. The interior wall was used for electronic surveillance and the outer wall contained the same black windows as the rest of the floor. No one could see in, no one could see out. If they needed help, they could alert the floor Aide team, which helped with clerical work.

She chose the desk furthest from the door. Shadow took the other. Sitting down, she sighed at the soft leather of her office chair. That was a small bonus.

"How do you propose we start?"

He smiled. "Well, I think we should look at all the data we've collected so far to determine what we are missing and what we need to get."

"What do you have?" The more she focused on him, the less he would ask her. The less she would have to lie to her new partner.

"I have a log of their positions in the field. I have which teams were paired with whom, I'd like you to review those as you know their personalities better than I do. Why don't we start there?"

"Sure. Send them to my watch so I can look at them."

A few seconds later, she was combing through that data. She looked it over thoroughly but quickly, noting that the first report didn't list the scouting positions, and the second report listed the assignments accurately. She wondered why the first was changed and the second was not?

"Something wrong?" Shadow could see her confusion on her face. That was one of the reasons she wanted to work alone, especially now.

"No, nothing, just thinking."

"What about?"

"I'm just wondering why these are all we have. Where are the security recordings?"

"They said they were destroyed by the traitor in the original file. Didn't you read it?"

"Right, but how did the traitor get access to everything? Are we sure nothing survived?"

He thought about that. "Why would the agency lie?"

"I'm not suggesting fault, only that the odds of every recording being destroyed seems slim. Right?" She made her face extra quizzical.

"You think someone missed something?"

"Maybe. Someone with the skills to retrieve damaged data might be able to find out something." Like Will had done, on Stead's tablet.

"I suppose we should check, just to cover our bases. That does seem strange that nothing was left. I'll get to work on it."

And just like that he was silent, combing through hours of destroyed video files that would take days for him to get through. Satisfied with herself, she stood to go. "Where are you headed?"

"Doing what I do best. I'll talk to my classmates some more."

"Update me each time you change locations. I can be anywhere in the city within fifteen minutes. Director wants to make sure we are both safe. Remember, we have nine days left to gather the evidence and inform the Director."

"Will do." She walked out of the office, a small smile spreading on her lips. Maybe having someone like Shadow working for her wouldn't affect her that much.

She walked out of the building and started her shiny, black car. She opened the door, sitting in the control seat for the first time in her life. It was basic, but it was hers. She ran her hands over the dashboard, appreciating her luck.

The door on the other side opened and someone sat next to her. She turned, ready to scream, but the familiar glowing eyes calmed her. "Mayne."

"Hello, Arda."

"What do you have to do with all of this?"

"About your boyfriend being a traitor? Nothing."

She squinted at him. "I'm serious."

"So am I. Look I have contacts that know things but I don't have a vested interest in the outcome of this contract. What I do have is a need to see you grow with your organization, because one day, I will need you to help me save…save people."

"If you want me to last long enough to do that for you, then maybe I could borrow your seemingly all-knowing contacts for the duration of this contract."

He looked ahead and behind them. "I could be persuaded to do that. In exchange for a favor."

"Fine, I owe you a favor."

"Oh, yes, you do, *ma colombe*, but I mean another favor. A more *immediate* one."

She ignored the strange foreign words, for now. "I do something for you, and you do something for me?"

"That's the idea."

"Can the information you have save Willful's reputation?"

He thought a moment on that. "I don't know about that,

but it will save his life."

"What are you talking about?"

He laughed, full and throaty. "Ardora, do you really believe that the government of the districts will just let a traitor walk? They kill them. I mean, they work them to death in work camps, but they still end up dead."

"We were told those didn't exist anymore."

"Nightmares yet walk the earth even in our enlightened age. And they have only gotten in deeper with the shadow."

"What does that mean?"

"There's an old set of rules, it predates the founding of the Districts. I know them because I know some pretty old people. It's called the Mythic's Code. Have you heard of it?"

"No."

"Well, one of my favorite rules, which you already apply to your life, is called 'Three Coins in the Fountain.' It means to look for the hidden coin or agenda. There are always three sides to a conflict, so to speak. Your whole organization runs on this rule. If all the evils in the world were over, gone, why would they need Project R.E.D.D.?"

She thought on that for a moment. "They wouldn't."

"Exactly. Now about that favor?"

"What do I have to do?"

"Something very simple." He took a watch out of his pocket. It looked identical to her watch in every way. "Keep this on you. If you're ever around the Director again, switch the watch with your normal one."

"What does this watch do?"

"Sends me recordings of everything it analyzes, and the director is a grand source of needed information. Deal?"

It was risky, but she could do it. "Deal. Now, what do you have to help Will?"

He pulled a tablet out of his coat. "This has all of the unedited video from the field." He nonchalantly handed it over, as if it were inconsequential.

Her eyes widened. "How did you get this?"

"Your surprise shows your ignorance. If you're going to find the third coin, you really need to think deeper about these things. How do you think I got it?"

She took a moment to think on it. "You had a contact in the field."

"I had several contacts in the field, most of them doctors."

"Why?"

"The key to succeeding in this world is information. I make a habit of having as much as possible."

She nodded, understanding his answer, impressed at his ability but also a bit fearful of what he could do with it. "Anything else?"

"Now that you mention it, I have one other thing to tell you."

"What?"

"All the info that I have, all the contacts I can give you, you have to assume that your enemy has those contacts as well."

"Who is my enemy?"

"That's the hidden coin you need to figure out. You know who was working for them, at least."

"The Dark Riders."

"Yes. If I were you, I'd focus my efforts in that direction. But that's just me." He opened the car door and left. She sat for a moment, knowing now was not the time to turn the tablet on or access the information. If she was going to get this done in nine days, she needed a network. She needed help.

Thinking for a moment, she started her car and plugged

in her course. There was a personal matter, now that she was a full agent, that she had to take care of, then she would find the right people for the job, someone she trusted with her life.

Minutes later, she stood in front of Stead's house. They hadn't spoken since the night she'd signed on for the Project. He was her father, the one who raised her, and she didn't like the fact that the last words they'd shared were said in anger. To her, family should come first.

Knocking on the door, knowing it was still early, knowing he hadn't gone to work yet, she waited. He opened it a moment later, staring at her for a moment before he recognized her. "Arda." A smile lit his face and he hugged her tightly. "Come in, come in."

She did so, sitting down at the kitchen table, as she had always done after academy. "How have you been this past year?"

"Wonderful. Your mother and I miss you terribly. I want to apologize for my reaction the night before you left. Working in security, we hear horror stories about Project R.E.D.D. The fact that my little girl would be involved…" He looked at her, taking her hands. "It was too much, but here we are, talking. You're back home, so I take it you finished your internship early?"

"Yes. Today is my first official day as an Agent."

"Congratulations, but don't tell your mom. She knows a little bit from what I've told her in the past, but I wouldn't want to worry her, you know?"

"You won't tell?"

"No, I won't tell."

She smiled, trying to hide her feelings from her face. He really had no clue what his wife did for a living.

"Well, I wanted to officially come by the first chance I could and see how you and mother were doing. Is she home?"

"Faith!"

She waited until her mother came in to see her. "Oh, Arda, honey." Her mother's eyes welled with tears. "It's so good to finally see you!" She hugged her as if they hadn't just talked last night. Tears welled in her eyes, too. It was comforting to be back in her family home.

"I know, mother. It's been forever." She hugged her back.

"Now, how is your life going?"

"Good, I can't talk about the job though. You understand."

"Oh, sweetie. Are you hungry? Do you want some eggs?"

"No, I'm fine, I just wanted to see my two favorite people."

For the next hour, they caught up on the last year of their life. Arda shared as much as she could without saying anything that would harm Stead. When she left the house, she felt much better about her home life. Now, she could focus on her second objective of the day.

She walked into Chaste's room not even ten minutes later. He was sitting on his bed, looking through a box of his belongings. "Hey, Arda."

"Tyrus told me to come to you and that you could get info to him?"

He nodded, placing a lid on the box and setting it under the bed. "What are you looking at?"

"Nothing." He turned and smiled at her. "Sit down." She sat on the bed. Instead of sitting next to her, he leaned against the wall. He was being very careful with her. "What did you need me to tell Tyrus?"

She removed Mayne's tablet from her pocket. "I think he should be the one to hang on to this. I haven't even looked at it yet. Once he's reviewed it, I'm sure he'll send me what I need."

"What's on it?"

She waited a moment. "The field recordings. All of them. Unedited."

He was surprised. "How did you get something like this?"

"I have contacts." A small brag.

"Obviously. I'd love to have your contacts. Arda, this is great."

"Just...get it to him, quickly. Chaste, if the wrong people got a hold of this, they could make it say whatever they wanted. The official record states that the traitor destroyed the records. Don't let yourself get caught with it."

"Got it. Was that it?"

"No, tell him I've been promoted, and Shadow is on the case now, too."

"Will do. Anything else?"

"Not right now." She stood to go. He placed a hand on her arm, trying to stop her. "Arda…"

She turned and faced him, her normal pleasant expression gone. Anger shone in her features. Before she could stop herself, she'd slapped him. Though he was fast enough to stop her, he didn't. Backing away, she thought before she spoke.

"Listen, Chaste, I know you did what you thought was necessary, but you *drugged* me. That is a serious violation of my rights. I need space. I'm furious with you."

He rubbed where she'd slapped him. "You got some power behind your swing. That's good, but you should learn to punch."

"You're not *mad*?" She was practically vibrating with it, yet he stood there, unperturbed.

"No. *You're* mad. I'm…so sorry that sorry seems

inadequate, paltry. I…did what we all believed was necessary, but… I may have lost you, in it, Arda, and I know that. All I can do is wait here if you're…ever ready to forgive me."

A weight lifted off her shoulders. She'd been dreading this conversation without even realizing it. "Thank you." She wanted to say more, but the anger was still there, potent like lava underneath her skin. She couldn't forgive him, not yet. "I'll come back tomorrow to update you."

He nodded, and she walked out. Getting back into her car, she let a few tears slip down her face. She knew his reasons, understood being ordered to do something, but he had been her best friend. She didn't know how to start the path to forgiving him, how to let go of the anger. For him, and Thea, who she had been getting along well with. Wiping the tears away, she started the car and input her next destination, pushing those thoughts to the back of her mind. Save Will, then fix what she had with them.

On thoughts of her only female friend, she entered the address of the hospital. Thea was there, currently receiving treatment to remove the physical scars from her body. Though this would be a hard conversation to have twice in a row, she knew she needed to offer her support, to be there for her while she was so vulnerable, especially if she could get Thea's side of Will's story. She needed to understand why they weren't all congruent, where her anger with Will came from.

She walked into the elevator and went straight to the third floor. She knew the layout of the building, and she didn't want anyone seeing her that didn't absolutely have to. The doors opened some minutes later, and she walked onto a white, polished floor that spoke of new beginnings and healing. Plants hung everywhere. A VA played soft music in the corner.

"Welcome to Plastics. What can I do for you today?"

"My friend, from the war, she had surgery scheduled this morning. I'm interested to know how she's doing."

"Young Thea. Beautiful girl, considering." She tapped several times on her tablet and a frown lit her features. "Let me get an attending for you." She walked away to the back office and the screen lit like she was on a call. Several moments later, a door at the end of the hallway opened and a man in a white coat came out. "Ms. Prime. It's a pleasure to see you." He held out his hand to her. She shook it, noting the limp grip. She didn't like him already.

"And I have the pleasure of meeting…"

"Dr. White. I'm the head of this floor." His eyes and stance were guarded, and she felt a sinking feeling in the pit of her stomach.

"Dr. White, how is Thea."

"Ms. Prime, I'm sorry to inform you that complications during surgery caused Thea to expire. She died at 950 hours this morning."

She thought fast. He'd shook his head, which meant all or part of that statement was a lie. Two, who was watching, as there were cameras everywhere and what would they do if she pushed, here and now.

She found the tears by biting the inside of her cheek, hard. "Oh, that's just…awful." She grabbed a tissue he handed her and hid her face, sobbing. "Oh, Thea, why!"

After several uncomfortable moments of pats on the back, Dr. White said, "there, there, I know this is difficult, but she'll be honored like the others."

"What happened?" She gripped his shirt, perhaps a bit too hard.

"Well, the procedure was complicated…"

"What happens during a routine surgery to result in the

loss of life?" She let anger fill her eyes. Her hands became fists. She wanted him to think she was an emotional threat.

He wasn't prepared for that. Looking to his left, she was almost certain he was checking for something, or someone. "Uhm, well.."

"Tell me!" That's how she'd do it. She balled her hands into fists and pounded on his chest. "Tell me what happened! Tell me!"

As he tried to restrain her, she suddenly stopped fighting and rested against his chest, sobbing. As she did so, she took his ID tag from his pocket and skillfully slid it up her sleeve, so close that no camera could see it.

"Never mind. It's all just…too much..." Walking away, she turned to the elevator. She had to get out now, if the ID card would be of any use to her. Stepping into the elevator, she pushed the floor for the basement.

She couldn't do this herself. She would need Shadow, who hadn't been seen asking about Thea to do the work. She could figure out how to get this done. It was clear he was lying, and she believed it over her friend's dead body.

Walking to her car, she stepped inside. Turning it on, she hid the ID card below the mat on the other side. Turning the car on, it suddenly started moving on its own. She hadn't entered directions, though, had she?

The car took her where it wanted, without her being able to override her destination. The doors locked and she lost all control. Even the windows wouldn't lower. It went through two left turns before starting the wrong way down a one-way street. Arda was nervous now. If another car came, there could be an accident. Thinking fast, she pried up the headrest, an archaic safety measure, and began to use the end of the metal to smash the window. It didn't work at first, but adrenaline pumped through her as she saw another car turn down the street, headed straight for her.

Breathing quickly, she smashed as hard as she could with her elbow, one, two, three times. The glass finally shattered, and she pulled herself out of the moving vehicle. Her feet shoved her through the window and she landed, rolling away and protecting her head as much as possible. Whoever was in the other car wasn't so lucky. They collided and exploded, while she covered her body to protect her from the debris. Immediately people ran out of their homes. Nothing like this was supposed to happen inside the Capital. As soon as she was able, she stood, and hobbled over to her car.

"I'm checking this car." Better they think of her as a bystander. Looking as best she could through the window, she managed to find the ID card she'd taken. Up her sleeve it went, and she turned.

"Get that person out of that car!" She directed everyone to help the injured soul in the other vehicle. All eyes turned away from her. She could already hear the sirens approach. She knew it wasn't a good idea to be present when they arrived. Walking down an alley, while everyone was focused on the victim, she opened a manhole cover, her only option to stay in the shadow, and descended. Hopefully she could make her way through the underground and come up in Z4, where she could hand this off to Tyrus. Maybe he would know what the hell was going on.

Reaching the bottom, she paused a moment, feeling her forehead. Blood dripped from it, her arm suddenly hurting as the adrenaline left her. She'd broken something, or twisted something, or bruised something. She couldn't focus on that, right now, though. She closed her eyes and saw the city layout in her head.

She was on the border between Z3 and Z2. Z4 was

diagonally left and down from her location. She knew the sewers ran in only the four cardinal directions, north, south, east and west. She would need to plot in her head how to get there.

She determined the pattern, left, then right, then left, then right, until she'd traveled a distance of about five miles. Confident she could do this, she set off to the left. From her last visit, she knew that the caverns ran along the outside of the city. If she reached one, or any glowing eyes, she'd gone too far in any direction.

She counted the number of steps she took, and each time she turned in a given direction, keeping track of lefts and rights. She noticed a pattern and realized that she was spending more time moving left than right. She'd have to adjust to come out in the city where she wanted.

As her eyes adjusted, though, she found help. She knew that Mayne's people used these tunnels to get around. When she could finally see in the dark, she found arrows that led the way. How had she missed this the first time? Because she hadn't been looking for it.

Finding what she needed, she turned and bumped into another body. She froze, as they grabbed on to her and wouldn't let go. Lifting her eyes slowly, she noted it was Mayne, his long black hair more visible to her without his eyes lit up. She breathed a sigh of relief. "Thank goodness it's you." She relaxed against him, grateful to be able to take the weight off one of her ankles. It was definitely twisted.

"Are you crazy?" His tone was fearful, but his arms supported her at her elbows.

"No, I'm injured." Wasn't that obvious?

"I know, we can smell blood. You're lucky I was wandering the tunnels. You want to be a donor tonight, that's on you, but I didn't think you were into that."

"I don't even know what a donor is. Look, I need to get to Z4, and I needed to do that without anyone seeing. Can you help me?"

Without answering, he picked her up, supporting her weight easily, and began walking. "What happened?"

"My car went crazy." He stiffened at that. "Do you know something?"

"Just that all cars have the ability to be hacked, that's all."

"Someone hacked my car?"

"Someone *wants* you *dead*." She heard an edge in his voice at that.

"Any clue who?"

"Not at the moment, but when I can, I'll use my contacts to track the son of a bitch down." His anger intrigued her and earned him a speculative glance.

He noticed it, and added, "you think I went through all the trouble of getting you where you are to let some jackass kill you? No. I meant it when I said that you were special. If I find them before you do, they're dead."

She didn't know what to say to that. Her arm hurt, her feet hurt from walking, her head was pounding. As she relaxed, her vision swam. From a great distance, she heard Mayne say, "Arda, try to stay with me." Then she was surrounded by the dark.

She wasn't out for long. Mayne was still holding her, but the sun shone overhead. He was knocking on the back entrance of a building in Z4. Arda tried to lift her head, but it felt so heavy, as if it would fall off her shoulders at any minute.

The door opened and Tyrus stood before him. He didn't say anything for a moment, just stood with questions on his face.

"I believe you lost something." Mayne's voice seemed older, deeper than when he spoke to her.

"What did you do?" The growl in his voice was full throated and much more deadly than Mayne's earlier one.

"Nothing, Tyrus. I found her and brought her to you."

"How…do…know…" She knew what she wanted to say, but she couldn't quite get the words out.

"Mayne and I are old…friends, Arda. Things are starting to make sense now. Hand her to me."

Mayne cradled her head as Tyrus enveloped her in his arms. "I've got it from here. Get back underground before someone sees you. And Mayne," he paused as the young man turned to face him, "I owe you one."

Shutting the door, he shouted for Will, who came running in a few moments later. He placed her on the island in the middle of the kitchen and began to check her eyes. A moment later, the dark came back.

What had happened? Had she slept wrong? Opening her eyes, she realized this wasn't her room. She didn't know where she was. Panic settled in, as she started to remember.

The accident came back in bits and pieces. Her time in the sewer, finding Mayne. Mayne and Tyrus were friends. This whole thing kept getting stranger. Sitting up, her head ached. The world swam in front of her. That's right, she'd been bleeding.

Laying back down, she decided not to move for now. The door opened a few minutes later and Will entered with a tray of bandages. Seeing her eyes open, tears swam in his eyes. "Arda." The word was shaky and broken.

"I'm awake, but my head hurts."

He placed the tray on the ground next to her and kneeled at her side. Taking her face in his hands, he kissed her, deeply, for so long she feared she would pass out again. When her hand began to lower from lack of oxygen, he relented. As he moved away, she said, "wow."

"*Dammit*, Arda." It was angry, yet barely a whisper.

"Are…you mad?"

"At what happened, yes. What the hell went wrong out there?"

He started to wrap her ankle with bandages, to support it while it healed.

"My car, I think, my car was hacked."

"You couldn't override it?" She watched him skillfully continue, thinking about his dreams of being in Medical when he was younger. He was certainly gifted in triage care.

"No."

"How did you get out of the car? The other guy is in the hospital with second degree burns over thirty percent of his body." He finished, securing it with a piece of tape.

"Who was the other guy?"

"I think his name is Shadow." He looked over her face, now, at the wound on the top of her forehead.

She went cold, gripping his shirt. "Shadow?"

"Do you know him?" His eyes stayed fixed on her wound, as if he were wondering how best to treat it. She admired his focus and attention.

"He's my new partner. We started working together today. What the hell was he doing out of the office?"

"I could ask you the same thing." He took a tool from the tray, and turned a setting and positioned it above her eyes. "Eyes closed. This will burn, but I'm essentially sealing your head wound. It's too deep for glue but not enough to need stitches. This won't scar, as long as you can stay still. Eyes closed." It was hard, because Arda wanted to look at him, working intently like that. It caused a blush to rise to her cheeks, but the sting of the tool as the laser burned her skin closed removed it, refocused her thoughts.

"I went to see Thea." He moved on to her arm, which was badly bruised, at the elbow and the wrist. He picked up more bandage to wrap her wrist, first.

"And?"

She looked at him. The news hadn't reached him yet. "I think they're lying, but they're claiming she's dead" his hands froze "from complications due to surgery. Did I have an ID card on me when I came in?"

"Yes." He continued wrapping, gently making sure he didn't cause any additional pain. She felt admiration for him growing, like a small piece of sunlight in her chest.

"We need that. We have to figure out what really happened to her."

"Why would they lie about that?" More tape.

"At this point, Will, I'm wondering why anyone bothers to tell the truth at all. The better question seems to be, why wouldn't they lie?"

He tended to her elbow, creating a sling for her to recover. It wasn't out of place, but it would require rest for the elbow to recover. Lastly, he handed her a serum, which she knew was quick activating calcium designed to heal bone within hours, instead of taking the body weeks to do on its own. The drawback was that it caused a lot of pain, so he also handed her a numbing serum.

"I'm rounding up the troops. No way they take one of our own without a fight. I'll send Tyrus to find out what he can. You're staying right here, in this bed, until tomorrow at the earliest. I gave you some serum, but it's not the same as a hospital visit. It'll take at least twenty-four hours to heal that elbow." His tone, so authoritative and commanding, caused a rush of warmth to go through her. She wasn't going to tell him so, but Will being commanding, was... really working for her.

"I'm surprised you can do all this yourself." She let the admiration show in her voice, and he gifted her a half smile in return, with a brush of his knuckles across her cheek. "Yeah, we would be called back to the tents if enough people were wounded. It was good for me, as I was hoping to be in Medical. Now, I don't even want to plan a future. Who knows how long I'll be around."

A lump in her throat formed at the thought that he may be killed, that she may not get a future with him. How did they go from being safe kids in a safe District to being hunted and brutalized adults? She'd started building a network, but if she was going to survive this, if Will was going to survive this, they'd have to get a much larger network, much faster than she originally thought.

"Will?" He turned back on his way out. She cleared her throat and forced the words out. "Will, can you kiss me again, for good luck?" He smiled, and rushed back to her, placing his lips on hers, gently.

Chapter 14

She was in and out all day, a side effect of the serum she'd received. She vaguely remembered someone feeding her soup, but beyond that, she wasn't aware of much until the following morning.

She felt much better, though she knew from the sun's position that she'd slept in. Sitting up slowly, she was relieved that the world didn't spin anymore, though the headache was still there. Some fresh clothes, white loungewear, had been placed on a chair across the room. She gratefully put them on and opened the door.

A long hallway stood before her. It must be nice to be rich. She could fit four apartments on this floor alone. All of this just for Tyrus? How did a Sergeant in the Army afford a home in this district? She'd known they were lavish, but this was huge. Z4 housed upwards of over fifty estates like this.

Walking down the hallway to the staircase, a massive structure made of dark wood, she placed her good arm on the banister and walked downstairs.

She heard shouting coming from closed doors. She knew that voice. It had scolded her when she scraped her knee as a child, putting her in time out. Her mother was here. Listening, Tyrus chimed in, deeper, lower. A third voice was in the room but was so quiet and muffled she couldn't understand it.

"Arda," Will said softly from her left. She jumped anyway. "What are you doing?"

"Listening."

"Come into the kitchen and let me fix you some food. They'll be awhile, believe me." He motioned down the hall and she began to walk in that direction.

"Do you know who it is?"

"Your mother and the Director of the Project."

"How do you know that?"

"I'll tell you if you let me make you a bowl of soup."

"Was it you that was feeding me?" She placed her good arm in his and allowed him to take her around a corner and into the kitchen.

"Yes, that was me. You swatted at me a couple of times."

"I did not!" Her eyes were wide.

"You did. Swatted me on the side of the head. If you learn to punch, you'd be unstoppable."

"That's what Chaste said." She found herself regretting that encounter.

"When did you smack Chaste?"

"Oh, he deserved it. I'm sorry, though, for swatting you."

"I'll give you a pass as you were in recovery. Worse has been done."

"Why thank you." He motioned for her to sit on one of the bar stools around the island. Opening a pot, he poured a ladle of soup into a bowl and handed it to her.

With food in front of her, she felt ravenous. She took a sip, decided she liked it, and asked, "do you have-"

Bread was set down before she could finish asking for it and she ate it all, along with two bowls of soup. Satisfied, she sat back, looking at Will.

He stood on the other side of the island she occupied, leaning against the countertop near the stove. His hands were crossed over his chest, as were his ankles. He looked relaxed, his face calm but blank. It mirrored hers, actually, when she was working for the Project. "Arda, who do you think wants you dead?"

"I don't know if they want me dead. All I know is that they wanted to cause an accident that could have led to my death."

"Same thing." His eyes narrowed, and his intense gaze began to cause unwanted heat to travel along her skin.

"Not to me. Maybe Shadow was the target."

"Seems to me you were both the target. Someone is taking out your team. Was there anyone else working on the project with you?"

"Not directly."

"Who knew he was on the case with you?"

"The Director and my Mother. The assistants on the floor."

"Could one of them have fed information to someone in your building who could hack cars?"

"Probably. We were all taught how to, in our own version of basic training. How do we find out, though?"

"We tell the adults."

She laughed. "We are the adults."

"True, but Arda, we're still learning here. There are bigger resources we can call in."

"Like my mother and the Director."

"Yes."

"Who you know by voice, how?"

He opened his mouth, and Arda believed he would have answered, but shut it again as footsteps came down the hallway. She turned to see her mother run toward her, hugging her fiercely.

"Oh, honey, you're okay! What happened?" She winced as her mother hugged her a bit too tightly, jarring her elbow, which was still in its sling.

"I was in an accident." Her mother ran a hand over her

hair, smoothing it like she had when Arda would get sick.

"I heard. The poor boy you are working with is in the hospital, fighting for his life. Can you tell me what went wrong?"

"I was at the hospital, getting the bad news about Thea," she blinked twice at her mother, warning her, "and I got back into my car, turned it on, and it drove on its own. I think someone hacked it."

The Director sat down, across from her and placed both hands, folded on the island. "I agree. Whoever did so was sloppy, but likely thought they could get away with it, if there were no survivors." He almost reached out a hand to Arda, but at the last second, took it back. "Still, this doesn't seem like the hack job of someone in the Project. Too…open, too much of a show. I'd never advise any Cloaked agents to be so…idiotic about a hit like this. Someone was trying to shut this investigation down. Does anyone in this room know who would do this?"

A deep, sarcastic laugh sounded from her left. Tyrus came into the room. "Really, Director, you don't know what's going on under your nose? Maybe Faith should have gotten your job."

The Director's knuckles turned white, his jaw clenched. "Tyrus, now is not the time to discuss the past. Maybe later, in a sparring ring?"

Tyrus smiled predatorily as if he'd love nothing more than to go toe to toe with the head of a deadly, secret government organization. "Maybe later."

Faith moved around Arda toward the Director, placing a hand on his arm. "You were always the right person for the job." There was a softness in her voice that puzzled Arda.

"Now we have to help Arda figure out who is trying to kill her." The Director removed Faith's hand, but turned so only Arda could see, and winked at her. "Who do we know that comes around in wartime that would have a vested interest in shutting down agents?"

"Oh, no!" Faith said it softly.

"The Dark Riders." He stood, pacing back and forth. "We don't have the manpower to fight them."

"No, right now you don't." Tyrus crossed his arms in front of him. "You have a very small force, even if you call in all members from all districts. So, what do we do?"

The room was silent, as everyone tried to think of a solution. After several moments of no one talking, Will let out a long sigh, and locked eyes with Arda, sadness apparent in their depths. "We appease them." He said it so quietly, Arda wasn't sure she'd heard correctly.

"What do you mean, Will?"

He looked at Tyrus, Faith, and the Director, but he couldn't meet her gaze, again.

"What do you *mean*, Will?" Her voice was louder this time.

He finally glanced at her, and the way he looked at her, with a heaviness in his eyes, it crushed her heart. "We give them the traitor."

It took her a few moments to realize what he was saying. When she did, she spoke up. "No!"

"It's the only way. It'll get Thea back, resolve this without it destroying everyone."

She turned to her mother. "Tell him no."

"I want to, dear, but I can't think of anything else. He…may have a point."

"Director?" He seemed sad to have to shake his head, but did so, silently.

"*Tyrus, please*!" She felt the panic rise in her chest, the world beginning to swim again.

He stepped up, easing Arda back onto the stool, seeing the color drain from her face. "Listen, I meant it when I said that I don't want to sacrifice any more soldiers. So no, I don't think this is best. Let's take a day or two to think on our choices. This plan, Will," he stepped up to the younger man and clasped elbows with him, "Recruit, this is a last resort. Understood?"

"Yes, Sergeant."

She sighed with relief. "Thank you, Tyrus." He placed a soft hand on her good shoulder, and gave it a squeeze, then let go.

"Now, the way I see it, we have some decisions to make, some things to get done if we don't want to have the Dark Riders on our trail. First of all, we need to stay in groups. No agents go anywhere alone, Director. Two, we need to locate and extract Thea. Three, we need to figure out a way to get the Dark Riders to back off. That starts by figuring out who hired them."

"They're mercenaries?"

"And spies, yes. Thieves… Someone hired them to make the war end. Who was it? We find the hidden coin, we find our enemy."

She looked at him, oddly. That's what Mayne had said. "Tyrus."

"Yes, Arda."

"Thank you for helping us."

Faith laughed. "Oh, honey, that's just what he does."

"Is it bad that I want ice cream?"

Everyone around her laughed, but Tyrus pulled out some real ice cream from a real refrigerator. She even saw him top it with some dark liquid chocolate. When he was finished, he said, "Will, take Arda to the living room. Relax, take a break. You're safe here. We adults will brainstorm, see if we can find a way to fix all this."

Will picked up the bowl of ice cream, stealing a bite and motioned to her. "Hey! That's mine!" She walked after him into a large open room with the largest couch she'd ever seen. He sat in the middle, daring her to sit next to him, winking when she did so.

"Do you think Thea will be okay?"

He shoved ice cream in her face. She took a bite. "I think Thea can handle herself. When we got back, do you remember I had that black eye? That was from her."

"Thea did that?" More ice cream.

"Yes. Thea did that. I'm really more worried about the Riders that took her. You know, if she wanted to, she could tear you down with just her words."

That made Arda laugh a bit. "Seriously, though, do you think she's going to be okay?"

He wrapped an arm around her, drawing her closer to him. She took the spoon and gave him some. "Until we know for sure, we have to believe she's alive. I'd rather believe that and find her than think she's dead, give up and have her suffer."

"When did you get so wise?"

He tried to smile, but he couldn't. "When I lost three of my classmates to those bastards."

"Do you want to talk about it?" She licked the ice cream from the spoon, and he watched her doing it.

He shook his head. "No. I want to kiss you."

"But I want the ice cream."

"Hurry up and finish, then."

"Shh. My mother will hear you."

"That's okay. She told me I was her favorite." Wink.

"She tells everyone that." Eye roll.

"But when she says it to me, it's the truth."

They sat there talking for some time, until Tyrus came

into the room. "Arda still needs her rest. You should go take a nap upstairs." Standing up, she waved to Will. She turned and walked up the stairs. She stopped though, listening for a moment.

"And what are we doing while she naps?" It was Will.

"No, she needs the rest, but we've got a lot of work to do."

"Should we call Chaste?"

"We should call them all."

She walked quickly up the stairs when she heard footsteps. As she opened her door, she saw her mother sitting in a chair, looking out the window. "Mother?"

"Oh, Arda, I just wanted to quickly say good-bye. I fought Tyrus to get you to come home, but given the circumstances, well, I was overruled by the Director. With the level of security in Z4, you're safer here." She hugged her daughter. "If I had known," she backed away, "if I had known what would become of this, I would never have encouraged you to become a part of the Project."

Arda smiled at her mother. "Whatever happened to my life, my choice?"

"I'd have changed your mind."

"More likely that I'd have been bullheaded and done it anyway."

Faith tilted her head. "There's my daughter."

"I learned from the best."

"Flattery will get you nowhere. I'll be back tomorrow. Get some sleep, dear." She turned and walked out, shutting the door behind her.

Arda was in bed several minutes later, comfy and warm, when a knock on her door sounded. She had no clue who would disturb her now. "Yes?"

The door opened and Tyrus walked in. Sitting down on the edge of the bed, he said, "How's your head?"

"Better, now."

"Listen, I should explain something to you."

"You should. For example, how do you know Mayne?"

"I have contacts."

She laughed. "If I had a credit for every time I heard someone say that..."

He smiled. "It's true though. You live long enough, you know things, know people."

"You don't look old."

"Looks can be deceiving." His face was carefully blank.

"What do you mean?" A little probing wouldn't hurt.

"I mean that things aren't always as simple as they seem."

"What did you want to tell me?"

"We will find Thea. She's a soldier, one of our own. You won't be with us. I need you to do something else."

"She's my friend."

"Yes, she is, but we only have so much time before Will does something stupid and brave." He gave her a knowing look.

"Right." She nodded.

"He's a smart guy. We need to keep him breathing."

"I agree." And her muscles relaxed a little, knowing someone else valued his life as well.

"Good. So tomorrow, you're going to leave."

"What?"

"You're going to leave and find Mayne. You're going to hand him this tablet." He placed one on the desk. "Tell him that Tyrus is calling in a favor. When he asks you what favor, you show him this tablet and say that we found the hidden coin."

"Have we?" She was tempted to look through it.

"Yes, and it's going to take every single person we have

to take them down."

Walking down the stairs, it was so early that everyone was asleep. She saw all her classmates, some sleeping on the floor, against walls, all crowded in the room below. They were really all helping. The only issue was how to get around them all to get out the back door and down into the sewer unseen.

The first couple of people were fine, but then they started moving. It took several interesting maneuvers before she could reach the other side of the room. Walking into the kitchen, feeling relief, she stopped in her tracks to see Will already up, eating eggs, watching her intently.

"Why am I not surprised?" He smirked.

"You're up early."

"As are you." He looked at my clothing, the tablet. "Where do you think you're going?"

"To do my job."

"Your job is to get better."

"No, I'm fine. My job, and my mission, is to keep you alive."

He set his fork down and stood. "Arda, what are you planning on doing?"

"Don't worry. It's all part of the plan. Tyrus is sending me to deliver information. That's all."

He tilted his head. "Then why don't I believe you?"

She held the tablet out to him. "See? This is what I need to deliver. You need to let me do this while you go get Thea back. It's my part. It's how I can help fix this. You need to let me help." Tears welled in her eyes. She still felt shame at not making the cut a year ago. "You need to let *me* help."

"Over my dead body am I letting you leave this house,

alone and without back up. You were in an accident only two days ago. Arda, I watched you sleep. I wrapped your wounds. I heard you moan and cry out in pain. I'm not letting you go." She wanted to be angry with him but seeing his eyes, filled with fear, she lost her words. What would it have been like, if their situations were reversed? If she'd seen him come in from a car accident, hand to bind his wounds? She probably wouldn't have let him out of her sight for days.

"You have to," a voice said from the side. Arda turned to see Chaste. "Arda has to go."

"What do you know about this, Chaste?" Will leaned against the countertop, trying to breathe.

"I know that we're the soldiers and she's the spy. Let her *spy* while we take out the muscle."

"She could die."

"*Thea* could die." The anger in his voice was sudden and potent.

His face became stone as they stared at each other for a long, hard moment, their eyes cold. "I know that."

"You want Arda to take on *those* guys? You know, if we teach her to punch-"

"She'd have a mean right hook, no I know."

They smiled at each other. Arda was fairly certain it was at her expense. "I have to go. Now."

She walked up to Will, but he blocked her path. "Will…"

He touched her face, gently, stroking her cheek once. "If you die, Arda…"

"I won't." She took his hand, squeezed it gently, and lowered it away from her face.

"You better not." She walked past him and stopped, near Chaste. Without meeting his gaze, she said, carefully, "thank you for sticking up for me."

He began to reach for her, but she recoiled, so he stuck his hands in his pockets, instead. "Come back to us."

"I will." She walked out the door and opened the manhole cover, putting one foot in front of the other. The last thing she wanted to do was walk around the sewer, but she didn't have a choice. She needed to do her part, and the sewer was safer than the surface, with an unknown threat ready to attack.

It was dark like always, but Tyrus had given her special glasses that saw through the dark without alerting anyone to your presence. She loved them, but everything looked green. It helped her see while her eyes were adjusting to the darkness.

He'd also given her another knife. Weapons weren't common place in the Districts. Soldiers, sure, security, maybe, ordinary citizens, no. Project R.E.D.D. expected their agents to work through subterfuge, not direct conflict, so the only way to have weapons was through soldiers willing to part with theirs. Having two made her feel even more secure. One at her side, the other at her ankle.

She followed the pattern he had shown her last night. It was a complicated series of lefts and rights, which she'd had to repeat several times before memorizing. She repeated the pattern again as she walked, so she wouldn't forget which turn came next.

She arrived at the cavern as expected. Now came the hard part. Finding Mayne in this underground city. The good news was they slept during the day. He'd given her a series of turns for this part too, but it took a moment for her to remember it, and another moment to ponder if she was right or not.

Starting out, she ran down the street, turning where she thought she should. She ran as fast as she could, all traces of asthma gone from her system. Left here, right there, she wandered through the massive city until the pattern of turns ended and she was left standing in front of what should be Mayne's house, hours later. There was just one tiny problem.

Well, not tiny. Arda wasn't standing in front of a house, but a castle, surrounded by gates on all sides. For a moment, she just stared at the sight before her, as if willing it to turn into a simple apartment. Then, she tried the gate. It was locked. *Now what should I do?*

She searched around the entrance, worried that she would be caught, that she would be dragged off and used for blood donation. She wasn't even sure how that worked, but she didn't want to find out.

After several long moments cursing Tyrus for not preparing her, she found a small hole she could squeeze through. Coming out the other side, she decided the front door would be too risky, so she looked for a side entrance. Coming across one on the left, she tried the door. It opened, but it creaked loudly.

She waited in the silence that followed, breathing as quietly as possible, and on the fifth breath, when she didn't hear anyone moving around, she walked forward. She entered a kitchen, of sorts, hurrying through. Turning right, she walked into a great hall. It took all her effort not to change her breathing. The floor was covered in sleeping people. Looking around, she couldn't see anyone with long black hair, so she carefully stepped over them, as she'd done with the soldiers. Concluding Mayne wasn't among them, she continued to the staircase.

She silently climbed the steps, surprised that this building had the same layout as Tyrus's home. Strange. She slowly opened the first door she could find upstairs, but a woman was sleeping in there. The next door had a group of people sleeping together, limbs entwined, mostly nude. The third door was the one. She walked in and saw Mayne, sleeping soundly.

Now what? How did she wake him without waking

anyone else? She walked closer to him, checking his even breathing. She thought about Chaste's reaction to her, how he'd grabbed her wrist, and didn't want a repeat of that, so she stood close to the bed, cleared her throat, and whispered, so softly that she couldn't hear it herself, "*Mayne*?"

His eyes opened quickly, his eyes glowing in seconds. She couldn't move, his grip on her so tight that just breathing was difficult. He stood, wearing no sleep shirt, only pants. He had a well-muscled chest despite his thinner frame, and his arms were laden with black ink in patterns and swirls that lit blue with his eyes.

He eyed her, looking up and down, seeing the tablet. Then he moved with lightning quick speed to shut the door, standing in front of her again. The pressure in the air still held her still, as he found a shirt and placed it over his head. He walked toward her, placing a finger to his lips.

Speak, very softly. Even with the door closed, anything about a whisper will be heard.

It felt similar to what Tyrus had done, when he shared a memory with her, but instead, this was just his voice, as if he were right next to her, whispering it in her ear. Goosebumps spread along her arms, and she would have shivered, if she could have moved.

In her head, she shouted at him. *I can't move!*

He walked forward, a smile on his lips. For a second, she wondered if he intended to keep her there, frozen like that. Her eyes widened in panic at the thought.

As if sensing her fear, the smile faded and she could move again, instantly.

"It was a mistake to come here."

He placed a bar in front of his door. Turning back to her, he chided her softly. "Do you know what will happen if they wake up and you're here? Do you have any idea what they do to donors who stumble upon this place? You shouldn't be here."

She fought the urge to sigh and motioned to the tablet.

"What was so important that you had to risk your life?"

She practically shoved the thing at him. *"Tyrus needed me to get this to you. We found the hidden coin."*

He took it, glancing at its contents for a while. "Why did he send you?"

"Because the soldiers are busy saving a life."

"Who did they take?"

"Thea."

"Chaste will be particularly eager to get her back."

"Why is that?"

He looked at her but didn't answer her inquiry. "I'm grateful for the information, but right now, my concern is the time. Servants will wake soon. You won't be able to leave if-"

A knock at the door sounded. "Mayne, your breakfast."

Silently, he took her hand, leading her to a closet. He placed her inside and shut the door. She couldn't see past it, but she could listen.

The door opened and someone came inside. "How did you sleep?"

"Well, Sabine, thank you."

She couldn't see what they were doing, but she was setting up something on a tray. "Your father wishes to speak with you."

"When?"

"As soon as you've been given your bag."

"I see. Can you tell him I might be delayed for a few minutes?"

"What's the problem?"

"A matter has come up that needs my attention, that's

all."

"Is it that girl again?" Arda couldn't keep her heartbeat from racing. Was she talking about her?

"No, no. She understands her place now."

"I'm glad. Marci is a beautiful girl, but she isn't for you."

He chuckled. "Yes, madam."

"All set. Bon Appetit." She left, closing the door behind her. Arda waited a moment, unsure if she should leave her hiding spot. Then she heard Mayne whisper her name, so she came out quietly.

Arda, put the bar on the door. She looked at him and noted an IV was set up, draining blood into his arm. Placing the very heavy bar on the door took some effort, but she was eventually successful. She turned back to Mayne, who sat there smirking.

"What?"

"Nothing. Come closer."

She did, sitting in a chair close to him. "So it's true. The part about blood transfusions?"

He nodded. "This is how we must sustain ourselves." He reached out with his other hand and squeezed hers.

"Where does it come from?"

"Sometimes we raid the hospital, sometimes we charm people on the street. We do what we need to. Some people come down and willingly donate. We get by for the most part."

"How many of you are there?"

He searched her face. "Why do you want to know?"

"Aren't these the people you want me to help save?"

"I'll tell you one day, but today is not that day. We have to figure out how to get you back to the surface. I can get you so far through the hidden tunnels in the estate, but once we're in the city, we'll need to be incredibly quiet, incredibly careful to get you back to the sewers. From there, you'll be on your own. Do you know how to get back?"

"Yes, I just reverse the pattern."

He nodded. "We need to wait until this bag is empty."

She nodded back, sitting back in the chair in silence.

When he was finished, he stood, removing the IV and placing everything in a trash can. Holding out his hand, he waited for her to take it, then reached for a candlestick near the fireplace.

As she watched in surprise, the fireplace opened, revealing a hidden passage. They stepped inside and were greeted by darkness. Placing her glasses back on, she was able to see that it led to a series of stairs that went downward. She followed Mayne down two flights of stairs. Then they turned left and walked down a straight hallway.

Arda heard voices approaching. Mayne paused, waiting to see if they would come closer. A candle stick was lit at the end of the hallway, blinding her with the goggles on, so she removed them. They approached slowly, and as the candle's glow touched his feet, he leaned Arda against the wall, hiding her face, his arm tight around her waist. He leaned over her, as if he would kiss her neck, but only his breath touched her. She felt goosebumps rise on her skin from it. A small sigh escaped her before she could stop it. A shiver following it down her spine, stopped only by his hand at the small of her back. His breathing didn't change, and his body stayed frozen in front of her, barely out of reach.

When they had passed, he leaned away, slowly, and she thought she saw a twitch of a smile, but it was so dark it was hard to tell. He reached out a hand silently asking if she was ready to continue.

She put her goggles back on, took his hand and nodded. The passage led out to the grounds, and they walked quietly to the hole she had found. Understanding, she slid to the ground and came out the other side. He followed by jumping the gate, landing noiselessly. Arda's eyebrows lifted. She wished she could do that.

He took off his cape, handing it to her. "Put it on and keep the hood up."

She did so and he took her hand again. "No matter what happens, no talking from here until you're back in the sewers. Got it? Let me handle everything. They'll know if they hear your voice that you aren't one of us."

She nodded, and they began walking. They kept to alleys, side streets, avoiding people. They stuck to the shadows as often as possible. As people began to wake and start their day, conversation and movement could be heard. Some people pushed carts up and down the streets, some people congregated in groups. Others just walked silently by.

They turned down an alley, coming across a set of younger teens. They were throwing things, smashing things on the ground. Mayne tried to turn back, but a large group of adults were walking past. Quickly, they walked through it, trying to avoid the teens.

"Hey! This is our alley." The leader shouted at them. Mayne didn't even listen. He shoved past them and pulled Arda through. Someone grabbed her other arm, stopping their progress.

"Manners, man. You come to our house, you play by our rules." He tried to pull Arda away from Mayne, who reacted so quickly, Arda wasn't sure her eyes could follow it all. Before she knew it, all of the kids were on the ground, beaten and moaning. Mayne's breathing came rapidly, as he walked up to her and took her hand.

"Sorry, we didn't know."

He laughed but didn't look back. They continued through the city, coming to the entrance to the cavern after what seemed like hours of walking. Mayne walked with her into the sewers and turned to face her. "Now go. I'll look over the documents, see what I can do with it from here. Arda," he grabbed both of her shoulders and said, "please don't come to my home unescorted, again."

She nodded, hugging him. He didn't hug back at first, surprised, but he recovered, patting her back, then giving her a squeeze, so that she was pressed against his chest and stomach for a mere moment. "Thank you, Mayne."

He gave her a strange look and said, "Anytime, *ma colombe*. Keep the cape. Go."

She walked away, treading back out the sewer, repeating the pattern as she went. An hour passed, then two, as she continued her trek. Arriving at the manhole cover, she climbed the ladder and opened it, removing her goggles.

The sun hurt her eyes. She'd been in the darkness so long that the sun hurt. She lifted herself out of the sewer and shut the cover, then sat for a few moments in the alley, allowing her eyes to adjust. Turning, she opened the kitchen and was safely back in Tyrus's estate. *Finally, something is going right.* The time was late afternoon. She knew they'd be tracking Thea by now, and tonight the rescue would begin. Expecting no one to be around, she opened the refrigerator and removed some ice cream. Time to take a break.

As she was sitting on the couch, the doorbell chimed. She ignored it the first couple of times, as she wasn't supposed to be there, but whoever was there was insistent. After the fifth ring, she stood, deciding that it wouldn't hurt to see who it was. Glancing out the window, she saw her mother there, with a young, thin girl with long blonde hair standing next to her.

Opening the door, she saw that it wasn't a girl, but an avatar of a VA. She looked at Arda, tilted her head, and said, "Hello, Arda. It's good to finally meet you in person." Arda smiled, because she knew that voice. She looked at her mother, then back at the avatar. "My name is Joy."

Chapter 15

"How is this possible?" She rotated around the avatar. It was more advanced than the other artificial intelligence units she'd seen at academy.

"I am the prototype for one of her contracts. She's been working with my creator to make me…real."

Joy held out a hand to Arda, who shook it. "It's nice to meet you."

"It's nice to meet you, too." The avatar's handshake was stiff at first, but after a couple of shakes, felt more like a human hand. She was a fast learner.

"Arda, let's take Joy inside. I'd like to talk with you about a couple of things."

They walked through the great hall into the living room. Joy watched as Arda sat on the couch, then mimicked her movements, down to crossing her legs. Arda looked at her mother. "She's a prototype, and a lot of her code isn't finished yet, so she will have to learn through you."

"I see. Why?"

"I wanted to do something to make sure you were safe, so I gave you Joy. Her protocol is now registered to you. She is your avatar. Use her as you see fit, but I have installed a moral code that will make her stop whatever she is doing and protect you if it appears your vitals are elevated, signaling potential danger."

"I understand, though I feel like I can take care of myself."

"We have removed Shadow from the hospital. He's recovering at the project. I thought you should know. The official line is that he is dead. We'll use him as a Cloaked Agent from now on."

"That's sad. His family…"

"Yes, they will believe he is dead. We only have two Cloaks, Arda. This is a good thing. He will help so many people. This sacrifice was his choice, so we are giving it to him in exchange for everything that has happened to him in our service."

"I see."

"Also," she took her daughter's hand, as Joy watched, tilting her head, "I need to leave the District on official business. I'm getting advice from the other Directors."

"Will you be safe?"

"In the Director's helicopter? Yes. No one would dare."

"Too public, at least, for anyone who isn't incredibly foolish."

"Exactly."

Arda had a thought scratch at the back of her mind, but she ignored it, along with the fear that traveling may be risky. Flashes of the car accident threatened to overwhelm her, but she grounded herself, staying in the moment. "When will you be back?"

"Not for a week, I'm afraid. I've spoken to Stead, he's staying at security in a dorm bunk for the time being under the pretense that we have an infestation. I want you to stay here with Joy and listen to Tyrus. For now, he is your boss. As an agent, you're to do everything you can to support him."

"How exactly did you meet him?" A little probing may not be harmful.

"He's a family friend, and well connected. Beyond that, I can't say much."

Well, she'd tried. "I'll treat him as I treat the Director."

"Good. Now," she stood, smoothing down her suit, "I must depart. I'll be back in a few days."

Her mother walked out, and she was alone with her avatar. For a few moments, she didn't speak. In spite of speaking with "Joy" a million times before, she wasn't quite sure how to proceed now that she had a face and a body.

Finally, Joy spoke. It startled Arda a bit. "What can I do to assist you today, Ardora?"

She thought on that for a moment. "Can you show me anything published that lists the Dark Riders? Secure search please?"

"One moment." She tilted her head as she worked, and a few moments later, she opened her hand, displaying a virtual screen. "Wow." Arda was impressed.

"I have found five articles online referencing the Dark Riders that have merit. Project R.E.D.D. has a protected file, but I would have to unlock it, which would take some time. I also found several strange communication key words in a conversation from someone at Project R.E.D.D. to someone calling themselves, "Jockey." I assume that is a code name for someone who rides a horse. Hence, he may be a Dark Rider."

"Can I see that conversation?"

"I can play the audio file for you if you like."

"Play."

She began the recording.

"I heard from the boss today. Hen's out of the nest, so now is the best time." Though the voice's tone was scrambled, something about their patterns and diction sounded familiar.

"What have you heard of the migration?"

"As far as I can tell, fall is coming today. Birds are heading south for the winter."

"Unfortunate, but it had to happen."

"They're coming for the broken wing."

"I guess I get to get in some target practice then."

"I getting paid?"

"Yes. Sending the package now."

A few seconds ticked by. "received. Good day, Jockey."

"Good day."

The recording ended. Joy took a moment to analyze the data. "Ardora, based on the words spoken, I believe I have prepared an analogy that you may be interested in hearing."

"Go ahead."

"The hen could be your mother. If we assume birds equal people, the migration could mean the soldiers who came home. The broken wing bird might mean Thea."

"I see."

"Ardora, I believe that your classmates are walking into a trap. We should warn them."

"If we try to communicate via message, it may be intercepted. We'd have to do it in person. Did anyone track your movement?"

"Verifying…" silence. "Yes. I eluded detection by placing the trace back to the source. They will believe we are them."

"Good. How do we get to them to give them a message?"

"I will take you." Joy stood, turning, and began walking to the door. Her gate was too mechanical to be human. Arda was concerned that people would notice her. "Joy," she said, "before we go, I'd like to give you this."

She took off the cape and placed it around Joy's shoulders. "Thank you for the gift. I treasure your friendship." Joy reached out, giving Arda the equivalent of a hug. "We must go now, if we wish to intercept them prior to termination."

"Got it. Follow me and try to mimic my walk." The fear rose in her throat as she shut the door. Cars zoomed by, and the accident was again fresh in her mind. She balled her hands into fists and began to put one foot in front of the other.

They reached the bottom of the stairs and began to jog down the street. Arda felt more secure having an avatar with her, but it was still strange being out in the world again after several days of seclusion. Her jaw clenched as she looked over her shoulder, repeatedly, worried about all the ways someone could end her life in an instant.

"You do not need to worry. I am analyzing our surroundings as we proceed. If someone threatens you, I will be able to eliminate the threat."

That made her feel secure, as they turned left, heading toward the wall. Joy did not go through the main entrance, but instead, opened a manhole cover leading to the sewers. "This is the best method. Do you concur"

"Yes, Joy."

"I'll go first." Instead of using the ladder, she just jumped down. Arda followed, more carefully. Reaching the bottom, she took out her glasses and they walked to the next cover, crossing the wall from underneath.

Coming up the other side, they were in an alley near the bazaar. At least this was somewhat familiar for her. "Where do we go from here, Joy?"

"We are attempting to locate a warehouse on the other side of Z5. We must cross the entire Zone in one hour, as the sun is already setting."

Fear gripped her throat. "We won't make it in time on foot."

Joy looked over Arda and said, "Yes. Your biology would dictate that there is no possible way for you to run a distance of fifteen miles in one hour. We will have to adjust our strategy." Walking out to the middle of the street, Joy turned, and held out a hand as a car slammed to a halt in front of her. It was a public rideshare, for people without cars that didn't want to take the bus and that could pay.

"What the hell are you doing?"

"Your rideshare is ending. Please exit the vehicle."

"But I haven't made my destination."

"Step out, or I will be forced to remove you. Time is paramount."

Arda watched his eyes fill with anger and stepped in. "Listen, she doesn't mean that."

"I am not programmed to engage in false pretense."

"Joy, silence."

Arda focused on the driver. "I'm sorry, but we absolutely need this vehicle. Here."

She used her watch to move credits to the ride share and to the man. "That's ten times what the ride originally cost. Please end your ride so we can use the vehicle. It's an emergency."

The man, impressed, stepped out. He looked toward a local punch establishment and then back at them. "I suppose this one is as good as the other. Have a nice day." Then he walked away.

Joy and Arda sat inside the vehicle while Joy quickly entered the address. Sitting back, she hoped that they would make it on time. Though the rideshare was faster than walking, it didn't guarantee a lack of stops, for people crossing the street or turn priority. It could still take a considerable amount of time to travel the distance.

Approaching their destination, a warehouse not far from the restaurant they'd celebrated at, the rideshare halted.

Arda wanted to run, but Joy stopped her with an arm

placed across her body. Picking Arda up, she turned and walked into an alley way.

"Joy, put me down. We have to help them."

Joy set her down but refused to let her leave the alley way. Seconds later, a huge explosion rocked the warehouse, so loud and big that it blew out the windows of the restaurant, causing glass to fly into the alley beside them. Arda hid her face from the debris, but Joy created a shield that kept them both from being cut.

"What the… You knew it would explode?" She felt her eyes begin to burn, her stomach clench.

"Yes." It was emotionless.

"Why didn't you tell me?"

"I didn't have time. My moral protocol clearly states that I must protect you above anything else, even above your classmates."

"Allow me to pass."

Joy assessed the danger, and said, "please stay a safe distance away from the flames."

Arda ran past her and out of the alley, but the warehouse was gone, replaced by a burning chunk of charred material. Nothing moved. No one was screaming. There were no sounds except the roar of the blaze.

She fell to her knees, holding her face in her hands. Joy continued to monitor the area. "Oh, no." The sun set. That meant the odds of them being in the building were quite high. If they all died.... Tears welling in her eyes, she thought about not seeing Chaste, Thea or Will ever again. Her stomach emptied itself on the ground next to her.

Then came the shaking. She began to sob, crying in front of the road. People were running toward the explosion, water in their hands, hoses, anything to douse the flames. Some people even carried wet towels, smacking the flames back with them. "Why are they doing this?"

"It generally takes first responders a half hour to approach a fire in Zone 5, as it is so large."

Standing, Arda thought a moment. "If my friends are in there..." another sob ripped from her throat, "we should help."

"We should help." Joy repeated her words, then walked over to an old fire hydrant. She used her strength to loosen the bolt, and water came rushing out. Grabbing a pipe from the debris, she angled the pipe over the rushing water, creating a spout. The water shot up with such force that it landed on the fire at the warehouse. Joy was putting out the flames.

People saw her and began to cheer, but never stopped their work. Someone handed Arda a bucket, and she ran toward the fire, dousing flames, helping as she could. Though she grew tired quickly, she didn't stop. She couldn't stop. She needed to know.

By the time the responders arrived, the fire had already been put out, thanks to Joy. Arda sat on the ground, shaking and breathing heavily. A responder approached her, but with the soot covering her, she looked no different than any other resident.

"Do you need assistance?"

"No, I'm fine. I was near the explosion when it happened, but I didn't inhale any smoke."

"Can you tell me what you saw?"

"My friend and I were getting out of a rideshare and it just, exploded."

"Do you need me to call someone?"

"No, I've got her."

Joy walked over to her. "It appears the fire originated on the south side of the building."

The responder laughed. "How do you know that?"

"Check Arda's watch."

Arda opened her watch, starting a video file. It showed the explosion in slow motion. The responder's face was surprised.

"I'll need a copy of that sent to our office."

Arda did it while he watched. "Thank you miss, stay safe."

Arda and Joy walked away from the crowd, turning down an alley. Joy opened a manhole cover. "It's safest to go back to the estate through the sewers."

"If my friends are dead, what's the point?"

"Though I can't confirm their life vitals, I did note that no bodies were in the debris of the explosion. If your friends are dead, they did not die here. Public location services are restricted for soldiers. I can override it, but not if we are in the sewers. I recommend retreat, at which point, when you are safe, I can find your friends for you."

Arda breathed a sigh of relief. "Well, why didn't you say so sooner, Joy?"

"Was it not obvious to you, Arda?"

"No! Didn't the tears clue you in?"

"Tears…mean sadness. Grief, pain."

"Yes, Joy."

"Tears hurt you."

"Yes."

"Writing a new protocol to immediately address crying over other actions. Help will now come second."

"I did say to help, didn't I? Thank you, Joy."

She jumped down again, Arda following. Her friends weren't in the rubble. That was a relief. Climbing back down into the darkness, they made their way back to the estate. It was dark by the time they immerged and walked through the back door into the kitchen.

Tyrus was inside, talking to the director with a watch of his own. "I don't know where she is. I got back and she was gone."

"We need to find her."

"I already sent out teams looking for her. Where's Faith?"

"Out of the city I'm afraid."

"Arda isn't with her, is she?"

"No, I saw her off. She was alone. Let me know if you need my support."

"Tyrus out." He turned off his watch and turned. Jumping, surprised, he stared at Arda a moment, before tears welled in his eyes. "Where were you?"

Before she could answer, he hugged her, a huge bear hug, squeezing her so tight she couldn't speak or breathe, unconcerned about the soot now covering his clothing.

"Warning! Please release Ardora. She cannot breathe. Further attempts to harm her will result in removal."

He did, turning to Joy, surprise and familiarity filling his face. "Hello. You remind me of someone."

She held out her hand. "I am Joy."

He took it, muttering "*freakin' unicorns*." Arda didn't get the reference.

"She's an avatar of my personal VA. Mother gave her to me this morning."

He looked over the unit, clearly impressed. "Very accurate, very lifelike."

"We tried to warn you about a trap."

He smiled, placing his elbows on the countertop, leaning over them, exhaustion filling his features. "We already knew. We set it."

"Oh." Now she felt silly. She fiddled with her fingernails, adjusted her clothing.

"How did *you* know?" He looked at her, then Joy.

"Joy found a recording online between Jockey and the traitor."

"I see. Joy, delete the recording."

"Why?" Her eyes widened.

"Deleting." It was done before Arda could argue.

"But that's evidence."

He smiled at her sympathetically. "Arda, we were baiting Jockey.
We were sending the message on purpose."

She thought about the familiar voice. "It was Will. He was the voice."

"Yes, it was Will, baiting Jockey. We finished the mission early, sending him false data that the operation would occur tonight."

"Why didn't you tell *me* though?" She thought about how awful it felt, thinking they were dead. Her eyes burning again, and walked forward, one eye on Joy, and softly gave her shoulder a squeeze.

"We didn't anticipate that you would have an avatar combing the web. We thought you'd find Mayne and we'd be back here by the time you were done. Did you get the message to him?"

"Yes." She pushed the tears away. Everything was alright, and they were unnecessary.

"Good. Now sit down, eat something, and for the love of everyone here, stay inside, for now."

She nodded, turning toward the living room. Entering, she saw Thea on the couch. She was sleeping, bruised and bandaged. Arda walked to her, slowly taking her hand. She noted that she'd received the plastic surgery because the two fingers were no longer fused. However, now she would have new scars.

Tearing up, she placed her head on her friends hand and softly began to cry. Joy looked over and asked, "Arda, you are crying. Please tell me how to help you stop."

"I…Thea is hurt. It hurts me that she was hurt, but it already happened, so unless you can time travel, there is nothing you can do."

"Sometimes, I will not be able to protect you from tears?"

"Sometimes."

"Updating the protocol."

"Can you heal Thea?"

"I do not have the required medical programming, no. Uploading…I will have a complete knowledge of all current Medical conditions and treatments in approximately…. two days. "

"Just checking. Joy, can you go bug Tyrus for a minute? I'd like to be alone with Thea."

"How do I 'bug' Tyrus?"

"You ask him a lot of random questions."

"Understood." She walked out without another word.

Arda sat on the ground, taking Thea's hand in hers, and softly cried while her friend slept. She felt helpless again. She hated feeling that way. She swore that next time, when something happened like this, to change her whole world, she'd react quicker, faster. She'd anticipate better. With Joy at her side now, she was sure she would be able to keep anyone else from being hurt. She would be able to help, like she hadn't been able to at the hospital.

The last words Arda heard before passing out on the floor were from the kitchen.

"Joy, I don't understand-"

"What is the product of three multiplied by two thousand and fifty nine?"

"I don't know."

"What does the phrase, 'beat a dead horse' mean?"

"Joy…"

"Where do children come from?"

"Shut down! Joy, shut down."

"Shutting down."

Then there was nothing but silence. Arda smiled as she drifted off to sleep. She dreamt of sweet days filled with mysteries of childhood. Dreamt of being back in academy, worrying only about test scores and social interactions. She dreamed again of floating somewhere, of a star burning in the distance. For once, no Betas attacked, no monsters came to steal her away.

Slam!

Thea was still breathing evenly on the sofa, stirring, but not quite awake yet. Standing, she rubbed her eyes as Will and Chaste came through the great hall to the living room. It must have been the door closing that woke her.

On seeing her, they stopped, clenching their fists. "What... where were you?" Chaste was the first to speak.

"Long story. I'm here. I'm safe." She realized she was still covered in soot.

"We came back as soon as we were done with our assignment." Will said it softly, but his voice shook.

She looked down at her shoes. "I…heard about it."

Will was silent, folding his arms cross his chest. Thea stirred from her slumber, and Chaste ran to her. He knelt next to her, gently brushing her hair away from her face. "Thea?" His voice broke. I saw the love in his gaze, and it clicked. They had been dating like we had, then they'd gone to war…

"Chaste. You saved me." Tears burned in her own eyes hearing her friend's voice.

"Yeah. We did." They gazed at each other, suddenly kissing passionately. Arda turned, blushing, embarrassed at seeing something so private from someone else. Will walked over to her and said, "let's get you cleaned up. In the kitchen."

She nodded and led the way. Upon seeing Joy turned off, she said, "Joy, activate."

The avatar came to life as Will was walking into the room. He took a cloth and turned on a spout, water flowing into the sink, but only long enough to wet the cloth. Then he began to gently rub it over her face, the soot wiping easily away. Her eyes met his, and it was hard to look away, his gentle hands fueling the heat under her skin. She was suddenly aware of his body, his muscles, how much power he could wield, yet here he was, gently washing her face. A blush rose to her cheeks, and she looked away, then.

Not for long, because that gentle hand tilted her chin upward, and his lips touched hers. The whirlwind of emotions from her day caused her knees to weaken, and she gripped his arms to keep from falling. His hand was around her waist, the other in her hair, and the kiss deepened, until she was lightheaded, and the dark began to swim at the edges of her mind.

"Alert! Please step away from Ardora. Alert! Failure to comply will result in personal injury."

Will released her, his eyes angry. "You have a security drone?"

"I have an avatar." She smiled sweetly at him, seeing his frustration.

"I thought they were still in production?" He released

her carefully, now covered in soot himself.

"She's the first." Will left to inspect Joy, who inspected him at the same time. "Her name's Joy?" Will asked without looking at Arda.

"Yes, my name is Joy." She held out her hand. "It is a pleasure to meet you."

He shook it. "She's strong."

"Yes, I am. Would you like to run a diagnostic with me?"

"What diagnostic?"

"I can determine your force per blow and training levels in a sparring match." She adjusted her position, looking aggressive. "Would you like to proceed?"

Will backed away. "Maybe another time, Joy."

"As you wish."

"Joy, please defrag."

"Defragging." Her eyes dimmed and the unit was no longer aware.

Will used the cloth to wipe the soot away from the rest of her face, her neck, and her arms. It felt wonderful, the soft touch almost a massage. She sighed into it, and he chuckled.

"The word got to me that you went looking for us."

She suspected Tyrus would reveal that. "That's the cause of the soot, yes."

"You couldn't just stay put?" He tried to keep the anger out of his voice but was unsuccessful.

"You were in danger, so I thought. You expect me to sit back while you walk into a trap?"

He sighed. "I know you too well to know you won't investigate. We just thought giving you recovery time from the accident would be a good thing. Going out so soon, being in a vehicle…was it hard for you?"

"If I hadn't been worried about you, I suppose it would

have been difficult."

"Can you understand how we thought it best that you recover in peace without the additional threat to your life?"

"I can see that from your perspective, that may have been your goal." He continued to remove the soot, finishing, then checking himself. "The explosion…I thought you were dead."

"We set that explosion." His eyes watered, and he wrapped his arms around her. "Thank God you were too late to go inside." He squeezed tighter. "Don't do this to me again."

"I won't if you won't."

"Agreed. We tell each other everything."

They backed away as they heard footsteps approaching. Chaste entered the room. "So, you and Thea?"

He smiled. "We got very close during our scout assignment."

"She's always liked you."

"Well, I'll just be happy if all of us are alive a year from now when it's time to be placed."

"We have twenty-five left."

"One person will be alone, unmatched for an additional year." Surprise in his voice, and a twinge of sadness.

That made her sad, thinking someone would be left out as she was. "That sucks."

"It does." He stood for a moment, silent before adding, "uhm, Will, Tyrus wants to see us. Arda, Thea is asking for you."

She walked to the resting girl and sat on the floor next to her. "Hey, Thea."

"Hi, Arda." Her smile was bright. "I'm so glad I'm out of there. They told me what's happening. How are you doing?"

"I'm just worried about you."

"We'll I'm worried about you." She motioned to her

clothing, and the soot still covering her clothes.

"I'm ok. Small, tiny misunderstanding about an explosion."

They laughed. "I appreciate what you did. Telling them. I know when we were younger, we were so competitive, but now, I hope we can officially be friends?"

"I'd like that." Arda took her hand in hers. "Was it awful?"

Her eyes grew dark. "Yes. I…I'm just glad it was only a short time."

"Do you want to talk about it?"

"Maybe someday, but not today. I'd much rather hear about you and Will."

Arda squinted. "What about us?"

"Oh, come on. *Tell me.* He talks about you constantly. What's going on between the two of you?"

She thought about the heat from his body in the kitchen, how hard his muscles were. What he could do with them…

"I'm not sure." She knew her cheeks were red.

"Well, do you like him?"

"He's a good person."

"That's not what I meant, and you know it."

Arda blushed. "I'd rather talk about something else."

"Suit yourself. I'll tell you about Chaste and myself."

Arda sat for the next hour hearing about all the great and wonderful reasons Thea loved Chaste. She told stories of his heroism in combat, times he saved her, times she saved him, how he was funny and smart. Looking into Thea's eyes as she spoke, she could tell that the two of them had something special. Something she would probably never share with anyone.

Guilt had her glancing down. "What's wrong?" Thea asked.

"I just...you have this great connection with him."

"I do."

"I...worry I won't ever have that. That your...service created that, and I couldn't..." she rolled her eyes at herself, wishing the shame and guilt would just leave her.

"Arda, our connection would have happened anyway. You and Will, you'll get to where we are. It doesn't take a war to grow love."

"You already know you love him."

"Pretty sure, yes. I think about him all the time."

"Will you push for the two of you to be matched?"

"If things continue to go well, yes."

"I suppose they'll want us all to start dating again. What will you two do? Just date each other?"

The idea sounded so foreign, but if you knew who you wanted to be matched with, why not only date them?

"We still need to play by the rules. I'll accept dates. He'll date others. It's how the system works."

"Aren't you afraid he'll match with someone else?"

She tilted her head. "I think the large" her eyes widened, "amount of data we supply will eliminate other options. I don't have to worry. I know you two also shared a connection. I know he still cares. Even though you're angry, at us. I'm sorry, by the way."

Arda nodded, squeezing her hand. "Don't worry about it right now. You can make it up to me later. I...just want you healed and safe."

"If you decide to forgive him, and you want to continue to date... I won't be mad. It's how the system works."

"I...appreciate that, but it's not something that we need to worry over, at least not until everyone from the war is given their career options. We have another week, until they even begin to think about reactivating the Chemistry Chips."

"So where *are* they?"

"Talking to Tyrus."

"Will you fill me in if you hear anything?"

"Yes. Will you do the same?"

"Yes. Can you grab me some water?"

"Sure." Arda stood, walking to the kitchen to help her friend. The office was next to it, separated by a wall. She could hear bits and pieces of their conversation.

"What do you suggest we do, Will?" That was Tyrus.

"I suggest we find a way to end this before someone else ends up dead or tortured. I checked in the hospital. The other person in the accident with Arda, the other agent? He's dead."

"You think she's next?"

"I know she's next." His voice was almost a growl.

"What do you propose we do?"

"Does your contact have the data?"

"Yes. It's just waiting for him to have the time to act on it."

"Fine. When that happens, we secure Arda here, and take down the Dark Riders in the city."

"Hold on a moment." Chaste was speaking. "We can't just take them down. They're sanctioned by the same people that control the government of the Districts."

"I realize that-"

"We need to neutralize their influence." Tyrus stepped in. "That's exactly what we're waiting for my contact to do."

"We just sit here and wait?" The tension in his voice melted her heart a bit more.

"There are people, forces working behind the scenes to fix this that even you don't know about Will. Tomorrow, you head back to Project R.E.D.D. to deliver your report to the director. Chaste, I'll need you here watching over the house. I'll be in the sewers, helping to end this."

The door opened and Arda walked quickly to Thea, handing her the water. Chaste and Will entered the room a minute later. "Arda, can I talk to you?"

She gave him a carefully blank look. She couldn't quite believe what she'd just heard, although she didn't know why she hadn't seen it before, with his skills and abilities. No way he wouldn't have been recruited. Will was an agent, like her. The only question she had, was why would he lie about it? She'd told the truth. Maybe he wasn't the person she thought he was.

"Is something wrong?"

"No, nothing's wrong. Sorry. Sure. Let's talk upstairs." She took his hand, leading him to her temporary room. They sat down, facing each other, for a moment, the silence between them heavy. Arda wasn't sure why, but she had a feeling that their association with each other was about to change.

"What did you want to talk to me about?"

He didn't speak for a minute, his hands white from clenching them together. She grew tired of waiting for him to speak.

"Are you working with Project R.E.D.D.?"

He froze, then. "You were listening."

"How long have you been lying to me?"

"It…was a situational assignment, after the war. I was sworn to secrecy. I…couldn't tell anyone."

"Neither could I, and I still managed to tell you the truth."

"I understand that, but…this was…different." He sighed, knowing his words were insufficient.

She tilted her head at him, anger rising from her. "How is this different?" Her face grew cold.

"I was recruited during wartime, after the scouting mission was over. I was specifically told that I would join the agency for the time being as a liaison for the armed forces. They needed me. It was your mother that recruited me. She specifically told me not to bring you in. I was hoping she would have told you on the side, but that didn't come to pass, obviously." He wouldn't meet her gaze.

"I found the time to tell the truth."

"Yes, you did, and I'm grateful. Arda, I don't want to talk about work."

"No, you want to talk about ending us." She'd seen it, in his eyes, in the living room. The tension, the almost daily threat to their lives, was clouding his judgement. The conversation she'd heard was proof of that.

"I think it's best under the circumstances."

The anger overwhelmed her, then, even though her brain knew they needed to be thinking straight. With how he felt, he may decide to take on the Dark Riders all by himself and get killed in the process.

"Well, then, we're done." The instant the words were out, she regretted the need to say them.

His eyes, wounded, locked on to hers. "This is just a hard situation. I don't want you to depend on me when I might not come back to you."

She looked at him, thinking of all the things they'd been through together. Thinking of their first date, the dance, of the way it felt when his lips touched hers. She cared deeply for this man, but her anger over his deception, and the logic of the need to back away, confirmed her choice.

"I think, Will, that it is best if we go back to friends. This situation is too…intense for us to be blinded by our feelings. You're correct. We need to end this."

She turned her back on him, angry and hurting. He walked out quietly, shutting the door behind him. After a quick air shower and change of clothing, Arda sat on the bed, holding a pillow to her face. She lay down, sobbing softly. She'd fallen for a man she barely knew. She wept for the lost boy that had stolen her heart.

Chapter 16

She was still debating her decision the next morning as she walked down the large staircase to a silent house. No one was home. She entered the kitchen where Joy was making eggs. "Hello, Ardora." She chirped.

"Hello, Joy. Where is everyone?"

"They've gone on a mission."

"Oh?"

"Yes. Our orders are to stay here until they return."

"Really? We don't have a job to do?"

"No. I was told by Will, 'Do not under any circumstances allow Arda to leave this estate.' He was quite adamant that you remain here and safe. Eggs?"

Arda swallowed the eggs, fuming. It wasn't his call to make. It was her life. They ended their…whatever that was and he still thought he could control her? Not while she had any willpower left.

She wouldn't leave without a plan though. "Joy, tell me about their mission."

"They are currently in the sewer, on their way to speak to Tyrus's contact about exposing the Dark Riders."

They really wouldn't need her help for that. "Joy, search the city. Is there any evidence of Dark Rider activity?"

"Yes."

"Where?"

"Error."

"What?"

"I was told by Will, 'Don't give her any information she could use to leave the estate.'"

"Can't I override?"

"Not at this time, as the present danger level is set to highest."

Sighing, she turned and thought for a moment. "Joy, defrag."

"Cannot complete."

"Why?" This was getting ridiculous.

"I was told by Will, 'Do not turn off or defrag your hard drive while Arda is alone.'"

The infuriating man thought of everything. Joy walked forward, handing her a note. She opened it, and quickly read his apology. Crumpling it, she tossed it into the trash.

Grumpy, she turned and started toward the living room. Surprised, she saw Thea still on the couch. "I assumed you would have gone with the others."

"No, I'm still too injured. I can't even move."

Finally, there was something she could do. "I'll take care of you, then."

"Arda, I heard about you two breaking up."

Arda smiled. "I don't want to talk about it."

"I know but…" she paused, "Arda, he kept everything you sent him in a box under his bunk. He looked at them when we were going to sleep. You were all he could talk about. He kept a virtual image of you above his cot. When we talked about the war ending, he told me that the only thing he could think about was being with you again."

Tears welled in her eyes. "He wanted to end it, Thea. There is just... too much pressure on us, right now. I don't know what to tell you."

She gave her a gentle look. "Arda, I've learned a lot about guys this year, some stuff I never needed or wanted to know… but if there's one thing I know about Will, it's that he would die so you could have another breath."

As would I… "I…think you overestimate my value to him."

"I think you underestimate yours."

"I…can't process it being over but not over. It's too…much for me. It needs to be done, simple, a clean cut. I can't discuss this anymore."

Thea didn't have anything to say to that for a while, then she simply added, "give him time."

For the rest of the morning, into the afternoon, they talked of safe topics, easy days of war, what Arda's internship had been like. The sun was setting when they heard the door shut. Someone had returned.

Walking into the great hall, she was surprised to see a hooded figure she didn't recognize. "Can I help you?"

The hood peeled away, revealing Shadow, some burns still covering one side of his face. Even with Medical, it would take multiple surgeries to heal those.

"Shadow? What is it?"

"Your mother called me this morning. I'm sorry, but she has a contract for us she can't get to. I need your help."

"My avatar won't let me leave."

He produced a small device from his pocket. "This is her manual override switch. Hit it and she'll be down for at least a couple of hours."

Taking the switch, she placed it in her pocket, not quite sure if she should use it or not. "What is the contract?"

"We're heading to Z5, where we will narrow down the location of the Dark Rider base."

"I thought it was the warehouse."

"No, that was just a building. Their base is likely to be near the outskirts of the zone. We need to surveil activity in the area, look for anything unusual. Your mother said to take you with me."

"That's fine. Let me…"

Noise behind her had her rounding. "Thea, you shouldn't be on your feet."

Her friend leaned against the wall. It was clear that she was hurt. "Arda, what's going on?"

Great. "Thea, go back and sit on the couch. I have a couple things to check out for my mother. Please don't ask questions." Cloaked agents' identities were kept secret from everyone, save the Director of the Project, and any trusted Agents. If Thea pushed, there could be consequences.

Thea turned, and walked back into the living room, but Joy approached. "Get away from Ardora."

Shadow shrugged his shoulders, and she sighed, pressing the button in her pocket. Joy stopped mid stride and just froze there.

"She'll be out long enough to complete this and return. Let's go."

They walked outside, stepping into his car. She gave him a sideways look, but he pulled the lever to turn off auto drive. "Live and learn, right?"

She tried to keep track of lefts and rights, but it appeared to be a very intricate pattern that eventually she lost count. Soon, they were pulling out toward the Fringe, the farming area between Zone 5 and the wilderness beyond.

"Now comes the hard part." He put the car into park and turned toward her. "This is an emergency alert. Press this button, and in minutes, you'll be descended upon by every agency in the area related to the security of citizens. However, I need to ask you not to press it unless you know you are going to die if you don't."

He placed the small red button in her hand. "You're playing the damsel, and I'm the knave. Do you remember the stories?"

They'd been told plenty of those growing up. Old tales of knights saving tied up maidens while jokers and thieves were torn to ribbons.

Wait… "You mean I'm bait???"

He brought out the rope from the back seat, an apologetic look on his face. "Yes."

She sighed. "Prove to me you are acting on my mother's authority, and you can tie me up."

He hit a small button, and a short video played.

"Honey, I know this seems radical, but when we are dealing with a hidden coin, sometimes, we have to fight unconventionally. Please listen to Shadow and let him lead this investigation. His plan was solid, and you have the red button. I love you."

She sighed. "Fine. However," she maintained glaring eye contact while she said it, "if I have to use this button, the first thing I'll do afterward is kill you, again. Slowly. With knives. Your brand of idiotic cleverness better work, understood?"

He began to tie her, while she sat there and allowed it. He was thorough. She was surprised by his skill level. He played the failing knave well. When she was tied, he asked, "can you still squeeze the button if you need to?"

"Yes." He got out a gag for her mouth and she tried asking, "wait! Who is the knight-"

With the gag in, she couldn't continue. "If I tell you, your fear won't be real, and we desperately need the hidden coin to believe your fear is real."

Stepping out of the vehicle, he came around and picked her up, throwing her body over his shoulder. She could see the ground, cold concrete beneath her. The concrete gave way to grass, and then the forest enveloped her.

They walked for ages before coming to a small clearing, where he stepped onto old wood and opened a door. Setting her on the floor, he paced back and forth for a while, waiting. Clearly, they were meeting his contact here.

Moments later, he left the shed, shutting the door behind her.

The minutes passed, the sun setting. Soon it was dark outside. Shadow still wasn't back. After several long silent moments while she struggled not to panic, she saw the motion of flashlights approach the shed. She let her heartbeat pound loudly, her eyes wide with fear. She had no clue who was there. She heard some commotion, then some groaning. A moment later, the lights were gone, and Shadow was opening the door.

"See? What did I tell you?" He walked over to her, beginning to take her bindings off. "All set."

From behind him came another figure. Arda mumbled, but he didn't turn. The figure picked up a piece of broken wood and raised it high, bringing it down with a whack on Shadow's skull. He fell over, unconscious. She silently prayed this was part of the plan, that he would recover, that he hadn't just died for this operation.

Arda eyed the figure before her. "Well, who would have ever thought we'd be here?" The voice was familiar, but in the darkness, she couldn't make them.

Arda fought to keep her breathing even. "Do you know why you're here, Arda?" Tension and anger were clear in their voices.

She shook her head. "Of course you don't, how could you? You're just a little girl. Grab her." Another figure came in, placing a sack over her head and picking her up. As they walked out, she heard someone say, "When I'm done with you, they'll regret disobeying me. Every last one of them."

That was the last thing she heard before being shoved into the trunk of a vehicle. Then, they drove away. She had no clue how long she remained trapped in the vehicle. Time was moving strangely as adrenaline pumped through her system. Reaching around, as much as she could, she felt something prick her hand. That meant it was sharp. Feeling at it, she was able to pull it into her other wrist.

She wouldn't just sit there, under normal circumstances. Playing the part well meant she would attempt to escape. She used that logic to justify slowly cutting through the rope on her wrists.

The sharp instrument was not quick, but it was slowly breaking the fibers of the rope. Freeing her hands, she removed the gag from her mouth. There wasn't enough space for her to really reach her feet. Still, when they opened the trunk, they were in for a fight.

The car eventually came to a stop. The men exited the vehicle and for some time, Arda was alone in the trunk. She heard a door shut and close, voices in the distance, the sound of laughing. After what seemed like another hour, she heard the door again, followed by footsteps approaching the car. Getting ready, she grabbed the sharp and prepared herself.

When the trunk opened, a security guard for the house reached down to grab her. Arda attacked, but the guard's reflexes were incredible. He grabbed and twisted her wrist until she was screaming in pain, causing the shard to drop.

Another guard trained a weapon on her.

"Move, and I end your life." With voice chips, there was no way to tell from natural inflection if he was willing or unwilling to pull the trigger.

After a quick moment, she sighed, balling both hands into fists at her side. If she could survive without using it, she needed to. If this was still on plan, she wouldn't be responsible for it being over too soon. Still, she'd done what she would have, normally.

Though she was annoyed, she acquiesced, as the soldier once again bound her hands. Carrying her in, she fought the urge to smile, pleased that they hadn't thought to check her other palm, the button safe and still accessible.

She was laid onto a couch in a large sitting room, the guard occupying a chair across from her.

"Don't move off the couch."

"Where am I?" At least she could speak, could ask questions.

"My job is to watch you, not answer your questions. Just do me a favor and shut the hell up. Boss will be out to deal with you soon."

She briefly wondered what he meant by, "deal with her." Watching the masked face, she couldn't discern much. His body language was relaxed but guarded.

Looking around the room, she tried to take in as much as she could, mentally thinking through ways to escape if it became necessary.

"Don't even think about it."

"About what?"

"About pulling another stunt like that. We're watching you."

She looked away, doing so anyway. If he wanted to stop her from plotting, he'd have to use more than a warning.

A few minutes later, someone radioed to them to switch their positions. The guards did so, saying, "if you move from the couch, the gag goes back on."

Walking out, it was only several seconds before someone came in to replace them. These guards' clothes were disheveled, as if they'd just woken up. Great, they were nappers. That was a bonus for her. They might be sloppy in other ways.

"You want to tell me where I am?" He shook his head. Arda sighed, sitting back, knowing she wouldn't be able to make it very far without a better plan. Something about his body language was different, more guarded, not as relaxed. His shoulders were tight, his movements jerky. He was either new, or the plans involved something that made him uncomfortable.

After several moments, she heard voices approaching. The gag when back on as two men walked into the room. One was Mayne, the other, an old gentleman that she should know, but she couldn't remember his name.

"This is the girl?" Mayne eyed her very briefly, as if they hadn't known each other for over a year. She tugged at the ropes to cover the sigh of relief at seeing a familiar face. He had too many plans for her to let her die here. She was safe, for now.

"Yes, this is the girl I need you to take care of. I trust you have some… clean way to do so?"

"Of course, but it will cost you extra, Chief."

Arda's eyes widened. This was the current Chief of their District. That's where she knew him from, from the speech he gave before the war.

"Cat got your tongue child?" Chief…Richards. He bent down and removed the gag from her mouth.

"Chief…Richards." He patted her head like she'd been a good tied up loose end. She narrowed her eyes at him in anger.

"Yes I am." He turned back to Mayne. "Name your price."

"Exactly what are we discussing here?"

"You fixing this problem."

"I understand, but if you would elaborate, I could narrow down the amount I charge."

"Just give me a number."

"It's the difference between thousands of dollars. It isn't easy to hide a body in this city. What can you tell me about your expectations?"

"I want you to use her as bait to catch the remaining scout. Then I want you to kill them both."

"No! Please don't! I'm not hurting anyone." Mayne shoved her gag back in place, but winked as he did so.

"How?"

"I want you to take her to the sewer, set the trap for him, drain their blood for your people until there's nothing left. Then do whatever you do with dead donors." She screamed against the gag, one guard came and made a motion as if he would slap her. She stopped, looking away, but the slap never came.

"Why would I allow you to place the burden of two deaths on my people?"

"Because you'll get a lot of money."

"What will money get me if you decide to frame me for her murder?"

"Oh, come on. Why would I do that?"

"So no one comes after you."

"I'm a Chief. My word is law."

"Is that what you told the Dark Riders?"

"They did their duty."

"Which was?"

The Chief eyed him suspiciously. Mayne saw it. "Look, the risk is all on me, so if you want me to do this, I need the truth."

"Your father wasn't so bossy."

"I'm not my father."

"Clearly." The man paced back and forth, his belly jiggling as he went. "Their duty was to end the war. It had gone on for too long. I was tired of sitting back and waiting for nature to take its course."

"I'm confused."

"I'm not surprised. This generation is lazy, incapable of making the hard choices. I have to do it for you. Well, the truth is hard. We live in a hard world. With the wheat shortage…the other districts needed drastic population reduction. When it was clear that the timid soldiers wouldn't kill each other… I had to end the war. The Dark Riders did that for me, so they were paid."

"And this scout, the one who filmed it?"

"A loose end that could weaken the people's belief in me."

"A leader should protect his people, even from themselves."

He chuckled then, full and raspy. "As old as I am, people still manage to surprise me. The scouts, it's unfortunate, but they had the recordings."

"So why take the recordings in the first place?"

"Historians love to document everything. It's in our bylaws. Nothing I can do about it, as I had no control over whether the army recorded or not. Their autonomy from me has always been a thorn in my side."

"So what, they had to go?"

"They had to go. Can't have the population thinking the war was a farce."

"Now that concept is interesting to me."

"The war being bogus? Oh, if you knew how twisted some of these Chiefs have gotten…"

"Listen, she's not going anywhere, why don't I knock the price down, you can drug her, we can talk some more about this.

I'd love your insight to help me with my own people."

The two walked away. Arda couldn't believe everything she'd heard. Chief Richards stopped next to the guard nearest the door and whispered something in his ear. The guard nodded, walking over to the couch and picking her up.

She struggled against her bonds as the guard took her upstairs, though the rope bit into the flesh at her wrists and ankles. They put her on the floor in the nearest room, shut the door and locked it. She was alone. She wasted no time, crawling toward a desk, gripping the legs to get her to her feet.

Reaching her bound hands into the drawer of the desk, she gripped something long and sharp. A letter opener. Perfect. She grabbed it, and hopped over to the bed, worrying at the bonds once again.

It didn't take long this time for her to break through them. She looked at the raw, red skin of her wrists. Even rubbing them would hurt.

After a few moments, just sitting there, she carefully stretched all of her limbs. Now her job was to adapt. There was a bed, a desk, a door and walls. No windows, no weak points. She would have to wait for the guards to come back in, then attack with the letter opener. It was her best shot. She heard footsteps approach, so she gripped her weapon, ready to strike, "bait" be damned.

The door handle squeaked, and she crept behind it, ready to face anyone that came through. The door creaked open, the guard entered, and with a deep breath, she struck.

The guard was ready for her, grabbing her hand and disarming her expertly. He flipped her over his shoulder so she was lying on the ground and put the letter opener to her throat. Looking into his eyes, she whispered, "Do it. Kill me here. Then at least your boss has to clean up his own mess."

She thought she heard a sigh come from him, but she couldn't be certain. He kicked the door shut with his foot, then allowed her to stand. He placed the letter opener in his back pocket and leaned against the door, watching her.

"What?" she said it harshly.

The guard just shook his head. A knock and he stepped to the side. It opened, and he left, unconcerned that she'd freed herself from her bonds. Pounding on the door, she let her aggression go, until finally, she fell back, temporarily defeated. She hadn't thought ahead this time. She hadn't anticipated anything. Maybe she wasn't cut out for this line of work. Maybe she wasn't a great agent, like her mother.

The adrenaline left her as she realized she was trapped. Feeling useless, depression overcame her, and she lay down on the bed, falling asleep.

> She was in a meadow. That's strange. She knew what a meadow was, but this one was fantastic. Flowers were brighter, bigger, the air was sweet, the grass soft beneath her feet. A group of women were dancing below her. She recognized someone that looked like Joy, as well as her mother among the group. Walking down, she noted that she was wearing a white dress, covered in ribbons. Personally, she didn't care for the style, but who was she to judge.
>
> Closing in on the group, she shouted, "Hey!" Her hand waved to the ladies, who turned, hearing her, and waved back. Making it down the hill seemed to take an eternity. Time moved differently here.
>
> Reaching them, Joy embraced her. "You

finally made it here." She let go, holding her hand. "Your mother and I were just talking about you."

Faith smiled. "Yes, we were. Having a delightful discussion about you, flowers, and the air here. It's so sweet, isn't dear? Sweet like drinking in sugar."

Arda smiled. "It is. And the flowers…"

"Oh, yes, they're quite lovely. Have you smelled one?"

Arda was so mad at herself for not thinking of that. "No! I have to smell one."

"You do indeed."

She bent down to smell a rose, soft and white. It was the real thing. It reminded her of the café where Will had taken her. It smelt the same. "Oh, how lovely."

"That's what I said," Faith interceded.

Joy took Arda's hands in hers, twirling her friend around. "Oh, it's so nice to meet you. I've been visiting Faith for a long time. But you, Arda, you, are tricky. Something has been blocking me from getting to you."

She thought about that, and it made her angry. "That's awful. Who wouldn't want me to be in such a lovely place?"

"That's what I said," Faith laughed.

Arda turned and noticed another woman waiting to see her. "Grandma?" She was young again, but that was definitely Grandma Hope. "Is that you?"

"Yes, dear, how lovely to see you." She

embraced her granddaughter.

"That's what I said, "Faith repeated. The three laughed.

Joy turned her to face away from the group. "You must listen. I don't have much time before they put me back."

"Just tell them you want to stay here."

"I will but listen to me Ardora. I have a message for you."

"I'm listening," she said, annoyed. She just wanted to smell the flowers.

"Ardora, when you wake up, you'll have something in your hands. It's important that you keep it safe. Do you understand? It's very important that you keep it safe, for me, for your mother, for everyone. Can you do that for me?"

"Oh, sure, but not now. I'm smelling the roses." She bent down to smell the flowers, but a shadow crossed over the meadow. "Aww. Stop that." The shadow didn't listen, she sat on the ground, angry that it was ruining her fun.

The cloud swallowed the world, her mother, Joy, everyone fading away. Arda just sat there, upset she couldn't smell the flowers, clenching her fists, hanging onto a white rose.

She woke, unsure what time it was. She became aware of noises from the hall. The guards were awake and walking this way. She felt something hard in her left hand, the same hand that was holding on to the rose. Looking down, she caught her breath. In her left hand, lay a straight, twisting animal horn. Hiding it underneath the pillow for now, the footsteps approached.

The door opened and the same guard from the night before came in with a tray of food. Her hunger became real then, and she looked at the tray hopefully. The guard set it down on the desk and shut the door.

Walking to the tray, there was a piece of fresh bread, an apple and some cheese, along with a pitcher of water. She poured a glass, downing it in a few gulps, then took a huge bit out of the bread. She couldn't remember the last time she had eaten. It'd been back at the estate, but how long ago was that? How long had she been asleep?

Her mind drifted while she ate. She wondered where she was. She doubted he'd have been stupid enough to take her back in to the district. This had to be his country home. Though home was maybe the wrong word. This was more of a fortress.

She wondered if this was still part of the plan, or if she was on her own. She worried about the others, out looking for her, hoping they didn't get themselves caught. Her thoughts drifted to Will, briefly, her burning tears helping her push his memory away. Now was not the time.

The tray empty, the door opened again. She wiped a tear away from her eye before the guard could see it, and stepped away so he could take it. She couldn't leave without that horn, and she wasn't willing to use it as a weapon. She'd have to find out how to get both her and the horn out of here.

The guard looked at her sudden resolve quizzically. She was making no sense, she was too calm.

"What's going to happen to me?" She let her voice shake.

That seemed to appease him. He turned and shut the door. Alone again. Taking the horn out of its hiding spot, she looked over the object. It wasn't synthetic. It felt real, like the horn of a goat. That was ridiculous, though, because unicorns have never existed. Yet here she was, holding a multicolored horn in her hand with a white core that sparkled.

She closed her eyes, picturing the meadow, the soft feel of the grass on her feet, the sweet air, the beautiful flowers. She smiled as a warm glow came over her, and when she opened her eyes, a rose was blooming through the wall.

Standing, not sure if this was real, she walked over to it. Touched it, smelled it. It was real. That hadn't been there before, had it? No, that was crazy. She couldn't make roses grow from walls. She just hadn't noticed it before, that was all.

Freaking out, she put the horn back beneath the pillow. Whatever that was, she didn't want to touch it more than she had to.

The hours passed in silence, and she entertained herself by singing childhood songs in her head, repeating multiplication tables, anything so she wouldn't go completely crazy from the solitude. When she heard footsteps again, she was almost glad, hoping this would soon be over with. She quickly placed the horn into her shoe, tying rope around her calf, then pulled her pant leg over it. Hopefully, they wouldn't find it.

The steps approached as she finished. The same guard walked in, holding rope in his hands. Now what? "You tied my ankles so tight my toes turned blue. Let me do it, then you can do my hands." Long shot, but it might work.

The guard looked at her surprised that she had the guts to ask. He handed her the rope, backing away quickly as she took it, and wrapped her feet. When she was done, he checked the rope, satisfied, he tied her hands. "Just make sure I don't lose my fingers before you kill me, okay?"

He shook his head and continued. Finished, he picked her up, placed her over his shoulder and walked her downstairs to the couch, plopping her onto it. He placed a hand on her shoulder to keep her from moving. The hand squeezed once, then twice. That was her mother's signal. *How…*

Chief Richards came back in with Mayne before she could consider it further. They were laughing, and it was obvious that the Chief was drunk. Mayne turned to him. "So, so my dear friend, we're in agreement. You give me the gold and I will have this, rather, lovely girl taken care of after catching the rogue scout. Only one thing left to do my friend, and that is show me payment."

He motioned to one of the guards, who walked forward with a briefcase. Opening it, Arda was surprised at its contents. The briefcase was not full of credit chips, but rather, bars of pure gold. She didn't even know that much gold was saved after Omega Fire.

"I assume it's real?"

"See for yourself." He took a bar out and handed it to Mayne, who carefully inspected the metal. Satisfied, he placed it back in the briefcase and said, "If you'll excuse me, I prefer to work alone. Two guards will be sufficient, but you must return to the city now, my Chief."

"Good. I have too much to do to linger." Taking one last swig from his glass, he said, "you two, stay. Guards, let's go." He exited surrounded by a group of ten men. Arda was only upset she hadn't been able to do anything to stop it.

Mayne sat down, apparently unwilling to go anywhere or do anything. The guard behind her still had a hand on her shoulder and the other guard stared out the window as the vehicles drove away. This was it. She still had the button, but she doubted Mayne would let her die. She'd seen his reflexes, knew he could handle two guards. And then there was the double squeeze.

Her heart pounded at that thought. She suddenly

regretted her attitude towards Will. She shouldn't have let him leave. He was afraid. She should have calmed his fear, told him how strong they were, that they could get through anything together. She should have been braver, more resilient than the woman she'd shown him.

A tear slipped from her eyes, staining her cheeks, but she remained silent. Mayne locked eyes with her but said nothing. "Clear." The guard at the door stopped watching and came around, pulling up a chair. The other guard knelt beside her on the floor, squeezing her shoulder twice, again.

They slowly removed their masks, revealing Will and Chaste. Before she could speak, Will's hand covered her mouth. "Shh." He whispered it in her ear. "There are still guards on the grounds."

She complied, and he picked her up, so that she was cradled in his arms. Walking as a group to the back of the house, she felt his body against hers, and wondered why he'd taken this assignment, why he would end things but then choose... It was a challenge for her to be near him, to not rest her head on his shoulder as he carried her through the house. She knew her muscles were tense, knew he could sense it.

A small office room sat at the back, overlooking a beautiful forest. Like he'd done before, Mayne pulled a candlestick and the fireplace in the room gave way.

"I didn't think those actually existed." Will said softly, surprised.

"I knew about the ones in the council offices, when my dad was Chief." Chaste walked ahead of them. "He just said that it was a secret, so I didn't mention it to anyone."

"I understand." Arda stayed silent as they descended into the hidden pathway. They walked for a long time, coming out in the middle of the forest. "Here we go. We should be fine now, this far away from the city." Will set her down and untied her.

"Arda," he warned as he did so, "I couldn't tell you I was there, or the Chief would have caught on."

Her eyes narrowed, so he added, "if you attack me when I release you, I swear I'll tie you back up."

She didn't answer, her frustration clear in her eyes, which she rolled. When she was free, she rubbed her hands and turned to Mayne. "What are we doing in the woods?"

"The estate has been compromised. Thea and your avatar are already at the camp. We're going there tonight. We should make it by morning if we hurry."

"Camp?"

"It's a safe place, outside the city. It's existed for centuries, off the grid. No one, save a select group of people, know it's there, and the trees cover it from above. We'll be safe as we look over all the evidence and devise a final plan to not only remove him from office but force him to take responsibility for his actions. We also got about twenty pounds of stolen gold back for the people of the city. This is a good day."

"That gold was stolen?"

"Over time, yes, stored away and taken from the people. Heirlooms were melted down into bars that the rich could store away and hoard. We can't give people their history back, but gold is good currency, untraceable on the net."

"What do I do with this?" She showed them the red button.

Mayne chuckled. "You can hit it if you want, but it won't do anything."

"What?" She hit the button, and nothing happened. "Then why go through all that effort of giving it to me?"

Mayne knelt next to her. "Because, Arda, it kept you focused, kept you calm while chaos surrounded you. The truth was you didn't need it. We were there the whole time."

She nodded, upset at being deceived, but she knew they couldn't stay there, and now was not the time to process her emotions.

"Let's get going then."

Mayne turned and said, "follow me."

The trek through the woods was long and arduous. The noises out here were different from the city, and the last time she'd taken a stroll, they hadn't seemed welcoming. She had to calm herself, remind her fear that she was among friends. Or at least, she believed she was. Will was behind her, followed by Chaste trailing the back. They walked silently, quietly. Mayne knew exactly where they were going. She caught herself reaching for her knife several times, but of course, it wasn't on her. She felt exposed without it.

They stopped for a couple hours during the late night to rest their feet. No fire, just sitting in the dark, though Mayne said he could see. Arda could make out each one of them, and watching Will, her heart broke again. He wouldn't leave her side, and it was…unnerving her.

"I…have to…you know. Please don't follow me."

She walked away, far enough that she knew they couldn't hear, then lowered her pants and quickly relieved herself. When she stood and zipped her pants, a cracking branch alerted her. She'd told them not to follow. Grabbing a sharp branch, she walked toward the sound, praying it wasn't another wolf, or some of the guards realizing they'd left the compound. If they found the others, if they were dead…

She focused her thoughts, listening as she slowly moved through the forest. A dark shadow rounded the tree in front of her and she aimed, throwing the branch as she would a knife, hoping it would hit its mark.

A groan let her know she was successful, but when she rounded the tree, it was Will, leaning against the trunk, slowly pulling the branch out of his shoulder.

She sighed, exasperated with him. "What the… *Will?*"

Through gritted teeth, he said, "I was just making sure you were safe. I didn't…peek or anything."

She walked in front of him and helped him pull the branch the rest of the way out. "I could have…hurt you."

He laughed. "You know how to throw, I'll give you that."

She wanted to laugh, which made her angrier. "Will, what are you doing?"

He covered the wound with his hand. "What do you mean? Someone had to make sure nothing happened to you."

"I mean, all of this. Taking point on this job, carrying me, making sure you're so close to me I can't breathe…"

His shoulders slumped a little, and she knew he was beginning to understand. "Will, we decided to end our romantic attachment, but you're acting as if we are still…us. It's…difficult for me to move on when you're…close by." The lump in her throat stole her words, as her eyes began to burn.

He sighed. "I…it's difficult for me, too. Knowing you were being put in danger, especially after everything that happened…I couldn't… Every instinct I have is telling me to protect you, even if we aren't…Arda, I…"

He stepped forward, jarring the injury, then groaned loudly.

"Don't move, or you'll *hurt yourself…*" The last words were little more than a whisper, as her emotions swelled.

He gripped her around the waist with his good arm, drawing her toward him, and she let him. He touched his forehead to hers, as the moon moved enough to light his face.

She saw his eyes, watering, his face twisted in pain.

She took his head in her hands and said, "I can't stand that you're hurting because of me."

He smiled then, the smirk coming back to his face. She wondered why for a moment, then he said, "well, you're the one that threw the stake at me."

She narrowed her eyebrows, and he just laughed louder. "That's not what I meant, and you know it."

She stepped back, walking toward the camp, as he said, "you won't help me back?"

"Find your own way!"

They moved on soon afterward, but Arda wouldn't look at him, or step near him. As morning dawned, she saw a large fence getting closer as she stepped forward. The trees here were ancient and taller than some buildings in the city. They stretched so high. She didn't know trees could grow that tall. No wonder they couldn't see this camp from the air.

Reaching a gate, Mayne knocked rhythmically. The door opened and they stepped inside, quickly, then a quick thud made her jump as it closed. Will placed a hand at the small of her back to steady her on a reflex, but she withdrew quickly. He no longer got access to physical touch with her. As they walked forward, several red dots appeared on her chest. The camp was protected by men with guns.

They were approached by a large man, bulky and strong. "Mayne." They shook hands.

"Edon. How are you?"

"Taking care of my people." His voice was strange, lower and rougher than it should be.

"You run this Haven well."

"Yes, I do."

"Is Tyrus here?"

"Follow me." Turning away, they walked further into camp, which was a massive city of cabins and tents, lined with green foliage on the roofs. They did a great job of making these homes invisible. They were fairly far from the city and Arda wondered, why wasn't this touched by Omega Fire? Why was this camp spared? They'd always been told that the fire had burned everything until there was nothing but ash. Had they lied to her or was this place special, like the land of the Capital?

He led them to a central cabin, larger than the rest. Stepping outside, Tyrus came to greet them. Walking to Mayne, he asked, "were we successful?"

"Yes, we were."

"Good." Turning to her, he smiled, "I'm sorry for the confusion. Arda, you'll be staying here for a few days. The estate was compromised this morning. Thea is here too, somewhere. Are you okay?"

She nodded, suddenly remembering the horn. If there was anyone that would understand its significance, it would be Tyrus, the ancient yet unageing man with a plethora of contacts and secrets. "Can we talk somewhere privately?"

He seemed surprised but complied. They walked into the large cabin and sat down by the fire. "What is it, Arda?" His tone was soft, sympathetic, concerned.

She had so many questions, but she knew she needed to prioritize this. Without really choosing to do so, she reached down to her pant leg, pulling up her pants and exposing the horn.

Tyrus stood, backing away. "Is that…"

She untied it. "I don't know what it is, really. I can only guess. I think it grew a rose."

"Where did you get it?" She handed him the horn and he took it gladly.

"I don't think you'd believe me if I told you."

He looked at her then. "Arda, this is something very precious to a dear friend of mine. I'd like to know, if you'll tell me."

She told him her strange story, expecting him to laugh in her face. Instead, his eyes welled with tears, and he hugged her tightly. "You have no clue what a good thing you've done. Arda, we can get her back now. One of the five. This is the first step in getting them back!" Tears flowed from his eyes freely now, but she had no clue what he was talking about.

"Who are the Five?"

"I'll tell you, after this is all over. For now, I need to keep this safe." Walking to the center of the room, he opened the floor to reveal a vault. Using his handprint, he opened it, and placed the horn inside. "We'll keep this locked away until I find her and return her horn."

Chapter 17

Walking out of the cabin, Chaste and Will were waiting for her. "We're to show you where we'll be staying for the time being."

"We?" It came out more defensive than she would have liked.

"The four of us, Thea, Chaste, You and I are bunking in the same cabin. No one gets their own." He moped away, making her heart break and her anger rise.

"Chaste, Will can show me where to go. Why don't you go check on Thea? I haven't seen her since Shadow took me, and I'd like to know she's okay."

"Roger. I'll send her to you when I find her." He walked away happily, and she started after Will.

He walked straight into the cabin with his back to her, and she had no choice but to follow if she wanted to talk to him. Inside, he sat on the bottom right bunk, his head in his hands. Was he crying?

"Will?"

"Yes, Arda." He said it softly, as if he were afraid of her.

"If you didn't want to end us, then why did you?"

"Cause I'm an idiot. Cause I thought I was helping you. I thought that I wouldn't make it through this, and I…thought it would make your grief…easier, somehow."

"You're saying this is some twisted sense of sacrifice?"

"Yeah, I guess so. It seems… silly when I say it out loud."

She sat on the bed next to him, silently for a few

moments. "Back in the house, when I was locked in the bedroom…were you the one who disarmed me?"

"Yes. I didn't hurt you, did I?" He looked at her then, and his eyes were red, worried.

"No, it's just, I didn't get that training. My asthma is gone now. When this is over, if there's time, I was hoping you would help me learn to do that. I…need to be just as strong as all of you. Spy training in the city, was…woefully inefficient."

"You… want to learn how to fight?" His face changed, relaxed. That's what she wanted.

"This world isn't the one I grew up in. That world was full of peace, of selflessness. Everyone helped and everyone contributed. This world is madness. This world is death, destruction, and misdirection. The hidden coin is everywhere. How can I hope to survive it all if I can't fight?"

He took her hands in his, and said, "I will teach you, if you teach me to throw that well. But you have to know you are *already* surviving. You've grown so much this year, and I'm incredibly proud of the woman you've become. You may not be able to fight, in the traditional sense, but in this world, the only thing that reveals that coin, is knowledge, information. You fight with what you know, and you know secrets. It's in your blood."

"Because of my mom?"

"Not only that." He opened his mouth, shut it, thought, and then said, "sing me the song we used to sing in grammar school. The one about the Urchin Queen."

She struggled to remember the words for a moment, then she began to sing.

The pot was burning, charred as night,
The urchin queen came in to sight.
She rallied all the sheep to sleep and
Lions slumbered 'nay a peep.

Oh, walk, oh walk to shelter dear
The urchin queen has led you here
The trees will grow again so high
When urchin queen draws nigh.
When urchin queen draws nigh.

He smiled. "You always did have a nice alto voice."

"What does that have to do with me?"

"Your heritage, Arda. Your ancestor, the one raised by Dr. Jackson."

"Regina. Queen. I see."

"Some people think the last line is special. That it means the urchin queen will come again."

"And I'm her descendant. I get it, but isn't that a little silly? What am I supposed to do?"

He shrugged his shoulders. "I don't know, but the people that believe in it, to them, it's powerful."

"Doesn't seem very safe. Someone could take that, twist it."

"Or someone could use that, mold it, to liberate them." He gave her a strange look then, of admiration, and something else. It wasn't love or passion, or affection. Almost like wonder.

She nodded, making a decision, then she reached over to give his hand a squeeze. "Will?"

He was suddenly very still, as if he was unsure of her. "Yes, Arda?"

"We promised to tell each other everything. Please, no more bait, no more damsel in distress, no more lies, not for the sake of a mission, or for anything. Clue me in, and I'll do the same for you."

He placed his hand on top of hers and said, "This was…not my call, but I will do everything to keep you in the loop from now on, to the best of my ability."

"I appreciate that. And…whatever is…between us, we will try to sort out, as we go."

"Deal." He moved a strand of hair behind her ear. She looked at his now wrapped shoulder. "I'm sorry, about that."

He gave her that smirk again, and she readied herself for the retort…

"Guys?"

They turned to see Thea enter the tent. "Hey, you're alive." Thea ran to her and gave her a hug, pushing Will away in the process. He groaned, as the movement jarred his injured shoulder. "Arda, I was so worried."

"I was worried about you!"

"Oh, no! I was fine."

"I wasn't, but I am now."

"I want to show you the camp." Taking her friend's hand, the girls left the cabin. "It's great here. The air is so fresh. There's even a lake. It's got clear water. Great for swimming. I know when he's here, Tyrus takes a swim in the morning."

They passed rows of tents, makeshift cabins, old cabins, some being constructed for more people. Everyone was working, helping, some fishing in the lake, some running laps on the dirt track around it.

"What do you know about him?"

"I know he's older than he looks. He's a great leader, great soldier. He never seems to get injured. There's a story that someone accidentally stabbed him with a knife once, and they swear, the knife bent from his frame, didn't even break skin."

"That's not possible though, is it?"

"No, it's just a story they tell recruits to make them behave. Why do you ask?"

"I don't know. He's very smart, but sometimes he almost seems, crazy."

She stopped walking and turned to Arda. "I think maybe it's just because you haven't been where we've been. Out of all the soldiers here, I trust Tyrus more than I trust anyone else, even Chaste. That should say something, right?"

"Sorry if I offended you. You're right, I'm sure I'm just…seeing what I want to see." She felt awkward, and adjusted her sleeves, hiding her hands as much as possible.

"No problem, and Arda, you don't have to be sorry. We're friends. I'll always be here if you need to talk about anything. Now, let's take the official tour."

An hour later she knew where the kitchens, gardens, bathrooms and lake were. Other buildings were off limits, like the strategy room and the armory. You weren't allowed in someone's cabin unless you were invited, or they were there. You could always enter your own. You were expected to help every day, doing something you were good at, but every so often they would announce a day of rest. If helicopters came by, you were to take shelter in the nearest building until the "all clear" was sounded.

"Oh, and one more thing Arda. The Betas are real. They don't really come around here, but just in case, I wanted to let you know what to do."

"We don't kill them unless we have to. They're people, too. If you don't move, they can't see you. They don't hear very well either. They will attack you if you touch them, so the protocol is to freeze in place, wait for them to leave, then walk away slowly."

"They're real." Flashes of her nightmares returned to her.

"Very. You'll want to keep this on you in case you need it." She handed Arda a knife. She put it in her pocket, grateful for her friend's foresight. She missed her knives.

Sitting down on a rock, she said, "So, now that you know where everything is, I have to ask, how are things between you and Will?"

Arda sighed. "With everything going on, it's hard to talk, sort everything out. I think we're ok, for now."

"I told you he was nuts about you."

"I guess he is, if he risks his life for me when we aren't even dating."

"You two still aren't…back together?"

"Afraid I can't say that, no. We are…working on it, slowly."

"That's ok. I can still dream about a double ceremony."

She took Arda's arm, linking it with hers, and the girls sat talking about their futures Every girl had some idea of the bonding ceremony she wanted, but Arda was one of the few that didn't plan it down to the last detail. It was an inevitability, like a job or a family. You just knew it was going to happen. She didn't see how someone could get that excited about anything.

But Thea obviously was. Arda almost wanted to say yes to the double ceremony, just so she wouldn't have to plan anything. Thea would probably even pick a dress for her, if she asked. And if it was with Will…

That thought crept up without her wanting it too. She had to remember to be sensible. She was not paired with him yet. She had no business thinking about a bonding ceremony. No business dreaming of flowers or songs or pretty dresses. For all they knew, she wouldn't even get him as a choice. She'd be stuck with someone else. Someone that didn't know her, didn't care.

Her eyes welled with tears, without her wanting them to. "Oh, Arda, what is it?"

"Nothing, I'm just being dramatic over something that likely won't happen."

"You can tell me. We're friends."

"What… happens if they don't pair you with Chaste?"

"Well, they have to."

"No, no they don't."

Thea thought about that for a second, and tears welled in her eyes too. "Oh, no! What if you're right and we don't end up with them."

Now they were both crying, and naturally, Tyrus picked that time to approach them. "Uh, ladies?"

"What?" It was said in unison.

"Uhm," he backed away from the two, unsure of himself. "We are ready for dinner, if you'd like to eat."

Drying their tears, Arda said, "thank you."

The two friends stood and left, arm in arm, sniffling together as Tyrus watched, bewildered, following them carefully at a distance.

Dinner was simple, chicken and rice. She ate gladly. She looked around, seeing Mayne was no longer among them. "Did Mayne leave?" She turned to Tyrus.

"Yes, he left to go back to his people. He'll return in a few days so we can plan how we're going to fix this."

"What are we doing in the meantime?"

"Maintaining the camp."

"Anything else?"

He looked at her, his eyes narrowing thoughtfully. "*you* aren't doing anything else for the next two days. Relax. You need it."

While that didn't help her feel relaxed, he was telling the truth. The past two weeks had drained her of all her energy. She had three days left. Three days before the soldiers were expected to be placed. Whatever was happening, whatever they decided, if they wanted to have a future, they had to finish all of this nonsense by then.

After Dinner, as the sun set, they entered their cabins for the night. Thea and Arda would sleep on one side, and the two boys would sleep on the other. A sheet came down, separating the tent for the night. At least they had a little privacy. Getting into her bunk on the bottom, Arda sighed, content, the first time in ages.

She had no clue how much weight she'd put on her shoulders until it was lifted off. She was surrounded by armed guards, in the middle of a forest, outside the only city she'd ever known, and somehow, she had found peace here. For the first time since they were called to war, she felt as if she wasn't truly alone. Here, she was just another person. She could belong here. They could form memories here.

The meadow came back into view. *Oh, wonderful. The flowers are so big here.* Walking down the hill, she searched for the group of women, but only one woman stood. Walking up to the human Joy, she picked a rose on the way, sniffing its beautiful fragrance.

"I have your horn."

Joy turned and smiled. "I know. You gave it to Tyrus like I knew you would."

"Any other cryptic messages you want me to send?"

"No, Arda, I just wanted to let you know something."

"What is it, Joy?"

"You are very special. But you aren't the Urchin Queen."

"I could be. You don't know." She was annoyed.

Joy just smiled. "I'm just saying, people are going to believe you are, and eventually, those people will be wrong. You are no god but are a very special girl. Keep your head on your shoulders. Stay grounded and listen to your friends. I'll see you soon."

The image faded away. It was still late. The moon was high in the night sky, stars glowing brightly. You couldn't see all this in the city. She heard movement next to her, and Will whispering to her. "Arda? Are you awake?"

"Yes."

"I can't sleep."

"Why not?"

"Knowing you're this close to me, it's just...challenging."

She thought about that for a second. "Should I ask to be assigned to a different cabin?"

The sheet was pulled away, and he sat beside her on her bed. "Don't do that to me."

She smiled. "Why not?"

"It's the least you owe me, considering my injury."

"Oh, I see. I *owe* you."

He chuckled. "No, Arda, that isn't quite the reason."

"I...I know the reason, but...we..." She sighed, not sure how to say it.

He knelt on the floor next to her, placing an arm over her waist. "You know, sometimes you...make noises. In your sleep. Sometimes, they sound like crying. I...want to comfort you, and it's difficult, being so close, but unable to."

"Oh," Arda said. "I see."

"Do you want me to go back to my bunk?"

"No, I'm up now. We can talk."

"About us?"

She sighed. "I don't know what to do or where to go with that."

He nodded. "We...both care about each other. That we agree on, right?"

"Yes, definitely."

"Then, maybe the label isn't as important as we think, at least, not until we are placed?"

"I guess not." He wasn't wrong. Why was she putting so much pressure on herself? Together, not together... the world was burning around them.

He moved his arm, placing it against hers, and began to run circles over the back of her palm with his fingertips. The light, gentle touch created goosebumps on her skin, in spite of the warm covers. She shivered from the sensation.

"Are you cold? Do you need more blankets?"

The concern in his voice melted her heart. "Blankets, no, but perhaps, some of you, next to me?"

He smiled as she wrapped her arms around him. He eased her over, groaning a little in pain. "Are you okay?"

He smiled, his face inches above hers. "Arda...I've never been better."

He dipped his head, and she could feel him smile through the kiss. She smiled back as his body relaxed onto hers. His warmth spread all over, and she moaned softly feeling his body against hers. She gripped the muscles of his good arm, tracing his biceps, triceps, then over his shoulder and his back.

He wiped her hair away from her face, then began to kiss

her eyelids, then her forehead, moving downward to her cheeks, her mouth, her chin. She gripped his good shoulder tightly, her nails digging in, just a little.

He hissed in a breath, but didn't stop, moving from her cheek to her earlobe, nipping lightly at it before kissing her racing pulse. She moaned out loud, a bit too into it.

"Aw, guys, come on. Other people trying to sleep here." Thea said it from the top bunk.

He backed off, but she felt the tension it took for him to do so. For a few more moments, they simply snuggled, feeling each other's warmth and closeness. She kicked him out, and when she heard him snoring, she drifted off, a smile still on her face.

Two days later…

Why had her friends left the cabin without waking her? She readied herself for the day and left, searching for them. Finding a large group surrounding the strategy tent, she approached, only to be stopped by guards.

"Sorry, but we've been given orders to keep you from the tent."

"Why?"

"I don't know Miss."

"I understand." She rolled her eyes as she walked away, annoyed that this was happening, again.

There were other ways to listen in. Walking casually around the area, she meandered to the side of the forest, near the back entrance to the wall. As she walked along it, a small gap lay between the building and the wall, big enough for her to fit through. Squeezing in, she found a small hole in the wood that allowed her to listen to the conversation inside, without being detected.

"The plan, now that the video is in place, requires two teams. I'm leading team A, Mayne will lead team B. Your assignments are in your packet, which I expect you to delete when memorized."

"I will lead team B to the security site. There we will use stealth and non-lethal force to enter their central hub. There, we can deploy the video, as a last resort. We'll have to hold the position until team A has finished their mission."

"Team A will infiltrate the estate of the Chief. Non-lethal force as well, but we have to be able to get to the Chief before team B is overwhelmed. In the event you must use lethal force, keep casualties to a minimum. We don't want to give him any leverage to use against us."

"When we have the confirmation that the Chief has agreed, team B will connect to the recording device team A will have in place. The Chief will be broadcast to the whole District on a one-minute delay. We will have the ability to cut the feed off if he tries anything. Hopefully, this will be solved tonight, and tomorrow, you will be able to go back to your lives as honorable men and women."

"It goes without saying that anyone that isn't in this room isn't to have access to this information."

"She isn't going to like that." Will spoke up.

"No, no she's not, but this is a military operation. We don't need her."

Arda had heard enough. The person that kidnapped her, wanted her killed, they were taking him out. And she wouldn't be there to see it? Not on her life. She'd been taught to negotiate as part of her training, and her ability to read people was surpassed by no one. They didn't *need* her? They wouldn't be able to pull this off *without* her.

Standing, she walked away, plotting the best course of action that would allow her the least resistance. She'd be in on this. That bastard that tried to kill her would stare her in the eye as she took everything from him, and she'd smile as he fell.

She watched the operation unfold from a distance, as vehicles were packed with the equipment they would need. She watched the soldiers test their equipment, watched as her friends readied their gear. When that was done, they approached her.

"Hey, Arda." Thea had her hands in her back pockets. She didn't know what to do with them.

"Hey, Thea. Big day."

"Yeah, I guess."

"What are you all up to?"

"We can't really talk about it. I take it you guys slept ok, last night, after?"

"I slept well, thank you for asking." She was proud that she didn't blush. She wouldn't let Thea change the subject.

Will sat next to her on the large log. "Sorry we can't include you." He put an arm around her. One look at his face told her he was, that he would tell her, if she pushed. They'd promised each other, but she also knew other people weren't included in that promise. She didn't want his loyalty tested, right now. Besides, she had what she needed, from the tent.

She smiled at him. "I understand." She smiled, softly touching his arm. It was almost completely healed.

"Look," Chaste sat on the other side of her. "We have this one night that we have to act, and then hopefully everything will be solved. We can all go home tomorrow, and really start our lives again. Get back to normal."

She kept her face blank, but she wondered if even a part of him believed that things would be normal, ever again. "That sounds like a great plan. I don't want you to worry about me. You focus on what you need to do to get this done." That part was at least true. If they worried about her, she wouldn't be able to do what she needed to do.

"You're really not mad?" Thea locked eyes with her.

"I'm really not mad." She was seething inside, but not at them, at Tyrus, for leaving her out. Still, they didn't need to know, so she kept her face even. She wasn't a soldier, but she was a damn good agent.

Will kissed her forehead. The other sighed with relief. "That's my girl. Now let's go get some food. I'm starving."

Arda smiled at them. She let Will take her hand and guide her to the kitchen. No need for them to suspect anything. They'd only try to stop her, and there was no way she was letting anything stop her. This time, she'd be an asset. She'd be the spy.

Tyrus watched her carefully during the day, waiting for her to show some sign that she was upset or plotting. She knew what he was doing. He was an intelligent man that had to know she was plotting. Still, she relaxed, giving away nothing. Let him wonder. He wasn't in her head, he couldn't know.

A few hours later, they started to prepare for the trip to the city. As she watched, she could tell she had a shadow, someone following her. A guard had been placed on her to watch her. Great, one more thing she needed to get around. Confident, she assessed everything, using every advantage she could think of until the plan came firmly into view.

The guard was easy. She'd take out a couple boards from her cabin. While he watched the door, she'd slip away underneath. She'd have to have perfect timing, though. She'd do it while everyone was gearing up at dusk.

One of the vehicles stood close to the cabin. This was her ride. She would have five minutes to get in the vehicle and hide. The benches in the back had hidden compartments. She could lay down in one of these with a blanket over her, and in the dark, no one would be the wiser.

Once the hard trip was over, she would wait for them to clear the area, and follow behind. They'd station guards at each point, so she would have to avoid being seen. They also had night vision goggles, which meant she'd have to be invisible. This was easy. She could use the vents which ran through every estate. The entrance was always the same, as each had the same layout. She would use the vent to bypass the troops and make her way through them to the office at the back of the first floor, where the official negotiation would take place.

It was low tech, but it would work. She just had to bide her time, patiently, and be very, very careful. She walked to her cabin, ready to start prepping for her operation.

Will found her an hour later, sitting in the cabin, shuffling cards. She smiled at him. He sat down next to her, taking the cards from her hand.

"I need to talk to you."

"No, you don't."

He stopped, confused. "We agreed."

She smiled, wide. "Will, you promised to tell me everything, yes. But...this op isn't under your direction, is it?"

"No. It isn't, but I don't want to hurt you, again."

She saw the worry on his face, knew she had to ease it, for them both to do their jobs. "I'm ok staying back. Sitting this one out. I'm...tired. From everything. And if I'm safe here, you can do your job. You can be careful, without worrying about me, and come back in one piece. I'm ok."

"Tyrus seems to think you're...plotting."

"Tyrus is a smart man, but honestly, I don't know how I could with all these guards around."

"That's what I said, but he was adamant that I come talk to you before dinner."

"Well, you have. I hate that you're doing this without me, but I understand. You don't need me."

"I need you, Arda," his eyes seared into hers, "just, not for this operation."

She blushed at that. "Well, you don't have to worry. I'll just be here, shuffling cards."

"You promise?"

She looked at him, took both of his hands in hers, and lied. "I promise." She silently prayed he would understand and forgive her as the op unfolded, after all, she had promised him as well.

He smiled. "There's something else I'd like to talk about."

"Which is?"

"Arda, if I don't come back, if something happens tonight and everything goes wrong, I need you to be brave, and trust the people here to take care of you."

"You're talking about Edon."

"And Mayne."

"Okay. Are you planning on dying tonight?"

He laughed. "No, no I plan on doing whatever I can to come back alive for you."

"Then let's hope for the best." She ran a hand through his short, fuzzy hair. "I miss the long hair."

"Me too. I don't know if I'll grow it out again, though. I got used to the buzz cut. Less work."

"You look great either way."

He turned and hugged her, rubbing her back as he'd done at the dance. She relaxed into him, letting his lips meet hers. "Arda," he murmured softly, "if you are planning something, and

I find out, I swear I'll tie you up to keep you from following me."

"I'm not," she whispered back. She kissed him deeply, letting her admiration of him reach the surface. "I only want you to come back to me alive."

He stood, walking out without another word. Convinced that she'd convinced him, she sat on the floor, working on loosening the second board with a hammer she'd hidden days ago. No way was she sitting this one out. She wasn't some helpless asthmatic girl. She was a female agent, and she'd help where she could.

Dusk began to approach, and she walked out of her cabin, satisfied that she'd loosened enough boards to complete her first step. Walking into the kitchen, she sat down for dinner. Taking a plate of food, Mayne, Tyrus and Edon sat around her. *Ah, the intimidation approach.* She'd studied it. Because she knew what it was, she could remain calm.

"Arda, how is your day going?"

"Better than yours, I hear."

Tyrus laughed. "Well, we do what we have to, right?"

"Right." She ripped into a piece of bread, a bit viciously, letting them see a bit of anger, which would be expected.

"I know you've got something up your sleeve, Arda."

"I tried, honestly, to think of something, some way to be involved. I did."

"And?"

"And I just don't know how I would have made it work."

Mayne stepped in. "Arda, how do you feel about staying here?"

"Crappy, but I'll live."

"Her heartrate is stable. She isn't lying." Edon said this. If Arda couldn't control her heartbeat, a basic skill they'd taught her, she wouldn't be very good at her job. She carefully avoided letting her mouth twitch in a smile.

"Of course, I'm not. You think I'm lying?" This was the perfect time for her to get angry, to storm away. "What do I have to do to convince you that I'm okay with this? Yes, it hurts that I'm being left out, *ah-gain*, but there's nothing I can do, so why don't the three of you just leave me the hell alone!"

She stood, clenching her jaw and her fists, and walked away. They didn't follow her. Storming straight to her cabin, she even slammed the door for good measure. No one would bug her, having too much to do. They'd give her space to calm down. Arranging the pillows to look like she was sleeping, she crawled under her bed and under the cabin. The blanket she'd stored was there, black as night. Crawling to the back, she rolled out from under the cabin and into the shadow of the trees.

This was her five minutes. Placing the blanket around her shoulders, she ran softly to the vehicle. The driver was inside it, watching, waiting for the operation to start. She kneeled, careful to displace her weight evenly. She was up and under the bench in a smooth move. The driver got out, looking for a disturbance, but she was already in position. He didn't see her.

She waited there, breathing evenly while everyone loaded into the vehicles. The weight on the bench made it impossible for her to move, but she could breathe, carefully. She could hear the soldiers talk as they got ready.

"I still feel bad." That was Thea. "You sure we shouldn't say goodbye?"

"She was pretty angry. Let's just focus on our work and leave her be." Chaste, ever the sensible one.

"We just reached an equilibrium again. I had to lie once, but it almost destroyed her. I don't want to be that person."

"I've known her all my life, brother," Chaste said, comforting him. "Give her space. Her head will prevail over her emotions, but she feels deeply. She needs that time alone to process."

She felt a twinge of guilt at his words, but she wasn't the first person in this group to lie through her teeth. If she forgave him, hopefully he could forgive her. The car started, and the operation was underway. From then on, the troops were silent. They filed in, and she ended up staring at combat boots. She wondered which was Will, if he was seated near her.

She saw the lights of the wall, even under here, knew they were approaching the city. Tyrus must have made an arrangement with someone to look the other way while the trucks came through. When the last truck was inside, they turned left, and she knew this was the way to Zone 4. Another wall separated that Zone from the others.

The sound of the gate shutting let her know they were through. Suddenly, the trucks were surrounded by lights, turning on all at once. She could see it blinding through the holes in the blanket, and she lay very still, barely breathing. A lot of shouting, asking them to put their hands up, to surrender.

Tyrus shouted, "Stand down!"

She didn't think this was part of the plan. Lying still, she waited as she heard them being taken away. She waited as the soldiers searched each vehicle, holding her breath. Another pair of combat boots stepped up, and she watched as they walked forward, then back. Though they looked under some of the benches, they must have gotten annoyed, and gave up before finding her. She was very lucky in that. When they had left, when the lights had turned off, when the night was silent again, she scooted out and peeked through the holes in the canvas.

She couldn't use the vents because they hadn't eliminated the guards that secured the estate's perimeter. Worse, team B would be waiting on them to finish. If they questioned the soldiers, someone might talk, and then she'd be alone. No, she had to finish this, do the work of all the soldiers and somehow convince him to record himself stepping down.

She waited for a break in the guard rotation, and silently rolled out, walking quickly to an alleyway, where she softly opened a manhole cover. If she was right, there was a hidden entrance in the sewers. As soon as she was in, she hit the button and it closed soundlessly.

She walked down, turning right, looking for passages heading upward. Finding one, she knew it would lead to his office, where she prayed there was a lever, something, to get into the office so she could finish this. She'd been right about one thing. They did need her. Confident she had made the right decision, she began to hear voices. This was her stop. Just ahead would lie the office of the Chief, traitor of the people, and it was up to her to bring him sweet justice.

Chapter 18

Through a small hole in the moving wall, she could see inside the room. She listened in, biding her time. She couldn't open the lever until the Chief moved far enough away.

"Tyrus, we meet again. I was afraid you'd try something like this. When will you learn your place, old man?"

Tyrus was on the floor, kneeling, while two guards held him in place. His face looked beaten. The camera they were supposed to use lay on the desk, the Chief out of view. She guessed he was in the chair, watching while someone loyal did his dirty work.

"Your time is up, Chief." His voice was lower than normal, almost animalistic.

He laughed. "You must have me confused. Your men are locked away in my cellar, you're alone. I won this time."

"Do you really think I didn't have a back-up plan?"

"What are you talking about?" He sounded concerned.

"We have another team infiltrating the compound at this second. Your men are already being taken out. Check your radios."

They did, and static greeted him back. "Go see what's happening." One of the two guards left. One down, one to go.

A shout from the hall had the Chief reaching into his drawer, grabbing a gun. "Don't move, Tyrus."

"You can't win this." Tyrus's breathing was labored from the beating.

"It doesn't matter. If one of yours comes through the door, I shoot you and they lose a leader. If one of mine comes through, I get to kill you knowing that none of them are left.

Either way, old man, we'll finally find out if you're immortal like the stories."

Tyrus looked directly at the hole in the wall and winked. He *was* smart. Fumbling for the lever, she found it, and hit it, at the same time, readying her knife.

The chief jumped from the sound of the fireplace moving, an old, creaky noise that had his gun firing upward, missing Arda. While his back was turned, Tyrus stood to attack, the guard behind him aiming his weapon. Arda released the knife from her grip more on instinct, watching in slow motion as it connected with the soldier near his throat. He dropped instantly, leaving only the three of them.

Tyrus grabbed the Chief, knocking the gun out of his hand and across the floor. It landed at her feet as the soldier fell and Arda grabbed the gun, securing it as Tyrus restrained the Chief.

Will and Chaste entered the room. "It's secure." He placed a black box on the desk. They saw her, tilting their heads. Tyrus hadn't told them. She smiled, waved, as they filled in, Will standing to her right, Chaste helping Tyrus.

They shoved the man into the office chair, as he snarled at them both. Tyrus held his hand out for the gun Arda was holding. She handed it over gladly. She hadn't been trained to shoot, yet.

She stepped back, and felt Will lean in, whispering, "couldn't stay put, could you."

She smiled. "Tyrus knew I would be here."

He gave her a look but was silent. She would make it up to him when this was over. Now the negotiation would begin. The door was locked behind them, and the place was secure.

"Are the men free?"

"Yes. Combing the compound for any other guards as

we speak."

"Excellent." Tyrus sat down in the chair opposite the Chief. "Now we get to sit and talk. Will and Chaste, guard the door. Arda, would you take the camera, please?"

"Like mother like daughter." He muttered it under his breath. She wanted to tell him off, but she knew better than to engage. He was just stalling for time. She stood behind Tyrus, ready to record.

"Now, we are going to accomplish two objectives with this negotiation. How we do that is up to you. One, you will be stepping down as Chief."

He laughed. "Are you insane?"

"No, I'm thinking clearly. Two, you will call off the Dark Riders, tell them to leave our agents and our soldiers alone."

"And why would I do that?"

"You can make a video, here and now, that will be broadcast to the entire District, and we spare your life. You take your possessions that are most valuable, and you get to leave for District 2. We have an agent, in the helicopter right now, waiting to take you to your new life." Was that what her mother was doing?

"And if I refuse, you, what, kill me?"

Tyrus smiled, but it was cold. "I think I can do better than that." He reached for the black box, facing it toward the Chief and opening it slowly. Inside was a large syringe filled with orange liquid. It moved, particles constantly in motion.

"Are you out of your mind? It's illegal to use that on anyone."

"And what do you call it when *you* allow *your* scientists to use it on the people you pull from Zone 5 and the Fringe?"

Next to her, she felt Will's breathing change, growing harsh, rapid. She wondered if anyone he knew personally had been a victim of this.

He looked at the liquid, the fear in his face genuine. "I'll tell everyone the truth the moment you let me go."

"Oh, no you won't. See, I'll release you to the sewer to let them deal with you. Have you ever been deprived of food? Tortured, just for your body to heal so quickly that they can do it again a day later? You want to go through that? Or do you want to take your wife and son, leave the district and start over? Your choice."

"No sane person would do this." His voice broke. "Fine, I'll film the stupid video." His eye twitched, his head jerking to the side.

"He's lying. He's not convinced yet." He glared at her as she examined her knife.

"My agent thinks you're full of it."

Anger shone in his face. "I won't destroy my legacy, not even in death."

"So be it." He motioned to the others. "Hold him down." He said it without any emotion, as if it were as natural and mundane as talking about the weather.

As he turned away, the Chief screaming for help, he gave Arda a small smile. Seeing what he wanted her to do, she placed the camera down and kneeled in front of the Chief.

"Please, please choose to live. He'll do it. You don't know what he's capable of, but I do. I was there. In the compound. Please, I…" She teared up. "I don't want anyone to die here."

"I need one minute to prep the delivery system. Hold him still. Arda, back away."

She stayed, even as Chaste gripped her arm. "Please, I'm the only one on your side here. I am, but you have to give him something so he doesn't inject you. Please, please, do the video."

She shook, visibly fearful. That did the trick.

"Fine, I'll do it. I'll do it!" He shouted it, and his body language supported his words.

"I suppose we still can…" Tyrus motioned to Arda to start recording. She did so, and the Chief made his final address to the public.

"To the Citizens of District One, I stand before you a troubled man. The trials of leadership are terrifying, and I am afraid I have failed you. Failed to maintain the levels of honesty and compassion needed to run this office with grace. I am stepping down as Chief. May the election bring a new, brighter tomorrow."

Tyrus signaled her to cut the recording, and she did so. "Take him to the car. Get him to Project R.E.D.D. Faith will meet you there."

Will and Chaste left, leaving Arda and Tyrus alone. She sat, breathing for what seemed like the first time since the evening started. Tyrus rubbed her shoulders. "Relax, kid. You did good."

"You knew I was in the truck?"

"Your mother pulled the same stunt in a different operation when she was your age. The Chief was right about that. Like mother, like daughter. The Primes have always been rebels."

"You knew I would go through the sewer?"

"I didn't know, but I was really hoping. It was either the sewer or the vents, and…"

"With the guards, it made the sewer the easier choice."

"I counted on you to do what your blood told you to. And you did. Now, how about as we leave, you sit in the front of the vehicle?"

"My mother was in on this?"

"How do you think we got the security codes for the

network? Mayne's team is great, but they don't have access to those. Your mother called in some favors, and there are a lot of high-ranking individuals that owe Blind Faith a favor."

"Blind Faith?"

"Her nickname. The agents she grew up with, the Director, it's their pet name for her. Something about being able to throw a knife blindfolded. I don't know, I wasn't there. Maybe she'll tell you about it if you ask once this is all over."

"Do you think we'll be safe now?"

"I think that for the time being, the Dark Riders are a force we don't have to reckon with. We can go back to living like we did before this all started, and we can make life better for the people of this district, instead of worse."

"What was in the vial?"

"Something awful. Something that would give you nightmares. The vial is liquid boogeyman."

"Tyrus?"

"Yes, Arda?"

"How old are you?"

He laughed. "Older than I look."

"That's not an answer..."

"Maybe one day you'll be ready for the whole story, Arda, but today is not that day. Today, you get to sleep, knowing we made a difference, knowing that we did something for the people they couldn't do for themselves. Today is your day. What are you going to do with it?"

"I'm going on a date."

"Really?"

"Hey, I owe Will, after lying to him."

"Sounds like a plan."

"One more question, Tyrus..." This made her nervous.

"Yes?"

"The Director."

"What about him?"

She thought of his eyes, grey and cold. She thought of his hair, its color and structure. She thought of the way she'd seen him twist his fingers when he was nervous. She had to know.

"Is…Is the Director my father?"

"Stead's your father."

"No, I mean my biological father."

Tyrus took her hand, gently placing her hair behind her ear. Leaning in, he softly whispered into her ear…

Arda walked out of the estate. Will was waiting for her. "Hey." She said it quietly, unsure if he was angry with her or not.

He turned from his conversation with Chaste and punched her arm, gently. "Hey. You surprised me tonight."

"I surprised myself, I think."

"Did you and Tyrus plan this?"

She looked at the older man. "I guess you could say that."

"Well, bravo. You had perfect timing tonight."

"I did, didn't I?"

He laughed, taking her hand. "Arda?"

"Will?"

"I forgive you." The playful look on his face told her he was half joking.

"For *what?*" She felt the edges of her lips pulling upward.

"Lying." He winked.

"Good. I didn't like doing it."

He laughed again. "You aren't even going to apologize?"

"For doing the right thing? No. I won't."

He pulled her close and kissed her. "Then I won't

apologize for kissing you in public."

Tyrus shouted for the soldiers to load up. She would be in the last car. The cushion was a relief after the bed of the truck. Looking out the window, she was smiling as they drove back, in reverse this time, so the lead was the last to leave.

They left the city smoothly, everyone inside, watching the video repeat itself. She felt the weight of the world leave her shoulders. Looking up at the night sky, she saw a star, millions of miles away. Its light twinkled at her. She reached up to touch it, knowing how far away it was.

The forest surrounded them, the other cars far ahead. Suddenly, a tree fell in their path. The vehicle stopped, and Tyrus turned to her. "Stay here. Don't move. This time I mean it."

She waited, as they exited the vehicle, searched the forest. She waited as the shuffling sounded, as the other cars called to them. She waited as two men came back to the truck. "Is everything-"

That's as far as she got, before a cloth with a foul-smelling odor was placed over her mouth. Almost instantly, she was gone.

Time was hard to discern here, in the dark, chained to a damp, cold wall. She was in someone's cellar, or maybe underground. Standing, she couldn't move more than two feet in either direction. The hours passed, and finding no way out, she rested, retaining her strength for the unknown that lay ahead. The damp sunk into her bones, made her body shake from the chill. Her stomach was rumbling, and she worried she would starve to death, down here, alone and forgotten.

The silence was deafening. Each second lasted an eternity, and she focused on her breathing. Just as she felt herself beginning to go mad, footsteps in the hall returned her sanity. The door opened and a woman stood before her.

"Well, well." She walked inside, shutting the door behind her. "You're the special girl he's keeping to himself, huh?"

"I don't know-" A slap to her face had her biting her tongue.

"Shut up, just *shut up*. You don't speak to *me*. You're food." She grabbed Arda by the hair and pulled, a shout of pain leaving her throat before she could stop herself. "You're just a *donor*."

Well, thanks to this crazy woman, Arda knew where she was now. "Marci?"

The girl stepped back. "You…you know my name?"

There you go. "Of course, I do. Mayne talks about you all the time." She grabbed on to the chains, hoping she'd get a chance to use them.

"He…he talks about me? Really?" The woman was gone, replaced by a little girl. She jumped up and down, clapping her hands. "What does he say?"

Crap. "He says that you're beautiful."

"Yes, yes, I know that, but what else does he say?"

"He says…your eyes."

"My eyes what?!" She stomped her foot impatiently.

"He says your eyes are like deep pools of…water…to your soul."

She giggled. Turning in a circle, she spun until she was dizzy. Walking closer, she said, "what else did he say?"

She leaned in close to Marci and whispered, "that you're an idiot."

She pounced, grabbing the woman by the throat with the chains. Unfortunately, Arda didn't plan on the crazy woman having super-fast reflexes. In a matter of seconds, she'd been flipped over Marci's shoulder and was in pain, lying flat on the ground, the air knocked out of her lungs.

The woman sat on top of her, crushing her chest. "What a foolish donor. Don't you know you're all just meat to us?" She grabbed one of Arda's hands and placed her mouth at her wrist. Looking back, her eyes began to glow, yellow instead of Mayne's blue, but the calm feeling didn't come. "Oh, don't worry, donor. It will only hurt…so, *so much.*"

She bit down, drawing blood. Arda screamed in pain, as it raced up her arm and into her neck. The woman began to drink, and the world swam in front of her. When the blackness came for her again, she was grateful for its cold embrace.

She woke sometime later, her head aching, her lips parched. Was she even alive? If she was dead, you'd think she'd feel better than this. She must still be alive.

Sitting up, the dizzy feeling returned, the room spinning. Probably from a lack of blood. Feeling her wrist, she touched where the woman had bitten her. She didn't think anyone really did that. Probing it gently, she winced in pain.

She let her mind drift, thinking over the events of the last few weeks. If anyone had told her she would end up in a dark dungeon, clinging to life as vampire food, she'd have laughed in their face. Why was she there? Was it Mayne who'd taken her, or one of his people? Who the hell let Marci in there to drain her blood?

She thought of the trees, the forest, and it calmed her. In her mind, she was back in the cabin with Will, laughing and embracing as they had that one night. She saw his face, held on to it in her mind, as long as the happiness would hold. Tears slipped from her eyes, unwanted. She didn't even know if she was going to see him again, and that made her heart ache, made her chest contort in pain. Laying down, she began to cry softly, so softly so no one would hear, so no one would feed on her again.

She awoke suddenly, hours later, to the sound of footsteps coming down the hall. Fearing it was Marci, she lay down, feigning sleep. She kept praying for the guards to pass by her, not to open her door, not to make her go through that again. She had no clue how long she'd been in the dark, but it had felt like days. Her stomach was in so much pain from lack of food. Softly whispering, she repeated over and over, "*don't let them pick me.*"

Her prayers would go unanswered, however. The door to her room opened, and two guards stepped in. Remaining limp from lack of energy, with slow even breath, she allowed them to undo her bindings and carry her out the door. She wasn't sure where they were taking her, but she only hoped it would be better than the dark, better than the cold.

As they exited the dungeon, she heard wailing and howls from other prisoners, asking for their death, or the occasional brave soul asking to be released, demanding to know why they were there. The whole time, Arda remained passive, using her ears instead of her eyes to envision what lay past the dark.

They stopped at a door and one of the guards knocked. A moment later, someone opened the door, and they stepped through. Turning left, they continued down a hallway, lit by candlelight. Even with her eyes closed, the light stung her.

The two guards began to climb up a series of stairs. She didn't dare open her eyes, but she did make a mental map of how many steps they'd taken, in case she needed it later. Reaching the next floor, they headed to the right and walked down the hallway. After fifty steps, they stopped at a door, and one guard said, "this is the one."

Opening the door, they set her on the bed, placing her head on the pillow. "Careful. She's someone's pet."

"I am being *very* careful." The guard sniffed her hair, and she wanted to vomit, but she stopped herself.

"No playing around. Come on. We've got better things to do than babysit."

The two guards left, and a lock clicked into place. It was only then that Arda opened her eyes. The chains were gone. She sat up and looked over her new cell. The bed was made of wood, four poles stretching up to the ceiling. Curtains hung down the sides of the bed, shielding her from the rest of the room. Who put curtains on a bed?

Her feet touched the rug underneath, and she slowly tried to stand. She was weak from blood loss, and her stomach rolled. Walking away from the bed, she found a chair nearby and sat down, panting heavily. This would be harder than she thought.

A few moments passed, and she managed to get around the room enough to map it. The bed was in the center of the large space, with dressers full of beautiful clothes. A fireplace stood in the back corner, grey stone and real wood. No windows in the room. A full-length mirror showed her frail bones, light skin, almost grey from lack of food and blood loss. She had lost weight. At the front of the room was a door to a small bathroom, with a tub and shower and a toilet. They were old-fashioned, working on water instead of air.

Unable to do anything else, she opened the drawers, looking for something to wear. Her clothes were soiled, stained with dirt and blood. Pulling out a dress that looked like it was made for some society five hundred years old, she decided it would do. At least it was purple and pink.

Taking off her clothes was difficult. All her strength was gone, taken from her by Marci who drained her blood. Her muscles ached when she used them, weak from hunger, sore from working so hard on so little.

With her clothes off, she avoided the mirror. She knew she must look like a skeleton, and she didn't want to see herself that way. She was depressed enough. Placing the dress over her head, she allowed it to fall, covering her bones and restoring some warmth to her body. Although she'd picked something that looked like her size, it was still too big for her. Tying the bodice together, she tightened it as much as she could, and the dress fit snugly against her frame.

Turning, she glanced in the mirror, and thought, even with the malnutrition, that she looked pretty and feminine in this dress. Something about it made her feel soft. They had no patterns like this in the city. Even her dress for the dance social hadn't been nearly as lovely. Turning, she looked at herself from every angle.

A knock on the door froze her. She walked back toward the fireplace and her breath quickened. After a moment, the door was unlocked and opened slowly to reveal a round woman, old and weathered, who had a tray of food in her hands. "This is for you." Her accent was strange, one that Arda had never heard before, but it was songlike.

"What is it?"

"Food. Do you wish to eat or starve? I will pick it up in one hour. If you try to use knife on me, I will not bring you anymore. Understand." Arda nodded, and the woman left, locking the door behind her.

Arda looked at the food, sitting on the tray. There was bread, warm bread, freshly churned butter, mixed fruit in a bowl, chicken, cheese and even some chocolate cake. A full pitcher of water and a glass with ice were awaiting her.

Arda smelled the bread, grabbed a chunk and spread butter on it, watching it melt. Placing it to her lips, she bit down, the first taste of food in ages, and it was so, so delicious. She ate quickly, washing it down with the fresh water.

When the woman came back an hour later, she noted the clean tray and turned to her. "That's a girl after my own heart. You enjoyed my cooking?"

"Oh, yes, very much."

The old woman smiled. "Good. Good. I will bring you more in the morning. You may use the shower, then you should sleep. Your master will want to see you soon."

Arda nodded, and the woman shut the door. Walking into the bathroom, she fumbled with the knobs on the shower until she found a way to get the hot water to flow. Why would anyone want to have to solve a puzzle every time they cleaned?

Taking off her clothes, as she assumed was the protocol, she stepped in and let the water wash over her. It felt so strange on her skin, like a massage. Others had swam in the lake at the cabins, but she'd never worked up the courage. This was the first time in her life that water flowed over her skin. Sighing, she understood why people would choose this. It was relaxing. The sound the water made as it touched the ground calmed her nerves.

Looking around, she saw several bottles with instructions for their use. One was labeled, shampoo. Taking a small dab, she put it in her hair, and rubbed it around, cleaning her head. Then she let the water rinse her hair clean. Another was labeled conditioner, and promised to leave her hair silky smooth, whatever that meant. She repeated the same procedure, rinsing her hair clean when she was done.

Another bottle said body wash. She used it as directed,

admiring how effective it was at removing dirt from her skin. She cleaned the wound on her wrist, red lines running away from it, a sign that it was starting to become infected. When she was out of bottles, she solved the puzzle of the knobs again to get the water to stop, and stepped out, grabbing a cloth from the drawers and using it to dry her skin.

When she stepped back into her room, somehow, night clothes had been laid out for her. It was a pretty night dress with frills and lace and ribbon in soft pink. Putting it on, she had nothing else to do but lay down and rest. She would need her strength for whatever lay ahead of her. Though it was hard to sleep, she was exhausted. After hours of tossing and turning, the world finally faded away.

Knock, knock-knock.

She sat up in the large bed and pulled the covers over the thin material of her night dress.

The same woman walked in, carrying a tray of food. This time, it was pancakes, sausage and bacon, with eggs and a glass of yellow juice. Smiling, Arda found her mouth watering.

The woman set the tray down and turned to her. "Ah, you have color in your cheeks. This is good. You are too skinny. We must make you beautiful, yes? You enjoy my food. I will pick it up in an hour." Smiling, the woman left.

Arda was once again ravenous. Though she'd eaten the night before, it felt like she hadn't in ages. She wasn't sure why she was so hungry, but she ate every bite of food, savoring the way the pancakes felt in her mouth as the fluffy bites touched her tongue.

When the woman came back, Arda decided to be brave. "Do...you know why I'm here?"

The woman looked her up and down, and said, "no. But I know what I was told."

"Can you share that with me?"

A soft, kind expression crossed her face. "Ah, so young. You are beautiful, yes. Someone, they see that beauty, they must have it for their own. Don't worry. If you are a good pet, your master will treat you well."

"Who is" she swallowed hard, forcing the words out, "my master?"

"I do not know, but they must be important if I am feeding you."

"Thank you."

"You're very welcome. Get dressed. You never know when your master will call you."

She nodded, and the woman left. Grabbing another dress, she quickly got ready. She didn't care about pleasing some unknown control freak, but she did care about no one seeing her in her night dress. Sitting in the chair by the desk, she waited.

Minutes turned to hours, as no one came for her. She sang, danced around, did sit ups, pushups, crunches, and stretched her muscles which were no longer aching. Looking in the mirror, she still looked too fragile, but she felt like her old self again.

She paced the room for what seemed like ages, but no one called for her. It wasn't until much later that a knock finally sounded on her door. Stepping back, she waited for it to open, but it was just the woman with another tray of food.

"No master today?"

Arda shook her head.

"Well, they will claim you soon. I have your dinner. Red meat to put on your bones. You are still too thin. Bon Appetit."

The same process continued for two days. The woman

came, giving her delicious food, and Arda would eat it as if she were starving. She would shower before bed and, every night, a new night dress would be laid out for her. It wasn't until the third day that something changed…

Chapter 19

That morning, the cut was no better. More red lines had started to form up her arm, indicating the infection had spread. When the woman came back, Arda decided she had no choice but to ask for help.

"I think my wrist is infected. Can you bring me anything for it?"

The woman set the tray down and turned. "Here, let me take a look for you."

Arda held out her arm and the woman saw the bite for the first time. "Oh, this is not good. No. For someone so pretty, you should not have to lose an arm. We will fix this, you and I. I will bring the good doctor to you, after I have taken your food. It is good of you to tell me. I can help you, beautiful girl."

Arda sighed with relief. Maybe meeting the doctor would provide her with more answers. She waited, and an hour went by, then two. Finally, someone knocked, entering without permission.

"Hello. I am Dr. Black. I'll be treating you today. I must advise you against trying to flee. While my scalpel is sharp, the guards are far superior in speed to you. Do you understand?"

She nodded. "Good. I will treat you now. Hold out your wrist so I can inspect it."

She did so, noting the red lines were all the way to her shoulder. He sighed. "I can save the arm, but it will not be a pleasant experience for you. Unfortunately, the skin at your wrist will have to come off. As I have no anesthetic, it will be incredibly painful. Do you understand?"

She nodded again. Taking something round from his

bag, he said, "lay back and bite down on this, hard." She did so. The doctor secured her wrists so she couldn't move, and then began.

As the scalpel sliced into her arm, the pain burned as it had when she was bitten. She tried to hold back, but she couldn't, and she began to scream, biting hard on the object in her mouth. Luckily, the doctor worked quickly, and after only five very long minutes of agonizing pain, the bitten flesh was removed. She was shaky, her breath coming in gasps, sweat dripping down her body, but she was alive.

"Unfortunately, we are not done. For now, I will wrap this wound. You are not to get it wet. I will put this salve on it to speed up the healing process, but I will also need to give you several shots so your body will fight off the infection. Tomorrow I will return, and you will get more. Do you understand?"

She nodded and he wrapped her hand. Producing a syringe, he said, "This is for the infection." He jabbed it into her shoulder, then squeezed. Heat poured into her veins. Reaching into his bag, he produced another and said, "and this is to help as well." Same process, same burning. When he left, she was exhausted from the pain, so much so that she didn't even get under the covers, or shower. She fell asleep.

On the visit, the doctor stitched her hand back together, but still, no "master" came for her. She was beginning to think that she would never leave the room. She couldn't take it anymore. When the woman entered, she asked, "Is there anything I can do while I'm in my room?"

"What do you mean, do?"

"Do you have any instruments I could play or something I can do to not go crazy?"

"Your master has still not claimed you. How odd. I will ask around, see what I can do for the beautiful girl who loves my food. Whoever your master is, they are a fool."

Arda waited for her to return. When the knock sounded on her door, a guard entered with a cello. "Will this do?"

She nodded, delighted. "Oh, yes. Thank you."

The guard set it on the bed and left the room, locking it as he went. Now at least she had something to do. Sitting down, she began to practice her scales. Eventually, when that was not enough, she began to play random notes in sequence, until it pleased her ear. It was a haunting sound, the cello's voice singing a sad tale that reminded her of her captivity. When she stopped, she wanted to cry.

It was the next day that she finally left that room. Two guards came to escort her, somewhere. Happy to be leaving, as the yellow wallpaper was driving her crazy, she willingly left with them. Still, they grabbed her arms, almost lifting her off of the ground. Down the hall and the stairs, they went, to the small office in the back of the castle. *Just like the estate.* The guards put her inside and shut the door.

She sat, apprehensively. She would finally find out who had taken her. Looking for weapons, finding none, her hopes dropped. Today may not be the day she got her freedom, but at least she knew more about the layout of her prison.

The door opened sometime later, and a tall, raven haired man stepped through. He looked like he was in his forties, but she knew he must be older than that.

"Ms. Prime. It's a pleasure to finally meet you." He actually held out his hand. Strange. She took it, and he shook with a firm grip. "Please sit down so we may speak."

She did so, waiting, holding her voice back until she

needed it, but the anger was there, ready. "I see we have done you a disservice. You're much too thin, even for being in the dreadful dungeon for two days. We will fix that. You must be so scared, right now, but believe me, I have nothing but good intentions for you."

"Is that why you let Marci bite me?"

"Excuse moi?" His eyes widened in disbelief. He hadn't known.

She spoke slowly, carefully, letting venom drip from her words. "Marci came down to my cell and almost killed me draining my blood."

He looked genuinely surprised. After a moment, he asked, "where did she bite?" His eyes glanced up and down her form, looking for the wound.

She held out her bandaged hand. He looked at it, aghast. "Oh, no, this will not do. We cannot have this. No, no." He grabbed her hand, removing the bandage. Seeing the stitches, he said, "Ah, the good doctor has tried to right this wrong. Wonderful. If you have a scar, I shall heal you."

"How?"

"It is my power. To heal. But we must wait and see. I do not wish to force any more of our tricks on you. No, you are a Prime and a guest in my home. If you wish it, I will heal you, but not until it is necessary." He turned away, pacing the room.

"Can we kill Marci?" She said it flatly, sarcastically, but inside, she meant it.

He laughed, fanning his face. "Oh, Ardora Prime, spicy as advertised. To kill another vampire, this requires…more than a bandaged wrist. For now, I must ask you to delay your revenge, for me. For only now. One day, you may very well be able to do what we have not yet done."

She hadn't expected a yes, anyway.

"Why am I here?" she asked softly.

He faced her. "You are here, Ms. Prime, because I need you as leverage. I need you to save my people."

"Then why didn't you ask nicely?"

He laughed then, full, throaty. "Because I could not get near you with Mayne hovering around."

"You…know Mayne?" Did he know she was here? Would he come rescue her?

He laughed again. "Oh, how little he has told you of us. I know Mayne. I know him well."

"He wouldn't like it if he found out I was here."

He smiled broadly. "No, no, I doubt he would. Which is why you will remain in your room until the precise moment I need you."

"When will that be?"

"Oh, I do not know. Days, weeks, maybe years. Do not worry, you will be cared for. No one will bite you again, unless of course you choose to be a donor."

"No thank you." She swallowed hard, trying not to vomit.

"I did not think so. Before you go, I need one small thing from you."

"What's that?"

"Oh, it is a trifle, a small gift. A lock of your hair."

"You want my hair?" *Vampires are weird.*

"Not all of it, no. Just a small piece." Producing a pair of scissors, he walked behind her and cut. "There. I took it from underneath so no one will see. Guards!"

When they entered, he instructed them to take her back to her room. Surrounded by the same damn wallpaper, Arda paced back and forth, playing the cello.

It was six long days before she again left that room. She was practicing, when two guards came to escort her away. Instead of taking her to the office, they continued down to the entrance, where the great hall should be. The older man was waiting there.

"Ah, beautiful one, you are here, so we can go." He held out a hand, and said, "do not try to run, for my men are faster than you." She nodded and let him escort her out of his castle. Turning, they entered what she thought was called a carriage, pulled by horses. She didn't think those creatures existed outside the habitats. She was tempted to touch one, but she didn't know the animal's temperament.

Once they were inside the carriage, the driver clucked, and the horses began to move. For a while she sat in silence, until she felt compelled to speak.

"Where are we going?"

"You are traveling with me to see the Council."

"The Council."

"They run the government in our world, setting down laws and rules for our people to follow. It is not like your Chief, on the surface. We are not led by the most noble, but by the most cunning."

"Who leads?"

He was quiet a long moment. "That is none of your concern. For this trip, I must insist that you stay by my side and agree to wear these chains." Opening a drawer inside the seat, he produced them. She didn't want to be chained again, but she hadn't regained enough strength to fight him, and the memory of Merci's bite and the pain and agony that followed sent potent fear through her. For now, it was best to comply, until she found a way out. Still, her breath became uneven, and she feared she may pass out.

"Shhh. Sweet girl." He tilted her chin up, and added, "I promise, she will not touch you again." The same sense of calm Mayne could illicit came out of her, as his eyes glowed a darker blue. "I know your autonomy has been violated, but I swear, on the life of my son, you are safe with me."

"Fine." She held out her hands, waiting to be chained.

"Good. Now, let us chat. How is the surface these days?"

"Bright, sunny. The trees grow tall." She felt a lump in her throat form as her eyes burned. She missed the camp.

"I miss the trees. It has been ages since I've seen a forest. Tell me more."

"The sun shines with yellow light."

"Yes. Go on."

"The flowers bloom in pots across the city."

"Ahh," he sighed. "It sounds lovely."

"It is." She said it as her chest crushed under her sudden sadness, forcing tears to fall from her eyes.

"Oh, I have hurt you with talk of your home. Je suis désolé. Have a tissue." He gave her one and she wiped her tears away. "That's better. Now, don't worry. When the Council has resolved this issue, all will be well. I will see you to the surface myself, and you will be free again. This I promise. This whole thing, is temporary."

"Really?" A sliver of hope shown on her face.

"I would never cage a firebird who needs to fly. No, ma colombe, you belong to the sky."

She wondered what he meant but didn't have the heart to speak again. She sat back, sobbing, consoling herself. The driver pulled up to another large building, and the carriage stopped. He exited, holding out his hand. She took it and stepped down, though it was awkward with the chains on her wrists and ankles.

The inside of the towering black structure looked very different from his home. It was dark, scary, full of skeletons, and tons of people. Everyone crowded inside. "These are the citizens, come here to accept the ruling of the Council. They will be waiting days to see someone. We have a civil unrest between Council members. One I am hoping you will help me solve. Come."

He let her go first, directing her to the right. Several times, a hand tried to grab at her, but he slapped them away. Coming to the end of the great hall, they walked down a small hallway and outside to a large yard, with a crescent shaped table of ebony, some forty feet long.

Chairs of white stood behind the table, and lavish, important looking people sat in them, adorned with jewels and precious gold. He walked to the right end of the table, and sat down, motioning for her to sit on the floor beside him. When she hesitated, unsure, he pulled her down.

"Do as I say, if you wish to see the surface again. You must look like my good pet, beautiful firebird." He stroked her hair, and it took all her strength not to react. As she lowered herself to her knees on a pillow, he began talking to the member next to him.

"I don't think I've seen this donor before. Are you sharing her tonight?"

"I think not. She is no donor, but my loyal pet." He touched a tendril of her hair, as if checking its quality.

"Oh, I do enjoy pets. Mine passed away a year ago, sadly. I just haven't had the heart to find another. Is she well behaved?"

"She is still in training but progressing nicely." He stroked her head, and it took all her strength not to let the anger overcome her, to sit still and look forward. She felt her body shake from it.

"Shh. Sweet girl." He tilted her chin toward him, and the calm resolved her shaking.

"I was going to say, while she's no child she is definitely still young. What luck you've had lately, Scythe."

"Indeed. I recommend pets. They keep you healthy. Much better than a donor. They are good for the soul."

"Well, you've convinced me. Tomorrow, I shall search for another. I can't wait to see their loving eyes as they sit next to my fireplace with me."

"You have a good heart."

"As do you, my old friend." She fought not to roll her eyes. The thought of another being taken down here, against their will, enraged her.

The conversation ended as a horn sounded. The Council was silenced, and someone shouted from the top of the castle. "All hail, our Emperor."

"Hail!" They shouted back.

"The cunning, the sly, the master of us all."

"The cunning, the sly, the master of us all."

The doors opened, and a cloaked figure walked out, taking a seat in a white chair opposite the council members, in the middle of the crescent. A large group of guards surrounded the entire area, keeping the council members from attacking or fleeing the emperor. The figure sat on his throne, others mirroring him. From her spot on the floor, she could see very little.

A council member rose and began to speak. "We are here to discuss the civil unrest facing our society. We, as council members, must stand united under our emperor to conquer the hidden coin in our mists. Let us act in accordance with all laws and rules of governance, so we may conclude this council satisfied, with light hearts."

"That's a great speech from someone who steals my donor blood!"

The emperor only needed to move his hand and the men stopped speaking. A court member came forward, unfolding a scroll. "This is a petition from the Larkov estate."

A member stood. "Present."

"They wish to address the lack of donor blood received from the hospitals."

The Emperor waved his hand.

"Cunning one, with those fleeing the war torn districts, we are overburdened and underfed. All of us have been rationed since the Fifth War ended. I beseech you, sly one, to find a solution, before we all starve. I ask the council to debate and settle this matter tonight."

Three members stood, as the first was seated.

"We have taken in too many refugees. That is the real problem."

"The problem is the lack of hunting. We starve while there are perfectly good donors we could compel on the surface."

"The real problem is our payment to the hospital. They ask for more than we can give."

After the three were heard, the scroll bearer approached the Emperor, so that only he could hear. After writing down a long string of words, he approached the council, the Emperor's mouthpiece. "Hunting humans will remain prohibited." The council stirred, clearly unhappy with that decision. "The emperor has acquired a large sum through his dealings on the surface. He will barter with the hospitals, on our behalf, personally. The refugees will remain."

She was pleasantly surprised. After her treatment, she didn't think anyone cared about the humans on the surface, or any refugees. The cloaked figure had her respect, for now. A wave of his hand, and silence fell again. The scroll bearer opened another.

"From the Draken estate. A gift for the emperor."

Standing, Scythe turned to the group and said, "if I may address the council?"

The emperor nodded. "I have a gift, one I hope will put an end to this civil unrest, one that I am sure will be seen by all as a sign that our time of exile is at an end. If we join together, we are sure to be great. Sure to regain our home. Sure to prevail and find an ending to your curse."

"Not all of us consider this a curse, Scythe." This from an older woman in the middle.

"No, but all of us wish to get to the surface, to stay there."

There was nodding and murmuring among the members at this. "I propose a truce, that you back our emperor, that we squash these rebellions together, and remember that our future is together, united. Our future…is the surface."

"You make great speeches, Scythe, you always have, but what gift have you brought us that is so treasured that it would end my quarrel with this buffoon who keeps stealing from me?"

Instead of saying a word, he stepped toward the Emperor and began to sing. The words chilled her to the bone, her breath coming unevenly.

"The pot was burning, charred as night,
The urchin queen came in to sight.
She rallied all the sheep to sleep and
Lions slumbered 'nay a peep.
Oh, walk, oh walk to shelter dear

The urchin queen has led you here
The trees will grow again so high
When urchin queen draws nigh.
When urchin queen draws nigh."

By the time he was finished, the Emperor's hands were clenching his chair. The others murmured for a moment before someone finally spoke up.

"You speak of ancient prophecy. It's a silly fable."

"Ah, but it is not, and I have the proof."

"What proof do you have of the urchin queen returning?"

He walked toward her, and she feared what he might do. It took all of her willpower to stay still, to not give in to squeals or screams. Grabbing her chains, he forced her to stand. Walking her to the Emperor, he said, "this is Ardora Prime, daughter of Faith Prime, granddaughter of Hope, great-grand-daughter of Patience, and great-great-grand-daughter of Regina."

As he ended, he forced her to kneel before him. "I offer her to our Emperor, as a gift, to help us conquer the light."

The council murmured, but it was some time before someone spoke. "If this is true, Scythe, then we happily withdraw our quarrel."

"We do as well."

After five minutes, it seemed that all members were suddenly best friends again. Arda didn't know what to do, so she didn't move. When the council members had quieted down, she dared to lift her head up.

Even from closer proximity, she couldn't see a face. The shadow surrounded him completely. The Emperor did not speak, but with a wave of his hand, a guard appeared, grabbing her chains and dragging her into the giant castle. Setting her in the kitchen, they chained her to the wall, and left.

It was a long while before anyone came for her. She had waited so long that her arms were starting to lose feeling. When the guards returned, they unchained her and walked her to a carriage. Placing her inside, covering her eyes, chains bound to the floor, they murmured something to the driver, and she was leaving the castle.

She'd given up on memorizing directions. By now she was so turned around that she couldn't remember how to leave if she wanted to. She had no clue which cavern she was in, where it was underground, or which direction would lead her to the surface.

Eventually, all movement came to a halt, and another set of guards were escorting her out of the carriage and through the dirt, then onto a smooth, cold floor. A door shut behind her, and though she couldn't see, she knew she was likely inside another residence. Taking the blindfold off, they removed her chains. An older gentleman walked toward her, in a suit and tie.

"Welcome to the Edge of Madness, the Palace of the Emperor. While you are here, please address your questions and concerns to me. I will be happy to answer what I can, but the Emperor is very busy, and will not be pleased by nonsense. Come. I will show you to your room."

She followed as he continued to speak. "I am the keeper of his house. If you have any issues with any staff, tell me. Also, you will notice that there are guards everywhere, in every room. You will not do well to think of escaping this place. You will be hunted down and brought back by the best trackers we have to offer. You may freely roam the palace tomorrow, after your first night's stay. No doubt, the Emperor will wish to see you upon his return."

He opened the door to her room, and she gasped. It was huge compared to the one at Scythe's house, larger than her apartment in the Project. A great room open to the second floor stood covered in purple, blue, and black furniture. A fireplace burned brightly, while a wall of actual books lay in the corner. She could see a large bed decorated in the same shades up the staircase, and another open door gave her a glimpse of a tiled bathroom.

"Yes, our Emperor treats his pets well. I shall have dinner brought to you. Are you allergic to anything?"

"No."

"Good, good. I will instruct them to bring a little of everything. Enjoy your stay." He left, and she heard the door shut and lock.

Now all she could do was wait. The hours passed, dinner was brought, ate and the tray taken away. It grew so late that she began to feel tired. Taking out a night dress, she slipped it on and crawled into bed. The dark came quickly, but nightmares of Marci, of burning cars, and betas disturbed her sleep.

A yell woke her, had her jumping out of her skin. She walked down the staircase, her ear to the door. Two voices were arguing downstairs, but she couldn't make out what was being said or who they were. Eventually, the shouting ended, with a door slamming shut. Footsteps traveled up the stairs and stopped in front of her door. She took several steps back, carefully trying not to make a sound.

Her heart was pounding. She could barely breathe. She would finally find out who this man was, and what they wanted of her. Joy's words resounded in her head. She was a fool not to listen. She'd even been warned that believers were dangerous. Would he be one? Would he expect miracles of her that she couldn't give? Would he punish her when she failed?

The door opened, and the hooded figure from the Council walked in. A crowd of women stood behind him, trying to get his attention. He silenced them with a flick of his hand, and they backed away from the door. He shut it behind him, locking it into place. Arda stood tall, her hands folded in front of her, choosing bravery, even though she was visibly shaking from fear.

"I hope you know…" the words were weak so she cleared her throat, "I'm *not* a god. I'm no one special. I don't know why everyone is making a big deal out of me, but I'm not. Really. I just want to go *home*." Her voice cracked on that last word, the tears threatening to fall. She clenched her hands together as her body began to quake, as her legs locked to keep her from falling down and apart.

The man turned toward her slowly, his head downcast. He walked forward, until she either had to back away or stand within arm's reach. Her frozen feet refused to obey her, so she held her head high, prideful, instead, even though her body was visibly shaking. She was terrified of another bite, another stay in the dungeon. Terrified that she would be used and discarded like Marci had done, but she wasn't a coward.

When he was close to her, towering over her, he removed his gloves, long, slim fingers wearing black polish. With one of them, he reached up. Slowly, his hand grasped his hood, pulling it away from his face, to reveal a familiar pair of sky blue eyes.

"*Mayne*?" Arda asked, her knees buckling.

He caught her, cradling her in his arms. He took the stairs two at a time and carried her to the bed. Laying her gently on it, he moved to back away, but she needed the comfort. She grasped tightly around his shoulders, and he gave in to her, one hand stroking her hair, the other around her waist, rubbing up and down her back.

"I had no idea." She realized he was shaking, as well.

"Arda, I'm so sorry."

She gripped his robe, keeping him close to her, as her body slowly began to relax. "I…it…Marci…" She couldn't get the words out.

"We've been looking for you for days. The soldiers, Tyrus, Will, my people, we had no idea you were here, or I would have stormed his castle and saved you myself, I swear it." His hands ran up and down her arms, around her waist, covering her face, wiping at the tears that fell. "Arda… je suis vraiment désolé, ma colombe." He leaned in and kissed her forehead softly, and for a moment, each of them allowed their nervous systems to reset, the shaking to end.

"It's really you." She relaxed into him, as he continued to stroke her hair. She let go of his shirt, reaching up with her bandaged hand to get a strand he couldn't see out of her eyes.

He stopped her, gently turning her wrist upward, seeing the bandage. He unwrapped it, careful not to cause any more damage. Noting the stitches, he said, "Marci…did this?"

Before she could answer, his eyes began to glow, and she found herself reliving the moment that Marci entered her cell. She felt everything as if it was new. The pain, the headache, the sore muscles, dread fear that she may never leave, the cold dark... When he let go and she was alone in her mind, the tears flowed anew.

Seeing it, he said, "I'm sorry. I'm so sorry." He picked her up off the bed, and sat, laying her on his lap, trying to comfort her. "I swear she will pay for that." The slight growl in his voice left no doubt in her mind that he would.

"I believe you…Emperor?"

He scoffed. "No. You will not call me that. I am your Mayne. Your friend. Your informant. Arda, please never call me that."

"As you wish..." she tried to pull another archaic word out of her vocabulary from early history. "My liege."

He groaned, but a smile slowly spread on each of their faces. Tilting her chin upward, he locked eyes with her and said, "Arda... She will pay dearly, but for now, I must ask you for more bravery, just for a little while."

"Why?"

"Because I need you. My people...need you."

"For what?"

He set her down on the bed, and began to pace, back and forth. "When they said we needed a miracle, they weren't lying. I don't want you to fear me, or fear being here," he gave her a guilt ridden glance, "but I'm asking you to stay, for a little while. No prison, just...as my liaison to the surface. I'm asking you to save my people."

"I'm...I'm not the Urchin Queen."

He stopped pacing and nodded. "I know. I know who you are. Don't forget, I've tested your blood. I know everything you are capable of, Arda. Even things that..." He drifted off, as if looking for the right words. "Things that you haven't learned of yourself yet.

"Arda, you are no god, but you are special. Extraordinary. You navigated Project R.E.D.D. like your mother did before you, earning recognition and taking down a corrupt District Chief. In the first three months of your time as Agent. I need you here. I need your help."

"What exactly do you expect me to do?"

He looked at her, earnestly. Holding her hands in his, he said, "you are stronger now. You are smarter. You are ready. Together, we are going to dismantle Protocol: Orange."

2 Urchin Queen

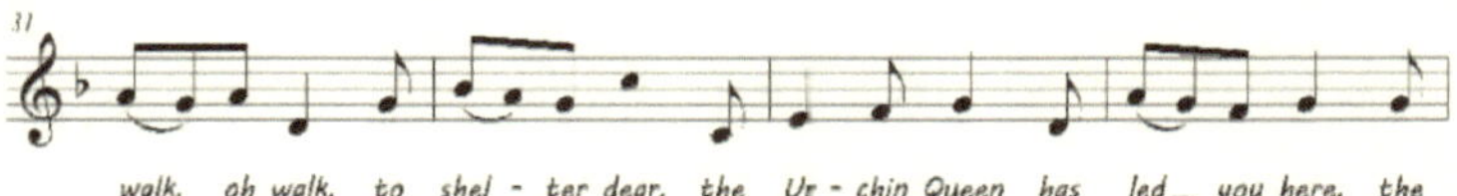

www.ingramcontent.com/pod-product-compliance
Lightning Source LLC
LaVergne TN
LVHW100512110826
845146LV00002B/603

* 9 7 9 8 9 8 8 3 1 3 5 6 4 *